TWO PEOPLE ARE W

ONE OF THEM HAS B   )E.

For over thirty years, a man named Harry Black lived quietly in a small town on the Gulf of Thailand. Then, while walking on the beach on his eighty-sixth birthday, he's shot and killed by a sniper firing from half a mile away.

Why would someone send a highly skilled sniper to kill an insignificant old man? Maybe he wasn't really as insignificant as everybody thought he was.

Inspector Samuel Tay was once Singapore's best-known homicide detective, but he's no longer a cop. He was too much of a maverick for straight-and-narrow little Singapore and his bosses forced him into an early retirement. When a guy who once did Tay a big favor asks him to look into Harry Black's murder, it's his chance to get back in the game.

Tay's mother wants to help. Tay has always had a somewhat fraught relationship with his mother, but he figures they get along pretty well now, particularly considering she's dead. Tay doesn't believe in ghosts, of course, and when his mother shows up in the dark of night to give him advice about his cases, he knows perfectly well that her appearances aren't real.

But here's the thing. Some of her advice is so good he can't help but listen to it anyway.

This time, Tay's mother warns him he's fishing in dangerous waters. 'I'll help you, Samuel,' she tells him, 'but you are about to expose secrets that will change the way people see the world. No one is ever going to thank you for what you're doing.'

That sounds pretty overwrought to Tay, and besides, his mother isn't really there, so why should he believe her?

Harry Black was just an old man who lived in complete obscurity for the last thirty years of his life. What secrets could he possibly have known that were so important somebody might have murdered him to keep them hidden?

But that also raises a really awkward question Samuel Tay needs to think about.

If he discovers the secrets someone killed Harry Black to bury, why wouldn't they kill Tay to silence him, too?

WHAT THE CRITICS SAY

ABOUT JAKE NEEDHAM

"Needham deftly morphs 1930's American Sam Spade into Inspector Samuel Tay, a world-weary 21st century Singapore homicide detective." — **Libris Reviews**

"Inspector Tay is an endearing flawed protagonist, and the storyline full of twists and turns kept me up all night." — **Cosmopolitan Magazine**

"Jake Needham is Asia's most stylish and atmospheric writer of crime fiction." — **The Singapore Straits Times**

"Jake Needham's the real deal. His characters are moral men and women struggling in an increasingly immoral world, his plotting is top-notch, and his writing is exquisitely fine. Highly, highly recommended." — **Brendan DuBois, New York Times #1 bestselling author with James Patterson of THE SUMMER HOUSE**

"Needham writes so you can smell the spicy street food mingling with the traffic jams, the sweat, and the garbage." — **Libris Reviews**

"Needham exudes the confidence of a man who has seen it all, done it all, and still bristles with energy and butt-kicking tales well worth writing about." — **Singapore Today**

"Tight and atmospheric, Needham's novels are thrillers of the highest caliber, a perfect combination of suspense and wit." — **The Malaysia Star**

"No clichés. No BS. Thrillers written with a wry sense of irony in the mean-streets, fast-car, tough-talk tradition of Elmore Leonard." — **The Edge, Singapore**

"Mr. Needham seems to know rather more than one ought about these things." — **The Wall Street Journal**

"For Mr. Needham, fiction is not just a good story, but an insight into a country's soul." — **The Singapore New Paper**

WHO THE HELL
IS HARRY BLACK?

JAKE NEEDHAM

This one is for Aey, too.

Just like everything else.

History is hard to know because of all the hired bullshit, but every now and then, the energy of a whole generation comes to a head in a long fine flash for reasons that nobody really understands at the time—and which never explain, in retrospect, what actually happened.

— *Hunter S. Thompson, Fear and Loathing in Las Vegas: A Savage Journey to the Heart of the American Dream*

History would be an excellent thing, if only it were true.

— *Leo Tolstoy*

WHO THE HELL
IS HARRY BLACK?

ONE

Harry Black, whose name was not Harry Black, stood on the grass and squinted at the cracked concrete steps down to the beach.

The iron handrails were pitted and corroded from decades in the salt air, and the steps themselves were steep. Each of them sloped a bit differently, which made climbing down them tricky. Had these steps always been so steep and difficult to climb down? When had he used them last?

Harry Black made a little snorting sound, something about halfway between a laugh and a grunt.

Yesterday.

He had used them yesterday.

Just as he had used them damn near every day for the last twenty-five years.

And now he was standing here muttering to himself about some concrete steps he had walked down ten thousand times before.

You're turning into a cranky old fart, Harry Black. You really are.

He'd had a lot of names over his life, but he had used the name Harry Black for so long he thought of himself as Harry Black now. There were times when he still thought about the

1

other names he had used, the other people he had been. Sometimes he even thought about the name he had been born with, but something about that made him uncomfortable so he tried not to do it.

What was the point, anyway? He had turned into who he was pretending to be, and the name Harry Black was as good as any.

What did matter now was that he was eighty-six years old, and it was far too late in life to waste time thinking about anything as insignificant as the name by which people called him. What mattered far more was that there was almost no one left to call him anything at all. He had no friends anymore. He had lost track of almost everyone he had ever known. Most of them were probably dead anyway.

He had no family either. Not really. He had buried two wives, a son, and a daughter. There was no one left but a granddaughter who lived in Hong Kong. At least she had lived in Hong Kong a couple of years back when he found her there. Maybe she lived somewhere else now. He hadn't seen her in a while. How long had it been? He would have to stop and work it out to be sure, and he didn't want to do that. How the hell was he supposed to remember?

His granddaughter had been a grown woman before he ever met her. His daughter had always told her he was dead, which he supposed he was in a way. He didn't blame his daughter for that. He had done enough damage in lifetime. The least he could do was let his granddaughter grow up without the burden of knowing who he was.

When his daughter was killed in a plane crash, however, he weakened. After all, his granddaughter was the only family he had left now. He used some old contacts and spread a little money around, and that was how he found her living in Hong Kong.

When he got in touch with her, she was skeptical. He didn't blame her. For her whole life, she had been told her grandfather was dead, and now some old man calls up and claims to be her grandfather? Of course, she was skeptical. She would have been an idiot not to be.

After a few telephone calls, he thought she might be getting more comfortable with him, and he suggested they meet in Bangkok where he arranged for her to stay at the Oriental Hotel. Since he had gone through so much effort to disappear, he couldn't bring himself to tell her where he actually lived. He imagined she thought he must be living somewhere around Bangkok since he chose the Oriental for their meeting. That was fine with him.

After their first meeting, they exchanged emails or calls every few weeks, and they met twice more, both times at the Oriental. Then they didn't meet for a while, and the emails and calls became fewer and further between. Eventually, he stopped hearing from her altogether. There was no reason for that, not really. They certainly hadn't quarreled.

Life just worked that way. If he had learned nothing else in his over eight decades on this earth, he had learned that. You kept up your ties to someone despite not seeing them very often, until one day you realized you had stopped keeping them up. Then you had to decide what to do. You either made the effort to rebuild those ties, or you just let them go. Usually, you let them go. No reason, really. It was just easier.

He didn't want to put it all on her. He could have called or written and tried to salvage their connection. Telephones and the mail worked in both directions, didn't they? So why hadn't he done that?

He supposed sometimes he simply got tired of being Harry Black. He had lived most of his life wearing other men's suits. He wasn't even certain he had a suit of his own anymore. Maybe being Harry Black had gotten too hard. Maybe he just didn't have the energy to be Harry Black any longer. Maybe that's all there was to it.

"Harry Black," he said out loud.

Harry Black sounded exactly like the name of some irascible, cranky, eighty-six-year-old bastard you did your best to avoid running into any more than you absolutely had to.

He said it again, louder this time.

"Harry Black!"

He laughed, got a firm grip on the iron handrails, and started carefully down the concrete steps.

I t was early morning and Harry Black was alone on the beach. The light was thin and watery. The day seemed to be struggling to arrive. He knew exactly how it felt.

The beach was wide and flat, and it was nothing at all like the powdery white beaches edged by crystalline blue waters that were a staple of travel posters touting exotic tropical beaches. The sand was hard and gritty. Perhaps it was uncharitable to call it a mud flat, but that was pretty close to what it was.

Harry Black slipped off his sandals and walked, swinging them from one hand. Just above the waterline, he spotted a set of tracks. One person moving in the same direction he was. It couldn't have been long since they were there or the incoming tide would have already washed out the tracks, but he didn't see anyone down the beach in front of him.

Had someone come and gone already? The thought gave him pause. His neighbors were not early risers and his walks were almost always solitary, which suited him fine. But someone out on the beach so early they were gone before he got here? That had never happened before.

His eyes instinctively flicked over the tracks as he walked. He could tell whoever it was had been wearing sports shoes that were on the small side. Could it have been a woman? Maybe. That was interesting.

The spacing and depth of the tracks told him that whoever it was had been moving quickly, perhaps even running. That was probably it, he thought. Someone running on the beach in the first light of morning. Which meant it wasn't a local. The locals didn't run unless somebody was chasing them.

A jogger then. Probably a woman. Almost certainly a European or an American. He would have to keep an eye out, Harry Black thought to himself. He was always open to possibilities. He wasn't dead yet.

The water was gray and flat, and the sky was streaked with ragged bands of musty looking clouds. A small blue and white fishing boat lay beached at the waterline. The paint was old and faded, but the hull looked sound and a mast with a boom for hauling nets sprouted from the center of its deck. The boat had been there for weeks. It didn't look abandoned, not exactly, but he had never seen it move either. Maybe the fishermen didn't go out early in the mornings when he was out walking the beach. Maybe they only took the boat out at night when he was tucked up in his house with a whiskey and a cigar. Did people fish at night? He had no idea.

There was no surf, just ripples rolling gently onto hard sand rutted from an eternity of tides washing over it. Ridges of sand had formed along some of the ruts which trapped pools of seawater when the tide receded. The pools were scattered out in front of him like water-filled craters from a mortar barrage.

The unevenness of the ground caused his ankles to ache. It was like that almost every morning now, but he was sympathetic with his ankles and never called them out. After all, they had reliably supported his weight for over eighty years, and that weight had increased steadily throughout his life, as did most everyone's. He could hardly blame his ankles for getting damn tired of hauling him around.

Getting old wasn't for sissies. Most mornings when he woke, he lay still for a few minutes and took a cautious inventory. Was everything still where it was supposed to be? Check. Was everything still working like it was supposed to work? Close enough. Was everything still functioning well enough to give him a fighting chance of getting out of bed? It was worth a shot.

That was why the first thing he did every day was to walk a mile or two along the beach. It was like starting up an old car. The engine might grind for a while and then it would probably run rough at first, but if you gave it a few minutes and just let it tick over, eventually the fluids would flow, the sound would smooth out, and the familiar power would return. The problem was that every day it seemed to take a little longer to get his decrepit old engine running, and there was less and less power there when it finally did start to run. Harry Black accepted that. It was only fair. It was the way of the world. You made your way through life, and then eventually you came to the end of it. He was ready for that.

Well … almost ready. He had a couple of things to do first.

The beach curved ahead of him out to a headland with a small, wooded hill a couple of hundred feet high. Right at the top of the hill was a Buddhist temple, an extravagant and fanciful structure capped with a steep red, yellow and green tiled roof with golden spires rising from each of its four corners. The temple sparkled in the morning sunlight. He remembered someone once telling him that was from the shards of colored glass embedded in its tiles.

He had been there once years ago. It had beautiful views of the coast in both directions and was very peaceful. Except for the damned monkeys, of course. They were everywhere. Shrieking, chattering, and clambering around in the trees. That was why the locals called the place Monkey Mountain. One visit has been enough for him. The temple was lovely, but the monkeys were nasty and disgusting.

He was just thinking about the temple when a sudden flash of light near it caught his eye. The flash was there and then it was gone again, like a momentary reflection from a mirror, but he doubted that was what it was. All around him, the rising morning light was growing stronger, and he thought it more likely that the first rays of the rising sun had struck a piece of glass embedded in the temple's roof tiles and been arbitrarily reflected at exactly the right angle to hit his eye as he walked on the beach a half mile away. One more inexplicably random occurrence in a world built of inexplicable random occurrences.

Distracted by the flash, Harry Black's foot came down in a depression filled with seawater and he stumbled. He flung out both arms to keep his balance and lost his grip on his sandals. They flew several feet and landed in another waterhole.

"Shit!" Harry Black muttered.

At least he had kept his feet somehow, although he was not certain how he had managed that. His sense of balance had started to fail him, and he had become more and more self-conscious when he walked. He could only imagine the humiliation if he slipped and fell somewhere. It would show the whole world he had become a helpless old man for whom even putting one foot in front of another was a constant challenge.

He retrieved his sandals and tried to shake the water off. That didn't work very well, so he bent over and tried slapping them several times on the hard ground. That didn't work very well, either.

As he was straightening up, another flash of light near the temple caught his eye. It was brighter and more sharply focused this time. Not at all like the sparkling light he was accustomed to seeing up there. Something about it troubled Harry Black, but he was not sure what it was.

Probably it was just some tourist with a pair of binoculars looking down at the beach, and what he was seeing was the rising sun glinting off the lenses. But that meant the binoculars had to be pointed at him or he wouldn't see light reflecting off them, didn't it? Surely there was some other explanation. Why would anybody be watching him through binoculars? An old man stumbling down a not particularly attractive beach in the early morning light? That was ridiculous. He wasn't nearly interesting enough for anyone to pay the slightest attention to him.

That thought made Harry Black laugh right out loud.

Because before long, that was going to change.

Because before long, his name was going to be one of the best-known names in the entire world.

Because of what he was about to do, soon people everywhere would turn to each other and say...

Harry Black?

Who the hell is Harry Black?

TWO

The breeze stiffened and Harry Black stopped and stood savoring the tang of salt and fish from off the ocean. He thought for a moment of all the places across that ocean that he would never see again if he went through with this.

Was he really going to do it?

He had thought about it for a long time, years really, but it was a poem he had read as a young man and then accidentally stumbled over again recently that had caused him finally to decide for sure.

A poem.

Harry Black shook his head at the absurdity of it, then raised his arms and recited to the sea:

> And would it have been worth it, after all,
> After the cups, the marmalade, the tea,
> Among the porcelain, among some talk of you
>   and me,
> Would it have been worthwhile,
> To have bitten off the matter with a smile,
> To have squeezed the universe into a ball

> To roll it towards some overwhelming question,
> To say: "I am Lazarus, come from the dead,
> Come back to tell you all, I shall tell you all."

T.S. Eliot wrote *The Love Song of J. Alfred Prufrock* when he was only twenty-two years old. The thought of that always made Harry Black shiver. How could anyone understand at twenty-two what Eliot understood about the quandary that aging brought with it?

Did you finally tell people the truth before you left this world? Or did you just leave quietly and take the truth with you? This was a world made of secrets, and Harry Black knew some of the biggest ones.

He shouted the lines from Eliot into the wind again:

> I am Lazarus, come from the dead,
> Come back to tell you all, I shall tell you all.

And he was. He was going to tell them all.
He was going to tell the world what he had done.
He was going to tell the world what *they* had done.

Harry Black sighed and started walking toward Monkey Mountain again. His eyes drifted over the temple at the top. No more flashes. Maybe the binocular-wielding tourist had left. If there had been one there in the first place.

He had thought for a long time about the best way to tell the world what he knew, and he had decided that publishing a book was the only way to go about it. It was all far too complicated simply to blurt out a few stories to some blow-dried moron on television. Besides, putting what he knew in a book offered him an additional benefit that he had decided was critical: he could arrange for it to be published only after he had left this world.

The thought of becoming a public figure filled him with

horror, and that was exactly what would happen to him if he did this while he was still alive. It would set off an earthquake.

Do I dare
Disturb the universe?
In a minute there is time
For decisions and revisions which a minute will
reverse.

Damn right, he dared. And nobody was going to reverse anything. Once he told the story, it would be out there forever. Everything would change.

He just didn't intend to be standing here when the bomb went off.

Being besieged by the world's media was the most uncivilized thing he could think of. It would be like an attack by a tribe of savages. Those people were utterly unconstrained by allegiance to anything other than their egos. They would scream and yell and abuse him and poke microphones and cameras at him, and it would be hell on earth.

No, he would never subject himself to that. He would write what he knew, he would tell the truth, and he would leave it for people to read after he left the building. He had passed through this world in the shadows, and he would pass out of it the same way. The light would come on after he was gone.

Harry Black knew that many people wouldn't believe him. They would dismiss him as just another crazy old fart trying to breathe life into a conspiracy theory long ago reduced to a cliché. He wouldn't have that either.

That was why the book had to be credible. The evidence would have to be presented methodically. He needed to make the case for his guilt completely bulletproof.

The thought made Harry Black laugh out loud again.

That was either a terrible choice of words, or the best choice of words ever.

. . .

Harry Black understood it wasn't nearly that simple, of course. Deciding he would write a book raised one major problem. Well, two, actually.

The first was that he had no idea how one went about getting a book published.

And the second was that he couldn't write for shit.

Neither problem was insurmountable. There had to be a lot of people around who understood how to get a book published. He would find one he could trust. How hard could it be?

And he could solve the second problem exactly the same way. There were a ton of successful writers around who couldn't write for shit either, and that certainly hadn't stopped any of them. He would solve his problem the same way they solved theirs. He would get somebody else to write the book for him. Pay them to do it, if he had to.

A sudden hair-raising shriek jerked Harry Black back to the present. He swiveled his head back, searching for its source, but he saw no one. He was completely alone on the beach.

Then the shriek came again, and this time Harry Black smiled. A seagull was surfing along on the breeze above his head. Its wings were spread wide, its beak was half open, and its dead black eyes were scanning the sand for food as it howled at the wind. He laughed and went back to thinking about his book.

He had spent a long time methodically developing and discarding ideas. Thank God for ebooks. Even out here on the edge of the civilized world, if you had an internet connection, you had instantaneous access to virtually every book ever published, at least those from the last decade or two, which was all he cared about.

In choosing a writer for his book, the first requirement, of course, was that it be someone alive. Someone who had a profile and a platform, but someone still young enough to have a significant career in front of them. A big-time writer from twenty years ago was probably either dead now or a drunk, so as a rule of thumb, he stuck to writers who had been publishing in the last decade.

He bought hundreds of books, maybe thousands, and downloaded every one of them to the Kindle app he had on his iPad. He read some of each book, all of some of them, and he began keeping a list of writers to consider.

It wasn't long before he found ways to focus his search. He quickly ruled out writers of fiction. He could only imagine the jokes if some big-time spy novelist wrote his book. And it was not long before he also ruled out writers known for books about politics and history. They had baggage, and their baggage would make it more difficult for him to shed his own.

It took only a few weeks of reading for him to realize that what he needed was a writer known for what publishers called *true crime*, frequently lurid tales of bizarre killings and tragic affairs. So he started buying and reading every true crime book he could find, concentrating first on the biggest sellers since he needed a writer with credibility, and nothing built credibility for a writer like selling a million copies.

Within a couple of months, he had found his writer. He had no doubt of it.

Tilly Talbot was British and had published a string of wildly popular true crime books. She checked all the right boxes for him. He didn't want his story to be written by an American, or by anyone over sixty. Their views would be suspect. Many people would assume they had an ax to grind or a personal theory to push. But a youngish Brit woman from an impeccable background with a reputation as a successful crime reporter? Perfect.

She had made her bones with an enormous international best-seller called *House of Horrors* about Fred and Rose West. The couple had tortured, raped, and murdered an unknown number of women between 1967 and 1987, most of them in their home in Gloucester, which the British tabloid press quickly tagged as the House of Horrors. Nine sets of bones were found under the patio and in the cellar of their house. Later, police learned that the Wests had begun their killing spree at another house, and under the floorboards of that house police found more bodies, including that of Fred's eight-year-old daughter.

Fred West killed himself in prison while awaiting trial on twelve murder charges. Mother-of-eight Rose was sentenced to life in prison for murdering ten young women, including her sixteen-year-old daughter Heather and her eight-year-old step-daughter Charmaine.

Tilly Talbot had written about all of it with both style and sensitivity. Even Harry Black was enthralled when he read *House of Horrors*, and he had next to no interest in two Brit douchebags who were famous for no reason other than murdering a string of people that included their own children. Tilly Talbot's skill as a writer had made him care anyway. That was the kind of writer he needed to tell his story. Most people would see him as a monster. Tilly Talbot could make people see him as more than that.

But it got better, at least as far as Harry Black was concerned.

Tilly Talbot's follow-up to *House of Horrors* had been a book called *American Mobster*. It had sold well, although not nearly as well as *House of Horrors*. Stories of the men who drove the mafia in America in the 1960s and 1970s were interesting, but they didn't seem to hold the same appeal to the public as a lurid book about a psychopathic couple who committed gruesome and revolting murders. Harry Black figured that said more about readers than it did about writers.

Well, never mind. He could make the names Tilly Talbot knew from writing *American Mobster* the number one topic of conversation in the world. Maybe she would even decide to do a new edition.

The real problem, Harry Black knew, wasn't finding a writer, even a good writer. It was convincing her to become *his* writer. How many nut jobs must a famous true crime writer hear from, people claiming that they had information about the crime of the century? And every one of them probably told her the same thing. They would share it with her, for a price of course, and she would become even more famous than she already was.

Harry Black had to distinguish himself from the crazies or he knew she would ignore him. He had to show her right from the start that he was different from the kind of people she usually heard from. And he *was* different.

First, he didn't want money. Not a cent.

And second, he actually *did* know about the crime of the century. With what he could tell her, she could publish the biggest-selling true crime book ever written.

So, what could he tell her?

He could tell her who really had committed the crime of the century.

He could tell her for the simplest of all reasons.

It had been him.

H e started by setting up an email address that was as close to untraceable as such things got these days, which was to say not untraceable at all. He understood it wouldn't withstand an attack by people with the right expertise, but it ought to be good enough to get him through the initial steps of establishing contact. She wasn't going to call MI6 on him, at least not right at the beginning.

But getting in touch with Tilly Talbot had been a lot harder than he expected. Who knew that best-selling writers had such an army of agents, assistants, minders, and managers protecting them? It had taken him several weeks and dozens of emails to work his way from one to another until he finally received a reply from someone claiming to be Tilly Talbot herself. Of course, the email could have come from anyone. He understood that. So, he insisted she telephone him.

He was being cautious, but he understood that eventually he would have to take a leap of faith. Even if she called, how would he know it was really her? A female voice could belong to anybody. It could be just another assistant to whom she had palmed him off.

He had to do something which would draw her in enough to make certain she called, and that she did it personally.

And he knew exactly how to do that.

In *American Mobster,* Tilly Talbot had devoted an entire chapter to Sam Giancana. Giancana was an American Mafia boss who ran the Chicago Outfit from 1957 to 1966.

During the 1960s, the Central Intelligence Agency recruited Giancana to develop a plan to use Mafia assets to assassinate Cuban leader Fidel Castro. Other mob figures had been involved, of course — Handsome John Roselli from California, Sam Trafficanto from Florida, and Carlos Marcello from Louisiana — but Giancana was the boss, and he had the final word.

It was the ultimate conjunction of interests between the government of the United States and organized crime. The government wanted Castro dead, but they couldn't simply murder him. Governments didn't assassinate each other's leaders anymore, at least not if there was any chance they would get caught at it. But organized crime wanted Castro dead just as badly as the government did. He had seized their casinos and run them out of Cuba, and they wanted back in. There was a lot of money to be made there.

They called the plan to kill Castro and topple the Cuban government Operation Mongoose. The methods proposed to assassinate Castro included scenarios so bizarre they seemed like ideas for slapstick movies: cigars poisoned with botulinum toxin, a tubercle-bacilli-infected scuba diving suit, a booby-trapped conch shell placed on the sea bottom, and an exploding cigar.

Of course, they also considered the traditional mafia-style approaches as well: a shot from a sniper during one of Castro's frequent public speeches, or perhaps blowing him up somewhere.

Operation Mongoose eventually resulted in several actual assassination attempts. They all failed, of course. Most of them comically.

In 1975, Senator Frank Church launched an investigation into Operation Mongoose and other activities of the Central Intelligence Agency. On the night of June 19, 1975, shortly before Giancana was scheduled to testify to the Church Committee, a gunman entered his house in Oak Park, Illinois, and shot him in the head seven times with a .22 caliber pistol.

No one was ever arrested or charged with his murder. The precise motive was never determined either, although naturally there was considerable speculation that someone didn't want Giancana appearing before the Church Committee.

Harry Black ended his email to Tilly Talbot with the number for a throwaway phone he had acquired solely to receive a call from her. It had an American SIM card so that the number would tell her he was in the US, which of course he wasn't.

It was an elementary precaution, but a necessary one. If she freaked after she saw his email, he didn't want her to have any information that might allow somebody to track him down.

And why would she freak?

Because of what he wrote after he gave her the number to call.

I know who killed Sam Giancana.
I was there in Oak Park, Illinois, on the night of June 19, 1975.
I know who killed Giancana, and I know why they killed him.
And I'll tell you.

THREE

I t didn't take Tilly Talbot long to call. He knew it wouldn't. How could she resist bait like that?

Her voice was pleasant, warm and well-modulated. Her accent was full-on upper-class Brit, bubbling with weekends spent at the manor house and visits to the Royal Box at Ascot. They had a pleasant conversation and he admired her for injecting just the right amount of skepticism into it.

He knew he could have been talking to just another assistant or researcher, but he was almost certain that wasn't the case. She was approaching him in exactly the right way, in exactly the way he would have approached her if their positions had been reversed. Besides, what he had dangled was too big. If there was anything to it, she wouldn't risk losing him by letting some research assistant pretend to be her.

No, he had Tilly Talbot on the line. He was sure of it. Now what he had to do was reel her in.

She said nothing disparaging or insulting, but she expressed just enough doubt about his claim to challenge him to convince her. So, he did. He told her some things about the murder of Sam Giancana. Most of them she could confirm from public sources, but some of them she couldn't since there were details that had never been made public. In every high-profile murder, there were *always* details that were never made public.

He told her how many shots had been fired and where they struck Giancana. He told her Giancana's body had been left on the floor of his basement kitchen. She could confirm both of those things easily enough, he was certain.

But he also told her what Giancana had been doing in that basement kitchen. He was frying sausages and peppers for his dinner. That would be a little more difficult for her to confirm, but when she did, he would be well on the way to convincing her he was for real.

You really know who shot Sam Giancana? she asked.

Yes.

Who?

Harry Black couldn't resist pausing for a few seconds. It was corny as hell to do that, he knew, but he did it anyway. He probably would have thrown in a drum roll before he answered if he could have.

I did, he said.

There was a silence after that. He would have expected nothing less.

Eventually, of course, she asked him why he had done it. He told her it had been for the simplest reason possible. He was hired to do it.

By whom? she asked.

And he had remained completely silent.

She had been unfazed by that. A true professional. He couldn't have asked for more.

Are you telling me you're a hitman for hire? she had asked after a few moments had passed.

Of course, she had. He had been ready for that question, but it still made him uncomfortable to try to fashion an answer she would understand. The obvious answer, he supposed, was yes. But if someone had asked Michelangelo if he painted ceilings, the obvious answer to that question would have been yes, too.

He needed her to see it was more complicated than that. He didn't hire out to angry wives who wanted to dispose of straying husbands. Harry Black had once been a man at the very top of his profession. When a targeted kill was needed to change the course of history, or perhaps to protect the course of history, Harry Black was the man who came to the minds of people who were powerful enough to do that changing or that protecting.

Not many people knew that Harry Black existed, of course. Just the people who needed to know.

He wasn't an ideologue. He didn't employ his skills to advance a particular philosophy. He didn't judge those who brought him a problem to solve or substitute his judgment for theirs on whether a targeted killing was the right and just solution.

Harry Black was a craftsman. Other people designed the future. He just built it for them.

All right, she had said. *Let me check out what you've given me, and we'll talk again.*

No, he had said then, *we won't. Check whatever you like. If you decide I might be worth your time, send me an email. Use the same address you used before. One word only. Just say …* okay.

And what happens if I send that email?

We'll meet in person, and I'll tell you the rest of it.

The rest? You mean, who hired you to kill Giancana?

Yes.

Harry Black tossed in another pause for effect.

That and a lot more.

He had waited for her response to that, half expecting her to laugh, but she had remained silent.

If you send that email, he finished, *I'll meet you at the Oriental Hotel in Bangkok a week from today. Next Thursday. Four in the afternoon. In the Author's Lounge. If you don't send the email, we'll never speak again.*

One week? she had said. *You sound like you're in a hurry.*

I am, he had told her. *I don't know how much time I have left.*
The email came the next day.
Okay, was what it said.

H arry Black had reached the spot on the beach where he usually turned around, but today he kept on walking. He felt stronger than he had in a while, and something about the morning drew him on.

He and Tilly Talbot had gotten on well when they met in Bangkok. She was younger than he expected and far better looking. She was also smart and charming. If only he had been about thirty years younger … well, he wasn't, so why think about it?

They met in the Author's Lounge of the Oriental Hotel. The name gave a touch of irony to his choice of meeting places that was perhaps a bit on the precious side, but he didn't care. He liked the place. It was where he usually met people when he didn't want them to know where he lived. And, for years now, that had been everybody.

It was a brilliantly blue Bangkok afternoon. They had tea on the terrace beside the Chao Phraya River and talked for over an hour. He had told her many things, but what he had not told her was who had hired him to kill Sam Giancana. Or why.

If you won't tell me that, she said, *I've got no story.*

I don't want you to have just a story, he told her. *I want you to have the biggest true crime story anyone has ever had. I've committed far more important crimes than that, and I intend to tell you about every one of them.*

More important than killing Giancana?

He had nodded.

Oh my, she said.

That was when he told her about the notebooks he had kept. He had made a detailed plan in a separate notebook for every single one of his assignments. They were ordinary little red notebooks like school children once used. Cardboard covers, tight spirals of metal rings, white paper inside lined with faint blue rules. Ordinary. Unremarkable in every way.

Except for what they contained.

No one knew about his notebooks. Christ, the people he worked for would have shit themselves if they had known.

He gave her one of them. The one that contained his detailed planning to kill Sam Giancana.

Take it and read it, he told her. *Decide if you want to write my book. If you do, I'll tell you everything. I'll tell you about things that are so big that you'll forget about Sam Giancana.*

She had raised her eyebrows at that, but she said nothing.

If you decide to do it, just send another email to the same address with the same one-word text: okay. *Then I'll tell you where we can meet. You'll need to plan on staying for a few days. There's a lot to cover. I'll hold nothing back. I'll even give you the rest of my notebooks.*

You're saying you have material like this — she tapped her finger on the notebook he had just given her — *for other murders?*

He had nodded.

And you'll show it to me?

I'll give it to you, he told her.

She took that in, but she still said nothing.

Harry Black hadn't kept all those notebooks, some of them for more than fifty years, to use them against anyone. He was a professional, perhaps the most successful ever at his chosen profession. He had kept them for the sake of history. Harry Black had changed the world. The world ought to know that, he thought, eventually.

I do have some conditions, he told her.

I thought you might.

There are only two. First, you must not share what I tell you with anyone or show anyone the notebooks I give you until the book you write is published.

That sounds reasonable.

And second, you will not publish the book until after my death.

She considered that for a long time and then nodded slowly.

That might be a while, she had said.

No, he had told her, *it won't.*

Two days after they had met in Bangkok at the Oriental Hotel, he got another email from Tilly Talbot.

Okay, was what it said.

S he was coming to his little beach town later today. This would be her third trip here, their fourth session altogether, including their first meeting in Bangkok.

In their second session, the first time she came to Hua Hin, he told her about killing John Roselli. And he told her about his involvement in Jimmy Hoffa's murder.

In their third session, he told her about a woman named Mary Meyer he had killed back in 1964 while she was taking an afternoon walk along the towpath of the old C&O Canal in Washington DC. The name Mary Meyer had meant nothing to Tilly Talbot when he told her the story, but then he hadn't expected her to recognize it. Not many people did.

What he did expect was that she would research Mary Meyer online overnight, and she had. When they met the next day, she looked nervous. He could understand that, because now she knew who Mary Meyer was.

He could see her starting to put it all together.

This would be his fourth session with Tilly Talbot. He figured the time for the big finish had arrived.

He had spent the last couple of days going through the notebooks he was going to give her. He hadn't looked at them in decades. Reading them was like reading history, somebody else's history. But it wasn't somebody else's history. It was his.

Everything was there. The planning, the execution, and — perhaps most important — who he had been working for. But it was important to him she not just *know.* She had to *understand,* too.

When people talked about covert action, they usually meant

things like the CIA's Bay of Pigs operation or the Israelis campaign in retaliation for the massacre of Israeli athletes during the 1972 Munich Olympic games, but those weren't real covert actions. Everyone knew who was behind them. The real covert actions, the ones that mattered, were the actions so well hidden that only a handful of people ever knew about them. The real covert actions were the ones you didn't know happened.

The people who set events like that into motion always did it in the name of freedom and democracy, some fucking city on some fucking hill, but every action shared the same common denominator: making the masses think someone else was responsible. The things they did could never come back to them.

That was where men like Harry Black came in.

H e suddenly realized he had walked a lot further than he customarily did, and he was getting weary. Maybe it was time to go back.

The next few days were going to be the most important of his life. He had a lot to tell Tilly Talbot, and some of it would be hard. It would force him to revisit places he buried deep in his memories, places he had hoped never to visit again.

He stopped walking and stood still for a moment. His eyes went as they usually did at this end of the beach to the temple on top of Monkey Mountain, and he watched the rising sun glinting off the shards of colored glass baked into the tiles.

He noticed he was breathing harder than he usually did when he walked. He was getting close to the end. Very close. He could feel it coming.

Harry Black raised his arms, turned his head into the wind blowing off the sea, and shouted another passage from *Prufrock*.

I grow old ... I grow old ...

I shall wear the bottoms of my trousers rolled.

Shall I part my hair behind? Do I dare to eat a
    peach?

I shall wear white flannel trousers, and walk upon
    the beach.

I have heard the mermaids singing, each to each.

I do not think that they will sing to me.

And, oddly enough, after the eventful and consequential life he had lived, that was the very last thought Harry Black ever had.

The 285-grain Hornady bullet arrived at exactly that moment from a sniper rifle fired more than half a mile away.

The bullet had left the rifle's muzzle at three thousand feet per second, generating five thousand foot-pounds of energy. By the time it arrived at Harry Black a full second and a half later, it was down to one thousand feet per second and a little less than two thousand foot-pounds of energy.

But that was plenty.

The bullet shattered his skull, bored through his frontal lobe, and exploded out the back of his head.

Harry Black crumpled to the hard-packed sand a lifeless mess.

Harry Black had left the building.

FOUR

Tilly Talbot had been called Tinks by nearly everyone she knew for as long as she could remember. She had no idea where she got that stupid nickname. Her mother always claimed it was because of her sunny disposition, but she didn't think that was it. She was pretty sure there was a joke there from her childhood that no one wanted to tell her about. Still, nicknames that sounded ridiculous were the norm in the London social circles in which she had grown up. She had gone to school with a Spunky, a Grunter, a Bumpy, a Flea, and a Stiffy, so maybe she hadn't come out too badly after all.

When she hit it big as a true crime writer, she had done her best to bury that nickname. Tinks Talbot didn't ring with credibility, did it? She thought Tilly Talbot sounded more serious — well, at least a little — and so that was mostly how people knew her now. Only her closest friends called her Tinks anymore. Either the people who were her closest friends, or a few who wanted to act like they were.

Credibility mattered in what she did. True crime was a funny genre. It fell somewhere between serious journalism and entertaining fiction. The beginning was all journalism, of course. You found people and you convinced them to talk to you. It was your credibility that got you through the door. Then you got them to like you, to trust you, and to talk to you. It was just that simple, and just that complicated.

The trust thing bothered her sometimes. She always tried to act honorably, and most of the time she did, but she knew she got people to tell her things that later they would wish they hadn't, and then she used what they told her to build up her story. There was a rather glib line about the writing profession that was widely attributed to Joan Didion: *Writers are always selling someone out.*

Tilly didn't know whether Joan Didion ever actually said that, but if she hadn't, she probably should have, because it was true.

You took the things other people trusted you enough to tell you, built on them, and spun them into a tale enticing enough to get a ton of people to buy the goddamn book. That was the only thing anyone cared about: how many people bought the book.

It wasn't the money. At least, not exactly. She had grown up with family money and plenty of it had come to her. She didn't need any more. But the amount of money you made reflected how many books you sold, and it was the number of sales that made a writer or broke a writer. Whether it was the money you cared about or not, it was the money that mattered in the end.

Nobody wanted to know a writer who didn't sell books, and everybody wanted to know one who did. She hated thinking about it that way. It sounded so crass. But it was the simple truth of the profession she had chosen, and she had learned to accept it without flinching. However you looked at it, personal credibility was still at the bottom of everything. If you wrote true crime books and people didn't talk to you and trust you with their stories, you had nothing.

When she was digging up the details of crimes someone had committed, the people she had to get to trust her weren't people who would have felt comfortable talking to somebody called

Tinks Talbot. That sounded like a toffee-nosed Sloane Ranger who lived in Chelsea and swilled champagne with her friends at lunch.

The people who had something to say about the brutal crimes she mostly investigated were more likely people who had never even been to Chelsea and wouldn't have felt comfortable there if they had. Somebody named Tilly Talbot sounded more like a person they might have encountered somewhere in their life. Somebody who wasn't a toffee-nosed Sloane Ranger.

Tilly Talbot sounded more like the name of an ordinary person than Tinks Talbot did. Sort of.

This was her third trip to Hua Hin to see Harry Black. Hua Hin wasn't an easy place to get to, but it was looking like all the effort she had put into getting there would be worthwhile.

The airport in Hua Hin was a sleepy little spot with only one runway, although she supposed one was all you needed unless you had the kind of problem she didn't want to think about. It had very little scheduled air service, only a few flights every day, and no international flights at all except for a couple of weekly flights from Kuala Lumpur since there was major traffic in Malaysian golfers traveling up to sample the well-known courses that dotted the area.

Most people who came to Hua Hin by air flew into Bangkok and then took a bus or hired a taxi for the two or three-hour highway trip south along the Gulf of Thailand, but she couldn't bear the thought of that. No story was worth spending three hours in a rattletrap Toyota with a Bangkok taxi driver. Well, that wasn't entirely true. This one might be. But she still preferred to fly from London to Kuala Lumpur and then join the Malaysian golfers on a short Thai Air Asia flight direct to Hua Hin rather than take a taxi down from Bangkok.

She still wasn't quite certain what to make of Harry Black. The first time they had met at the Oriental Hotel in Bangkok, he claimed to have killed Sam Giancana. Since she had written a book about mobsters in America, she already knew a good deal about the murder of Giancana, and what he told her was consistent with what she knew. Then, when she checked the other details he gave her with the sources she had drawn on for her book, they turned out to be exactly correct, right down to what Giancana had been cooking for dinner when somebody pumped seven .22 caliber bullets into his head and neck.

That proved nothing, of course. Information wasn't that hard to get, and if you did it right, you could easily parlay crime details you had gathered through diligent research into masquerading as someone you weren't. She had been fooled before. Only once, but it had happened, and she wasn't going to let it happen again.

Her bullshit detector had remained encouragingly silent when Harry Black claimed to have killed Sam Giancana. When all the details he gave her checked out, she decided to stick with it for a while and see where it went.

In their first session in Hua Hin, Harry Black claimed to have killed Johnny Roselli, another prominent American mobster and one closely associated with Sam Giancana. He had also claimed to have been involved with the abduction and murder of Jimmy Hoffa, although he insisted he had not personally pulled the trigger.

When she checked the details he gave her about those killings with her sources, they again checked out perfectly. It was beginning to look like this grandfatherly figure she was chatting with in an out-of-the-way beach town on the Gulf of Thailand actually had once been a mafia button man of some importance. That was no small thing. A guy sent to murder some of the most significant figures in American organized crime during the 1970s had to be someone trusted by people who carried even more weight than Giancana, Roselli, and Hoffa. And there hadn't been many such people.

Harry Black was still refusing to tell her who his orders to kill Giancana, Roselli, and Hoffa had come from, but she was sure he would tell her, eventually. It was important to him that this book had a tremendous impact, and he understood that without knowing who had ordered those hits, she didn't have a story worth telling.

He was going to tell her when he was ready, she was sure of it, and then she would have one hell of a book.

She was starting to feel it in her bones.

On her second visit to Hua Hin, everything changed. Harry Black told her about killing someone named Mary Meyer in Washington DC in 1964. She had never heard of Mary Meyer, but when she looked into the case and found out who Mary Meyer was, she started getting scared. Dealing with a button man for the mob who killed prominent mobsters back in the 1970s was one thing, but suddenly their conversations were moving to a frightening level of conspiracy and collusion.

Mary Meyer had been John Kennedy's secret lover when he was president. It was rumored she had kept detailed diaries of her conversations with Kennedy, including his plans to reduce the power and influence of the CIA after the fiasco of the Bay of Pigs. Within an hour of Mary Meyer's murder, a neighbor of hers discovered CIA counterintelligence chief James Angleton ransacking her row house in Georgetown. She assumed Angleton was looking for the rumored diaries, but it appeared he didn't find them. The consensus was that no one had ever found them, if they existed at all.

She had heard the conspiracy theories about collusion between the American mafia and the CIA, of course, and she knew some of them went back to a series of abortive plans to kill Fidel Castro in the 1960s. She also knew that Sam Giancana and John Roselli were the mobsters usually fingered for working with the CIA in most of the stories she had heard, but the research for her mafia book hadn't turned up enough solid evidence of a connection for her to include those tales in the book.

Now she was talking to someone who actually did appear to have been a hitman for the mob and who claimed he was sent to kill both Giancana and Roselli. But he also claimed to have been sent by someone to kill John Kennedy's lover, a woman who had stashed away secret notes detailing Kennedy's intention to break the power and influence of the CIA.

Was the mob trying to grab Mary Meyer's diaries to blackmail the CIA into giving them cover for their activities? In a world filled with often strange and inexplicable connections, it would be hard to find one any more sinister than that.

No wonder Harry Black wanted her to write a book about what he had done, and no wonder he didn't want it published until after he was dead. This was dynamite. If there was someone out there powerful enough to send Harry Black after Giancana and Roselli and then send him to grab Mary Meyer's diaries to blackmail the CIA ... well, whoever that had been was probably dead now. It was nearly fifty years ago, after all, but there were no doubt people still alive who knew about it and wanted to keep anyone from ever finding out it happened. Powerful people. Powerful enough to come after Harry Black to shut him up.

Right now, no one knew Harry Black was talking. No one but her, and she sure as hell wasn't going to tell anyone.

But after the book was published, all that would change. Overnight, Harry Black would become one of the best-known names in the entire world. His anonymous life would be over, and she was certain there were people out there who would come after him.

The only safe way for Harry Black to tell his story was to do it after he was gone.

They couldn't kill a man who was already dead, could they?

FIVE

The first time Tilly Talbot came to Hua Hin, Harry Black arranged for her to stay at the Hyatt. It was a very pleasant hotel with a large, open-air lobby from which two low-rise wings of rooms with large balconies spread out to embrace an unobstructed view of the Gulf of Thailand and Hua Hin beach.

Their initial conversations had been there, sitting on lounge chairs on a gently rolling, pea green lawn just above the beach that was as tightly mowed as a putting green. It wasn't until her second trip that Harry Black seemed comfortable enough with her presence to invite her to his house. To get to it, they had walked south along the beach for no more than half a kilometer. She gathered that convenience was probably the reason he had chosen the Hyatt. Whatever his reason, she had liked the Hyatt just fine, so she had returned to it for her second trip and now for her third.

She unpacked in her room on the second floor at the very end of the south wing. When she was done, she took a shower to wash away the smell of the overnight flight, changed into knee-length khaki shorts and a pink polo shirt, and walked out barefoot onto the balcony. She considered ordering some breakfast from room service, but instead she just leaned there on the rail, wiggled her toes against the cool tiles underfoot, and took deep breaths of the salty air blowing in off the Gulf of Thailand.

No, forget the breakfast, she thought. She felt ready right now for her next conversation with Harry Black.

She took out her telephone, waited while it logged into the local cell system, and called to tell him she was there.

No answer. No voicemail.

Odd, she thought. *That's never happened before.*

He was expecting her and he knew she would arrive early this morning, so why wasn't he picking up? Had he forgotten?

No, of course he hadn't forgotten. Harry Black was a meticulously organized man and he would be waiting to hear from her. Perhaps he was just in the bathroom.

After a few minutes, she rang again.

Still no answer.

She went inside and got the notes she had made after their last conversation, came back out, and settled into a chair on the balcony to read through them and refresh her memory a little. After about twenty minutes, she called again.

Still no answer.

Now she was beginning to worry. Harry Black was an eighty-six-year-old man. When an eighty-six-year-old man who is expecting your call doesn't pick up the phone over a period of a half hour, you worry. You can't help it.

She thought about it for a few moments and decided the right thing to do was to get herself to Harry Black's house and make sure everything was all right. She was sure he wouldn't mind. There was probably some completely innocent explanation for him not answering his telephone, but all the same, it was best to make sure. He lived close enough for her to walk, but it had been a long and wearying day of travel and she decided she would ask the hotel to telephone a taxi instead.

The driver had no difficulty finding the house, which was a relief. She had asked the hotel doorman to describe to the driver where it was. He had smiled and nodded, and then the taxi driver had smiled and nodded when he heard the doorman's instructions, but then Thais always smiled and nodded when they were told something, even when they had no earthly idea what you were talking about. She didn't know a single word in the Thai language and had no idea what she was going to do if the doorman's explanation hadn't gotten her to the right place. But it had.

After the taxi drove away, she mounted the steps to Harry Black's front door and rang the bell. Nothing happened. He didn't answer. No one answered, and she heard no sound of movement from inside. She wasn't hopeful, but she rang the bell a second time anyway. Still nothing.

She was just trying to decide what to do when a woman's voice called out.

"He's gone down to the beach, dear."

Tilly looked over her shoulder and saw a small woman who was probably somewhere in her sixties or seventies watching her from the porch of the house next door. She was lean and tanned, and Tilly's first impression was that the woman appeared quite fit, like she had just returned from a cross-country bicycle race she had almost certainly won.

The woman pointed toward the beach, as if Tilly might somehow be unable to work out where it was.

"Just go down the steps and turn right. He always walks that way. To the right."

She thanked the woman, thinking that she must keep a pretty close eye on the comings and goings in the area. She not only knew that Harry Black had gone down to the beach, but she knew the direction in which he had walked.

Tilly retraced her steps from the front door back down to the driveway and took the short flight of concrete steps at the bottom down to the beach. She looked both ways, but she didn't see Harry Black, so she turned right as his neighbor had suggested.

At least that was the direction that would take her back to the Hyatt. Even if she didn't find him, she would end up in some place she wanted to be.

Tilly hadn't gone very far when she saw a small crowd of people gathered on the beach ahead of her. There were probably a dozen people altogether, maybe a few more than that. It was a mixed group of foreigners and Thais, and she noticed it included several men wearing the tight brown uniforms of Thai police. Uniformed policemen on a beach were a jangling sight, so she looked closer.

That was when she realized they were all looking down at something lying on the sand.

My God, she thought, *has someone drowned?*

As she watched, two more policemen appeared, walking from the opposite direction. One of them seemed to be older and more senior, and the crowd respectfully parted as he arrived so that he could inspect whatever it was they were looking at. When it did, she caught a glimpse of a man stretched out on the beach. His bare feet were pointed directly toward her and they weren't moving. No one in the group appeared to be attending to him, so it seemed likely to her that he really was dead.

It is a drowning, she thought. *What a very sad way for this visit to begin.*

She immediately scolded herself for the silly self-absorption of that thought. Some poor man had just died, and here she was thinking about it ruining her trip.

Tilly Talbot hesitated for a moment. She would just as soon have turned around, but the way back to her hotel led right past the little group gathered around the man's dead body. It would have been silly to walk back to Harry Black's house and then have to figure out how to get a taxi from there, so she carried on.

As she drew closer, the older policeman who was standing with his hands on his hips staring down at the body suddenly looked up and met her eyes. He kept his gaze on her as she walked toward the group and she wondered if it was just because she was a foreign woman or if there was some other reason.

Mostly to shift her eyes away from the policeman, she glanced down at the body. She didn't want to, but that was where her eyes went. A space in the crowd around the body opened just then, and she got her first completely clear view of the dead man.

Tilly caught her breath and stopped walking.

She was looking at Harry Black lying dead on Hua Hin beach.

And he hadn't drowned or even had a heart attack or a stroke. Her profession had brought her into contact with enough violent death for her to have no doubt about what she was looking at. Harry Black had been shot in the face, and his skull had exploded, leaving blood and brain matter smeared over the beach behind where he had fallen.

It was all she could do not to gasp and turn away, but she could feel the policeman's eyes on her and she didn't want to attract any more attention than she already had. After only a few seconds, she knew exactly what she had to do.

She got moving again. Not too fast, and not too slow. She walked past the group gathered around Harry Black's body without another glance and went directly back to the Hyatt. Within ten minutes, she had packed, telephoned the front desk with a hastily invented story about a family emergency, and asked them to get her a taxi that would drive her all the way to the airport in Bangkok.

Someone had brutally murdered Harry Black, and she didn't have the slightest doubt that his murder was connected to the things he had been telling her. It had already occurred to her that those things might well be enough to get Harry Black killed if anyone knew he was talking about them, but no one knew, did they?

Now she saw she was wrong about that. Someone *did* know. And if they knew Harry Black was talking, they probably knew who he was talking *to*.

Was someone looking for her now as well? And did they know she was right here in Thailand?

There weren't many international flights in and out of Hua Hin, and she sure as hell wasn't going to sit around a day or two waiting for one of them. She didn't care where she went. She had to get herself on the first flight she could find that would take her out of the country, anywhere out of the country, and that would be a flight leaving from Bangkok.

When she was safely out of Thailand, she could get lost for a while and stay lost until she figured out what to do next.

She certainly didn't want to end up like poor Harry Black, and suddenly that seemed like a serious risk.

SIX

His coffeemaker loosed one last blast of the slobbering noises that Samuel Tay always found so deeply consoling. They signaled that the little machine had once again successfully converted his limited hopes and diminishing dreams into coffee. He filled a white ceramic mug and walked outside into his garden.

Tay lived in Singapore's Emerald Hill neighborhood on a quiet dead-end street. It was a sleepy area of classic row houses steeped in dignity and tranquility, yet it was barely a hundred yards from busy Orchard Road. Motor vehicles were banned from the bottom of Emerald Hill Road where Tay lived and no one but pedestrians and an occasional bicyclist passed on the street in front of his house. During the week, it was almost always peaceful, but on weekends, that changed.

The lure of free street parking led people headed to the dozens of massive shopping malls that lined Orchard Road to cruise the area to the north of his neighborhood to avoid the extortionate prices charged by the city's commercial garages. After they parked their cars, most of those people seemed to end up walking straight down Emerald Hill Road, right past Tay's house. The trickle of pedestrians during the week swelled to a torrent on weekends.

And then there were the tourists. The weekends brought them out in droves, too. A lot of Singapore guidebooks described the houses along Emerald Hill Road as fine examples of early colonial architecture, and Tay supposed that was true enough. Still, finding mobs of tourists taking photographs of his house every weekend disquieted him.

Tay hated the weekends. The weekends made him feel like he was living in an amusement park.

He had inherited the house from his mother, who had in turn inherited it from his father. It was a three-story structure of vaguely nineteenth-century appearance with a tiny front garden that was surrounded by a high wall of white-painted brick. A heavy gate of filigreed black iron bars filled a low archway. Through it, Tay could see out to Emerald Hill Road. If he wanted to. Which he almost never did.

On the opposite side of the house was a back garden, which over the years had become his sanctuary from an unpredictable world. It was paved in bricks, now somewhat uneven from more than a century of the earth shifting beneath them. The garden was surrounded by a high wall constructed of the same brick, and it was lined with a thick barricade of banana trees and bamboo that had the effect of dampening stray noise almost to the point of complete silence.

A violent storm had swept across Singapore during the night, pushing curtains of rain across the city. Gusts of wind bent and twisted the banana trees and bamboo so violently that the big leaves had slapped out the rhythm of the storm against his bedroom windows, and that had roused him far earlier than he was accustomed to getting out of bed. Now pieces of the leaves that had succumbed to the violence lay scattered over the bricks. He would have to sweep them up later. Or maybe not. It was too damn early to think about doing anything that might be even remotely productive.

The morning air was hot and heavy, but the brick pavers felt chilly against his feet and the living room lights cast a pale and calming glow out through the panes of the French doors. He walked to the teak table where he drank his coffee every morning, pulled out a chair, and sat down. Then he pulled another chair over and swung his feet onto it. As he took his first sip of coffee, he stared balefully at the heavy ceramic ashtray that had held pride of place in the center of the table for as many years as he could remember.

Tay had smoked Marlboro Reds for most of his life. Smoking had never been a habit for him. It was a choice. He liked everything about it. He liked the crinkle of the foil as he peeled open a new pack; he liked the smell of tobacco that wafted from the pack when he broke it open; he liked the sound of a wooden match flaring into flame; and he liked the taste of the first draw of nicotine into his lungs. It was a ritual for him, a comforting routine, one rife with small meditative moments that offered momentary escape from an unreliable world.

It always made Tay feel a little downhearted to reflect on the way the world had passed him by. Smoking had gone from commonplace, to unusual, to unwelcome, to an abomination. Smokers had become pariahs, social outcasts targeted for extinction by the very large number of people in the world who seemed to know what was good for everyone else and who stridently demanded that everyone else behave in exactly the way they told them to. When he had been sitting here in his garden enjoying an evening cigarette, he half expected to see people coming over the walls to demand that he stop smoking immediately and beg their forgiveness for ever having done so in the first place.

It was no longer necessary for Tay to imagine his garden under assault by militant non-smokers. He hadn't had a cigarette in months. Despite that, he had left the big ashtray exactly where it had been for decades as a reminder of what his life had once been. Better times should always be remembered.

Tay hadn't stopped smoking out of any concern about the social approbation it brought with it. If anything, he missed all that now almost as much as he did the taste and smell of tobacco. Smoking had been a mark of his disdain for social fashion. Without it, he was just another cranky old man.

Tay had found quitting easier than he imagined it would be. Or maybe the health scare that had driven him to it had simply frightened him enough to make it seem easy. He had experienced several episodes of coughing up blood, and when those episodes showed no signs of stopping on their own, he knew he had to see a doctor.

When all this happened, he was in Hong Kong, and a man he knew slightly there had arranged for him to be examined in a private clinic. He would always remember the sound of that doctor's voice when he told Tay that they had found a mass in one of his lungs. *A mass.* That was a hard phrase to put out of your mind.

There has been no trace of cancer in the mass, but there easily could have been. He had realized then that he wasn't quite yet ready to die and perhaps that was what had made his choice to give up cigarettes seem relatively easy. He had to admit he sometimes wondered now if he had made the right choice. What was the point of prolonging his life if he had to give up the things he loved to do it?

He drained his coffee cup and pushed himself to his feet. He reached out and gave his big ashtray an affectionate little pat, then went inside to get himself more coffee.

Tay refilled his cup from the coffeemaker in the kitchen and thought about what to do with his morning.

Should he get out his bicycle and do a few miles around the neighborhood? He had started riding when he quit smoking to stave off the weight gain everyone told him was inevitable. Age had already gifted him with quite enough extra pounds. Being miserable without his Marlboro Reds was bad enough, but the thought of being both fat *and* miserable was too much to bear.

As he understood it, the nicotine in cigarettes had the effect of speeding up your metabolism as well as limiting your taste for food, and that was why when people quit smoking they felt hungry all the time. That hadn't happened to him. Food had never been all that important to him, and it became no more important after he quit smoking. Perhaps he simply wasn't a man who was driven by his appetites.

Of course, maybe all the warnings he had read about the effects of giving up smoking had simply been wrong. He had also read that he was likely to experience anger, frustration, and irritability, but that hadn't happened either.

Or maybe it had. Anger, frustration, and irritability were already fundamental elements of his life. Not having his Marlboro Reds didn't seem to make them any worse.

W hen the bell at Tay's front gate rang, it startled him. He had very few visitors, and absolutely none he didn't expect.

He looked at his watch. It was barely eight o'clock in the morning. Who in the world would ring his front gate bell at that hour? It was either someone who had the wrong house or someone he wouldn't be happy to see. There was no other possibility.

The bell rang again, and he walked through to the living room and opened his front door. Down the short walkway and through the black iron bars of his front gate, he saw an elderly man with a Chinese-looking face. The man lifted a large brown envelope and wiggled it at him.

A delivery or some sort? He wasn't expecting anything.

He took the steps down to the walkway and went out to the gate.

"You Inspector Tay?" the man asked in a sing-song voice.

Tay nodded, and the man held up the envelope and wiggled it again.

"For you."

"From whom?"

"For you," the man repeated and poked the envelope between two of the bars.

Tay took the envelope and examined it. It was a plain brown envelope of the sort that people used to exchange documents, not a commercial envelope from one of the local courier companies. It wasn't very heavy and there was a lump in one corner as if it contained only a single small item that had fallen to the bottom. Across the center of the envelope, his name had been printed in block capitals using a heavy black marker pen. There was no return address.

When he looked up, the elderly Chinese-looking man had disappeared. Tay leaned against the gate and peered as far as he could in both directions up and down Emerald Hill Road, but there was no trace of the man. He had vanished as completely as if he had never been there at all.

Tay carried the envelope into the kitchen, poured himself more coffee, and examined it again. There was absolutely nothing to show where it had come from.

The lump in the corner was about the size of a pack of cigarettes. Surely not, Tay thought. He couldn't think of anyone he knew who would either be that cruel or think it was funny to send him a pack of cigarettes. But what else could it be?

Well, he might as well open it and find out. Surely, it was nothing sinister. Since he had retired from the Singapore police, he didn't rate sinister anymore.

He ripped the end off the envelope and dumped the contents onto the kitchen counter. There was nothing in it except for a single sheet of paper folded over once, and a mobile phone.

Tay picked up the phone and examined it. It was a black flip phone. He didn't even know they made those anymore. A cheap model, it was the sort of phone people bought to make a call or two they didn't want to be traced to them, and then threw away. People who felt the need to make it clear they were younger and hipper than he was always seemed to insist on calling them burner phones.

He unfolded the sheet of paper. The typeface was one of those annoying ones that tried to look like handwriting when everyone knew it had come out of a computer printer just like every other piece of paper did these days. Why did anyone bother? Nobody was fooled.

Worse, this printing was very small and Tay had to squint to read it. Did he need glasses? Surely not.

Maybe decreased vision was another symptom you suffered when you stopped smoking. There had to be a connection, didn't there? He hadn't had any difficulty reading small print a year ago, and now he was having great difficulty. That must be related to the lack of nicotine in his system. Had to be. He might be getting old, but he wasn't getting old *that* fast.

Tay took the note over to the window to get more light on it and moved it in and out in front of his eyes as if he were playing a trombone. Finally, he found a position in which it was more or less legible.

I need to talk to you. I will call you on this telephone in a few minutes.

Jones

J ones was the acquaintance in Hong Kong he had asked to suggest a doctor when he started coughing up blood.

Tay had been in Hong Kong trying to locate a young girl who had gone missing, and one of the people he was working with had introduced him to Jones. Jones was supposed to have some contacts that he might be willing to use to help them. He did, although it was never entirely clear to Tay what, or who, those contacts actually were.

He and Jones had gotten along very well. Jones was intelligent, thoughtful, soft-spoken, and witty. Despite their limited acquaintanceship, when Tay started coughing up blood, Jones had arranged for him to be examined discreetly at a private clinic. He had also turned out to be a warm and caring friend when Tay had been very much in need of one.

It wasn't all quite that simple, of course.

Jones was a triad crime boss. Although the details were murky, it was obvious from the resources Jones marshaled to help them find the missing girl that he was high up in the triads. Very high up.

Jones wasn't his real name, of course. It was just a name that he gave Tay because it seemed to amuse him. Tay didn't even know what the man's real name was. And he was happy enough not to.

The irony of turning to Jones when he needed help wasn't lost on Tay. He might be well-dressed and soft-spoken, but he was still a gangster. And Tay was a policeman. Well, he *used* to be a policeman, and it was hard for him to stop thinking of himself as one even now.

The worst part was that it had left Tay in the position of owing Jones a favor, and now it looked like Jones was coming to collect. Having a triad crime boss calling in a favor couldn't be a good thing, and certainly not when whatever the man wanted required the use of a disposable phone.

Did Jones seriously think Tay's phone was being monitored

by someone? If it was, Tay figured whoever was listening had long ago died of boredom.

Still, it bothered him that Jones, with his significant connections in such matters, apparently thought there was at least some chance his phone actually *was* being monitored. Had some investigative agency like Interpol that had the power, formally or otherwise, to listen in on telephone calls somehow linked him to Jones and the triads?

That *really* wouldn't be good.

Tay was just telling himself that when the black flip phone rang.

SEVEN

"How are you feeling these days, Inspector?"

"I'm fine."

"No recurrence of the …"

Jones paused while he hunted for the right word.

"… the trouble."

"I'm fine," Tay repeated.

"I am so glad to hear that. I know what you went through was a bit of a scare for you."

"It was enough of one that I've stopped smoking. For now, anyway."

"Good for you, Inspector."

"But I'm still not an inspector. At least not anymore. I'm retired from the Singapore Police, as you know perfectly well. I used to be a police inspector who smoked. Now I'm neither."

Jones chuckled.

"Then what would you like me to call you? Perhaps Non-Smoker Tay?"

"Sam will do just fine."

"Somehow that doesn't appeal to me. I much prefer Inspector Tay. It has … well, it has a touch of gravitas to it that the name Sam simply lacks, don't you think?"

Tay didn't bother to argue. He gathered Jones was used to getting his own way about almost everything. Whether he was going to call him Inspector Tay or Sam was hardly the hill on which to take a stand. He would save that for a time when it mattered.

"Why all the melodrama?" Tay asked instead.

"Melodrama?"

"A disposable phone hand-delivered by an anonymous man who vanished before I could ask any questions. You don't honestly think my telephone is being monitored by someone, do you? There's not a soul in the world who has the slightest interest in what I say on the telephone."

"Perhaps not, but there are quite a few souls in the world who are very interested in what *I* might have to say on the telephone. Even if there is only a slight chance that my call would cause you to be linked directly to me, I wanted to avoid putting you in that position."

Tay hadn't thought of that. Maybe Jones had a point there.

He cleared his throat. "Yes, well, then perhaps this is best after all," he said.

"And, Inspector, just out of an abundance of caution, would you please deal with the phone when we have completed our conversation."

"Deal with it? What does that mean? Are you going to have someone pick it up?"

"Oh goodness me, no. Normally, I'd just ask you to remove the SIM card and break it and that would be that, but I've always thought you can't be too careful."

"So, what do you want me to do?"

"Break up the SIM card, and destroy the phone. Beat it to death with a shoe or something. Then get rid of the pieces."

Tay flinched at a triad crime boss telling him to beat something to death with a shoe even if it was just a telephone, but he kept that thought to himself.

"Now, shall I get to the point of this call?" Jones continued without waiting for Tay to say anything else about the phone. "I need to ask you a favor."

Tay said nothing. He just waited.

"You will be relieved, no doubt, to hear the favor is not for me, but rather for an admirable young lady of my acquaintance named Renée Couvier. Everyone calls her Renny. She owns an art gallery here in Hong Kong, and I assisted her with financing the gallery because it promotes the work of young local artists who deserve to be recognized."

Jones paused as if he was waiting for Tay to say something, but Tay remained silent, and after a moment Jones continued.

"In the spirit of complete disclosure, let me add this. Nothing is lurking here in the background that I'm not telling you. My relationship with Renny is purely a business one, and I like to think a friendship. Other than mutual respect, there is no personal relationship between us."

Tay wasn't certain he believed that, but he was even less certain why it made any difference, so he let it go.

"What is this favor?" he asked instead.

"Renny's grandfather was recently killed. As I understand it, he retired a long time ago to a little beach town on the Gulf of Thailand called Hua Hin and he has lived there quietly for something like the last twenty-five years. A few days ago, he was taking his usual morning walk on the beach and someone shot him."

"A robbery?"

"No, not as far as Renny knows. Besides, people walking on a beach aren't usually carrying valuables that would make them a suitable candidate for a robbery, are they? Certainly not a violent one."

"Have the police arrested anyone?"

"In your usual incisive manner, Inspector, you have put your finger right on the problem. Renny says the Thai police don't appear to care very much about the case. Foreigners getting killed aren't of much interest to them unless the foreigners are prominent for some reason, and her grandfather certainly wasn't. He was just a harmless old man of eighty-six, quietly living out his remaining years at the seaside and bothering no one."

Tay wasn't certain he believed that either. In his experience, very few people were killed for no reason at all. Nobody bothers to shoot nice old men quietly living out their lives walking on the beach. People got killed for a reason. Maybe it was something they had done in the past, or perhaps it was something someone feared they might do in the future. But a random shooting of an eighty-six-year-old man for no reason at all? He had never heard of such a thing.

"I would be very grateful if you could find the time to go to Hua Hin and look into what happened, Inspector. It was diffi-cult enough for Renny to lose her grandfather when she had just found him, but knowing that his killer is probably going to walk away is very hard on her."

"What do you mean, she just found him?"

"Well, there's a complicated family story involved. I'll leave it to her to provide whatever detail she thinks is appropriate, but as I understand it, she met her grandfather for the first time a few years ago when he tracked her down and introduced himself. Her parents had always told her he was dead. That was the first she knew of his existence."

"Why would her parents say he was dead when he wasn't?"

"She doesn't know."

Tay considered that. The oddities were piling up. Maybe this woman's parents really thought the man was dead. Or maybe they didn't, and they wanted her to think so because of some-thing about his past they didn't want her to know. Could the reason they told this woman her grandfather was dead have anything to do with his murder? Of course, it could, but so could almost anything else.

"Will you do this for me, Inspector? I really would be most grateful."

Jones was polite enough not to remind Tay that there was a favor owed. A big one. Tay didn't like the whole idea of being in Jones' debt, and this at least seemed a relatively benign way to balance the books.

"I have no authority in Thailand, Jones."

As soon as he had spoken, Tay realized what a silly thing that was to say. He had no authority anywhere anymore.

"The Thai cops aren't going to listen to me," he went on. "It's more likely they'll be resentful that I'm there asking questions since that will cast doubt on the competency of their investigation."

"As I understand it, there wasn't much of an investigation."

"That will just make everything worse. The Thai cops will hardly welcome a retired Singapore cop poking around in a case they've already closed. They'll make it as difficult as they can for me to accomplish anything."

"I have some friends there. I think I can safely promise you will have the full cooperation of the Thai police."

Tay wondered what that meant, but he didn't ask. He wasn't even certain he wanted to know.

"So, let me make sure I've got this straight," he said instead. "You want me to go to the place where this man was killed and see if I can find out why it happened and then put together a case as to who did it?"

"Precisely."

"And then you want me to turn the case I've built over to the Thai police so they can arrest whoever was responsible."

"Oh dear me, no. I want you to tell me who was responsible and turn the case you've built over to me. I'll take it from there."

Tay was pretty sure he knew what *that* meant.

Tay poured himself some more coffee while he thought about Jones' ask. He could stall for a bit, say he needed to think about it maybe, but what would be the point of that?

He knew perfectly he would eventually agree, so why drag it out?

He took another sip of coffee. It was getting cold, but he drank it anyway. Coffee, hot or cold, was still coffee.

He was grateful to Jones for everything he had done when he most needed his help, and that help had been willingly given with no strings attached. Now Jones was calling the favor, but he was graceful enough not to remind Tay that was what he was doing. Tay had to admit he liked that.

He also liked the way Jones remained silent while giving Tay the space to think. The man might be a triad crime boss, but he wasn't callow and crude. He carried an air of refinement and intelligence about him, and he exhibited a sense of old-fashioned courtesy that Tay rarely encountered anymore. All of that sucked Tay in. He knew it, and he was sure Jones knew it.

Besides, being retired was a pile of crap. He missed being a homicide detective and here Jones was handing him a homicide case of his very own to investigate without a bunch of nervous bosses looking over his shoulder. The case even sounded like it had the making of being an interesting one. How could he possibly say no to that?

Tay took one more sip of cold coffee and cleared his throat.

"What is the name of this place again?" he asked.

"Hua Hin. It's a beach town on the Gulf of Thailand, about a two-hour drive south of Bangkok. I think you might even like the place."

Tay very much doubted that, but he kept the thought to himself.

"I'm sure it's very pleasant, Jones, but I'm not really a beach town kind of guy."

"It's not flashy," Jones continued, as if Tay hadn't spoken. "No showy hotels crammed next to each other along the beach with a bunch of expensive restaurants and trashy bars. It's an old-shoe kind of town. I'm willing to wager you'll find the atmosphere there very much to your liking."

Tay put down his coffee cup and shifted his phone to the other hand.

"So how do I get to this paradise on earth? Fly to Bangkok, then hire a taxi to drive me down there?"

"Oh dear me, no. I've already got everything organized for you. I'll send a plane to pick you up in Singapore and fly you directly to Hua Hin. It has a small but quite adequate airport. The plane will remain there and take you wherever your investigation leads."

Wherever his investigation led?

That sounded like Jones knew already that Tay would discover things that might require him to travel somewhere else to complete the investigation. Did Jones know something he wasn't sharing?

"I'll have someone pick up you at the airport," Jones went on. "He will remain with you for the duration of your stay to act as a local guide, and he will drive you anywhere you want to go. I've also arranged for you to use a house we have down there that we sometimes lend to our friends. It's rather nice. I'm sure you'll be very comfortable there."

Tay thought about asking who this *we* was that Jones was talking about, but he decided he would just as soon not know, at least not for sure.

"And you've organized all this in the thirty seconds since I agreed to do this?"

Jones chuckled, but to his credit, he said nothing else.

"Look," Tay said, "even if I look into this for you, I'm not sure how much I can accomplish. I don't know anything about Thailand. I've never even heard of this beach town you're talking about. I certainly don't have any contacts."

"Don't worry about that. We have lots of friends there."

There was that *we* thing again.

"How soon can you be ready to go?" Jones asked.

"I guess … well, tomorrow afternoon would be okay."

"Fine. What time?"

"Uh … four o'clock?"

"There'll be a plane waiting for you at Jet Aviation at Changi Airport at four o'clock tomorrow afternoon."

"All right, I suppose I—"

"Just a couple of other things," Jones interrupted. "Do you still have those Interpol credentials you were carrying when you were here in Hong Kong helping with the search for Emma Lau?"

When the daughter of the Chief Executive of Hong Kong had disappeared a few months back, some people he knew who had vague connections to American intelligence had been quietly trying to find her without causing a stir. They had convinced Tay to help, and they had provided him with an Interpol ID so he could explain his involvement if he needed to. It was a fake, of course. Tay didn't have anything to do with Interpol. But how did Jones know about those fake credentials? Sometimes Tay discovered Jones knew things he couldn't see how Jones could possibly know, and it made him a little wary every time he did.

"I'm not sure that would be a very good idea," Tay said after a few moments of silence.

"Which I take it to mean you *do* have them. Bring them. It *is* a good idea. People in Thailand respond to status, and official credentials give you status. You'll find them quite helpful for getting people to talk to you."

Tay sighed, but he said nothing.

"The other thing I need to mention is that Renny is in Hua Hin now waiting for you. I think you'll like her."

"Having a relative of the victim hanging around when I'm conducting an investigation isn't a very appealing idea."

"Renny is smart, and she's tough. She's also discreet."

"I'm sure she is, but it's still not a good idea to involve her."

"I understand your reservations, but I think Renny can be of help to you. I'm sure you'll like her."

"You just said that."

"Did I? I must be getting old and forgetful."

There's absolutely no chance of *that*, Tay thought, but of course he didn't say it out loud.

"Don't forget to destroy that phone you're using now," Jones went on. "The man who meets you in Hua Hin will give you a new one when you get there. You can use it to contact me whenever you need to, but I think the one you have now has reached the end of its useful life."

"Just beat it to death with a shoe, I think you said."

"Or perhaps a cricket bat. Whatever you have that's tough enough to destroy it."

"Then perhaps I should use my sunny disposition."

Jones laughed. "Thank you for doing this for me, Inspector. I won't forget it."

"I know I owe you. It's been nice of you not to say anything about it."

"Did I mention I think you'll like Renny?"

Jones laughed again, and then he hung up.

EIGHT

Tay wasn't accustomed to traveling by private plane, but he thought he would have no difficulty at all becoming accustomed to it. No check-in lines, no security lines, no lines of any kind. You just strolled out to the plane and told the pilots you were ready to go.

He had no idea what kind of plane it was. He could have asked the pilots, of course. They seemed friendly and approachable, but he figured that people who were used to flying on private planes already knew what kind of plane they were flying on, and he had no intention of outing himself as a yokel by admitting he didn't.

The only other time he had flown on a private plane was when he went to Hong Kong to join the search for Emma Lau. That one had been nice, but this one was something else entirely. Bulkheads that looked like lacquered teak, table tops of polished granite, and seats upholstered in caramel-colored leather so buttery soft it felt like silk.

Right behind the cockpit there was a cabin with four seats, each of them the size of a small car. They all rotated and tilted and folded out into what amounted to single beds. They probably did all sorts of other things, too, but Tay's limited ability to relate to machinery prevented him from figuring out what those things were.

The four chairs were arrayed around an oval table with a top made from what looked like fine-veined brown granite. Tay figured it probably functioned as both a dining table and a conference table, and he was pretty sure the sort of conferences that had occurred around it didn't bear thinking about. At least not by a retired cop.

At the back of the plane, separated by a door that looked solid enough to be soundproof, was a private cabin. Tay peeked inside and saw a double bed covered with a snow-white duvet trimmed in gold piping. There was a built-in desk that looked like rosewood, and opposite the desk was another large recliner like the ones in the front cabin. On the wall separating the cabin from the front of the plane was a large flat-panel television screen. Could you watch television on an airplane? Tay had no idea.

He was still playing with his seat about twenty minutes after takeoff when one of the pilots opened the door from the cockpit, stepped back into the cabin. It was the younger of the two pilots. He was wearing a white shirt with epaulets on both shoulders and navy slacks with creases so sharp you could use them to slice cheese.

"Can I get you anything, sir? Coffee, tea?"

Tay gathered the junior man was probably the one who got stuck doubling as the stewardess.

"We have some very fine malt whiskeys in the bar, too, sir, if you'd like something stronger."

Tay glanced at his watch. Four-thirty. A little early for him.

"No, thank you," he said. "I'm fine."

"Well, if you change your mind, sir, just pick up that handset." The man pointed to what looked like a telephone receiver tucked into a recess in the console that ran along the side of the plane under the windows. "It will connect you directly to us up front and we'll get you whatever you need."

"Thank you."

"Our flight plan today calls for a trip of just over 800 nautical miles, and we expect a flying time of two hours and twenty-three minutes, which will put you on the ground in Hua Hin just after five-thirty, local time. As I'm sure you already know, there is a one-hour time change between Singapore and Thailand."

The man repeated his salute, then returned to the cockpit and closed the door.

Tay reset his watch. He found the right buttons to lift the footrest and tilt his seat back, then he closed his eyes.

The landing in Hua Hin was so smooth that Tay might not even have realized they were on the ground if he hadn't been looking out the window. As they came in over the beach, he could see the blue of the Gulf of Thailand against a range of low hills covered in a heavy blanket of deep green vegetation. The airport was a sleepy little place with just one runway and a tiny terminal building. There were a handful of small airplanes parked off to one side in front of a hangar, but he didn't see any commercial aircraft.

As they taxied in, a white Mercedes S500 sedan appeared from around the terminal building and rolled slowly toward them. The pilot nosed in toward the terminal and cut the engines, and the Mercedes stopped about fifty feet away. A man and a woman got out and stood waiting by the front fender while a ground crewman trotted out from the terminal and did whatever ground crewmen did to secure an airplane that had just landed.

The man looked quite young, which was a surprise to Tay. When Jones told him he would have someone there to drive him and act as a local fixer, he had pictured someone who looked like a triad soldier in a Chinese gangster movie: squat, broad-shouldered, swarthy, and wearing a rumpled suit.

This young man didn't look a bit like that. He was of medium height and slim, with a deep tan and long light brown hair casually disheveled. Dressed in dark green chinos, a pink polo shirt, and light brown loafers without socks, he looked less like a triad soldier than he did a male model on his way to shoot an ad for Ralph Lauren.

The woman could easily have been there to appear in the same ad. She was tall, slightly taller than the man, and she had short dirty blonde hair cut in a no-nonsense style that Tay thought women called a pageboy. She wore yellow sandals with low heels and a white sundress with a flared skirt that bared her shoulders and stopped just above her knees. Tay couldn't help noticing that they were very nice knees, indeed.

The cockpit opened and the same pilot who had come back before unlatched the aircraft's forward door and held down a red button on the bulkhead. A motor whirred into life, opened the door, and extended a set of steps down to the concrete parking apron. The pilot pulled Tay's carry-on out of the small cupboard at the front of the airplane and placed it next to the door.

"There you go, sir. We'll be right here whenever you need us again."

He handed Tay a business card. Tay glanced at it and saw nothing printed on it but two telephone numbers.

"Just give us an hour's notice on either of those numbers and we'll have you back in the air headed anywhere you want to go."

Tay pushed himself out of the big leather chair, pocketed the card, and rolled his shoulders to loosen them up.

"Where do I go for immigration and customs?"

"Oh, you don't need to worry about that, sir. That's all taken care of. Your car's waiting right outside. Just get in and go on about your business."

Entering Thailand without bothering to go through immigration and customs? Tay gathered there were all sorts of benefits to traveling under the auspices of a triad crime boss.

Tay climbed down the steps and stopped at the bottom for a moment. The air tasted different here from the air in Singapore. He could smell the Gulf of Thailand in it, but there was something else in there, too. He breathed deeply, searching for whatever it might be. He would have liked for the moment to last, but the woman came toward him with her hand outstretched.

"Inspector Tay, I'm Renée Couvier. Please call me Renny. Everyone does."

Tay briefly considered launching into his standard patter about being retired and no longer an inspector of anything, but making that explanation was getting tiresome for him. He could only imagine how tiresome it must be for the people he made it to. Perhaps the time had come to accept that the title of inspector was now a permanent part of his name, in the same way titles like general or judge or ambassador stuck to people for the rest of their lives even when they were no longer any of those things.

He shifted his carry-on bag to his left hand and shook the hand Renny was holding out with his right.

"Thank you for coming," she said. "I'm really very grateful. Eddie speaks very highly of you."

Eddie?

Jones' real name was *Eddie?* Surely not. A triad crime boss wouldn't be named Eddie, would he?

The woman must have seen his reaction to the name in his eyes because Tay saw a hint of puzzlement in hers.

"He said he's sure you can help me find out what happened to my grandfather. I've known Eddie Woo for years and he's very economical with his endorsements."

Eddie Woo? *Seriously?* This just kept getting better and

better.

"He did me a very great favor recently. I'm just balancing the books. Whether I can be of any help to you is another matter entirely."

Tay was spared from coming up with another round of platitudes to fill the empty air when the young man stepped forward and extended his hand, too.

"Welcome to Hua Hin, sir. You can call me Max."

As they shook, the young man continued. "I'll be your driver while you're here. Uncle Eddie asked me to be available to you twenty-four hours a day and help you in any way I can."

Tay couldn't hold his tongue any longer.

"*Uncle* Eddie?"

"Oh, Mr. Woo's not really my uncle, of course. My father and Uncle Eddie are old friends. They used to work together."

Tay put aside the implications in that for later consideration.

"Your English is very good, Max."

"It should be, sir. I graduated from Harvard last month."

Today was turning into one surprise after another. And Tay hated surprises.

"Really? Well, congratulations. And you're working in Thailand now?"

"No, sir. Not working. Just staying at my family's home here in Hua Hin and taking a little downtime."

Tay frequently regretted that the concept of *downtime* had originated a generation too late for him to benefit from it. He figured he could have made quite good use of the idea when he had been Max's age.

"I have the police report and the autopsy waiting for you in a file on the backseat," Max went on before Tay could say anything else. "On top of the file is the phone that Uncle Eddie asked me to get you. It has a local SIM card that's prepaid, which makes it pretty much untraceable."

In Tay's experience, no phone was untraceable. Depending

on who was doing the tracing, some phones just took a little longer than others.

"The police report and the autopsy are all in Thai, of course, so I've prepared translations of the most important points, and you'll find those translations at the end of the file. If there are any specific details you want to look at more closely, I can go back and translate everything in those sections for you."

Tay had to admit he was impressed. Young Max obviously had some smarts and, maybe more important, some connections. Police reports and autopsy findings weren't just left lying around for anybody to pick up, even in Thailand. You had to know somebody with a little authority to get access to things like that.

"We'll go straight to the guest house and give you some time to read the reports," Max finished. "And, of course, to meet Apple."

"Apple?"

"Apple's the housekeeper. She looks after the guest house."

"And her name is *Apple*?"

"Thais sometimes have nicknames that seem strange to people who aren't Thai. Apple's a real character, but she doesn't speak a word of English. If you need something from her, you'll just have to act it out."

Tay tried to imagine himself acting out a cup of coffee. He couldn't quite manage it.

M ax grabbed Tay's bag and headed for the big white Mercedes. Tay and Renny followed and Renny got into the front passenger seat. Unless Tay was going to drive, which of course he wasn't, that left him in the back seat by himself.

Now that he had met Renny, he had distinctly mixed feelings about that. It occurred to him he'd been sucking in his gut ever since he climbed down the steps from the airplane and found her waiting there for him, and he shook his head slightly.

Really? he chided himself. *At your age?*

After Max loaded Tay's bag into the trunk, he held the rear door for Tay.

"You must have pretty good connections with the local police to get those reports," Tay said to him.

"Not me, sir. It's my father who has the good connections. I just trade on them."

That's interesting, Tay thought, and maybe a little disturbing.

Max's father, whom Max said had worked for years with Jones or Eddie Woo or whatever the hell his name really was, has good connections with the Thai police? Tay had always held a doubtful view of the Thai police in general, both as to their competency and their integrity, but a direct connection between the Thai police and a high-ranking triad guy was in a whole different universe of doubtful.

"Does your father still work with ... uh, Mr. Woo?"

"Oh no, sir. Not for a long time."

That was a relief to Tay, but he couldn't resist venturing just one more question.

"What does your father do now?"

"Oh, he's in the cabinet, sir."

Tay wasn't certain he had heard right.

"He's ... what? In cabinets? He sells cabinets?"

Max chuckled.

"No, sir. I said he's in *the* cabinet. He's part of the government here. He's the Minister of Justice for Thailand."

Tay was too flabbergasted by that to say anything else. He just got into the back seat of the Mercedes and let Max close the door.

NINE

The description *guest house* conjured up for Tay an image of a small structure located somewhere behind a far larger structure. Probably pleasant and well-decorated, but on the modest side when it came to size. When Max stopped the Mercedes in the circular driveway of a sprawling house built of large panels of heavily tinted glass separated by slabs of sand-colored concrete, Tay got out and stood looking around.

"Is the guest house in the back?" he asked Max when he came around to get Tay's bag out of the trunk.

"No, sir. This *is* the guest house."

Before Tay could figure out what to say to that, the front door opened and an elderly woman came out and shuffled over to where they were standing. She looked like she could easily be eighty years old, but Tay imagined she was probably closer to sixty. She planted herself in front of Tay and brought her palms together before her face in that graceful form of greeting Thais called a *wai*.

Tay, like most non-Thais, found the gesture a little confounding. He understood it was nuanced with all sorts of layers reflecting the relative status of both the giver and the receiver of the *wai*. How high the hands were raised and how long the palms were held together both flashed such signals, Tay had been told, but you had to understand what the signals meant and he didn't have a clue.

There were other layers, too, and they made it even more complicated. The subordinate *waied* the boss, and the boss never *waied* the subordinate, but the younger also *waied* the older rather than the other way around. What Tay didn't understand was what happened when an old subordinate had a young boss. Which took precedence, age or position? Thais effortlessly kept all the plates spinning, but non-Thais struggled.

Long ago, Tay had decided that the best way for him to interact with Thais was to ignore everything. He wasn't a Thai, and no one expected him to get it right anyway, so he didn't even try. When someone *waied* him, he inclined his head very politely in acknowledgment, and that was that.

"Inspector Tay," Max said, "let me introduce you to Apple."

Max switched smoothly into Thai and rattled off several sentences to the old woman that were, of course, entirely incomprehensible to Tay. When he finished, Apple bobbed her head once, grabbed Tay's bag, and made for the front door.

"Wait," Tay said, making a grab for the bag himself, "I can—"

"If you would allow me, sir," Max interrupted, "you should let her carry the bag up to your room. It's her job. If you take the bag back yourself, she'll think you don't trust her. She would be very hurt."

Tay hadn't thought of that. He wasn't in the habit of letting old women carry things for him, but he certainly didn't want to offend Apple before he had even gotten inside, so he let her take the bag. He held onto the file Max had put on the back seat for him as well as the phone that had been with it. Surely Apple wouldn't be offended at him carrying those, would she?

"Apple will show you to your room," Max said, "but of course the entire house is yours. She will take care of everything, but if there is anything else you need, just use gestures and I'm sure Apple will understand."

"I've made a reservation for dinner at seven-thirty," Renny said, "so we'll pick you up at seven."

Max extended his hand, and they shook.

"It's a pleasure to meet you, sir. We'll return for you in exactly one hour."

Tay followed Apple through the front door and saw that the house was as aggressively contemporary on the inside as it was on the outside. Tay had little fondness for contemporary architecture and even less for sand-colored concrete and tinted glass. In his view, they made the house look like the world's largest Taco Bell. At least it sat a few feet above the beach and had an unobstructed view out over the Gulf of Thailand. That helped. A little.

Apple was already halfway up an open staircase in the center of the large living area, so Tay didn't stop to admire the view and trotted up the stairs right behind her. The bedroom into which she led him was generously sized and had sliding glass doors opening onto a balcony with the same view as the living room. Apple swung Tay's bag up onto an upholstered bench at the foot of the king-size bed and opened it. When Tay realized she was about to unpack for him, he stopped her.

"That's not necessary," he said. "Thank you, but I'll take care of it myself."

He didn't want this woman unpacking his bag. Something about letting an old lady do that seemed rather undignified. She could carry the bag if she really wanted to, but he drew the line at her sorting out his underwear.

Apple gave Tay a blank look. Then she pointed at his bag, turned and pointed at a huge oak wardrobe opposite the bed, and raised her eyebrows in a questioning look.

"No, thank you," Tay repeated, shaking his head slowly in

that sort of exaggerated way people do when trying to make themselves understood by someone with whom they don't share a common language. "I'll do it."

Apple looked at him for a long moment, but she finally nodded and stepped away from the bag. Then she mimed herself drinking from a cup and did the thing with her eyebrows again.

This time, Tay nodded.

"Yes," he said. "Thank you. I'll have it downstairs."

That brought a look of puzzlement, so he also mimed drinking from a cup and then pointed down.

Apple remained expressionless, but she did the head bob again and left, closing the door behind her.

Tay wondered briefly if the imaginary cups from which they had been drinking contained coffee or tea. He assumed he would find out when he got downstairs.

He took a quick shower and changed into a clean shirt. He hadn't asked Renny how formal the restaurant was, and he wondered for a moment if he should put on a tie.

No, this was a beach resort, wasn't it? He was pretty sure no one in a Thai beach resort ever wore a tie. He doubted they even wore dark dress slacks like he was wearing, but he had nothing more casual with him, so they would have to do. He mentally kicked himself for not doing a better job of packing, but the truth was he hated packing and was lousy at it. That was just one more good reason, as far as he was concerned, to stay home.

Tay grabbed the telephone Max had given him and stuffed it into his pocket, then he scooped up the file with the police report and the autopsy and headed downstairs. He smelled the coffee before he got even halfway down and smiled. Maybe his miming skills would be up to this after all.

. . .

A pple had set out a silver coffee pot with containers of milk and sugar. Tay settled down on one of the couches, poured himself a cup, and opened the file.

There were half a dozen photos of the scene attached to the police report, but they weren't very helpful. All they showed was Harry Black's body crumpled on the sand from several different directions. There was no context to any of them. It could have been any sand anywhere. The only thing that Tay took away from the photos was that the devastation to Harry Black's head was massive. The handgun that killed him must have been a large caliber and fired at almost point-blank range.

Tay drank coffee while he flipped through the rest of the file. The police report was all in Thai, of course, so he had no idea what it said, but it seemed to him to be very short for the report of a murder investigation. Back when he was dealing with homicides in Singapore, the investigative report for a gunshot death would have run to a hundred pages. This one was four pages. The autopsy report was a little longer: six pages. Happily, Tay noted, it did not include any autopsy photographs.

He poured himself another cup of coffee and turned to Max's translations. As he already suspected, there was nothing at all useful in the police report. Place of death, cause of death, approximate time of death, how the police came to be notified, and a list of all the police officers who attended the crime scene. That list was very long. There probably weren't many gunshot deaths in a little town like Hua Hin, and it looked like every cop within fifty miles had shown up to have a look.

There were no witness interviews. None at all. Which seemed strange to say the very least.

Perhaps there had been no witnesses to the actual shooting, but surely there were people who had seen Harry Black on the beach that morning and who may have seen someone talking to him or at least showing an interest in him. Harry Black couldn't have been the only human being on the beach, but the Thai police appeared to have been remarkably incurious about who else might have been around.

The autopsy report was marginally more interesting. Harry Black had been a remarkably healthy man for eighty-six. Tay doubted he was as healthy now, and he was thirty years short of Harry Black's age.

Tay skimmed the gruesome details about the utter devastation to Harry Black's skull that the bullet had caused until he came to the last line. At first, he wasn't certain he had read it correctly, so he went back and read it again.

His mouth dropped open.

THE SUBJECT WAS STRUCK BY A SINGLE ROUND, MOST LIKELY OF .338 LAPUA CALIBER, FIRED FROM A SIGNIFICANT DISTANCE AWAY.

When Jones — or Eddie Woo, or whatever his name really was — told him that Harry Black had been shot on the beach, Tay naturally assumed he had been killed by a handgun. What else? But that wasn't what had happened at all.

The .338 caliber was a rifle round, not a handgun cartridge. And it was a very special rifle round. It had been developed specifically to provide military snipers a round capable of delivering high-powered hits on targets at extended ranges. Shooters called it the death laser because it could maintain pinpoint accuracy for more than a mile.

Harry Black wasn't killed by a mugger. He was killed by a highly skilled sniper. Just how highly skilled was underscored by the autopsy finding that he had been hit by a single shot. With the target down and helpless on the sand, most shooters would have taken a second shot just in case the first hadn't been fatal. This shooter didn't. One shot was all he needed, and he knew it.

Why would an expert sniper, almost certainly either military or at the very least ex-military, have been lying in wait for Harry Black that morning on Hua Hin beach? The entire purpose of a sniper was to take out threats anonymously and at a distance before they could do any harm. How could an eighty-six-year-old man strolling along a beach on the Gulf of Thailand be a threat to anyone?

Samuel Tay didn't know what the answer to that question was, but he was reasonably sure he did know at least one thing now that he had not known before.

There was something big and messy out there, and he was walking straight into it.

"Did you get a chance to read the police report and the autopsy yet?" Renny asked.

She was sitting in the back seat with Tay when Max drove them away from the guest house a half hour later, something Tay saw as a change for the better.

"Have *you* read them?"

"I don't read Thai, but I read the translations Max did while we were waiting for you at the airport."

Tay doubted Renny had seen the significance of the medical examiner's conclusion as to the caliber of the bullet and the number of shots. You had to know something about guns and shooting for that to mean anything. He didn't know much. He wasn't a gun guy and killings in Singapore seldom involved firearms, but after twenty years as a homicide investigator, he had picked up a little. Renny owned an art gallery, for God's sake. He doubted she knew much about gun calibers and bullets.

"Did you learn anything from them?" Tay asked, cautiously testing his theory.

Renny shook her head.

He had been right. She hadn't seen it.

"I wasn't expecting for there to be anything in them," she went on. "The Thai police don't seem very interested. They don't seem to want to get involved."

"I'm not sure what you mean by that. They're the police. They're involved whether or not they want to be."

Renny's laugh had no humor in it.

"I may not know much about Thailand, Inspector, but even I know that the Thai police are automatically going to break into a trot in the opposite direction when they find a foreigner dead of a gunshot wound. Thais don't much like dealing with foreigners, even when they're alive. Dead ones raise all sorts of problems, and dead foreigners who live in Thailand can be downright dangerous. Sometimes they're connected to people and things the Thai police don't want to know anything about."

Renny had just put her finger right on the number one thing on Tay's to-do list.

He needed to find out exactly who her grandfather had been connected to. He must have posed a danger to somebody, and it must have been somebody pretty important if they could call in a skilled sniper to kill Harry Black.

He would tell Renny about the significance of the autopsy finding about the gunshot eventually, of course, but he didn't want to do it yet. First, he wanted to have a quiet conversation with her and draw out everything she knew about her grandfather. Maybe there would be something in what she recalled that would point him toward the threat her grandfather had been, and to whom. Tay just hoped the restaurant they were going to didn't turn out to be big and noisy.

TEN

The restaurant was a place called Let's Sea that was right on the ocean. It was very quiet, but not because it was empty. It was actually fairly busy.

It was quiet because most of it was outdoors. A collection of tables, chairs, couches, and even lounge chairs were scattered across two wooden decks, and more tables dotted a grassy lawn that sloped gently down to an overhang a few feet above the beach. The beach was floodlit, but beyond it, the darkness of the Gulf of Thailand rolled off to the horizon.

Renny and Tay walked through a small interior bar area and out to a round table on a wooden deck that faced the ocean. Max had stayed in the car, which was fine with Tay. He had wondered briefly if he should invite Max to join them, but Renny had made the dinner arrangements and she said nothing about it, so Tay kept his mouth shut. When Max dropped them off, he seemed to assume he would stay with the car, and Tay decided saying nothing had been the right thing to do.

Tay smiled to see that the two chairs pulled up to the table were old-fashioned wooden rockers with woven cane backs and seats. Nothing suited Tay better than old-fashioned. That was who he was. That was who he wanted to be.

When the waiter brought the menus and offered drinks, Tay assumed Renny would order the obligatory glass of white wine that young women always seemed to order. It surprised him to discover he was wrong. She ordered a beer. Not just any beer, but something called Beer Lao, which Tay gathered must be a brand of beer from Laos, the tiny land-locked country that bordered Thailand on the north.

Tay ordered a Bushmills neat. He had briefly gone out with a woman from Dublin he met while standing in line at the bank and she had given him a taste for Irish whiskey. Even after he lost his taste for the woman from Dublin, his taste for the whiskey remained. Irish whiskey smelled to him of days just slightly off-center. It was particularly beguiling if you liked earth, rain, sadness, and despair, and who doesn't like all that?

They made small talk for a while and sipped their drinks the way people do who don't know each other very well. Tay couldn't take his eyes off Renny's hand and the graceful way it curled around the brown glass of the Beer Lao bottle. She had long, slender fingers, and her nails were finished in a blood-red polish that caught the light when her hand moved. It was the way her fingers held the bottle that took his breath away. Was it possible to fall in love with a woman's hands? He hoped not, because if it was, he was about to do just that.

Tay was a little relieved when the waiter arrived to take their orders. Not only did that allow him to escape his developing obsession with Renny's hands, it put at least a temporary end to the small talk part of the evening. The setting was lovely, and slowly rocking back and forth listening to the sound of the ocean while looking at Renny's hands was all very pleasant, but he was lousy at small talk. Trying to make conversation without having an actual subject at the center of it made him feel stupid and awkward.

When the waiter collected the menus and left, Tay quickly steered the conversation toward firmer ground.

"How long have you been in Hua Hin?" he asked.

"Since Monday. It happened on Sunday, and the police called me the next morning. I flew to Bangkok right away, and Eddie arranged for Max to meet me and drive me down. I got here Monday night. Eddie offered me the guest house where you're staying, but I ..."

Renny hesitated, then shrugged.

"I said I'd rather stay at a hotel. I didn't want to rattle around in a whole house all by myself."

She shrugged again, as if in apology, although Tay couldn't see what she was apologizing for.

"Where are you staying?"

He was sure the answer wouldn't mean anything to him, but he thought it would be polite to ask.

"Max arranged for me to stay right in the middle of town at the Centara Grand. It's a wonderful old hotel that doesn't look like it's changed in a hundred years."

"Have you met with the Thai police yet?"

"Max took me there first thing Tuesday morning. I talked to someone who was supposed to be the senior officer in charge in Hua Hin. Colonel Something-or-another."

She trailed off and Tay remained silent, waiting for her to go on.

"He was very polite, but he didn't tell me very much. Murders here seem to be unusual, so maybe he just didn't know very much. Maybe he didn't even know what to do."

"I'm sure he could have called for help from somewhere," Tay said. "If he thought he needed it."

"I got the impression that all he cared about was closing the case, particularly because it was a foreigner who was murdered. Finding out what actually happened appeared to be far less important to him than filing it away."

"So how did you leave things with this police colonel?" Tay asked.

"He took my telephone number and told me he would let

me know if the investigation turned up anything. Then he asked me to identify the body formally."

Renny shuddered as if a chilly wind had suddenly blown over her, which in a manner of speaking Tay knew it had.

"It was awful, Inspector. It was the worst thing I've ever seen. His head had been …"

She hesitated again and looked away. She bit her lip and gathered herself, then she went on.

"I don't think I'll ever be able to forget what I saw."

Tay didn't know what to say. It was the right time for him to offer some words of comfort, but he had no idea what those words might be, so he said nothing.

"Anyway," Renny went on after a bit, "I felt completely overwhelmed. That was when I called Eddie. I told him about how little interest the Thai cops seemed to have in finding out who killed my grandfather and that I was afraid whoever killed him was just going to walk away. Eddie told me he knew someone who could help."

She shrugged.

"Then you got here today. And now you know what I know."

"Not really. I know nothing at all about your grandfather."

"Neither do I."

"You probably know more than you think you do."

Renny considered that for a moment as she sipped her beer. That she had ignored the glass and was drinking straight from the bottle made Tay smile. This woman was full of surprises.

"I didn't know him very well," she said. "My mother had always told me he was dead."

"Why would she do that?"

"I don't know. I asked him, and he said my mother had always disliked him and they had very little to do with each other. I'm sure there was more to it than that, but he never told me what it was."

"How did you find out he wasn't dead?"

"He tracked me down and introduced himself. Otherwise, I probably never would have found out. After my parents were killed, my grandfather—"

Tay stopped rocking.

"Killed?" He interrupted. "Your parents were killed, too?"

"They were passengers on Malaysian Airways flight 17, the plane that was shot down over Ukraine in 2014."

Tay knew his face must have been blank because Renny gave him an odd look.

"Don't you remember when that happened?"

Now something vaguely came back to him, but not nearly enough to claim a memory of anything specific. Renny bailed him out before he had to admit he didn't remember.

"It was a flight from Amsterdam to Kuala Lumpur that was shot down over eastern Ukraine by a surface-to-air missile. No one could ever say with certainty who had fired the missile. It might have been the Ukrainians, or it might have been Russian separatists fighting the Ukrainians, or it might have been the Russians themselves."

She shrugged slightly.

"I guess it doesn't matter. The missile destroyed the plane and killed everyone on it. Nearly three hundred people, all gone forever. Knowing who really fired the missile won't change that."

"I'm sorry," Tay said.

"Don't be. It was eight years ago, and you didn't have anything to do with it, did you?"

There was a bitter edge behind Renny's flip remark, so Tay said nothing.

The waiter arrived with their salads, and they fell silent while the man fussed around setting them out. He produced a pepper mill from the front pocket of his apron and offered them ground pepper. Then he wished them *bon appetite* and withdrew.

. . .

"Can we talk about something else?" Renny asked as they both started eating. "Just for a while."

"Sure," Tay said. "What would you like to talk about?"

"Well ..." Renny chewed thoughtfully at a piece of lettuce and considered that. "Why don't we talk about you?"

"*Me*? Why would you want to talk about me?"

"I know almost nothing about you. Eddie told me you were friends, and that you had been a homicide investigator in Singapore until you retired recently. Frankly, you look too young to be retired. I expected some old guy to come off that airplane."

"I *am* an old guy."

Renny stopped chewing and examined Tay carefully. She looked like a woman contemplating a purchase who wanted to make certain she wasn't overlooking a defect in the product.

"No," she said and went back to eating her salad. "I don't think so."

Tay didn't know what to say to that. Was this woman flirting with him? Surely not, but he really had no idea.

He had never been very good with women. They made him uncomfortable. He thought it was mostly a matter of proximity and practice. He hadn't been around that many women in his life, at least not at close quarters, so he had very little experience in trying to figure out how not to come across as a complete meatball on those occasions when he was at close quarters with one.

Even if Renny was flirting with him, she was much too young for him to take it seriously. He knew that. Still, for just a moment, Tay felt himself wishing he were a younger and better-looking man. For just a moment, he wanted to be everything other than what he was. The folly of age spared no one, he realized, certainly not him.

He finished the rest of his whiskey to cover his awkwardness and thought about ordering another. It sounded as if he might need it. Maybe this confident young woman who drank beer out of a bottle and wanted him to talk about himself was a little too much for him to deal with.

He suddenly wished very much that he had a pack of Marlboros and a box of matches in his shirt pocket, but he didn't. That left him with nothing to do that might deflect, or at least to stall the disconcerting direction the conversation had taken. Having no better idea what to do, he took a deep breath and dived in.

"Okay," he said, putting down his fork and folding his arms, "what do you want to know?"

"Uh-oh." Renny flashed a smile and giggled slightly. "When you ask a man to talk about himself and he folds his arms like that, his body language tells you the story before he's said a single word."

Tay quickly unfolded his arms, but now he had no idea what to do with them. He dropped them into his lap, realized how awkward that looked, then tried propping his elbows on the table. That looked even worse.

When Renny laughed out loud, Tay flagged the waiter down and ordered another Irish whiskey. He wasn't sure he was going to drink it, but holding it would give him something to do with his hands and arms.

To cover himself until it arrived, he grabbed his glass, wrapped his hand around it, and lifted it as if it wasn't already empty. He felt like a fool holding an empty glass, but at least it occupied one arm. Then he just had to figure out what to do with the other one.

"Okay, Inspector, start out with something easy. Why did you retire from the police force so young?"

"They offered me a promotion from Inspector to Deputy Superintendent in charge of traffic enforcement. They told me I had to take the promotion or retire. Remaining a detective in CID wasn't an option."

"CID?"

"The Criminal Investigation Department."

"And you were a homicide investigator in the Criminal Investigation Department for—"

"Sixteen years."

"Did you like it?"

"You can never do anything else as a cop that matters more. Homicide is the major leagues, the center ring. It's the show. It always has been."

Renny thought about that. She sipped at her beer, put the bottle down, and said, "They really wanted you out, didn't they?"

Tay hesitated. He started to say something, but then he settled for merely nodding.

Renny went back to eating her salad. She didn't ask *why* they wanted him out, and Tay liked her very much for that.

"Maybe we should start somewhere else then," Renny said after a bit. "Where were you born?"

"I was born in Singapore."

"Brothers and sisters?"

"No. Only child."

"Married? Divorced? Children?"

"No, no, and no."

Renny looked at Tay with a half-smile on her face.

"You never married? Seriously?"

"Why does that surprise you?"

"You have to admit, it's unusual in a man your age."

Tay didn't think he had to admit anything. Maybe it was unusual, maybe it wasn't, but the concept of this young woman thinking of him as *unusual* was deeply unappealing.

The waiter returned with his drink, and Tay was glad of the interruption. The conversation was getting far too personal for him. He didn't like talking about himself and he was generally able to avoid it, but somehow this woman had pushed right past all his well-practiced defenses before he even realized it was happening.

He sipped at the whiskey, said nothing else, and he let his eyes slide out over the dark ocean.

"Are your parents still alive?" Renny asked.

She wasn't going to let it go, was she?

"My father died of a heart attack on a business trip to Vietnam in 1975. I hardly knew him. My mother died a few years ago. In New York. I think she had a stroke."

"You think? You don't know for sure?"

"My mother and I weren't close. When my father died, he left her very well off. She didn't know that he had been investing in property for many years and had accumulated quite a valuable portfolio, but she had no difficulty at all adjusting to her newfound wealth. Within a year or two after he died, she moved to New York and bought an apartment on Park Avenue. Eventually, she married again. He was an investment banker who was a widower."

"Did you like him?"

"I don't know. I was at university. I didn't go to the wedding."

The truth was that Tay didn't remember being invited to his mother's wedding, but that was beside the point. Even if he had been invited, he wouldn't have gone.

"But surely you met him later whenever you visited your mother in New York, didn't you?"

"I didn't visit my mother in New York."

"Not ever?"

"No."

"That seems ... well, if you'll pardon me saying so, a little odd."

Tay shrugged. "Never married, no children, didn't visit my mother. I'm sure if you keep your eyes open, you'll find a great many more odd things about me."

The moment the words were out, he could have bitten his tongue. He hadn't meant to sound so harsh, but he had, and now he didn't know how to get the words back. He glanced at Renny's face, but she was expressionless.

Before Tay could think of a way to recover from his blunder, the waiter returned with their main courses. Neither he nor Renny said anything while the man fiddled about the table serving their food. By the time he was gone, it felt like it was too late to say anything. Tay picked up his fork and sighed to himself. He just wasn't any good at this sort of thing, was he?

They ate in silence until Tay finally grew so uneasy that he broke it.

"I'm not very comfortable talking about myself."

Renny glanced up at him for a moment without expression and said nothing.

"And I'm even less comfortable talking to women. When a woman asks me to talk about myself, sometimes I feel awkward and ..."

Tay trailed off, shrugged, and fell silent.

Renny glanced at him again, but this time her face was softer.

"Just sometimes?"

When Tay looked back at her, he saw she was smiling. He was suddenly gripped by an overwhelming sense of relief.

He smiled back, took a deep breath, and settled in to await developments.

There were no developments.

ELEVEN

Max was driving them back to the guest house before Tay realized he had never gotten around to steering the conversation back to the subject of Renny's grandfather. He still knew practically nothing about the man, and tomorrow morning he was supposed to start investigating his murder.

"You're thinking that I didn't tell you very much about my grandfather," Renny suddenly said.

Tay turned his head and stared at her.

How did she do that?

"There's just not much I can tell you. I hardly knew him."

"You never saw him after he tracked you down and you discovered he wasn't dead?"

"Oh sure, I saw him. We met three times, but always at a hotel in Bangkok. I just assumed he lived somewhere around there and it was a convenient place for him to meet me."

"Then you've never been here to Hua Hin before this?"

"No, never. I didn't even know where he lived until after the Thai police called me. The man who called to tell me he had been shot had to explain where he was calling from."

"Your grandfather never gave you his address?"

"I just had an email address and a telephone number. That's all you need to stay in touch with somebody these days. Where they really are doesn't seem to matter that much anymore."

"You didn't ask him where he lived?"

Renny gave Tay a look he couldn't quite put a name to. "You think I should have, don't you?"

Tay wasn't about to offer an opinion on that, so he ignored Renny's question and asked another of his own.

"You didn't think it strange that he never gave you his address or invited you to his home, even when you were coming down from Hong Kong to see him?"

"Not really. I thought maybe he had a girlfriend at home he didn't want me to meet. Do you invite everybody you know to your home?"

Tay didn't invite *anybody* he knew to his home, but he didn't think it was necessary to tell Renny that, so he just tried to look thoughtful.

"How did the police know to call you?"

"The man who telephoned said my grandfather had put me down as his emergency contact the last time he renewed his residency permit. At least I think that's what he said. His English wasn't very good."

"But they found your grandfather on the beach. There was no one with him. Was he carrying identification?"

"Maybe. Honestly, it didn't occur to me to ask."

"I think I can explain that, sir," Max spoke up.

Tay and Renny both looked at Max, but since Max was driving, he kept his eyes on the road.

"As I understand it," he said, "a neighbor saw the commotion on the beach. When she walked down to see what was going on, she realized the dead man was Mr. Black and she identified him to the police. Since he was a foreigner, I'm sure the first thing the police did was check his immigration status to see what information Thai Immigration had about him."

Tay thought about that for a moment and then turned back to Renny.

"Do you know why your grandfather was living here in Hua Hin?"

Renny slowly shook her head.

"Did he have friends or relatives here? Was he working?"

"I doubt at his age that he was working, but otherwise —" Renny shrugged. "I don't know why he was here. I just don't know."

"Do you think he was hiding from someone?"

"I guess it's possible. He's been here a long time. Twenty years. Twenty-five years. Something like that? That's a long time to hide if that's what he was doing."

"Did he ever give you any idea who—"

"Look," Renny interrupted, "maybe this is going to sound weird, but I'm going to say it, anyway. Something gave me the feeling that Harry Black wasn't even his real name."

"Black wasn't your mother's name before she married?"

Renny hesitated and looked abashed. "I don't remember. Does that make me an awful person?"

Tay wasn't about to go there, not with his track record of dealing with his own mother, so he took that as a rhetorical question and moved right along.

"Why do you think his name wasn't Harry Black?" he asked. "Did he say something specific that made you believe that?"

"No, not really. It was just a feeling." Renny shrugged slightly. "See, I told you it was going to sound weird."

"Perhaps he wasn't really your grandfather."

"I thought about that, but I'm sure he was."

"Another feeling?"

"Yes, I suppose so. That's natural, don't you think? A blood relationship should make you feel something, right? A connection of some kind."

Tay wasn't so sure about that, so he said nothing.

"Besides," Renny went on, "he knew all sorts of things

about my mother that I don't think he could have known if he hadn't been her father. And what reason could he have had for trying to pass himself off as my grandfather if he wasn't? He didn't want anything from me. He certainly never asked me for anything."

"Maybe he was just waiting a while to put the bite on you."

"I don't think so. When I started slacking off about keeping in touch, he just let it go. It was almost like he was leaving the decision about whether to keep the connection going entirely up to me."

"And you didn't keep it going."

"There wasn't any reason, not really. I just got busy with the new gallery, and he was in Thailand while I was up in Hong Kong, so ..."

Renny trailed off. She turned away from Tay and sat silently staring out the car window, watching the dark landscape slip by.

"And now I feel like a right shit because of what I did. He was my grandfather, for God's sake. All he wanted from me was to *be* my grandfather. I didn't let him, and now he's dead and I *can't* let him."

Renny kept on staring out the window. Tay stayed silent.

"I guess that's why I feel so damned guilty. I let the connection slip away even after he had made the effort to find me. And now it looks like the Thai cops are letting his murderer slip away. I will *not* let him be forgotten twice. He deserves better than that."

Tay watched Renny's reflection in the car window.

Oh, dear God, he thought to himself, *please don't let her start crying. I'd look like a fool. I wouldn't have the first idea what to do then.*

After a few moments, Tay cleared his throat and tried to get the conversation back on track.

"How much do you know about your grandfather's life?"

"Nothing really." Renny turned away from the window and looked at Tay. "Nothing at all."

"Do you know where he was born?"

"I think he was born in France. Mother was. I'm sure of that. But she got married and ended up living in Australia."

"Is that where you were born?"

"Yes. I grew up in a fairly small place called Palm Beach. It's right on the coast a little north of Sydney."

She smiled slightly.

"Like all kids, I didn't want anything other than to get away from the place where I grew up. When I somehow got into the University of Melbourne, I couldn't get out of Palm Beach fast enough."

"How did you end up in Hong Kong?"

"I graduated from Melbourne with a master's degree in journalism and somehow landed an internship on the South China Morning Post. I started covering the local art scene for them, mostly because it was a job no one else wanted. After a couple of years, I decided the art business offered me a better future than the newspaper business, so I quit to manage a gallery."

"Did your parents support that?"

"I don't recall them saying anything about it one way or another." Renny hesitated. "I wasn't close to my parents. From what you said about your mother, I'm sure you understand how that can happen."

Tay did understand, but he didn't say anything. He just nodded.

"I knew from the beginning that I wanted my own gallery," Renny went on, "not to work in someone else's. I had just gotten the money together to open one when my mother and father were killed in the crash."

"And your mother had never mentioned your grandfather to you?"

"I remember asking her once about her parents and she said they had both died before I was born. After that, it didn't seem like there was any reason to bring it up again."

"And you have no idea why she would tell you that?"

"Maybe she thought it was true." Renny pursed her lips and considered that as if for the first time. "It looks like my grandfather went to ground here in Thailand a long time ago. Maybe he was hiding from something. Maybe he wanted her to believe he was dead."

"What do you think he might have been hiding from?"

Renny slowly shook her head, but she said nothing else.

M ax stopped the Mercedes in front of the guest house, walked around to the rear passenger door, and opened it for Tay.

When Tay got out of the car, it suddenly occurred to him that no one had given him a key. Before he could ask Max what to do, he saw Apple was holding the front door open for him.

"What's the plan for tomorrow, boss?" Max asked.

"I'd like to look at the crime scene. Can you talk to someone and arrange it?"

"I don't have to arrange it. We can just walk down the beach anytime you want."

"How do you know exactly where it was?"

"I could tell from the pictures."

Tay remembered nothing distinctive about the pictures, just the body of a man lying on the beach, but maybe there was something he had missed that meant more to Max than it would have to him, anyway.

"How far is it?"

"Not far." Max pointed off to the right. "Maybe half a kilometer down the beach. That way."

Renny had stayed in the car and now Tay bent down and looked in at her.

"I just want to get a sense of the crime scene tomorrow, but there's no need for you to go. I know it might be difficult for you to—"

"I'm sure you think you're protecting me, Inspector," Renny

interrupted, "but I don't need protecting. I'll be back with Max tomorrow morning and we can all walk down together from here. Is eight early enough for you?"

Truth be told, Tay thought, it was way *too* early for him. Tay was not by nature an early riser. He had always thought all that hokum about the virtue of making an early start had been invented by people who were too lazy to work late.

What was the difference between starting at six and working until four in the afternoon and starting at noon and working until ten at night? Both periods consisted of exactly the same number of hours, but that didn't seem to register with the early-morning lunatics.

The guy who started work at six in the morning invariably got credit for being an energetic go-getter no matter how early he quit, and the guy who started work at noon was labeled a lazy bastard no matter how long he kept at it. It was damned unfair.

Tay didn't say any of that, of course. He just arranged his face into the most sincere expression he could manage on short notice and nodded earnestly.

"Eight would be great," he said.

TWELVE

Apple greeted him with a deep *wai* when he went through the door.

Caught off guard, Tay responded with a clumsy gesture that was equal parts *wai*, nod, and bow, without being exactly any of them. He gave Apple a long look. It was almost as if she had been standing there for hours doing nothing but waiting for his return.

She hadn't been, had she? Surely not.

Apple closed the door, pointed into the kitchen, and pantomimed making Tay coffee. Or maybe it was tea she pantomimed making. It didn't matter since Tay didn't want either.

What he wanted was a Marlboro. He had a lot of things to think about and the act of smoking had always been intimately tied up for him with the process of reflection. But of course, he didn't have any Marlboros. He had given up smoking, damn fool that he was.

Tay considered briefly whether Apple might be a smoker, but she didn't have the look and he hadn't caught even a whiff of tobacco odor either in the guest house or from her clothing. If there had been, he was sure he would have noticed it.

Perhaps he could ask Apple if she at least knew where he might buy some Marlboros around here at this time of night, but he quickly dismissed that thought, too. That was a bridge too far in light of the limited ability they had to communicate. If he was going to fall off the wagon, he didn't want to start by having to play a demented game of charades to find a cigarette. He would save the big gesture of falling off the wagon for some occasion on which he could at least communicate his weakness with dignity.

Tay went up to his bedroom and brushed his teeth. Then he got into bed and read for a while from a biography of Napoleon that he had been working on for the last week or so. He had just closed the book and was reaching to put out the light when he heard an electronic noise start up downstairs. It was a sort of bleating sound. In the nighttime silence of the house, it sounded like some kind of alarm had gone off.

Was there a security system he hadn't noticed that he had accidentally triggered? Could it even be a fire alarm that was sounding?

Tay had no idea, but just lying there and waiting on Apple to deal with the problem didn't seem to him to be the wisest course of action, so he pulled on his robe and went downstairs.

H e realized almost immediately that the noise he was hearing was from the cell phone Max had given him.

He had left it lying on the living room table alongside the police report and the autopsy, and now it was ringing with a noise that sounded like a goat being strangled to death. Whoever had selected the default ringtone for that phone was clearly a sadist.

Tay scooped up the phone, dropped into a chair, and answered it.

"Hello?"

"Inspector? I hope I didn't wake you."

The first thing that popped into Tay's mind was the punch-line to a joke that had been old when Adam and Eve were children.

No, you didn't wake me. I had to get up to answer the phone anyway.

But he didn't say that. It was late and he was tired, so he played it straight.

"Jones?"

"Of course. You were expecting someone else, maybe?"

"I thought it might be Mr. Woo. Or perhaps Uncle Eddie."

Jones laughed.

"Where did you get this number?" Tay asked. "I don't even know what it is."

To Jones' credit, he didn't bother to respond to that.

"Well, what do you think?" he asked instead.

"I just got here. I don't think anything yet, Jones. Or maybe I'll call you Uncle Eddie. I kind of like that."

"You can call me Aleksandr Solzhenitsyn as long as you figure out who killed Renny's grandfather."

Now it was Tay's turn to laugh.

"Look," Jones went on, "I didn't call to lean on you. I just called to make sure you have everything you need and to thank you for doing this for me. I won't forget it."

"I haven't done anything for you yet. Nothing at least that's worth being thanked for."

"Oh yes, you have. You're there. I asked for your help as a friend and you stepped up. That means a lot to me."

Tay wasn't sure how he felt about a triad crime boss characterizing him as a friend, but he let that pass.

"I owe you quite a lot," Tay said instead, "and I pay my debts."

"I'm sure you do, but that's not really the reason you're there, is it?"

Tay didn't want to go any further down that road. In his experience, probing for someone's deepest motivations in the middle of the night never ended up going anywhere good. He changed the subject.

"Max seems to be quite a sharp young man. He said you and his father have a long relationship."

"Yes," Jones said.

"And now his father is the Minister of Justice for Thailand."

"Yes," Jones said again.

A single word spoken twice, but Tay had no doubt that word encompassed a narrative as labyrinthine and entangled as *Hamlet*.

"You know a lot of people, Jones."

"Everybody knows a lot of people."

Tay chuckled. "You're not going to tell me a thing about your relationship with Max's father, are you?"

"I don't think you want me to, do you?"

No, Tay supposed he didn't.

"If you need anything," Jones went on, "just tell Max and he'll get it for you. The plane will remain on standby for as long as you need it, and it will take you anywhere in the world you need to go. Whatever resources you need are available. Just find out who killed Renny's grandfather, and why. Then tell me."

Anywhere in the world?

Why would Jones think he might need to go jetting around the world to solve the murder of an elderly man living in a provincial backwater in Thailand? Did Jones know something he wasn't telling him, or had that been just a figure of speech?

When he had agreed to come to Hua Hin, it all sounded pretty simple. The old man was no doubt shot by some unsuccessful mugger. No matter how unlikely it might seem that such a thing might happen on a beach, what other reasonable explanation was there?

If Tay could identify the shooter, he had already decided he would turn whatever he had over to the local police. He had no intention of painting a target on the back of some poor fellow who was probably already scraping along at the bottom of the social order by pointing Jones in his direction.

Tay knew, of course, why Jones wanted Tay to tag the killer to him rather than identify him to the police. He liked Jones, but not enough to become an accessory to murder for him. After all, Tay was a cop — well, he used to be a cop — and he was damn well going to act like one.

But now Tay wasn't so sure what he thought anymore. This thing wasn't nearly that simple, was it? He hadn't even been here for twelve hours and already he could see that all this was going to be anything *but* simple. Renny's grandfather had been shot by a top-tier sniper who had patiently laid in wait for him. This wasn't a mugging gone wrong. It was an assassination. Did Jones already suspect that somehow?

"What is it you're not telling me, Jones?"

"Oh dear me, Inspector, there are a ton of things I'm not telling you, but none of them have anything to do with this."

"Did you know Harry Black?"

"No."

"Do you know why he was killed?"

"No."

"No idea at all?"

"No," Jones said for the third time, but this time he hesitated a beat before he did. Tay heard the hesitation, and he wondered what it meant.

Regardless of who killed Harry Black and why they did it, and regardless of whether Jones already had some ideas of his own about one or both of those matters, Tay was certain now of at least one thing. A bunch of provincial cops in a small town in Thailand were way over their heads on this one.

The Thai cops would never find out who murdered Harry Black. Even if by some miracle they did, they would never make the killer face justice. Whoever he was, he was protected by layers of hidden power. Maybe the only justice Harry Black would ever get would be the kind of justice Jones and his friends stood ready to deliver.

It pained Tay to realize he was thinking that, but he didn't have to decide right now, did he? He could put aside worrying about what he would do with what he learned until he had actually learned something. He realized there was a healthy dollop of sophistry in looking at it that way, but he figured he could live with it.

So, Tay kept it simple. He promised Jones he would keep him informed, and they said their goodbyes and ended the call. Then he went back upstairs to bed.

THIRTEEN

Something woke Tay from a sound sleep. There was a clock with green phosphorescent hands on the bedside table. He shifted his eyes to it without moving his head. Just after four o'clock.

He wondered what had roused him. Everyone has similar thoughts when they are abruptly woken deep in the night, and in the blackness of the empty hours, the explanations that crawl from our imaginations are seldom things that soothe or comfort.

Had there been a noise? Tay strained his ears, but nothing came to them now. No unexplained bump or mysterious creak. His room was so quiet that he could hear the dull rumble the sea made as it sloshed against the beach far down below. Had there been a sudden flash of light from outside? If there had been, there was no sign of it now. Only a watery gray half-light seeped around the edge of the draperies.

That seemed to eliminate the usual temporal events as likely causes for his waking, which left Tay with only one other explanation. And it was one he did not much like.

Recently, his mother had become a wellspring of unsolicited advice. Sometimes it concerned his personal life and sometimes it concerned his professional life. He would not normally have thought that particularly remarkable since mothers had been giving their sons unsolicited advice more or less from the beginning of time, but the circumstances here were a little unusual.

More than unusual, actually, since Tay's mother was dead, and had been for years.

When she was alive, his mother hardly ever communicated with him, but now that she was dead, she simply wouldn't shut up. Worse, her visits always seemed to come at some God-awful hour in the middle of the night. If she felt she simply *had* to talk to him, why didn't she show up for coffee one morning or even come around for lunch? Her nocturnal manifestations were driving him mad.

Sometimes his mother revealed herself to him as a voice in a clump of light. Most commonly, she appeared as a shadow, a hole in the darkness without clear edges or definition. On rare occasions, she even presented herself as a full-body manifestation and posed herself sitting primly on the foot of his bed or in a chair close by it. She hadn't done the burning bush yet, but he figured that was coming.

The full-body manifestations were the appearances Tay most dreaded. When his mother materialized as a complete human figure, she inevitably came filled with a litany of woeful portents. His mother didn't do the full body materialization thing to give him tomorrow's winning lottery numbers. She did it to tell him just how fucked he was.

Of course, Tay knew full well his mother wasn't really there, regardless of how she seemed to manifest herself. He wasn't a man who fraternized with ghosts. He did not see spirits in the street or anywhere else. In the whole of his life, he had only encountered one ghost: that of his mother.

There had to be a rational explanation for the phenomenon he thought he was experiencing, didn't there? The first few times his mother had appeared, or seemed to appear, he had written off the whole unsettling phenomenon to having eaten a bit more chili crab than was good for him. Eventually, however, it occurred to him he might not be suffering from indigestion at all, and he came up with a much more rational and intellectually satisfying explanation.

He remembered someone once saying that dreams were nothing more than tangible expressions of intuition, and he had come to suspect that in the silence of the night, his subconscious was simply making itself heard in the form of his mother's dream-like apparitions. The advice that seemed to come from her was nothing more than the voice of his own unrealized thoughts. And what was more rational than the realization that these imagined manifestations were simply his subconscious whispering to him in the night?

He did have to admit it sometimes bothered him a bit that his mother's appearances seemed ... well, quite real. Tay was not a spiritual man, but sometimes her presence appeared so authentic that he wondered, despite himself, if her presence might not actually *be* real.

When he sat in his garden on a sunny morning with a cup of coffee and a Marlboro and thought about the matter, the idea that his mother was manifesting herself to him from beyond the grave was laughable. In the darkness and the loneliness of his bedroom in the middle of the night, the idea of it was far less amusing.

Of course, Tay understood perfectly well that he was not speaking to the ghost of his mother, no matter how real the conversation might seem to be. He knew perfectly well he was simply looking in a mirror and speaking to himself.

There was no other reasonable explanation.

Except, of course, the possibility he wasn't looking into a mirror at all, but rather through an opening of some sort into a spiritual dimension so profoundly unfathomable that it called into question everything he understood, or thought he understood, about the whole phenomenon of human existence.

But Tay was not a spiritual man, so he knew that could not be true.

. . .

Tay cleared his throat and let his eyes roam the bedroom.
"If that's you, Mother, please go away."

He felt silly saying it out loud, but he said it anyway.

"I'm tired and I need to go back to sleep. I'm in no mood for your nonsense tonight."

There was no response, but a white light suddenly appeared near the ceiling directly opposite the foot of his bed. While Tay watched, the light began to pulse rhythmically and glide toward him. It came to rest at the foot of his bed about four feet above the floor, where it began to expand and spin until it looked like a sparkling disco ball straight out of a seventies dance party.

The first time his mother had appeared to him, it was in a swarm of lights that looked like a goofball effect from a low-budget movie. It had all been so trite he could hardly stand it. He told her that, but she ignored him and kept on doing the light thing regardless of his scorn.

"I know you're not really here, Mother."

The disco ball spun faster, and he heard his mother's voice coming from it.

"Sometimes you are so disrespectful, Samuel Tay, that I truly cannot believe I gave birth to you."

"We're not having a conversation tonight, Mother, because you're not here."

"Then where do you think I am?"

The metaphysical implications of that question were far too weighty for Tay to cope with at four o'clock in the morning, so he remained silent.

"It's a simple question, Samuel."

"Yes, but you didn't ask it because you're not here. And I'm not in the mood to talk to myself."

The disco ball bobbed up and down a few times. Tay imagined it was chuckling, which he saw as yet more proof that he was not talking to his mother. In life, she had never had a sense of humor.

All at once, the spinning ball vanished, and Tay's bedroom was filled with a dull, orange-colored glow. He glanced at the drapes to see if it was coming from the windows, but it wasn't. When he looked back to where the disco ball had been, Tay saw his mother standing there.

Uh-oh.

The full-body manifestation. This couldn't be good.

His mother stood as still as death. Which, Tay thought, made sense. After all, she *was* dead.

She was wearing something that looked like a church choir robe that was dark green with gold trim. But that wasn't what caused Tay's mouth to open slowly in astonishment.

That happened because his mother was smoking a cigarette.

"Cat got your tongue, Samuel?"

"That's an awful cliché, Mother. Please try to be a little more original."

"One advantage of being dead is that you care very little what anyone says about you. Your criticism used to hurt me, Samuel, but I have become impervious to it."

"I didn't know you smoked, Mother."

"There are a lot of things you don't know about me. No son truly knows his mother."

"Are you mocking me? Are you doing this just because I stopped smoking and now you—"

"This may come as a surprise to you, Samuel, but everything I do isn't about you."

His mother shrugged slightly and exhaled a long steam of smoke.

"Most of my friends smoke. I just thought I'd give it a try now that I don't have to worry anymore about cigarettes killing me."

Tay normally coped with these visits from his mother fairly well, but this one was rendering him practically speechless. That was partially from the shock of seeing his mother with a cigarette in her hand, an image that was both novel to him and one that for some reason he found a little disturbing, but it was also from discovering that people commonly smoked in ... well, in wherever his mother was. Call it *the other side* to avoid becoming too theological.

Smoking seemed to get closer and closer every day to being banned outright everywhere on earth, and yet on the other side ghosts were merrily puffing away? That hardly seemed fair. Did it mean they left you alone on the other side to do pretty much as you liked? If it did, maybe there was an upside to death, after all.

"I think I understand now why you smoked for all those years, Samuel. There's a real sense of peace to the whole process, isn't there?"

His mother took another puff and smiled at him. Tay would have sworn that he could actually smell the smoke there in his bedroom, but he knew that could not be.

For one of the few times in his life, Tay was at a total loss for words, so he said nothing.

These nocturnal visits from his mother had become more and more exasperating to him. Sometimes they seemed designed for no real purpose other than to throw him off stride. The last time she had appeared, he had resolved that the next time he would simply refuse to acknowledge her at all and remain silent no matter what she said or did. After all, refusing to carry on a conversation with someone who wasn't there could hardly be considered rude, could it?

It could not.

He'd had enough.

Tay rolled over onto his side, pulled the duvet up to his chin, and closed his eyes as tightly as he could.

. . .

H e had hardly shut his eyes when he felt the mattress at the foot of his bed compress as if his mother had just seated herself on it.

Was it possible, he asked himself, to feel the weight of his mother's spirit sitting on his bed? Weren't spirits supposed to be ephemeral things, weightless and gauzy? Hadn't the great painters depicted spirits as winged seraphim afloat in the heavens?

Of course, such a rendering here would require him to picture his mother as an angel. That was far beyond the power of his imagination.

"You're telling yourself again that I'm not here, aren't you, Samuel? You're probably blaming me on whatever you had for dinner. Well, if it makes you feel better, just go on telling yourself that."

The dead do not easily leave this earth. Tay already knew that for certain. He had been a homicide investigator for most of his adult life, and every time he stood over the body of a murder victim, he could feel around him the presence of the living being that had once inhabited that body. But his mother had been dead for years. Surely by now, she had found her way to … well, to wherever it was she was going.

"Stop being such a baby, Samuel! I have something to talk to you about and I don't have all night to do it. I have things to do, places to be."

That was interesting, Tay thought to himself. The dead have schedules and appointments? Did they meet people for lunch, or maybe go bowling with their friends?

"Open your eyes and sit up, Samuel! This is important!"

His mother wouldn't go away until he had heard her out. He knew that. Ignoring her wasn't an option. Ignoring his mother had never been an option. The only way to get rid of her was to get this over with as quickly as possible.

Yielding to the inevitable, Tay pulled himself up, pushed his pillow behind him, and leaned back against the headboard. He eyed his mother sitting on the foot of his bed. She seemed to him to have posed herself with a degree of care. Her legs crossed, her back straight, and her green robe wrapped around her like — there was no other word for it — a shroud.

She waved her cigarette at him. "Do you have an ashtray, Samuel?"

"You know I quit smoking, Mother. Why would I have an ashtray?"

His mother gave him an annoyed look. Then she flicked her fingers and her cigarette spun toward the ceiling, where it appeared to vanish into thin air.

"Never mind," she said.

Now she was doing magic tricks, for God's sake. What would it be next? Water into wine? Maybe, for his sake, she could make it Irish whiskey instead.

"How did you know I was here, Mother?"

"Oh, for God's sake, Samuel, if you've ever asked me a dumber question than that, I can't remember it. I'm a spirit. I have universal knowledge. We've talked about this over and over. I exist on a purely spiritual plane."

They had talked about that before, that was true enough, but he still wasn't entirely certain he believed what his mother was telling him. He could think of no single word that fit the woman with whom he had grown up so poorly as the word *spiritual*.

"So how are you, Mother?"

"How *am* I? I'm dead. I was dead the last time you asked that, and I'm still dead."

"I know you're dead, Mother."

"Then why do you keep asking me how I am?"

"It's called politeness."

Tay's mother responded to that with a snort so loud it seemed to echo in the room.

"If we're all done with the witty dialogue now, Samuel,

would you like to know what I've come to talk to you about? Are you listening?"

"I'm listening, Mother."

"You must walk away from this. Now."

"Walk away from what?"

"You're trying to find out who killed that poor old man, aren't you?"

"Yes."

"But *why*, Samuel? Why are you doing that?"

"Because somebody asked me to."

His mother shook her head and looked away.

"You have no idea what you're doing. There are deep and ugly secrets here, secrets that people have fought to protect for fifty years. Do you think now they're just going to let you turn everything out for anyone to see?"

"What secrets are you talking about, Mother?"

"Keep a clear head, Samuel. Do not let this pretty girl pull you into deeper waters than those in which you can safely swim."

"That sounds positively Biblical. Have you become religious since you passed on?"

She ignored him again, as he knew she would.

"Listen to me, Samuel," she went on. "There are beliefs and convictions that lie at the foundations of all societies. No one may bring those beliefs and convictions into serious question. Only the crazies talk about them, and we mercilessly mock them. Then, ironically, that very mockery becomes another layer of protection for the real secrets underneath."

"I have no idea what you're talking about, Mother."

"You're not a fool, Samuel. Don't pretend to be one now. If you persist in digging into the death of Harry Black, you will release forces that will fundamentally alter the way people see the world. No one is ever going to thank you for what you're trying to do."

"I'm only trying to solve one murder, Mother, not change the world."

"There is something bad waiting for you down the road you're traveling now, Samuel. Something very bad."

"But you won't tell me what it is, will you?"

"It's not completely clear to me."

"Oh, for God's sake, Mother, now you sound like a fucking fortune cookie."

"Language, please, Samuel. Language! You grew up in my house, not in the gutter."

"Besides," she rushed on, not waiting for him to mount a defense, "I reject your pretense of cynicism. It is unconvincing."

"Why don't you just tell me plainly whatever you have to say, Mother? And then go away so I can get some sleep."

His mother was silent for a minute. She uncrossed her legs and then crossed them back the opposite way. He felt her weight shift on the foot of his bed as the mattress rose and fell.

"You think you're just looking for the truth about this man's murder, Samuel, but there are secrets here so big that people will risk everything to protect them."

"And you're saying that Harry Black's murder is one of those secrets?"

"Not exactly."

"Then just spell it out for me, Mother. What *are* you saying?"

"That you're in danger and you're putting the people around you in danger, too."

"What people are you talking about?"

"I don't know for sure. I seem to bring more insight to the past than I do to the future."

"Stop with the fortune cookie slogans already, Mother. You sound ridiculous."

"You think finding the truth is everything. The truth will not set you free, Samuel. Sometimes it condemns you to purgatory."

"I think the truth is always worth fighting for."

"Then I can only say good luck to you, Samuel."

"Thank you, Mother."

"Don't let them get behind you."

"What does that mean?"

All at once, the orange light vanished as abruptly as if a switch had been thrown, and Tay's bedroom was plunged into complete darkness.

"Mother?"

Silence.

"Are you still there, Mother?"

Silence.

Tay did not ask again because he knew the answer. His mother was as gone as if she had never even been there at all. Which he was pretty sure she hadn't been.

He scooted back down in bed, punched his pillows into shape, and pulled the duvet up to his chin.

During the day, he was quite certain he didn't believe in ghosts. At night, however, he had to admit he was a little more open minded on the subject.

FOURTEEN

Tay was outside the guest house at eight the next morning when Max and Renny turned off the main road. He was looking out over the beach toward the slightly dingy waters of the Gulf of Thailand and drinking coffee out of a heavy white ceramic mug.

He was almost certain he had smelled a faint odor of stale cigarette smoke while he was eating his breakfast. He knew that couldn't be, but it did seem very real.

He was sick of being taunted by his imagination so he decided to wait outside where he could stop thinking about whether he really smelled smoke or not. There was a stiff, salty wind off the water. It made him feel a little better, but not as much as he hoped it would.

Were there actually people who got up at this hour every morning because they wanted to? He found that very hard to believe.

He had prepared himself for the day as well as he could, given the ungodly hour. He had drunk several cups of coffee and eaten a plate of fruit and two pieces of toast that Apple had insisted on making for him. He had even remembered to tuck the fake Interpol credentials into his back pocket, just in case.

As much as he wanted to, he couldn't stop thinking about the visit from his mother in the night, or rather the visit from his mother he had imagined occurred in the night. Perhaps whether it was imaginary or real didn't matter that much. Everything about it had left him shaken. The appearance itself, the cigarette she seemed to be smoking, and most of all the message she had delivered.

You will release forces that will fundamentally alter the way people see the world.

That made no sense. This was an investigation into the murder of one elderly man. What could it possibly have to do with how people see the world?

His mother's fortune cookie wisdom sounded even more ridiculous this time than it usually did.

"Good morning, Inspector," Renny said when she got out of the car. "Did you sleep well?"

"Yes," Tay said. "Just fine."

Max had gotten out as well, and he looked at Tay like he was having trouble believing that.

"It's only a short walk," Max said.

It sounded to Tay as if Max thought that might make him feel better. It didn't.

For just a moment, Tay felt a mad desire to tell Renny and Max the whole story. He wanted to tell them about his mother's occasional nocturnal visits, and he wanted to tell them about the dire warning she had given him last night concerning Harry Black's murder.

But, of course, he did nothing of the sort.

Instead, he just put his coffee mug down on the low concrete wall that separated the house from the beach and arranged his face into the most benign expression he could manage at that hour.

"Then lead on," he said.

. . .

Tay was not a beach person. Under the best of circumstances, a stroll on a beach was a long way down his personal list of preferred activities, and these were anything but the best of circumstances.

They were going to examine the spot where a man had been murdered, and that was bad enough, but the beach itself was an unpleasant place to walk. It was more like a wide dirt road than anything Tay thought of as a beach.

The sand was hard-packed, and it was rough and rutted. The tide rolling in and out had filled some of the depressions with seawater and walking there required Tay to thread his way carefully among the multitude of puddles while trying not to stumble on the uneven ground.

Tay still wasn't certain that taking Renny to the spot where her grandfather was gunned down was a good idea, but she had insisted, and he had no right to tell her otherwise. He watched her face out of the corner of his eye. Was she as tough and resilient as she tried to come across? He had no idea, but he supposed he was about to find out.

And that was what he had been thinking when Max suddenly stopped.

"It was just about here," he said, pointing to the ground.

Tay looked around. After all this time, he knew there would be nothing to see, and that was exactly what he saw: nothing.

"That's the Hyatt," Max said, inclining his head toward a grassy lawn that rolled down to a rock topped with a thick layer of concrete. "The photos placed the body just at the foot of those stairs down to the beach."

Max pointed to five concrete steps edged with sturdy-looking black iron hand railings.

At the top of the steps was a dark wooden sign with a stern warning painted in yellow letters.

Hotel Guests Only

Tay, unimpressed by the sign, walked over, climbed the steps, and looked around.

Here and there clumps of white lounge chairs sat facing the beach, but they were all unoccupied. Perhaps a hundred meters away, Tay could see the hotel's swimming pool and, beyond it, a large open pavilion with a peaked roof and two wings he assumed contained guest rooms. He saw no sign of human activity anywhere.

Maybe it was just too early for guests at an expensive resort hotel to be out and doing whatever it was guests at an expensive resort hotel did with themselves, or maybe the hotel wasn't very busy. When he hadn't seen any mention of witness interviews in the police report, Tay had assumed the local cops had been lazy, but now it occurred to him that might have been unfair. Possibly there was a simple explanation for the lack of witness statements. Harry Black had been out on the beach even earlier than this. Maybe there had simply been no witnesses.

Tay turned around and used his vantage point at the top of the steps to look up and down the beach. It was about twenty-five meters wide at that point and very flat. He wondered if the Hyatt ran some sort of machinery over it since this part of the beach was far smoother than the stretch on which they had walked here. He supposed that was possible. Other than the smoothness of the beach and the slightly gray-brown waters of the Gulf of Thailand sloshing against it, there wasn't a great deal to see.

Tay climbed down the concrete steps and walked back over to Renny and Max.

"I can't believe somebody mugged my grandfather right in front of the Hyatt," Renny said.

Tay's eyes drifted away and Renny caught it.

"What?" she asked. "There's something you're not telling me, isn't there?"

Tay already knew that Renny had missed the significance of the information in the autopsy report about the round that had killed her grandfather, but he also knew what it would mean when he explained it to her.

Knowing how her grandfather had been killed would forever change everything she thought she knew about him. Tay didn't want to be responsible for that, but he didn't see how he could avoid it.

"Tell me," Renny said.

Her voice was very firm, and Tay shifted his eyes back to her.

"Your grandfather wasn't mugged."

Renny said nothing. She just waited.

"Did you see the paragraph in the autopsy report that said a single round struck him? Likely a .338 caliber."

Renny nodded, but she stayed silent.

"The .338 is a rifle round, not a handgun cartridge. They developed it to give military snipers a round capable of delivering high-powered hits at extended ranges."

Renny just looked at Tay, still saying nothing.

"A highly skilled sniper firing from a considerable distance killed your grandfather, not a mugger with a pistol."

"A sniper?" she asked. "Seriously?"

"A highly trained one. It was a long-distance shot and there was only a single round fired. Most snipers would have taken a second shot as a safety. This one didn't. One shot was all he needed."

Renny looked out to sea for a moment, then turned back to Tay.

"He was just a nice old man, Inspector. He had lived here for more than twenty years, bothering no one. Why would somebody send a trained sniper to kill a perfectly nice eighty-six-year-old man who had retired decades ago to a tiny Thai beach resort and hardly left it since?"

Tay hesitated and took a breath, but then he just said it.

"They wouldn't. Not if that's really who your grandfather was."

"I don't understand."

"Neither do I, but my guess is your grandfather was something other than a nice eighty-six-year-old man who retired in a tiny Thai beach resort. He was something you knew nothing about."

"Such as what?"

"Something that made him a threat."

"A threat to whom?"

"To people with enough power to send a skilled sniper here to kill him."

R enny turned away and walked toward where the sea lapped against the hard-packed sand. Tay let her go. That had been a lot to take in, and the right thing to do was to give her time to do it.

"Do you really think he was shot by a sniper?" Max asked, keeping his voice low.

Tay nodded.

"But from where?" he asked. "There's no place out here where a sniper could shoot from."

Tay had to admit that Max had a good point. The Hyatt was only two stories high and there were no taller buildings anywhere around.

Besides, Harry Black was struck in the front of the head, so the shot must have come from somewhere out in front of him. Not from a building to his right, certainly not from the ocean to his left, but directly in front of him. And it was pretty difficult to imagine Harry strolling directly toward some joker standing on the beach who was pointing a sniper rifle at him.

"What is that?" Tay asked, pointing over Max's shoulder to

a small hill at the tip of the narrow peninsula that marked the end of the beach.

"That's called Monkey Mountain."

"Odd name."

"It's because of the monkeys that live out there. Hundreds of them. Maybe thousands."

"What's that building on top? The one with the red and green roof."

"It's a Buddhist temple. A small one."

Tay looked thoughtful, but Max shook his head.

"A sniper firing from a Buddhist temple, sir? I don't think so. That would be pretty hard for me to believe."

"Unless the shooter was standing on the beach, the shot had to have come from up there. Where else *could* it have come from?"

Max looked from Tay to the temple and back again to Tay.

"That must be at least a kilometer away. Is it even possible to shoot someone from that distance?"

It was possible, but it wouldn't have been easy. If that was where the shooter fired from, his shot would have to have traveled the whole kilometer with the wind off the ocean coming in almost exactly perpendicular to it. Wind drift at distance was the toughest thing about long-range shooting, and adjusting for the wind coming off the ocean over that long a flight path would have been a bastard.

Tay stood with his hands on his hips and looked around. There was nowhere else. Whatever the distance, whatever the wind drift, that was where the shot had come from.

"Can we go there?" Tay asked.

"Go where?" Renny asked.

Neither Tay nor Max had heard her walk up behind them, but at the sound of her voice, they both looked around.

"Go where?" she repeated.

"Monkey Mountain," Max said. "The Inspector thinks the shot came from there. Maybe from the temple on the top."

Renny's eyes roamed the beach. They flicked over the buildings lining the landside, glanced out to sea, and then returned to Max.

"I think he's right," she said. "Let's go."

Renny spun on her heel without another word and marched back down the beach toward where Max had left the car. Tay and Max just kept up as well as they could.

FIFTEEN

It was only a short drive to Monkey Mountain.

Just over to the main highway that ran through the center of Hua Hin, follow it south for a couple of miles, and then turn east onto a narrow two-lane road that circled around the back of the hill to give sightseers access to the top. Ten minutes. Maybe fifteen if you drove slowly. Max didn't drive slowly.

As they started up the low hill, the road twisted past a modest fishing village. The land side of the road was lined with little cafes that weren't more than badly weathered shacks with a few rickety chairs and broken-down tables. On the ocean side, a couple of dozen fishing boats that looked as if they had long ago seen their best days were moored to a dilapidated dock.

It was a simple economy. The men went to sea and fished, and the women stayed on land and prepared food to sell. It had probably worked that way for a century. It would probably work that way for another century.

As the big white Mercedes passed, heavily lined brown faces of indeterminate age, most of which looked as if they had seen their best days as well, turned toward them and silently clocked their passage. It occurred to Tay that these very people might have watched the shooter driving back down the hill after putting a bullet through Harry Black's head. How else would the shooter have left the scene?

This appeared to be the only road down and there was no obvious way to access Monkey Mountain except in a vehicle. The pampered guests of the Hyatt may not have been up and about early in the morning, but these people no doubt rose before dawn and started work before full light. They would have been right here when the shooter drove by.

But what would they have seen? A vehicle coming down the hill. Why would anyone remember it now, nearly a week later? The shooter wouldn't have exactly careened downhill in a red Ferrari waving his sniper rifle out the window. He would have been in an inconspicuous vehicle, and he would have driven so as not to attract any attention.

A professional hitter who could make a shot like that would depart unobtrusively. The fishermen and their wives might have looked up as the vehicle passed, but surely nothing about either it or the driver would have caught their attention.

Was it possible he was wrong about that? Doubtful. Regardless, maybe he ought to get Max to come back later and poke around, anyway.

Just in case he *was* wrong. As unlikely as that might be.

A fter the roadway passed through the fishing village, it twisted gently up the hill through dense vegetation that looked impossibly green to Tay, but what did he know about vegetation?

Tay was born in Singapore and he had spent all of his life in Singapore. For a city, Singapore had always seemed to him to be pleasantly green, but this was of another order of magnitude entirely. It was a jungle, one that looked as if a human being couldn't possibly walk through it.

They rounded a curve. Max braked sharply and came to a

complete stop. Monkeys were blocking the road. Dozens of them. Maybe even a hundred. There were big monkeys, small monkeys, and everything in between. They all appeared similar enough that Tay assumed they must all be of the same species, but as far as he was concerned, a monkey was a monkey.

Some monkeys walked back and forth across the road, some sprawled in the roadway examining either their own anatomy or that of another member of the tribe, and some had mounted each other and were busily engaging in bouts of carnal pleasure. Most of them were just sitting around, not doing much of anything. Probably saving up their energy for when it was their turn for the carnal pleasure thing.

What was the collective noun for a bunch of monkeys? A herd? A flock? A pride? No, none of those sounded quite right. It had to be something, but Tay had no idea what it was. He supposed it didn't matter. Whatever the right collective noun was, the little bastards were blocking the bloody road, and he wanted to get by.

"Hit the horn," he told Max.

Max beeped the horn a couple of times, politely, but absolutely nothing happened. A few of the monkeys may have given them a glance, but that was it. The pairs that were busily humping in the middle of the road didn't even bother to do that. None of the monkeys seemed remotely interested in the big Mercedes idling just in front of them and blowing its horn for them to move.

"Roll forward slowly," Tay instructed. "They'll get out of the way."

Tay honestly didn't know whether the monkeys would get out of the way or not, but he had no intention of simply turning around and going back down the hill. He wanted to find the place from which the sniper had shot Harry Black, and he certainly wasn't going to be stopped from doing that by a bunch of monkeys too busy humping in the road to get out of their way.

That was when Tay registered the smell.

Despite all the filters the Mercedes air conditioning system must have, the smell that invaded the car was sharp, hard, and rude. It was the pungent, musky odor of poop and piss mixed with something that made Tay think of piles of rotten fruit. He had heard of people keeping monkeys for pets, but if they smelled like this, he couldn't believe it. How could anyone live with a smell like this?

Max took his foot off the brake and rolled slowly forward. When none of the monkeys seemed inclined to move, he started beeping the horn again. The monkeys responded with magnificent disdain. They moved out of the way, after a fashion, but they did it ever so slowly, barely even bothering to glance at the big car that was threatening to run them over.

Tay had to smile to himself. Maybe the monkeys smelled like shit, literally, but he had to give them their due. He and Max and Renny were the interlopers here. They would soon be gone and the monkeys would remain. They were what mattered on Monkey Mountain, not them, and certainly not the Mercedes.

The monkeys moved because it pleased them to do so. Not because a car was rolling toward them and honking its horn. It was the monkeys' mountain, not theirs, and they would probably do well to keep that in mind.

Maybe, it occurred to Tay, the monkeys had seen the shooter. Well, yes, they probably had. Perhaps then he ought to send Max to talk to the monkeys at the same time he came back to talk to the fishermen. Tay figured he would probably get about the same amount of useful information out of both.

The road ended a kilometer or so further uphill in a small asphalt parking lot beside the Buddhist temple Tay had seen from the beach. There were no other cars in the lot, so Max pulled over, stopped pretty much at random, and they all got out.

The word *temple* had brought to Tay's mind an image of a grand structure constructed with the intent of creating something soaring and magnificent. Something that symbolized the puniness of human beings reaching for the heavens.

There was nothing like that here. Tay wasn't sure what he had expected to see, but whatever it was, it hadn't been this.

This temple consisted of nothing but a half dozen rather unpromising wooden structures of varying sizes scattered across a pitted and stained concrete pad. The structures weren't exactly dilapidated, but they were working toward it as fast as they could. The salt air and the constant wind coming off the ocean were taking a toll.

Laundry flapped from a rope line tied between two of the little buildings and a pile of discarded cardboard cartons lay outside another. It looked more like a collection of outbuildings for a luckless and unprofitable farm.

If it hadn't been for the giant standing Buddha on the far side of the concrete pad, the place would have looked nothing like a religious site. The Buddha must have been at least fifteen feet tall. It was painted bright gold and positioned so that it was looking down from Monkey Mountain over Hua Hin beach.

They walked over to the Buddha figure and stood at the edge of the pad behind a low concrete balustrade streaked with water stains. Hua Hin Beach curved away into the distance right below them.

Harry Black would have been walking directly toward a shooter positioned up here. No side-to-side motion at all. He was the next thing to a stationary target. From here, it was almost a routine shot for a well-trained sniper.

Yes, the distance was significant. At least eight hundred meters, maybe a thousand. But all the shooter had to do was correct for the bullet drop produced by the downward angle of the shot and account for the right to left drift from whatever breeze had been blowing off the ocean that day, and that would have been that. That would have very much been that.

It bothered Tay that there were certainly far easier ways to kill an elderly man walking alone on a beach in the early morning light than positioning a sniper nearly a kilometer away. Perhaps the use of a sniper to kill Harry Black was some kind of message. But if it had been, what was the message, and who was the message meant for?

From this elevated vantage point, the Gulf of Thailand took on the look everyone was familiar with from a hundred travel magazines and a thousand postcards. Azure blue water washing against a broad sand beach edged with glittering white luxury high-rises and sprawling resort hotels. Hua Hin certainly looked a lot better from up here than it did down at ground level.

There was a philosophical principle in that somewhere, Tay thought, but he let it go. He wanted to get on with this before the damned monkeys showed up again and swarmed all over everything.

"Is there somebody in charge at a temple like this?" Tay asked. "Like a priest or something?"

"They're called monks," Max said. "And they live in the temples. At least most of the temples I've seen."

"Is there a head monk?"

"The large temples have a senior monk called an abbot who's nominally in charge, but Buddhism isn't big on hierarchy and structure. The abbot is just an administrator. The job doesn't have any religious significance."

"I'm not interested in discussing religion. What I need to know is if anyone here heard or saw anything the morning Renny's grandfather was killed. If I'm right and the shooter fired from up here, someone must have heard the shot. Somebody may even have seen him. The abbot won't be offended if I ask about that, will he?"

Max looked around doubtfully.

119

"I don't think a little temple like this would have an abbot," he said. "I'm not even sure there are any monks here."

"Someone's here," Renny said, pointing to where two saffron-colored robes and a half dozen other unidentifiable garments flapped in the wind from the rope line tied between two of the little buildings.

Both structures were built of wood so weathered that it had turned almost gray from the relentless assault of the sea air. The larger of the two buildings had big wooden flaps propped open with stakes which looked as if they functioned as windows. Perhaps mosquitoes gave monks a pass.

"That's probably the living quarters where the laundry line is," Max said. "I guess we could start looking for someone there."

Tay turned slowly in a full circle and examined the entire compound. Nothing moved, and the only sound was the noise of the laundry flapping in the breeze.

"What's that?" Tay asked, pointing to the largest and most prominent structure in the compound.

It was up on a small rise at the top of two flights of concrete steps and occupied what seemed to be the highest ground in the compound. The building itself wasn't large, but the design was so whimsical that Tay could hardly look away from it.

They might have constructed the building from a drawing made by a child. A steeply peaked roof of red, green, and white tiles laid in concentric rectangles was supported above an open pavilion by polished teak pillars. The roof was edged with an elaborate gold frieze of spiraling shapes that ended at each corner in what looked like golden spears swirling up toward the heavens.

Flanking the top of the steps were two statues on concrete pedestals. They were human-sized figures, but there was nothing human about them.

They looked more like demons from a cartoon. Brightly colored costumes that vaguely resembled something out of a production of the Arabian Nights; golden shoes and pyramid-shaped golden crowns; faces covered by green masks; and two enormous swords held at the ready. They were the gargoyles guarding the castle.

"That's probably where the altar is," Max said. "It's where the monks come to meditate."

Tay wasn't sure why monks needed broadsword-wielding gargoyles to guard their meditation room, even symbolic ones made of stone, but he figured it wasn't his place to question the aspects of anyone's religion.

"Then that's where we ought to start," Tay said. "A little meditation would probably do us a world of good."

SIXTEEN

The silence was so complete that when Tay stepped into the pavilion it surprised him to find someone there.

A man wrapped in the saffron robes of a Buddhist monk sat cross-legged on a cushion facing a gold Buddha figure that was more or less the same size he was. The figure rested on a varnished wooden pedestal and was seated in a posture that was almost identical to that of the monk facing it.

Between the man and the figure was a low wooden table polished to a mirror-like sheen. Sitting on it were a variety of containers filled with flowers and fruit, half a dozen smaller Buddha images, and several silver framed photographs of what appeared to be very elderly men in monk's robes.

At the ends of the table there were brass bowls filled with sand. Burning sticks of incense stood upright in both bowls, and the sticks gave off coils of smoke that rose toward the roof of the pavilion until the ocean breezes caught them and swirled them away.

Tay saw that he had interrupted something, although he wasn't at all certain what it was. He stood silently trying to decide what he should do now.

When Max and Renny caught up with him, they each removed their shoes and left them at the top of the steps, then stood barefoot next to him with their palms pressed together in a gesture similar to the deferential *wai* with which Thais greeted each other.

Tay gathered he was supposed to do the same even if they were too polite to tell him, so he slipped off his shoes, too, and put them next to Renny's. He felt awkward standing there in his stocking feet since neither Max nor Renny were wearing socks.

Should he take off his socks, too? He figured he would feel even more awkward hopping from foot to foot and trying to remove his socks without sitting down, so he kept them on.

The silence was so complete it felt almost tangible, and it combined with the odor of incense spiraling up on both sides of the serenely posed Buddha figure to create a sense of peacefulness so overwhelming that it left Tay feeling like an intruder from another world. Which he supposed when he thought about it, was exactly what he was.

He examined the man in the saffron robe sitting cross-legged in front of the figure. He appeared to be quite tall, but he was very thin and his brown skin was stretched so tightly over his face and arms that he looked cadaverous. He was barefooted, and his hands and arms were bare of jewelry or even a wristwatch, but he wore a pair of yellow sunglasses with lenses that were tinted gray.

There was something about the man that hardly seemed real. He could have been almost any age from thirty to ninety. His face showed no expression at all, and his dark eyes seemed to be focused on something far away. His back was very straight and his posture was rigid, but there was still something effortless about the way he sat. He looked so in harmony with his surroundings that Tay half expected to see the man suddenly levitate.

Did Buddhist monks levitate? Tay doubted it, but right there and right then, it wouldn't have surprised him one bit to discover they did.

T ay tilted his head toward Max and whispered as quietly as he could. "Can we talk to that monk? Would it be rude to interrupt him now?"

"I'm not sure," Max whispered back.

"Why don't you try? Ask him if we can talk to him for a moment."

"Of course, you can talk to me."

The three of them looked at the monk. He had spoken without turning his head, and his words seemed to be issuing from the air rather than coming from his mouth.

"What would you like to talk to me about?"

Tay cleared his throat.

"It didn't occur to me you would speak English."

"Why not? I attended the University of Texas for two years. Despite that, my English isn't too bad."

Tay assumed that was a joke, but he wasn't completely certain, so he just nodded.

The man turned his head very slowly toward Tay and his face assumed a pleasant look that was almost, but not quite, a smile.

"Hook'em Horns," he said.

Max and Renny burst out laughing, and Tay managed a chuckle. He didn't have any idea what that meant or why it was funny, but the comment seemed to amuse everyone else, so he thought he probably ought to join in.

"Do you know about the man who was shot on the beach just below here on Sunday morning?" he asked the monk.

"No."

That stopped Tay. How often did somebody get shot in this sleepy little village? It had to have been big news. How could this man have heard nothing about it?

The monk read the disbelief on Tay's face.

"I live here alone. I do not read newspapers. I do not watch television. I know the things I need to know, and I do not know the things I do not need to know."

Tay couldn't argue with that. To tell the truth, that sounded pretty damn appealing to him.

"A man walking on the beach was shot and killed by a high-powered rifle very early on Sunday morning. I think the rifle was fired from here."

The monk thought that over for a moment.

"You're not a policeman," he said.

Tay noticed he had not made a question of it.

"I was. Just not a Thai policeman. I was a homicide investigator in Singapore for many years, but I'm retired now."

Tay watched the monk thinking that over. He expected he would ask why a retired homicide investigator from Singapore was investigating the death of a man in Hua Hin, or perhaps ask him who the man was who had been shot, but he did neither of those things.

The monk simply nodded slightly and said, "I heard the shot."

"I thought you didn't know about the murder."

"I didn't. I heard the shot. I didn't know what the effect of it was."

Tay felt the conversation moving toward a Zen-like meditation on action and its consequences, and he wasn't about to get into a conversation like that with a Buddhist monk.

"You're sure it was Sunday morning?"

"Yes. Very early. Just after sunrise."

"Why do you remember it so clearly?"

"We do not have a great deal of gunfire around here. When I hear some, I am likely to remember it."

"Some? Several shots?"

"No, just one."

"How do you know what you heard was a shot? Could it have been a car backfiring or perhaps something else?"

"It could have been," the monk smiled, "but it wasn't. I was in the military for three years. I know what a shot sounds like, and this was a rifle shot. Something in a large caliber. Not a handgun."

A Buddhist monk who went to the University of Texas, served in the military, and could distinguish the sound of shots well enough to identify large-caliber rifle fire? Tay wasn't sure what to make of that.

"So you were right, sir," Max murmured. "The shooter did fire from here."

"No, the shot didn't come from here," the monk corrected him.

They all looked back at the monk and saw he was pointing just over their heads.

"It came from above. From up there."

Naturally, they all swiveled their heads to look in the direction the monk was pointing, but there was nothing to see other than the other temple buildings scattered around outside the pavilion.

"Up where?" Tay asked.

"There is a trail," the monk said. "It leads to a lookout that's about a hundred feet further up above us. Occasionally, visitors go up there for the view. That is where the shot came from."

"Did you see anyone?" Tay asked.

The monk shook his head. "I was right here when I heard the shot. I finished my prayer, then I went over to the top of the steps. I stood about where you are now and looked outside."

"How long after you heard the shot was that?"

The monk thought about it. "A few minutes. Maybe five? Not long."

"And you saw no one."

"No, no one. Only a white car driving out of the parking area."

"A car? What kind of car?"

"I have no idea. I don't know one car from another. It was an ordinary car, a common-looking thing. It was of average size and white. That is all I know."

"You didn't get a look at the driver?"

The monk shook his head.

"Was there a passenger in the car with the driver?"

The monk shook his head again. "I only saw the car and only for a second. That is all I can tell you. I don't even know if the departure of the car and the sound of the shot had any connection with each other."

They found the pathway to the lookout easily enough. It was exactly where the monk had said they would find it. It began at the parking lot just about where Max had parked the Mercedes and curled around Monkey Mountain up to the lookout at the very top.

The footing was a combination of dirt and gravel, adequately graded for comfortable walking, and not particularly steep. A short stroll between walls of dense vegetation brought them to a small open area edged by a waist-high stonewall. It was directly above the building in the temple compound they thought was probably the monk's living quarters.

Hua Hin Beach was spread out below them. There were no obstructions at all. Tay could easily pick out the Hyatt and the wall that separated it from the beach, and his eyes went directly to the spot where Max said Harry Black's body had been found.

"Do you really think they shot him from here?" Renny asked.

Tay nodded.

"It's the only possibility," he said. "The monk heard the shot, and he knows it came from somewhere above the temple. This is the only place that *is* above the temple."

"It's hard to believe it's even possible to shoot someone from this far away."

"It wouldn't be that difficult for an experienced sniper. Especially not when the target is walking directly toward him and moving slowly."

Tay hesitated.

"I'm sorry," he said. "Referring to your grandfather that way was clumsy of me."

"Stop worrying about me, Inspector. I'm a lot tougher than I look."

Tay wasn't certain what to say to that, so he said nothing. He just nodded and walked over to the low wall that marked the edge of the lookout.

He let his eyes roam over the dirt behind it. Renny and Max stepped back and remained respectfully silent while Tay examined the place from which Harry Black had been murdered.

The dirt was scuffed and marked, and Tay could make out bits and pieces of footprints here and there. Did one or more of those prints belong to whoever had shot Harry Black? Yes, probably, but he had no way of telling which ones. He began walking slowly back and forth, his eyes scanning the ground.

"You don't expect to find something after all this time, do you?" Renny asked.

"I don't think anything," Tay shrugged, "but we're here, so I'm going to look."

Walking a crime scene told Tay things, but he didn't know how to explain that to Renny. He certainly didn't believe in premonitions, omens, clairvoyance, or whatever other names people wanted to call the feelings they got, nor did he believe that standing at the crime scene would conjure up a vision of what happened there.

What he did believe was that the dead leave this life reluctantly and that something of them lingers long after their physical body ceases to function. Many times over his career, he had learned things that led him to a killer simply by standing quietly at a crime scene and listening. He wasn't altogether certain what he was listening to, but he was certain that sometimes he heard things anyway.

Of course, in this case, there was another problem altogether to consider.

A crime scene was almost always a single location. The victim and the killer had been together in the same place. More than likely, they had confronted each other in some way, and the victim knew or suspected what was about to happen.

His last thoughts would have been of his fear and pain, and it was those last bursts of feeling that Tay had found remained at a crime scene long after the body had been removed. It was as if the victim's terror of passing into the unknown had metastasized right into the air. There were things you could never scrub away from a crime scene. The victim's final anguish was one of them.

But this crime scene was different from the others Tay had examined in his career.

Someone had crouched behind this stone wall and used it to brace a rifle barrel. Then they placed the crosshairs of a telescopic sight on Harry Black's head almost a kilometer away and fired a single round that blew apart his skull. After that, they had no doubt calmly packed the rifle away in some kind of case, walked down the path to their car, and driven off.

Harry Black hadn't died where he was shot. He died almost a kilometer away, and he died without having the slightest idea what was about to happen to him. One second, he was strolling on Hua Hin Beach enjoying the early morning light, and the next second, he had left this earth. Even if the ghost of Harry Black materialized in front of Tay, right here, right now, there was simply nothing he could tell Tay about how he died. He understood no more about his murder than Tay did.

Real death doesn't always come right before the end of the

movie. It isn't preceded by signs and signals and final words. It happens in the middle of everything else, before anyone is ready, when a thousand loose threads are hanging. You don't see it approaching. It just shows up out of nowhere in the middle of an ordinary Thursday. There is no orderliness to real death. And there was no orderliness to the death of Harry Black.

No, if Tay was ever going to find Harry Black's killer, he would find him by asking, not *how* Harry Black died, but *why* Harry Black died. Someone with a great deal of power was very afraid of Harry Black, which meant that Harry Black had a kind of power, too.

Figuring out what that power was, and who it threatened, would point Tay directly at his killer.

W alking back down the path, they came across a single monkey sitting in the middle of it scratching his stomach. It shrieked and plunged into the thick vegetation before they reached it.

Then, twenty or thirty yards further down, they came across two more monkeys. These sat unmoving at the side of the path and tracked them as they walked by with what seemed to Tay to be a certain amount of bemusement.

When they approached the bottom of the path, Tay heard the chattering of a much larger group of monkeys and smelled the same sour odor he had back on the road. They stepped out into the parking lot and saw that a dozen or more monkeys had made themselves comfortable on the Mercedes. Four or five sprawled on the roof, a couple sat on the trunk, and the rest occupied the hood.

They walked toward the car, and the chattering rose alarmingly in volume. The monkeys didn't wish to be disturbed. As if to underscore that, the largest of the monkeys stood up on the hood, turned to face them, and let loose an impressive stream of urine that he aimed directly at them.

Tay watched the yellow liquid flow down the hood, wash over the Mercedes logo, and splash to the ground. Then he opened the rear passenger door and got in. When he slammed it closed, the monkeys scattered.

"I hope that's not an omen," he muttered.

SEVENTEEN

Renny took her accustomed seat in the back of the Mercedes next to Tay and Max slid behind the wheel. "Where to now, sir?" he asked.

Tay looked at Renny. "I'd like to look through your grandfather's house if that would be all right with you."

Renny nodded absently, but she said nothing.

"Have you gone through it yet yourself?"

First, Renny looked surprised. Then she looked puzzled.

"No. Why would I do that?"

"For the same reason I want to. To see what it might tell us about his life and why this happened."

"I guess I don't think like a detective. Besides, I don't even know where he lived."

"If I may, sir?" Max interjected. "The address was in the police report I gave you, but it was in a part I didn't translate for you."

"Do you remember it?"

"Yes, sir. I remember it. And I know exactly where it is."

"I guess then that only leaves the problem of how I get in."

"The police gave me some keys they found in his pocket," Renny said. "One of them is probably his house key."

"Do you have them with you?"

"They're back at my hotel."

"Then let's get them."

Max started the car.

While Max drove them back down Monkey Mountain, Tay thought about how he would approach looking at Harry Black's house.

He appreciated the help Max and Renny were giving him, but he wasn't sure that all three of them trooping through the house together was the best way to do it. When he was with other people, which wasn't often, Tay realized how much time he spent on his own and how much he preferred it.

Solitude was seductive. Solitude was purity. Solitude was control. Solitude wrapped itself around you, gently at first, and then more insistently, until every alternative to it seemed little more than noise and confusion. It would be distracting to have other people around when he went through Harry Black's house. He wouldn't be able to absorb what he saw the way he wanted to absorb it.

When they reached the fishing village, Tay watched the men cleaning the boats and drying the nets on one side of the road. Then he turned his head and looked at the women and children working in the food stalls on the other side. An idea occurred to him that might solve two problems for him at the same time.

"While I'm looking at your grandfather's house," he said to Renny, "I want you and Max to come back here and talk to as many of these people as you can. Ask them about that white car the monk said he saw leaving the parking lot after he heard the shot fired. Maybe someone noticed the car because of the early hour and can tell us something about the driver. Physical description, age, ethnicity, anything would help."

"I'd rather look through my grandfather's house with you,"

Renny said. "I've got to do it sometime, and I don't want to do it by myself."

"I can take care of talking to these people, sir," Max said. "No problem."

Tay would have preferred to go through Harry Black's house entirely on his own, but he felt awkward telling Renny that. He wasn't a cop. He had no authority over her or anyone else, so who was he to tell her she couldn't accompany him when he went through her grandfather's house? This doing-favors-for-friends stuff was complicated. It was easier when he was a cop and just told people how it was going to be.

"That's fine," Tay said. "Maybe it will help to have two pairs of eyes looking around."

That wasn't an honest answer, of course, but he thought it was the only one he could give.

They stopped at Renny's hotel to get the keys the Thai police had found in her grandfather's pocket.

Tay was surprised to see that the hotel was a lovely old three-story colonial building with wide, shaded verandas around all three floors. Its white wooden walls were trimmed with polished teak and topped with a peaked, red-tile roof. He had been expecting another of the same kind of bland, high-rise monstrosities that had obliterated the beauty of his once-upon-a-time lovely and beloved Singapore, but he was pleased to see how wrong he had been.

Tay and Max waited in the car while Renny retrieved the keys. It was only a few minutes before she brought them out and handed them to Tay.

He looked at the plain metal ring with three keys hanging from it. One key looked like a common door key, and one of the other two was much smaller. Tay thought it looked like a key to a desk drawer, or maybe a box. It was the third key that puzzled him.

It was big and heavy, twice the length of any door key he had ever seen, and very thick. It had a wide handle and a long round shaft with a square plate at the end. The strange pattern of grooves and ridges on the plate didn't look like the business end of any door key Tay had ever seen before. It made him think of a key that might open some medieval fortress that had heavy timber doors studded with black iron bolts, bound with steel bands, and secured with an enormous iron lock. But surely it couldn't be that, could it?

T he drive from Renny's hotel to Harry Black's house took less than ten minutes. Just as Max had said, no place in Hua Hin was very far from any other place in Hua Hin.

The house, of course, turned out to look nothing like a medieval fortress. It was a three-story row house finished in white masonry that Tay thought was of an altogether undistinguished design.

It was the last in a row of perhaps a dozen nearly identical structures, all of which sat in a straight line joined together by common walls. The houses all faced on a wide driveway that led off the main highway, and on the other side of the driveway was a high stucco wall. Both the driveway and the wall stopped at a low concrete barrier a few feet above the beach. Harry Black's house held pride of place among the group. It was the last house in the column, the one furthest from the road and closest to the ocean.

Concrete steps led up to a low front porch covered with dark blue tiles. The porch was completely bare. No furniture, not even any plants. The front door was solid-looking and made of some sort of blond wood. It was at one end of the porch and you entered the house parallel to the front driveway.

The two floors above the porch had some scattered windows, all of them tiny and covered with either drapes or shades. They weren't windows designed for enjoying the view.

They looked almost like an afterthought, as if the architect had suddenly realized he hadn't put any windows in the front so he stuck a few in here and there at random.

It may not have been the kind of building Tay had pictured when he had seen the big key on Harry Black's keyring, but it didn't look very homey either. It seemed institutional to Tay, like a building you'd find in a suburban office park.

"Did your grandfather live here alone?" Tay asked Renny.

"You mean, did he have a girlfriend?"

Tay looked uncomfortable. For all he knew, Black might have lived there with a man, but he couldn't think of any way to say that without sounding like he was trying to be politically correct.

"Not as far as I know," Renny continued, taking Tay off the hook before he could decide what to say. "If he did, he never mentioned her to me."

"Did he own the house, or was he renting it?"

"I don't know. I suppose I'll have to find out now, won't I? Who would I ask?"

"Do you know if he had a will? If he did, a local lawyer may have drawn it up. Surely he would know."

"I haven't looked. I guess I should."

"Did your grandfather have a car?"

"I don't know that either. If he did, I don't know where it would be since there's no garage."

She looked over her shoulder and down the driveway toward the main road. Cars stood at the side of it in front of several of the other houses, but there was none in front of Harry Black's house.

"I guess that's another thing for my list. I'm not doing very well here, am I?"

"You're doing fine. You can hardly blame yourself for not being prepared for this."

"Yes, I can," she said. "Just try and stop me."

. . .

The three of them got out of the Mercedes and stood in a line in the driveway examining Harry Black's house.

"We probably look like Peter, Paul, and Mary standing here about to burst into 'If I Had a Hammer,'" Tay said.

No one said anything. Tay glanced first at Max, then at Renny.

"Who?" Renny asked.

Tay cleared his throat. "Seriously?"

Renny and Max just looked at him.

Tay was still struggling not to fall into the yawning chasm of decrepitude that had just opened at his feet when a woman's voice called out from behind them.

"Hello? Can I help you?"

Tay looked back and saw a woman watching them from the front porch of the house next door. His first thought was that the woman was a foreigner, not a local, but then he was a foreigner in Thailand, too, so maybe that didn't mean very much. What he meant, of course, was that the woman was white, not Asian.

She was wearing a yellow t-shirt and brown shorts, and her sun-bleached hair was back in a ponytail. She was small, not much over five feet tall, but she looked athletic, sinewy and solid, like a long-distance runner. She wasn't young, but Tay guessed her compact body probably made her look younger than she was.

"Are you friends of Mr. Black?" she called out.

Tay wasn't sure how to respond to that without saying more than he wanted to say, but the woman started talking again without waiting for him to answer her.

"I'm sorry to have to tell you this," she said, not looking all that sorry at all, Tay thought, "but he …"

The woman paused, apparently trying out and discarding several possible phrases until she settled on what she thought was the most innocuous one.

"… he passed away several days ago."

For all those years Tay had been a cop in Singapore, when he faced any challenge to going anywhere he wanted and doing anything he wanted, all he had to do was hold up his warrant card and announce *Inspector Tay from Singapore CID,* and that ended that.

But this was exactly what Tay had warned Jones about. He had no authority here. None at all. He had no authority anywhere, he knew, but that was a separate issue.

He could feel the fake Interpol credentials in his back pocket calling to him, but he hated to pull them out. There was an indignity to using fake police credentials when he had so recently been a real policeman. But it was a small lie, wasn't it? And he wasn't doing it to cause any harm to this woman, only for the sake of making their encounter less complicated. If he was going to do this at all, Tay figured, he'd better do it quickly before he drowned in his own sophistry.

He pulled the credentials wallet out of his back pocket before he could change his mind, flipped it open, and held it up toward the woman.

"Inspector Tay of Interpol," he announced in his most authoritative cop voice.

Despite Tay's initial reluctance to engage in the deception, he had to admit that had something of a ring to it.

Inspector Tay of Interpol!

The woman gasped audibly, and Tay suddenly wondered if he had gone too far.

"We're here investigating Mr. Black's death," he added quickly.

"Interpol?" she sputtered. "Really? Interpol? I heard Mr. Black was shot. Everyone has heard that. But Interpol? I thought that was just something in the movies."

She started down the steps from her porch toward where Tay was standing with Max and Renny.

"Oh my," she said, "how exciting!"

Tay lifted his right hand, palm out, like a traffic cop holding up a line of vehicles.

"Is that your house, madam?"

The authority in Tay's voice made the woman stop walking before she reached the bottom of the steps.

"Yes, sir," she nodded. "My husband and I live here, but he's playing golf right now."

"Did you know Mr. Black?"

"Yes, sir." Now she was nodding so vigorously that her head seemed to be in some danger of detaching itself from her neck. "Yes, sir, I did. We did."

"What is your name, please?"

"Fiona Campbell, sir. My husband is Duncan Campbell. We're from Scotland, but we're retired now and we live here. In Hua Hin," she added, as if Tay might not be entirely certain where he was.

"Well, Mrs. Campbell, please go back inside your house and wait for me. After my colleagues and I have examined Mr. Black's house, I would like to ask you a few questions. Will that be all right?"

"Oh yes, sir. I'll be happy to help you in any way I can. Very happy, sir."

"Then wait inside your house, please, Mrs. Campbell. I'll be there as soon as I can."

When she didn't move, Tay made a little shooing gesture with his hands. Mrs. Campbell immediately turned and scurried away.

After the woman's front door closed behind her, Tay put the Interpol credentials away and turned back to Max and Renny. He found them staring at him, their mouths slightly open.

"What?" he asked.

"Interpol?" Renny said. "Eddie didn't say you were with

Interpol."

Tay studied his shoes and looked embarrassed.

"I'm not," he said.

"But…" Renny gestured toward the credentials wallet he had just returned to his back pocket.

"As the cliché goes, it's a long story. The short version is that this Interpol ID is from an intelligence operation I was part of recently in Hong Kong."

"An intelligence operation? In Hong Kong? For who?"

Tay didn't know quite what to say to that, so he was enormously relieved when Renny rushed on without waiting for him to answer her.

"Is that where Eddie knows you from?" she asked.

Tay nodded.

"Then Eddie thinks you're with Interpol?"

"Oh, no. He knows the credentials are fake, but he suggested I bring them with me here in case I needed to establish my authority. Mostly because I don't have any authority."

Renny thought that over for a moment.

"This is all sounding a bit complicated," she said.

"Yes," Tay agreed, "that's because it *is* a bit complicated."

"I don't care how complicated it is," Max grinned, "that was *bitching*. You stopped that woman in her tracks and then got rid of her just by waving that fake ID and using the tone of your voice."

Tay looked away, a little embarrassed.

"*Is that your house, madam?*" Max mimicked Tay's tone as well as he could. "*Please wait inside until I come for you.* Damn, sir! That was so cool! I have *got* to learn to do that."

T ay mounted the steps to the porch and walked down to Harry Black's front door. He stood quietly for a moment and examined it. There were no pry marks or scratches or other signs of the door being forced. The lock looked sturdy. It wasn't one of those tinny, in-knob jobs, but a high-end deadbolt positioned about six inches above the doorknob. Still, it was no lock from a medieval fortress. The big, odd-shaped key had to be for something else.

Tay touched the door with one hand. It felt sturdy and substantial. He made a fist and knocked gently against it, then he knocked harder. It was solid, not hollow-core. It might even have been steel-reinforced. Tay wasn't certain.

He took the keys Renny had given him out of his pocket. Before he tried the one that looked like a door key, he wrapped his hand around the knob and gave it a turn. It moved smoothly and silently with practically no resistance. The bolt snapped open with a solid sound.

The door wasn't locked.

Max and Renny had followed Tay up onto the porch and now Max spoke up.

"That's not as unusual as it might seem to you, sir," he said. "People go walking on the beach here all the time without locking their front doors."

"But if he hadn't locked the door," Renny said, "why would he have taken his keys with him?"

It was a good question, Tay thought. Habit? Maybe. Maybe not.

Of course, the fact the door was unlocked now didn't mean that Harry Black had left it unlocked when he went for his last walk on the beach. Maybe he had. Max said that wouldn't have been unusual. But maybe he hadn't. Maybe someone had broken in after they shot Harry Black, looked around for something, and then left, not bothering to re-lock the door.

If that was true, then what were they looking for? Tay had absolutely no idea.

"I really wouldn't worry about it, sir. Leaving doors unlocked is common here. Hua Hin is a pretty safe place."

Tay turned his head and gave Max a long look, but he didn't say anything.

EIGHTEEN

After Max drove off to the fishing village to look for witnesses to the shooter's disappearance from Monkey Mountain, Tay and Renny went inside Harry Black's house and shut the door behind them.

The air was heavy and still. Was the air-conditioning running? Tay listened. Yes, he could hear the slight whooshing noise air made when it was pushed through ducts and out of vents, but the temperature and humidity suggested the system was set on a warmer temperature than he would have expected in a tropical country. He wondered why. Was Harry Black trying to save a little money or did he just prefer his house not being that cool? Or maybe Harry Black had nothing to do with it. Maybe someone else had been here and adjusted the temperature upward after they shot Harry Black. But why would they do that?

Searching someone's house, particularly someone who was dead, had always made Tay vaguely uneasy. He didn't know Harry Black, of course, and it shouldn't have embarrassed him to look through his things, but it did. Searching someone's house and going through their possessions, no matter how well justified, was always an invasion of privacy. Tay had never lost the feeling of discomfort it gave him. He was certain he never would.

The front door opened into a small entryway with a staircase on the opposite wall. There was a red and yellow oriental rug on the floor of some design Tay didn't recognize, but what immediately caught his eye was a huge framed poster on the left-hand wall. Mick Jagger's face leered at him from a kaleidoscope of psychedelic colors, his features distorted in a way that suggested either unbridled ecstasy or extreme pain. The poster touted a Rolling Stones concert in Auckland, New Zealand. Tay's eyes found the date at the bottom: March 1, 1966.

"Did your grandfather live in New Zealand in 1966?" he asked Renny.

"I don't know. He never mentioned New Zealand to me."

Was the poster simply decoration, or did it represent a memory for Black? Had he been at that concert in New Zealand on March 1, 1966? Tay did the math in his head. Renny said that her grandfather had been eighty-six, hadn't she? In 1966 then, he would have been … what? Somewhere in his late twenties, right? He certainly *could* have been there.

Did that mean that Harry Black was a New Zealander who lived in Auckland in 1966? Maybe, but he could just as easily have been a Norwegian who lived in Los Angeles in 1966, liked the look of the poster, and wanted something colorful to hang in his front entry.

Tay wanted this house to tell him who Harry Black was, of course, but he knew he wouldn't find the answer to that question conveniently written on the wall. What he had to do was what he had always done: observe with a nonjudgmental eye, absorb what he observed, and turn it all over in his mind until it eventually told him a story.

At least it used to work that way for him, but he was out of the game now. His instincts were going rusty from lack of use.

Maybe he had even lost them altogether. Maybe his day was done.

Tay shook his head at his own foolishness. Did he have to overthink everything? Yes, of course, he did. That was simply who he was.

"Let's do a quick walk-through first," Tay said. "After we get a general sense of the place, we'll go back and work our way through each room."

On the right side of a short hallway off the entry was a small but well-equipped kitchen, and just past that was the living room. The room's outstanding feature was the floor-to-ceiling glass wall that framed the beach and the Gulf of Thailand just beyond it. Tay had to admit it was a lovely view. The beach was empty and didn't look like it ever drew much of a crowd. The Gulf was gray-brown and flat, and it sloshed quietly onto the sand. Tay thought the calmness of it held a certain appeal. At least it did for him.

On the next floor up, there was a small guest bedroom close to the stairs that looked as if it had never been used. The rest of the floor was a single large room which Tay thought was very appealing. It was an old-fashioned study. The left side had the same floor-to-ceiling glass looking out on the beach that the living room had, but the opposite wall was covered with dark wooden bookcases, all of which were filled with books that looked as if they had been well read.

The entire top floor was made up of the master bedroom. Instead of the same treatment of floor-to-ceiling glass, the wall facing the beach had three sets of French doors that opened onto a balcony just wide enough to hold a small table with two chairs and a lounger. On the right was the master bath with a very large walk-in closet next to it, and on the opposite wall were more closets with shelves above them.

Tay couldn't see very much of any interest in the room. On the whole, everything was neat and clean. Harry Black was a man who hung up his clothes and put his shoes in the closet. There were minor examples of disarray here and there: a bed which was made, but not very well; an empty coffee mug on one bedside table; and a pile of loose change stacked on top of a few Thai banknotes on the other. But he wouldn't call it clutter. They were all things that humanized the room and reminded Tay that an actual person had lived there.

Other than just walking through the house and getting a sense of its layout, Tay had been doing one other thing he hadn't mentioned to Renny. He had been looking for security cameras, but he hadn't found any. That didn't surprise him. Black didn't appear to be all that security-minded since the house didn't even have an alarm system, but you could never be certain about cameras unless you looked carefully.

If there were any cameras, they were the kind that were so sophisticated they were the next thing to undetectable, but Tay doubted Black would go in for anything like that. Yes, cameras had become so common recently that they weren't even remarkable anymore, but he thought there was a generation thing involved in the choice, too. He didn't have any cameras around his house. He didn't see why they were necessary, and something about the idea of having cameras observing him, even if they were his cameras, just rubbed him the wrong way. He didn't know Harry Black, but he would bet Black felt the same way.

"OK," Tay said to Renny, "let's go back downstairs. We'll start at the front door and work our way carefully through each room. Tell me if you see anything that seems odd or out of place."

"I wouldn't know what's out of place. I've never been here before."

"You knew your grandfather. Perhaps not as well as you might have liked, but certainly better than I do. If anything strikes you as not fitting in with what you know about him, that's what I want you to point out."

Renny didn't look convinced, but she shrugged and followed Tay downstairs.

The furniture in the living room looked relatively new.

There were three loveseats covered with what appeared to be heavy cotton sailcloth, all very white, drawn up in a U-shape facing the big windows over the beach. Behind the three loveseats was a round glass dining table with four chairs, and opposite it were two leather armchairs set at right angles with a table and lamp between them. There were large abstract paintings on two walls, both extremely colorful, and Tay guessed they were decorator art rather than actual art. There were no photographs or other personal items anywhere that he could see.

On the whole, it was a soulless room. There was too much uniformity. All the rugs went together. All the paint was the same color. All the furniture looked like it had been selected from the same manufacturer at the same time. There were no books, no television set, no music system. It made Tay think of the way his mother had kept their living room when he was a child. It was a reception room for guests. Despite being called a living room, no one had done any actual living in it.

Had Harry Black used this room to receive guests? Tay doubted it. He hadn't learned much about Harry Black yet, but everything he had learned told him the same thing. He and Harry Black shared at least one personal characteristic. They were not men who invited many guests into their homes.

Tay walked across to the kitchen, stood in the doorway, and flipped on the lights. The kitchen wasn't very large, but it was equipped with all the usual things: coffeemaker, toaster, blender, electric can opener, and coffee grinder. The major appliances were all stainless steel and looked to be high-end. Tay somehow doubted Black had been a gourmet cook, and he imagined that most of the kitchen equipment, like the art in the living room, resulted from some decorator's choices rather than Black's needs as a cook.

He stepped over and opened the refrigerator. There were half a dozen large bottles of mineral water of some brand Tay didn't recognize, four cans of Coke Zero, a vacuum-sealed glass jar filled with ground coffee, a package of sliced ham, and a bottle of sweet pickles. The shelves in the door contained a dozen or so bottles of various condiments, most of which looked as if they might have been there for a long time. No, not a gourmet cook.

He bent down and pulled open the freezer at the bottom. An ice maker filled with ice cubes, two bottles of vodka, two pints of ice cream, and nothing else.

"What do you suppose he ate?" Renny asked from behind Tay.

Tay opened the cabinet beneath the sink where most people seemed to put their kitchen trash and found a dark green rubber trashcan. He pulled it out and looked inside. Some crumpled paper towels, a banana peel, a Coke Zero can, and a used coffee filter with the grounds still in it.

"No cartons or bags from food deliveries," Tay said. "Either he had just emptied the trash, or he didn't have food delivered. Maybe he went out most of the time."

"Or he didn't eat much," Renny said. "Oh God, I should have done something."

"Done something about what?"

"Just … helped him some way. He was an old man living by himself, and he was my grandfather. But I didn't do anything to help him or to make his life easier."

Recognizing a conversation that could go nowhere good when he heard one, Tay changed the subject.

"What did you find in the living room?"

"It's a room," Renny shrugged. "It could be anybody's room. There's nothing personal in it."

"I don't think he used this floor very much. Let's go upstairs and see if that part of the house feels different."

The small bedroom on the second floor had a single bed, a mahogany dresser with four drawers, all empty, a large framed mirror on the wall above it, and a wing-back chair upholstered in nubby gray-brown fabric with a brass floor lamp sitting next to it. The whole room gave off a sense of never having been used.

The study was another matter altogether. Tay settled himself in the expensive leather Aeron chair behind the desk and looked around. It was a room he could understand, but looking at it also renewed his sense of trespass against the dead. This was the room in which Harry Black had lived whatever his life had been. And, Tay was certain, it was in this room that he sat and thought about whatever it .was that had eventually killed him.

In front of the windows overlooking the beach, there was a round coffee table of gray granite. Arranged around the coffee table were three chrome and leather Le Corbusier lounge chairs. Square and brutal, they were beautiful and harsh at the same time. Tay didn't know how much Le Corbusier chairs cost in Thailand, but in Singapore each of those chairs would have cost as much as a small car. In Thailand, they would probably have cost as much as a considerably larger car.

On the wall opposite the table and the Le Corbusier chairs was a large flat screen television with a small chrome and glass table beneath it. The table held a new-looking DVD player and an old-fashioned VHS tape machine, and they were both connected to the flat screen above them.

Tay looked around the room, but he didn't see any DVDs or old VHS tapes anywhere. Why would you have players cabled to your flat screen if you didn't have something to play on them? That might be interesting. Or it might not be.

Floor-to-ceiling bookcases, each of them filled with books, covered the other wall. Unlike the art in the living room, Tay was sure the books weren't there because some decorator had put them there. These were well-used books. This was Harry Black's library. It had been a part of him.

Renny was busying herself going through the bookshelves, occasionally pulling down a volume and thumbing through it. Tay left her to it and turned his attention to the desk.

Working his way methodically through the drawers, he found nothing but the usual collection of junk that most people accumulated until he got to the top right-hand drawer. In it, he discovered an Apple charger that could have been used with either an iPhone or an iPad or maybe both, and an Apple laptop charger. But there was no iPhone, no iPad, and no laptop on the desk. Maybe they were upstairs in the bedroom, Tay thought.

The bottom right-hand drawer was a deep file drawer of the sort in which people kept personal papers like bank statements, insurance policies, and tax returns. It was the only drawer in the desk that had a lock, so Tay fished out the keys Renny had given him. He would bet that was what the little silver key on the ring was for.

But then Tay looked more closely and realized he didn't need the key. The lock on the drawer had been neatly but effectively broken by inserting something large and flat into it, probably a screwdriver blade, and twisting it.

He pulled the drawer open and examined the contents. Dark green hanging folders with neat tabs filled it: *Credit Cards, Health Insurance, Immigration Matters, Home Maintenance, Checkbook, Bank Statements,* and a few others.

The signs, however, were unmistakable. Someone had already methodically rifled through all the folders and already taken anything of interest. Tay pushed open the folder labeled

Checkbook with his forefinger. Empty. The folder labeled *Bank Statements* was just as empty.

Now Tay knew he wouldn't find Black's phone or his tablet or his laptop upstairs in the bedroom or anywhere else in his house.

Someone had gotten here before them.

NINETEEN

W hen Tay and Renny left Harry Black's house, Tay closed the front door and then hesitated.

Should he leave it unlocked as he had found it, or should he lock up? The more he thought about it, the less it seemed to matter. There wasn't much in Harry Black's house worth stealing, at least not that he could see, and even if there was something, Harry Black wouldn't care much anymore, would he?

As it usually did, however, habit won out over reason and Tay fished the keys Renny had given him out of his pocket. He selected the one that looked as if it might fit the front door and tried it. It worked fine. He locked the door behind them.

Max was waiting in front of the Mercedes with his arms folded.

"I didn't come up with very much, sir," he said before Tay even had a chance to ask.

"No one remembered the car?"

"The village is busy at that time in the morning. It's when the boats are getting ready to go out for the day. Everyone has their hands full with what they're doing and no one is paying very much attention to anything else."

"It was worth a try. It's a shame that no one remembers the car."

"That's not entirely true. One woman selling noodles to the fishermen says she remembers the car, but what she says she remembers doesn't make any sense. I think she was confused."

"What did she say?"

"She said she saw a small white car coming down Monkey Mountain that morning and that a woman was driving it. A *farang* woman. She noticed because she thought it was odd to see a *farang* woman driving there by herself so early in the morning."

Farang was the all-purpose Thai word for foreigner, Tay knew, and most people claimed it was a generic term with no racial connotations. But Tay also knew that wasn't true. Thais used the word *farang* solely for Caucasians. Other Asians, regardless of where they were from, were never called *farang*.

"Did she see anyone else in the car?" Tay asked.

"I asked her that several times in different ways, but she seemed very positive. She said there was no one else in the car except the *farang* woman who was driving it."

A Caucasian woman driving down Monkey Mountain in a white car at about the same time the monk saw a white car leaving the temple? Perhaps the white car had nothing to do with the shooter, Tay thought. It could have been just a coincidence the monk saw it leaving when he did. Maybe it was some tourist catching the sunrise from the temple who left about the same time the shot was fired.

But then what happened to the shooter? Surely, he didn't walk back down Monkey Mountain. Could he have been concealed in the car the Caucasian woman was driving? Tay supposed that was possible, but it seemed a bit of a stretch. Why send a driver for the shooter? Why involve a second person in the killing, particularly a *farang* woman, when the shooter could easily have driven himself away after he took his shot?

Tay was getting nowhere, and he was running out of ideas.

No one saw the shooter on Monkey Mountain. No one saw the shooter leaving Monkey Mountain. And he had found nothing in Harry Black's house that offered even the slightest hint of why someone might want to kill him.

He had discovered only one thing, but that was something important. Somebody was trying to clean this up.

They had searched Black's house, and they had taken away things like his laptop, his phone, and his checkbook. Things that might have told Tay what Harry Black was doing that made him worth killing.

Now all Tay had to do was figure out who had done the cleaning and what they had cleaned up, and he would have his killer.

Piece of cake, huh?

"Can I ask if you found anything of interest in the house, sir?"

Tay looked at Renny. "Did you see anything you haven't mentioned?"

Renny was staring out across the beach and just shook her head.

"Then the answer, Max, is no. We found nothing. Except that somebody was here before us."

"You mean somebody searched his house before you got here?"

"They made a neat job of it. I might not even have realized it if they hadn't broken the lock on a desk drawer to get into it. His checkbook and banking records were gone. They also took all his electronics. Cell phone and laptop. Possibly an iPad, too."

"Maybe he didn't have any of those things."

"I found the chargers in his desk. He had them, and they're not here now, so somebody took them."

"Did they get into the safe, too?"

"What safe?"

Max pointed at the ring of keys that Tay was still holding in his hand after locking the front door.

"The one that key fits."

Tay opened his hand and looked at the ring of keys.

"This big key is for a safe?"

Max nodded.

"How do you know that?"

"Because we have an old safe at home that uses a key just like that. You still have to work the combination, but after you set the combination you use the key to open it." Max shrugged. "Like I said, it's an old safe. I don't think they make them that way anymore."

"If it's there, we missed it," Tay said. "And if we missed it, maybe whoever searched the house before us missed it, too."

Tay looked at Max.

"How big would it be?"

"Ours is…"

He held out one hand, palm down, about four feet above the driveway.

"…about so high. But I imagine there are all sorts of sizes and shapes. It wouldn't be small, though."

"It must be hidden somewhere," Renny said.

"If it's there at all," Tay reminded her. "Just because there's a safe key on your grandfather's ring doesn't necessarily mean he has a safe."

"Then why would he have a key?"

Tay had no answer for that, so he settled for replying with a small shrug.

"Let's go through the house again," he said. "If your grandfather has hidden something that big, we certainly ought to be able to find it."

. . .

Max stood in the middle of the living room, a puzzled expression on his face.

"What am I looking for, sir?"

"If there's a safe here, it's hidden. Inside a piece of furniture, behind a wall, in the floor maybe. You said it would be big. It couldn't be that hard to find."

Renny worked her way around the living room in one direction tapping on the floor with her foot, knocking on walls with her hands, and carefully examining every piece of furniture. Tay worked his way around the room in the opposite direction doing the same thing. Max mostly stood in the middle of the room and looked baffled. Tay didn't expect to find anything here, but he still wanted to be methodical about conducting the search.

If Harry Black was going to hide a safe somewhere, it seemed unlikely to Tay that he would place it on the ground floor in a room that appeared seldom used. It was human nature to keep the things most valuable to us as close as possible. That's why burglars invariably headed straight for the master bedroom. If there were money and jewelry to be found in a house, that was where it would be, in the place the owner of the home thought was the most secure.

In this case, however, Tay would bet the safe was somewhere on the second floor in Harry Black's study. If there was a safe here at all, he doubted it contained money and jewelry. It was more likely to contain personal papers Harry Black had accumulated throughout his long and somewhat mysterious life. Maybe even a diary of some sort or perhaps a collection of photographs of ... well, what? Tay really had no idea.

Whatever it turned out to be, Tay had already convinced himself it would help him understand why somebody had organized the murder of Harry Black in such a spectacular fashion, and knowing why Harry Black was murdered was the place Tay knew he had to start. The *why* would point him to the *who*. It always had. It always would.

Tay moved into the small kitchen. He examined each of the appliances and opened all the kitchen cabinets. Nothing. He tapped his way around the floor, but he found no sign that it was anything other than what it appeared to be: a solid floor.

When he came back out into the living room, Renny stopped her stomping on the floor and knocking on walls and looked at him.

"There's no safe here," she said.

"I don't think so either," Tay said. "Let's try the study."

R enny and Max took the bookshelves, and Tay took the rest of the room. They removed all the books from the shelves and stacked them on the floor, then they carefully examined each empty shelf, tapping on the back and listening for hollow sounds. They even wiggled each shelf to see if it opened a portal into a hidden room like it would have in an Agatha Christie novel. Nothing.

Tay removed all the drawers from the desk, took everything out of the closet, and then went into the attached bathroom and searched methodically through it. He even lifted the lid on the toilet tank and looked inside. He felt foolish doing it, but he did it anyway. Nothing.

Tay was disappointed. He had almost convinced himself that they had caught a break, but now he was wondering if there was a safe here at all. Max might well have been right that the key on the ring was a safe key, but there could be another explanation for why Harry Black had it. It didn't necessarily mean that there was a safe hidden somewhere in this house.

They made quick work of the small guest bedroom and bath, and they moved on to the master bedroom on the third floor.

"You two take the room," Tay said to Max and Renny. "I'll take the bathroom and the walk-in closet."

He went into the closet first. It was very big, and Tay

wondered why an elderly man living in a beach resort would have so much clothing. Perhaps it was just an accumulation going back decades and Black had been reluctant to get rid of it for some reason.

Long chrome clothes poles ran down both sides of the closet. Pants over hangers to the left, and shirts on hangers to the right, all of them organized according to color. Harry Black had been a man with a very organized mind.

Tay shuffled through the pants first and then the shirts, but he found no sign of anything hidden behind them. Across the back of the closet were two chrome clothes poles, one slightly above head height and the other at waist level. Those poles were devoted mostly to suits, the jacket and pants sharing the same hanger, as well as a few blazers and other jackets on hangers of their own. There must have been thirty or forty suits and another ten jackets there. Did people ever wear suits in a beach resort like Hua Hin? Tay doubted it.

He shuffled through the suits and saw that most were of good quality, although they were all made of heavier fabrics that were inappropriate for a tropical country. Most of the suits looked old and out of style to him, too, but he was old and out of style himself, so he wasn't about to get judgmental.

It seemed apparent that these suits had been part of Harry Black's past, whatever that past had been, not his present. Tay pulled open several of the jackets and saw the same London tailor's label in each one. Tay didn't know what suits like this cost at a custom tailor in London, but he was sure it was a lot. And there were a lot of suits. He guessed he was probably looking at $100,000 worth of clothes right there. Maybe the tailor would have some kind of records that would be helpful. He should remember to look into that.

He gave the suits another push, saw nothing else, and moved on to the bathroom.

· · ·

157

When Tay flipped on the light, the whiteness of the tiles was so dazzling he had to squint until his eyes adjusted. Everything about the bathroom was pristine. It could have been the display unit in a new condominium. It felt almost wrong to upset the perfection of it, but Tay shrugged off the feeling and got to work. As with everywhere else in the house, he drew a blank.

He walked over to the sink and stood in front of the mirror. The usual array of items was lined up neatly beneath it: hand-washing liquid, a can of spray deodorant, shaving foam, toothpaste. Black's electric toothbrush was sitting in a charging stand, and Tay looked at the small red light on the bottom.

A few days ago, Harry Black had been standing in front of this very mirror brushing his teeth. Now he was on a slab in a mortuary. *Blink blink blink*, went the little red light, exactly as it had when Harry Black was alive. Here yesterday, gone today. The suddenness of his death hung in the room like a cloud.

Tay glanced in the mirror, then stopped and stared. His own reflection startled him. His skin looked sallow, his face drooped, and he had developed deep bags beneath both eyes. Tay was at an age when many people claimed to see themselves morphing into their fathers. He had never understood exactly what that meant since he had only vague and distant memories of his father. Is this what his father looked like? The slightly pinched face, the perpetual sense of fatigue, the dark intensity of his eyes.

It wasn't the look of someone people would approach for directions or to ask to recommend a place to eat. It wasn't that he appeared gruff or unfriendly. Not really. He was simply someone no one would notice. He might have a tired face, but it was also an eminently forgettable one, one that blended into the world until it disappeared altogether. It was the perfect face for a detective, or maybe for a spy.

Tay was on his knees tapping at the walls of the cabinet

beneath the bathroom sink when he felt a *ping* in the back of his mind.

He had seen something in the closet, but what was it?

He stopped tapping and sat on the bathroom floor. There was nothing behind any of the clothes. No place in the closet where a safe could possibly be. He was sure of it. But there was … something. What had he seen? Where had that *ping* come from?

He got up and walked back to the closet. He stood in the doorway and let his eyes roam the closet, but nothing caught his attention. There was a flashlight on one shelf, a big black one. It was a six-cell Maglite, one of those that used to be carried by a lot of cops until someone noticed how many of those cops were using them as clubs and started making cops carry smaller flashlights.

Tay picked up the Maglite, punched it on, and played the beam over the clothes. He panned over the shirts and the trousers, seeing nothing, but when the beam crossed the suits hanging from the top rail at the back, a glint from something just above them caught his eye. He moved closer, pushed the suits down to one end of the rail, and worked the beam method- ically over the wall behind them. Almost immediately, he found what had registered at some subconscious level the first time he examined the closet.

There were Phillips-head screws in the back wall of the closet.

At a glance, they looked as if they were just a normal part of the wall, but they weren't. The walls of Harry Black's house were built with Maxthe sort of wallboard typical of residential construction all over the world. Some form of gyp board was nailed to the vertical studs that framed the walls and then floated out and painted. All except this one wall in the back of the closet. This wall was white-painted plywood.

"I found it!" Tay called out.

A moment later, Renny and Max were standing behind him, one looking over each of his shoulders.

"What am I supposed to be seeing?" Renny asked.

"The screw heads."

They stared at the silver screw heads reflecting the bright Maglite beam.

"Yes ... but what about them?"

"You don't use Phillips-head screws to hold wallboard. You use nails. You use Phillips-head screws to hold something that you might need to remove from time to time."

"Damn," Max murmured. "It's a false wall."

TWENTY

Max went down to the car and got the toolkit. It was exactly the set of high-end tools you would expect to find in a Mercedes so it included several Phillips-head screwdrivers of different sizes. One of them was just what they needed to remove the screws in the back wall of the closet.

While Max was downstairs, Tay and Renny had shifted all the clothes hanging on the back rails into empty spaces on the sides of the closet and lifted the two rails out of their brackets. That gave them clear access to the back wall of the closet and made the pattern of screws securing a panel in the wall pretty obvious.

Max returned and immediately set to work removing the screws. There were only eight of them, so it didn't take long. When he was done, Tay and Max lifted the panel out of the wall. Renny pushed aside the pants hanging along one side of the closet and they propped the panel against the wall.

Then the three of them stood in silence for a moment and just stared at the gunmetal-gray safe the panel had concealed.

It was about five feet tall and three feet wide, the size of a small refrigerator. The entire front was a single large door with a black combination dial in the center that had numbers marked around it in white. Next to the dial was a large keyhole with a silver cover. On the left side was a V-shaped handle that opened the door once it was unlocked.

"Now all we have to do is figure out what the combination is," Tay said.

"Maybe not."

Tay and Renee looked at Max.

"Seriously?" Tay asked. "Are you about to tell us that safe-cracking is another of your hidden talents?"

Max pointed at the keyhole.

"Try the key without touching the dial," he said. "People who have these old safes sometimes get lazy. They set the combination once, then they leave it set and just use the key to relock the safe. At least that's what we do with the one we have at home."

Tay handed the flashlight to Renny and took Harry Black's keys out of his pocket. Taking care not to disturb the dial, he moved aside the cover and pushed the big key from Black's ring into the keyhole behind it. It slipped in without resistance.

When Tay rotated the key, the satisfying sound of a solid *CLUNK* filled the closet. He pushed up on the V-shaped handle, felt the bolts retract, and gave it a tug.

The three of them watched as the safe door swung open on well-oiled hinges.

The interior of the safe was also gunmetal gray, and five horizontal metal shelves divided it into six roughly equal-sized compartments. All the compartments except the top two were empty, and those two were nearly empty. Tay had been hoping to find something that would help him understand who Harry Black was, but there was nearly nothing here. He couldn't help but feel disappointed.

What he saw attached to the back of the safe's open door,

however, surprised and puzzled him enough to take his mind off his disappointment.

It was a gun rack.

The right-hand side of the rack held two long guns mounted vertically, both semiautomatic rifles with telescopic sights and wooden stocks. The left-hand side of the rack had six leather holsters for storing handguns. Four of the holsters were empty, but the grips of pistols were visible in the two at the top.

Both rifles looked old, but well maintained. Tay didn't know much about guns, but after several decades as a cop, he readily recognized the smell of gun oil, and he smelled it strongly now. Whatever Harry Black was doing with these two rifles, he had taken good care of them.

"Was your grandfather a gun collector?" Tay asked Renny.

"If he was, he never mentioned it to me."

"Do you know if he was a hunter, or perhaps a target shooter?"

Renny slowly shook her head, but she said nothing.

"I wish I knew what I was seeing here," Tay said.

"I might be able to help with that, sir."

Tay looked at Max. "You know something about guns?"

"A bit."

Max pointed at one rifle.

"May I, sir?"

Tay gestured at him to go ahead, and Max reached out and removed the closest rifle from its mount. Keeping the muzzle pointed at the ceiling, he opened the bolt and pushed his fingers into the receiver to confirm that there was no bullet in the chamber.

"This model is fed by an eight-round magazine which is inserted here ...

He pushed his fingers into a rectangular opening on the top of the rifle.

"...so it's not loaded."

"Do you know what kind of rifle it is?"

163

"Yes, sir. It's a Winchester. This is called an M1 Garand. It was a standard military weapon with the American army from World War II until around the mid-1960s. This one could be seventy or eighty years old, but it's in superb condition."

"Could he have used it for hunting?"

"Maybe. The American military used a slightly modified version of the M1 Garand as a long-range sniper rifle for years."

At the sound of the word *sniper*, Renny flinched.

Then Max realized what he had just said. "Oh my God, sir, you don't think there might be some connection…"

"I don't think anything yet," Tay interrupted. "For now, let's just stick to understanding what we are seeing and then later we'll try to decide what it might mean."

Max cleared his throat. "Whatever the reason he had this rifle, sir, I don't think it was for hunting."

"How could you know that?"

"Hunting isn't a big sport here in Thailand. And for a foreigner? I've never heard of a foreigner hunting here. No foreigner could ever get permission to own guns like these."

"Are you saying you think he didn't have permits for these guns?"

"I can find out for sure if you want me to, but I don't think there's any way he could have. If a foreigner is well connected and is willing to put a little money around, he might get a permit to own a handgun legally, but …"

Max gestured at the rack in the safe.

"… two high-powered rifles and two handguns? I don't think there's any way a foreigner could ever own four firearms like this legally here."

"Check the other guns," Tay said. "Tell me if you recognize any of them."

Tay and Renny stood back while Max examined the other rifle and both of the handguns. Tay couldn't help but notice that Max handled them all in a way that suggested he knew exactly what he was doing. Firearms might be closely regulated in Thailand, but Tay gathered being the son of the Minister of Justice probably meant that you had rights and privileges denied to others.

"And you don't know any connection between your grandfather and firearms?" Tay asked Renny while they were waiting for Max to finish.

"No, none."

Renny seemed to think about that, and Tay waited quietly to see if something else might be forthcoming, but it wasn't. After a few moments, she just shrugged and looked at the floor.

W hen Max had finished examining all four of the weapons, he returned the handguns to the rack in the safe and turned around.

"They're all unloaded, but they're all very well cared for and smell like they've been cleaned and oiled recently."

Tay's nose had told him the same thing from the moment they opened the safe, so he just nodded.

"The second rifle is newer than the first," Max continued. "It's an M14, the rifle that replaced the M1 Garand for most of the American military by the 1970s. It's been modified for use as a sniper rifle so technically it's called an M21. This one is chambered in 7.62x51mm NATO and uses a twenty-round box magazine rather than the eight-round magazines the M1 uses."

Max shot a glance at Renny because he had used the word *sniper* again, but she was still looking at the floor and he didn't catch her eye.

"What about the handguns?" Tay asked.

"They're both older military weapons, too, sir. One of them is a Springfield 1911, and the other is a Colt Commander 1911. They're both .45s. They've both been standard military sidearm in the United States in the past, but I can't tell you the specific dates."

"Would you guess they're the same vintage as the rifles? Around the 1960s? Maybe the 1970s?"

"Yes, sir. I think that's about the size of it."

"So, you're saying these are all antiques? Maybe this guy was a gun collector."

Max hesitated. "Maybe."

"But you don't think so."

"Not really, sir. Some people who shoot just prefer older guns. They like their reliability. They say there's something about the feel of them. These aren't a collector's guns. They're a shooter's guns."

"Then you think Harry Black was a shooter."

Max hesitated again. "I'm not a detective, sir. All I can tell you is what I see when I look at these guns."

"And what is it you see?"

Max didn't hesitate.

"I see guns that belong to a shooter, sir, not to a collector."

Tay looked at Renny. "What do you think?"

"I have no idea. I just feel completely overwhelmed."

Tay knew exactly how she felt, but he didn't think he should tell her that.

"Let me have the flashlight, please," Tay said.

He flicked it on and played it over the guns inside the door. Tay wasn't a gun guy, but he had to admit there was something graceful and beguiling about them. The rifles in particular. The polished wooden stocks gleamed warmly in the flashlight's beam and the telescopic sights had the look of something nearly extraterrestrial. They were beauty bred to savagery.

Back when he had still been a cop, he was the last man on the Singapore police force to hang onto his old revolver. To the considerable amusement of many, he had refused to exchange it for one of the newer semi-autos that became the standard police sidearms in Singapore. He took a lot of grief over that. It's a great gun, the other detectives had chuckled, if you get into a gunfight in an elevator. But he didn't really care. Most of the time he forgot to carry it, anyway. What was he going to do with it? Shoot the next cab driver who was rude to him?

Tay shifted the flashlight beam to the safe's main section and, starting at the bottom, moved it methodically through each of the compartments. He found nothing at all until he got to the second section from the top.

Tay tucked the flashlight under his arm, collected four small green and black boxes from the shelf, and handed them to Max.

"Is this the ammunition for these guns?"

Max examined the boxes, opening the lid of one to confirm that what was inside matched the description printed on the boxes.

"Yes, sir. These are.45 ACP rounds. They would fit either of the handguns."

Tay pulled something else off the same shelf. Eight brass-cased and copper-tipped rounds were seated in a black metal holder in two rows of four, and Tay found three of the holders. To his eye, the bullets looked huge, like little rocket ships. He had no trouble imagining a sniper using them to bring down a target a mile away.

He handed them all to Max.

"It's rifle ammunition, sir. These are the eight-round magazines that fit the M1."

That left four somewhat larger back metal boxes on the shelf and Tay collected them and handed them to Max, too.

"These are box magazines for the M21. They're each loaded with twenty rounds of 7.62x51mm NATO."

"So that's ... what? Eighty or a hundred rounds for the handguns, eighty rounds for one rifle, and twenty-four rounds for the other?"

"Yes, sir. About that."

Tay sighed. "That's a lot of firepower."

"It is indeed, sir."

"I wonder what he thought he needed it for."

No one answered him, but then Tay hadn't expected anyone to.

T ay picked up the flashlight again and played it slowly over the contents of the top shelf.

On the left side was a stack of spiral-bound notebooks with heavy red covers. They looked like the notebooks college students used back in his day to take notes in lectures. Did college students still take notes in lectures, he wondered, or did they just watch everything on YouTube and save the videos on their laptops? If they did still take notes, he doubted anyone had taken them by hand in a spiral notebook in a generation or more. He was pretty sure doing that these days rather than using some kind of electronic device would be considered terminally uncool.

He and Harry Black, however, had grown up in times in which people listened to what they were being told, organized their thoughts about it, and then wrote those thoughts down with a pen. The stack of red-covered notebooks beckoned to him. Whatever Harry Black had recorded in them might be exactly what he needed to understand who Black was and why someone wanted him dead.

Tay put the flashlight on the floor and reached into the safe with both hands to lift out the stack of notebooks. He blew the dust off of them and then handed them to Renny.

"Hold on to these for a minute, would you?"

He reached back onto the shelf and lifted out the only other thing he saw there: an old-fashioned microcassette recorder. He had used one just like it to record interviews back when he first became a detective.

This one was scratched and battered and looked as if it had seen some hard use. He pushed the eject button and looked inside. There was no cassette in it. Why would Black have kept an old microcassette recorder in his safe when it had no cassette in it? And if he had used it to record something, what had he done with the cassettes?

When Tay lifted the little recorder out of the safe, something caught his eye. He picked up the flashlight from the floor, turned it back on, and played the beam over the empty shelf. Where he had picked up the stack of notebooks, he could see a clear print in the dust marking where they had been. And just to the right of that, he saw a second and identical print in the dust on the shelf. Another stack of notebooks had been there once, but at some point, they had been removed.

Had Black taken them out and put them somewhere else? Or had whoever beat them to searching Black's house somehow gotten into the safe and taken the other stack of notebooks?

Tay doubted that. If they had found the safe and opened it, why would they have so carefully closed it back up, replaced the false panel in the closet, and moved all Black's clothes back into place in front of the panel? And why would they have taken one stack of notebooks out of the safe and left the other?

No, Tay didn't believe the earlier searcher had found the safe. He would wager that whatever had been removed from the safe had been removed by Harry Black. But what did he do with the other stack of notebooks, and where were the cassettes that went with the recorder?

M aybe something in the notebooks he had found would point him in the right direction.

Renny had taken the stack out of the closet to where the light was better, so Tay and Max followed her out into the bedroom. She was sitting on the side of the bed, one notebook open in her hands and the others scattered across the bed.

She looked up when they came out of the closet. "You're not going to like this."

She turned the notebook she was looking at around so Tay could see it. But all Tay could see were blank pages.

"I don't understand," he said.

"Neither do I. All the pages are blank. Why would my grandfather keep blank notebooks in a safe?"

Tay took the notebook from Renny. He flipped a few pages and then thumbed through the rest. Just as she had said, they were all blank.

To him, the pages looked slightly yellow and they felt brittle, as if the notebooks were decades old. Maybe they were. But old blank notebooks kept in a safe? That made no sense at all.

"I'm going to keep one," she said. "You don't mind, do you?"

Tay shook his head.

"Everything here belonged to your grandfather," he said. "What you take isn't up to me. But why a blank notebook?"

"It just seems more like him than anything else here." She thought about it. "I can't really explain it."

Tay shrugged and handed her back the blank notebook.

TWENTY-ONE

"Sniper rifles?" Renny asked. "We find two military sniper rifles in a hidden safe in my grandfather's house after somebody murdered him with a sniper rifle?"

They had put the blank notebooks and the cassette recorder back and locked the safe again, and now Tay was standing with Renny and Max on the front porch of Harry Black's house. They were waiting for Tay to tell them what to do now, but Tay had no idea what to do now.

"I know next to nothing about this man," Renny went on, "I thought he was a nice old man trying to be my grandfather. But he wasn't, was he, Inspector? He wasn't a nice old man at all, was he?"

Several times since Jones had gotten him involved in all this, Tay had wished he still smoked. He'd had no difficulty giving up smoking, but he had been out of the homicide business then. Now that he was back running a murder investigation again, he was missing smoking more than he wanted to admit. There were moments in every investigation when the only sensible thing to do was to light a cigarette, smoke it slowly and deliberatively, and look pensive. One such moment was this one right now, but he didn't have a cigarette and he couldn't do any of that.

"I don't know," Tay eventually said, mostly just to fill the silence.

"Whatever we find out about him," Renny went on, hardly seeming to notice Tay's feeble response, "it won't bring him back and it won't make up for me not getting to know him when he was alive, will it? Maybe I should just go back to Hong Kong and forget any of this ever happened."

"Are you trying to convince me or yourself?"

"Probably both."

Then suddenly Renny grinned.

"So, are you convinced?"

"No," Tay said, shaking his head. "I'm not even convinced you're convinced."

Renny looked at Tay as if she was seeing him for the first time.

"You really are a very empathetic man, aren't you, Inspector?"

"I don't think of myself that way."

"No, you probably don't. But you are."

Renny let her gaze wander across the beach to the ocean. After a moment, she shifted her eyes back to Tay.

"Thank you, Inspector, for pushing me past my moment of weakness. Now let's get back to work and find the bastard who killed my grandfather. Where do we go from here?"

Tay took a breath and let it out. He was used to not knowing things. That was the lot of an investigator. But this time he didn't even know what it was he didn't know. He felt unmoored.

Do what you always do, he chided himself.

Move forward. Put one foot in front of the other, even when you have no earthly idea where you're going. Hold fast to the conviction that eventually it will all make sense. Even when you don't know if it will. Especially then.

"We need to look for the people your grandfather associated

with here in Hua Hin," Tay said. "He lived here for a long time and somebody knows something about him. What we have to do is find them and get them to tell us what it is."

Tay pointed to the house next door where the woman had come out when they first got to Harry Black's house.

"I get the feeling that woman keeps a close eye on things around here. I'll bet she could give us a list of all your grandfather's visitors going back for years and tell us a good deal about each one of them. Let's find out."

F iona Campbell had changed clothes. Instead of a T-shirt and shorts, now she was wearing expensive-looking white slacks and a blue and white striped shirt. Tay would also swear she had applied a bit of makeup, but he might have been wrong about that.

Duncan Campbell, her husband, had either returned from his golf game or, more likely, Mrs. Campbell had telephoned him and told him to get his ass home right away because now he perched uneasily on the couch next to Mrs. Campbell.

Mr. Campbell had red hair, a redder face, and a golfer's tan on his arms and legs. He was wearing green shorts, a white Polo shirt, and scuffed brown loafers without socks. He was taller than his wife, but not much. Tay felt like he was interviewing two of the Munchkins from *The Wizard of Oz*.

"How well did you know Mr. Black?"

Tay asked the question without indicating whether he was directing it to Mr. Campbell or Mrs. Campbell. He made a bet with himself who would respond.

"Oh, not very well at all," Mrs. Campbell answered.

Tay collected his bet and moved along.

"How long have you known him?"

"He was living here when we moved in," she said. "That was ..."

She glanced at Mr. Campbell.

"It was six years ago now, wasn't it, darling?"

Mr. Campbell nodded, but he didn't say anything.

"Have either of you ever been in his house?"

"No, he didn't socialize with anyone around here. Oh, he was perfectly nice, and he would always smile and speak to me if I saw him outside, but he stayed to himself."

Tay shifted his eyes to Mr. Campbell.

"How about you, sir? Did you have any conversations with Mr. Black?"

Mr. Campbell seemed to think about how to answer that question rather longer than Tay thought it merited. Eventually, he gave a small shake of his head.

"He didn't play golf," Mr. Campbell said.

Tay enjoyed a good non sequitur as much as the next man, but this one left him speechless.

He cleared his throat and tried again.

"Then you're both saying that you lived next door to Mr. Black for six years and never had a conversation with him?"

"He was an elderly man who kept to himself, Inspector. He was polite and pleasant, but he wasn't friends with anyone around here."

"Did you see him very often?"

"He went for a walk on the beach at least once every day. Sometimes twice. Always early in the morning, and occasionally in the afternoon. And back when he parked his car in front of his house, sometimes I would see him going to and from it, too."

"There's no car there now."

"He started keeping it in the garage over at the Holiday Inn across the highway a few years ago. I really don't know why. Maybe he stopped driving much because of his age and thought it would be safer over there."

"Do you remember what kind of car it was?"

"It was a Volvo. A green one. With four doors."

"Did Mr. Black have many visitors?"

"He never had any."

Mrs. Campbell glanced at her husband. A look passed between them, and Tay caught it.

"There's something you're not telling me about his visitors, isn't there, Mrs. Campbell?"

She shot another look at her husband and shifted her weight on the couch.

"Duncan says it's none of my business, but there *was* someone recently. This girl came here a few times. She seemed young to me. Oh, not young like a teenager or something. She was probably in her 30s. But that's still pretty young for an 80-year-old man, don't you think?"

"Did she visit him a lot?"

"She was here a few times, but only during the last few weeks. I'm sure I would have noticed if she had come before that."

Tay was sure of that, too.

"Was she a local woman?" he asked. "A Thai?"

"Oh no, she was English."

"English? You mean she was Caucasian?"

Mrs. Campbell nodded.

"But you don't know that she was actually English, not specifically?"

"Of course, I do. I spoke to her, didn't I? She had an English accent. Quite a posh one. Oh, she was English, all right. No doubt about it."

"What did you talk to her about?"

"It was just the once, and it wasn't much of a conversation, not really. I just saw her knocking at Mr. Black's door and I told her he had gone for a walk on the beach. She thanked me and went down to the beach looking for him."

"Was this recently?"

"Oh, didn't I say? This was the day poor Mr. Black was killed. The very day."

Tay leaned forward. "This woman was here on the day Mr. Black died?"

Mrs. Campbell nodded again, vigorously.

"He was still on the beach when she got to his house. I told her he had walked to the right, and she went down the steps and went off looking for him."

Suddenly Mrs. Campbell gasped, and her hand flew up to her mouth.

"Oh God, you don't think this woman is the one who killed him, do you?"

"No ma'am," Tay said, "I don't. But she may have found his body, so I'd very much like to talk to her."

"The poor girl," Mrs. Campbell sighed. "Poor Mr. Black. It's all just so awful."

"Did this woman tell you her name when you talked?"

"No, and I certainly didn't ask. That would have been nosey, and I'm not a nosey person."

Tay bit his tongue and just nodded.

"Did it appear that this woman was staying with Mr. Black at his house?" he asked.

"No, I'm sure she wasn't. Each time she was here, she went to his house in the morning and left late in the afternoon. And she always carried that little briefcase. Like she was there for a business meeting. But it's my belief that was just what they were trying to make it look like."

She glanced at Mr. Campbell.

Mr. Campbell studied a spot on the wall somewhere over Tay's head and said nothing at all.

When they left the Campbells, Tay led them back to the car so the three of them could talk in private. He had something now. He just had to figure out what it was he had and what to do with it.

As soon as the car doors closed, he looked at Max and Renny.

"We need to find this woman."

"Why do you think she was coming to see my grandfather?" Renny asked.

"I've got no idea."

"But you think it's got something to do with why my grandfather was killed?"

"I've got no idea about that either. But look, he was a man who had almost no visitors. Then this woman starts coming to see him regularly, and a few weeks later he's murdered. Maybe that's just a coincidence, but maybe it isn't."

"If there was something romantic going on," Renny said, "I think nosey old Mrs. Campbell would have seen it. Maybe it really was a business meeting, despite her suspicions. He was an old man. Perhaps he was just getting his affairs in order. She could have been a lawyer. Or an accountant."

"Your grandfather had lived in Thailand for decades. If he was going to get his affairs in order, why would he have been meeting with someone who was English? Wouldn't he need a Thai lawyer or accountant to do that?"

No one said anything.

"No," Tay said, "it was something else."

"How can we possibly find her?" Renny asked. "All we know is we're looking for a woman in her 30s who might be English. We don't even have a name."

"We know by the way she came and went that she wasn't staying with your grandfather, so chances are she was staying in a hotel."

"Unless she lived here," Max said. "There are a lot of Brits living in Hua Hin."

"That's possible," Tay nodded, "but I'd bet against it. Mr. Black had lived here for decades, and suddenly this woman turns up several times just a few weeks before he's killed?"

"Maybe he just met her somewhere, and they became friends."

"That doesn't feel right," Tay said. "The pattern of visits and how recently they began makes it more likely she was coming to see him for some specific reason. We have to start somewhere, so let's start with that assumption. If it turns out I'm wrong, we can look at locals later."

Max and Renny didn't appear convinced, but they nodded anyway.

"Don't hotels here have to file a report with Thai Immigration about foreigners who check in or check out?" Tay asked Max.

"Yes, sir, they do."

"There can't be that many hotels in Hua Hin."

"There are a lot of them, sir. Hua Hin is one of the most popular beach resorts in Thailand."

"Okay, but we can narrow this down. If we stay with the assumption that this woman was someone who came here specifically to see Harry Black, she wouldn't have come to Hua Hin and sat around for a few days without contacting him. She would have gotten in touch as soon as she arrived. Since she went to see him the morning he was killed, almost certainly she arrived either early that day or the night before."

"And she probably took off the moment she discovered he had been killed so she wouldn't get pulled into the investigation," Max said. "I'll bet she saw his body when she went down to the beach. Then she went straight back to her hotel, checked out, and left."

"That gives you two possible check-in dates, a check-out date, a nationality, and a sex. Surely that will be enough to identify her if we can get access to the hotel reports."

"No problem, sir. Where do you want me to take you while I'm working on it?"

"How long will you be?"

"It shouldn't take more than an hour to see if immigration can find anyone who fits. If they can, they'll tell me her name and what hotel she stayed in. Then I'll need to go to that hotel and get a copy of her passport details they took when she checked in."

"Do you think immigration will do that for you?"

Max chuckled. "I'm sure they'll be happy to help."

From what Tay had seen so far, he had no doubt of that.

"Maybe Renny and I will have lunch somewhere while you're doing all that. Any suggestions?"

"What do you feel like eating?"

Tay looked at Renny and raised his eyebrows in a silent question.

"Anything," she said, "that doesn't come with rice."

"Got you covered," Max laughed.

TWENTY-TWO

W hen Max pulled to the curb in the middle of what passed for the Hua Hin business district, Tay looked out the car window and said, "Seriously?"

The modern two-story building looked pleasant enough. At the front there was an outdoor dining area separated from the street by thick stands of flowering plants in whitewashed planter boxes. It was the green awning that shaded the front area that had given Tay pause. It displayed the name of the establishment in large white letters.

Father Ted's Irish Pub and Steakhouse

"Renny said she wanted food that wasn't served with rice," Max said, "and Father Ted's fills the bill. It's pretty solid if you like Irish pub food."

Tay wasn't a big fan of Irish pub food, and the idea of Irish pub food served in a small town in Thailand made the concept seem even less promising than it normally would.

"You said it'll take you an hour to track down our visitor?"

"Probably a little longer, sir. Give me two hours just to be on the safe side."

"I can survive for two hours," Tay said, opening the car door. "I can survive anything for two hours."

To Tay's surprise, the food was quite good. Who would have thought that Irish pub food cooked up in the middle of a dusty, provincial little town in Thailand would be edible, let alone tasty?

He had a bowl of Irish lamb stew that came with mashed potatoes and two slices of absolutely delicious home-baked soda bread, and Renny ordered a steak and Guinness pie with a pint of Kilkenny Ale. Tay stuck to water. He wasn't much of a drinker to begin with and he couldn't even remember the last time he had anything alcoholic at lunch.

While they ate, the conversation was sparse and insubstantial, which suited Tay just fine. Conversing with women had never been easy for him. He wasn't ever sure what he should say, and what he should avoid saying, and the choices he made too often turned out to be exactly the wrong ones. Maybe he just didn't have enough experience talking to women to avoid making a hash out of it whenever he tried. But how did you get experience other than by doing it? And how did you do it if you felt like a fool every time you did?

When Renny finished her steak and Guinness pie, she pushed her plate away, folded her arms, and gave Tay a long look.

Uh-oh, Tay thought. *Serious conversation coming.*

"I'm sorry I got you into this," Renny said.

Tay busied himself sopping up the rest of his lamb stew with the soda bread and said nothing.

"I should have just stayed in Hong Kong. I don't know what I thought I was going to accomplish by coming here. And I certainly shouldn't have told Eddie about it."

She was having second thoughts again. Tay figured the right

thing to do was simply to let her talk it out, so he stayed silent and kept eating.

"Nothing I can do now is going to make up for the way I treated my grandfather when he was alive. I may even make things worse by doing this. I may dig up all kinds of things he wanted to keep hidden. My curiosity about who my grandfather was isn't a good reason to ransack his life."

Unhappy at getting no response from Tay, Renny drummed her fingers on the table and tried to stare him down. When that didn't work, she started talking again.

"Finding those guns makes me think maybe my grandfather was a killer himself. Maybe somebody caught up with him after all this time and got revenge for someone he killed a long time ago. What good would it do anyone for me to find that out now?"

Tay wiped up the last of the gravy from the lamb stew with the last bite of his soda bread and popped it into his mouth. He chewed as slowly as he could, hoping Renny might keep talking so he wouldn't have to say anything.

She didn't. She fell silent, sipped at the remains of her ale, and stared off across the room.

Tay knew he was going to have to say something eventually, but he had no idea what it ought to be. He had no dog in this fight. He was only here because Jones had asked him to look into the murder of Renny's grandfather, but now that he had started doing that, he didn't much want to walk away.

He had always believed deep in what passed for his soul that the role of the detective was to restore balance to the world. To impose order on a chaotic state. The detective was the vehicle for uncovering and revealing uncomfortable truths. It was almost a holy task, he thought. Uncovering truth. It was witnessing. It was standing up to the disdain of an indifferent universe.

On top of that, he kept hearing his mother's warning about there being something important here. He could feel in his bones that she was right. Or she would have been right, if she were real and had actually spoken to him.

Despite all of that, did he have the right to pry into Renny's family and possibly even blacken her memories of her grandfather if she didn't want him to? He wasn't a cop any longer. He had no duty here to investigate a crime. If Renny wanted him to walk away, then that was probably what he ought to do.

And yet …

Max burst through the door and stood looking around the room. When he spotted them, he darted over to their booth and pushed in next to Renny. He slapped a piece of paper onto the table and shoved it toward Tay.

"I found her, sir."

T ay picked up the sheet of paper and examined it. It was a copy of the identification page from a British passport.

The passport had been issued to Tilly Charlotte Talbot, a female citizen of the United Kingdom who was born on September 14, 1984. Judging from the passport photograph, Ms. Talbot appeared to be an attractive and agreeable person. At least as attractive and agreeable as anyone could look in a passport photograph.

"She checked into the Hyatt early on the morning Mr. Black was killed," Max said. "Then she checked out just a few hours later claiming some kind of family emergency and she asked the hotel to find her a taxi to take her to the airport in Bangkok."

"Perhaps we should show this photo to—"

"I've already done that, sir. I took the passport copy back and showed it to Mr. Black's neighbor. She said she was sure this woman was the one who came to Mr. Black's house on several occasions, including the morning he was shot. I hope that was all right, sir. I thought that was what you would want me to do."

It was very much all right. In fact, Tay thought Max

deserved a pat on the back for taking the initiative, but he didn't want to overdo it, so he settled for a small nod.

"The hotel showed me her registration information, and I copied down the address she used to register as well as the credit card she gave them."

Max took a small piece of notepaper from his shirt pocket and placed it on the table next to the passport copy.

The woman had given the hotel a London address, and she used a Mastercard issued by NatWest Bank.

"That's good work, Max. Now all we have to do is find out what this woman's connection to Renny's grandfather is."

Tay gave Renny a long look.

"That is," he said, "if Renny still wants us to do that."

Renny held out her hand. "Let me see that," she said.

Tay handed her the passport copy and Max's notes about the address and credit card she had used.

While she was looking at them, Tay turned back to Max.

"I don't have any contacts with law enforcement in the UK any longer. Do you suppose you could prevail on your father to put us in touch with someone to help us find out who she is?"

"You don't have to do that," Renny said, and both Tay and Max looked at her. "I can tell you who she is."

Tay's eyebrows lifted. "You *know* her?"

"No, but I know who she is. Or at least I recognize her name. I'm sure it's the same person I've heard of. How many people can there be in this world named Tilly Talbot?"

"Don't keep us in suspense," Tay said.

"Tilly Talbot is a writer. She's pretty famous. Neither of you ever heard of her?"

Tay and Max both shook their heads and Renny went on.

"She's something of a big deal, even in Hong Kong. She writes true crime books. She had a huge bestseller about an English couple who murdered a lot of people including their own children and buried them under their house. I think she also wrote a book about the American mafia, but I didn't read that one."

"How do you think she and your grandfather knew each other?" Tay asked.

"I've got no idea."

Tay thought that over.

"Then," he said, "I guess the only thing to do is ask her."

Renny looked again at the notes Max had taken from the Hyatt's registration information.

"We've got both an email address and a telephone number here. Which one do you want to try first?"

"Neither. If some stranger contacts this woman out of the blue and asks her why she fled Hua Hin when your grandfather was murdered, I imagine that would frighten her badly, and right now she's the only lead we've got. We need somebody to check that address and see if she's back in London now. If she is, it might be worth going there and catching her off guard."

"I'm sure Eddie would have a way to do that," Renny said. "He seems to know people everywhere."

Tay doubted Renny had any idea why her friend and supporter knew so many people in so many places. Big-time Chinese triad bosses were very well connected internationally, of course, but Tay wasn't going to be the one to tell her that was the reason.

"Okay," he said instead, "let's go back to the guest house so I can get my phone and call him."

Max pulled his iPhone out of his shirt pocket and offered it to Tay. "You're welcome to use my phone, sir."

"Thank you, but he asked me to use the local phone you gave me if I needed to reach him, and I think I should honor that."

Tay could see that both Max and Renny appeared a little puzzled by that, but he wasn't going to explain that to them either.

.   .   .

Tay and Renny waited on the sidewalk in front of Father Ted's for Max to bring the car around. It was a lovely afternoon. A slight breeze off the ocean smelled of salt and fish, and the cloudless, sapphire-blue sky seemed to go on forever.

Tay had to admit that Hua Hin was growing on him. He wasn't a beach resort kind of guy, but Hua Hin wasn't so much a beach resort as it was an agreeable provincial village that just happened to be near the ocean. He could see the attraction of the place for retirees looking to live out their final years, he really could, but he doubted he would ever be one of those people.

He had lived in the same house for his entire life, and he was sure he would continue to live there forever. Whatever love-hate relationship he might have with Singapore, it was still his home. He had been born there, and he was sure he would die there unless he stuck his nose into something he shouldn't and got killed somewhere else before his allotted time on earth was scheduled to expire.

And, ironically, that was exactly what Tay was thinking when that came very close to happening.

Max had stopped the car at the curb and was walking around to open the rear passenger door for Tay when a black and red motorcycle roared up and stopped in the road level with their rear bumper.

The streets of Hua Hin were filled with motorcycles and scooters of all sorts, so the appearance of one more did nothing to cause alarm. This particular bike attracted Tay's attention only because of the odd place it stopped.

Tay registered the rider as someone on the small side, less than average height and slightly built. He was dressed all in black, even to the black riding gloves covering his hands and a black motorcycle helmet with a dark visor covering his face.

Tay thought nothing of any of it until he saw the man's right hand go inside his jacket.

Surely not, Tay told himself.

Although it looked very much like the rider was reaching for a weapon, that couldn't be true, could it? Not right here in the middle of Hua Hin at lunchtime on a bright and sunny day. Then Tay registered the butt of the black semi-automatic handgun emerging from beneath the driver's jacket, and he realized it not only could be true, it was true.

Both of Tay's hands went to Renny's shoulder, and he gave her a shove behind the Mercedes.

She stumbled and fell to one knee just as the rider fired. The shot soared harmlessly over her head and dinged off a metal sign in front of Father Ted's promising 15% off tacos on Tuesday nights.

Before the rider could shift the muzzle to acquire Tay as an alternate target, Tay dived behind the car as well, and the second shot pinged off the Mercedes' rear roof support.

The rider didn't get off a third shot.

Before he could, Max produced a small handgun from beneath his shirt, leaned over the trunk of the car, and returned fire. Max's shot missed the rider, but it took out the bike's front headlight.

The rider didn't give Max a chance to improve his aim. He revved the bike's throttle, popped the clutch, and roared away.

Tay got back on his feet just in time to see the bike reach the main highway a block down, turn left, and disappear behind a bus.

Renny got to her feet, too, and the three of them stood in shocked silence, staring at the place where the bike had disappeared. Tay was the first to regain the power of speech.

"I didn't know you were carrying a gun," he said to Max.

"Could we discuss that later, sir? We should get out of here before we attract any more attention than we already have."

Renny was too much in shock to say anything, and Tay allowed Max to nudge both of them gently into the backseat of the Mercedes and slam the door.

When they reached the highway, Max turned in the same direction the bike had. He drove fast, but not so fast as to make them conspicuous.

Max pulled his phone out of his shirt pocket, punched a two-number speed-dial code into it, and spoke several sentences in rapid-fire Thai.

"I'm taking you and Renny back to the guest house, sir," he said after he returned the phone to his pocket. "I've asked a couple of our friends to provide security until we figure out what that was all about."

Tay nodded, but he didn't say anything.

Renny didn't even nod. She just sat staring at the back of Max's head.

TWENTY-THREE

"**Y**ou'll be safe here," Max said.

Tay was pretty sure that was true. Not only did he now know that Max was armed, but the two men Max described as *friends* had already taken up positions in front of the guest house.

One was at the top of the stairs on the beach side of the house covering any approach from that direction, and the other was facing up the driveway and covering that direction.

Both were middle-aged Thais dressed in short-sleeved white shirts hanging loose over jeans. They were altogether nondescript and forgettable men, but Tay's guess was that was rather the whole idea. He recognized the hardness in the men's eyes and the handguns printing beneath their shirts, and he saw the way they took in their surroundings. Neither man was physically imposing, but they both carried themselves with the sort of confidence that Tay knew from his experience as a policeman could morph into violence in a blink.

No one seemed to feel much like talking. Apple fussed around them in the living room of the guest house, serving coffee and plates of cookies. It all felt very civilized. No one had ever before served Tay coffee and cookies after someone tried to shoot him, assuming that was what had happened this time, which he doubted.

Tay finished his coffee and poured himself another cup.

"It never occurred to me you were carrying a gun," he said to Max.

"There hadn't been an occasion in which it seemed appropriate to bring it up, sir."

"Until now."

"Yes, until now."

Tay sipped at his coffee. It was strong and a little bitter. Just what the moment called for.

"Do you always carry a gun, Max?"

"No, sir. Not always."

Tay didn't see any point in belaboring the subject, so he just nodded and let it go.

Renny hadn't touched the coffee Apple poured for her. She was standing in front of the big windows looking out over the beach and the Gulf of Thailand, her arms wrapped tightly around herself.

"No one's ever tried to shoot me before," she said without taking her eyes off the Gulf.

"They didn't try to shoot you this time either," Tay said.

Renny turned and looked at him, her face as flat as a pie pan.

"What are you talking about?"

"Whoever sent that shooter didn't want us dead. They just wanted us to go away."

Renny took that in for a moment and then walked over and sat on the sofa next to Tay.

She picked up her coffee cup. Tay was sure the coffee was cold by now, but she drank some of it anyway and didn't seem to care.

"Think about it," Tay said. "Someone sent a professional shooter to kill your grandfather, a shooter who was good enough to do it with a single shot from nearly a kilometer away. If whoever did that wanted us dead, he wouldn't send some yokel on a motorcycle who was so incompetent he just sprayed a few bullets at us from twenty feet away without coming close to hitting anybody. That guy wasn't there to kill us. His job was to scare us off."

"Then he did his job very well."

Renny put the coffee cup down and the sound of it clicking into the saucer seemed loud in the quiet room.

"I'm in over my head here, Inspector. I should have never gotten involved in any of this, much less gotten you involved, too."

"Then what would you like me to do?"

"I'd suggest you do what I'm going to do. Just go home and forget any of this ever happened. I'm going to go back to Hong Kong and run my gallery. You should go back to Singapore and … well, do whatever it is you do there."

Renny got to her feet and looked at her watch.

"I'm sure I can get a flight back to Hong Kong tonight if I hurry. I won't ask you to drive me all the way to the airport in Bangkok, Max, but can you arrange a taxi to take me?"

"That's not necessary," Tay said. "You're forgetting I have an airplane waiting on me here in Hua Hin ready to go wherever I tell it to go."

"But you're going to use it to take you back to Singapore, aren't you?"

"If you're certain you want me to close up shop and go home, I need to sit down and talk to Jones. Remember, he's the one who asked me to do this, not you. I can't walk away without at least talking to him about it first."

"Would you like me to contact the pilots for you, sir?" Max asked.

Tay looked at Renny and raised his eyebrows in a silent question.

"I am certainly not going to turn down a ride home," she said. "I'll go back to the hotel and pack right now."

Tay shifted his attention back to Max. "Then tell the pilots we'd like to leave for Hong Kong as soon as possible. Say, an hour and a half from now?"

"I'm on it, sir."

"And can you arrange—"

"I'll take Renny to the hotel myself, sir. We'll come back for you as soon as she's checked out. It's only about fifteen minutes from here to the airport, so an hour and a half all in is easily doable."

"Then I'll pack and be ready when you get back."

After Max and Renny left, Tay poured himself another cup of coffee and thought about things. In particular, he thought about the woman who came to see Harry Black and then fled in a panic when she discovered he had been murdered.

Maybe curiosity was making him stupid, but he couldn't quite abandon the idea of having a conversation with her. That woman knew something. Either she knew why Harry Black had been killed or she thought she did, and she must believe that put her in danger, too. If she didn't, why would she have run like she did?

Tay had the copy of Tilly Talbot's passport that Max had talked the hotel into giving him, as well as her home address in London. Finding her wouldn't be that hard.

When Tilly Talbot had looked like their best lead to finding out something about Harry Black's life, Tay was going to get Jones to use his contacts to find out whether she had gone back to London.

He had to call Jones anyway to let him know they were coming to Hong Kong. Maybe he would pass along Tilly Talbot's details and ask him to see if he could locate her. Why not? What would it hurt? If she turned out to be at home in London, he could decide what to do with that information later.

Tay put down his coffee cup and headed upstairs to find the telephone he was supposed to use to talk to Jones.

J ones answered on the second ring.

"Were you just sitting there waiting for me to call?" Tay asked.

"Ah, Inspector, you are my first thought every morning and my last thought every night."

"I'm not sure I know how to take that."

"Take it as an expression of my admiration for you. Now, not to be rude, but as I have one or two other things on my plate, what do you have for me?"

Tay told Jones about the shots fired at them outside Father Ted's. He kept the story lean and the details to a minimum, and he emphasized his conclusion that the shots weren't intended to hit them, only to frighten them off.

"If that's what they wanted to do, it worked, because Renny now insists she wants to forget about everything and come home. I've asked Max to tell the pilots that we're going to Hong Kong, so we should be there sometime this evening."

"Do I hear in your voice that you're not entirely onboard with this?"

Tay hesitated, but then he just went ahead and said what he was thinking.

"When someone tries that hard to keep me from finding out something, I can't help but wonder why. I think we might have stumbled into something here that's bigger than any of us imagine, and I want to push just a little further before I walk away."

"Oh my, you do spin an intriguing tale, Inspector."

"Harry Black had been meeting with a woman Renny says is a famous author of true crime books. She came to see him on the day he died and then fled in a panic when she discovered he had been murdered. I think he was working with her on something, almost certainly a book. He may have told her some things about crimes he had committed in the past and was about to tell her even more things, things somebody wanted to remain hidden. I think now she's frightened that whatever he told her might cause his killer to come after her, too."

"You think someone killed Renny's grandfather because of the things he revealed to this writer?"

"Yes."

"And now you want to find out what he told her because you believe it will point to the people who killed him."

"Yes."

Jones was silent for a moment, thinking that over.

"Do you have any idea how to find this writer, Inspector?"

"Max talked the hotel where she was staying into giving us a copy of her passport, as well as her registration details. She used a London address when she checked in and several things point to it being her real home address. That's why I need your help."

"What would you like me to do?"

"I'd like to send you both the passport copy and the address. Perhaps you could use your contacts in London to check and see if she's there now. I have a London telephone number for her, but just calling her out of the blue after she ran the way she did doesn't seem to me to be a good idea. I'd only end up frightening her even more, and then perhaps I'd never find her again."

"Yes, I can see that."

"If she's in London, it might be worth me going there and catching her off guard. If I can do that, I'm sure I can convince her to tell us what she knows."

"Let me do what I can."

"Just get someone to confirm that she's there. I don't want him to speak to her or frighten her. And don't kidnap her, Jones. Just tell me if she's at the address I have, and I'll take it from there."

Jones didn't bother to respond to that, but then Tay hadn't expected him to.

"Is there a fax machine here in the guest house?" Tay asked.

"A fax machine? Seriously? What for?"

"I can fax you the copy of the woman's passport and her home address now if there's a fax machine here. Otherwise, I'll have to bring them with me to Hong Kong."

"My dear inspector, how old are you?"

"Why would you ask me that?"

"Because I don't know anyone who has used a fax machine in probably twenty years."

That stopped Tay. People didn't use fax machines anymore? How could that be? Didn't they still need to send documents to each other sometimes?

"Just message the stuff to me," Jones said.

"What are you talking about?"

"Photograph the documents with the phone you're talking on right now and send them to me as a message."

Tay hesitated. "Uh … I don't know how to do that."

Jones laughed, but not unkindly.

"I could explain it to you, Inspector, but we'll save a lot of time here if you simply ask Max to do it for you. Tell him to use the phone you're on now, however, not his own."

Jones insisted on sending a driver to meet them in Hong Kong.

He also offered Tay the use of an apartment he said he kept available for guests, but the idea of staying in a triad safe house didn't particularly appeal to Tay. He might not be a cop anymore, but he still had standards.

"I'd rather go to a hotel if you don't mind," he said. "Would it be too much trouble for you to have someone in your office make me a reservation somewhere?"

Jones chuckled, knowing perfectly well why Tay preferred a hotel to his guest apartment.

"You stayed at the Cordis the last time you were here, didn't you?"

"Yes, it was fine. Why don't you just get me a room there again?"

"Mongkok might be rather inconvenient for you this time, if I may say so, Inspector. The traffic is awful if you try to use a car to get around from there, and I'd wager you're not a big fan of riding the MTR."

"Where would you suggest I stay?"

"I'll put you at the Peninsula. It will be much easier for you to go wherever you need to from there."

"That's a pretty popular place, isn't it? If you can't get me in because it's the last minute—"

"There won't be any problem," Jones interrupted. "Didn't I ever mention to you we own a rather large piece of it?"

Then Jones laughed and cut the connection.

TWENTY-FOUR

As soon as Max got back, Tay asked him to message Tilly Talbot's details to Jones. Max offered to show Tay how to do it so he could send things himself in the future, but he told Max not to bother.

The world was full of things Tay didn't know and didn't want to know. Using a phone to send people copies of documents wasn't even close to the most interesting thing he didn't know and couldn't be bothered to learn.

The pilots had the plane ready to go when they got to the airport. Tay and Renny thanked Max for all his help, particularly for driving off the motorcycle shooter, and then went straight onboard. Ten minutes later they were wheels up for Hong Kong.

It was a three-hour flight with a one-hour time change, and they touched down at Chek Lap Kok a little before nine in the evening, local time. The pilots taxied directly to the Hong Kong Business Aviation Center, and they were directed to a stand where two black Range Rovers with darkened windows waited. The pilots shut down the engines, and Tay listened as they whined into silence.

Jones was leaning on one of the Land Rovers waiting for

them when they left the plane, and Renny walked straight to him and gave him a hug.

Tay evaluated the hug as subtlety as possible, but he detected nothing other than a hug between friends. It was none of his business one way or another, of course, but he couldn't avoid feeling just a little pleased to see that.

"You're all right?" Jones asked her.

"I guess so. It was an awful experience, and it's going to take me a while to get over it."

"Well, you weren't hurt. That's all that matters."

"I might have been if Max hadn't scared the guy off. I've never been shot at before. Have you?"

Tay caught Jones' eye over Renny's shoulder and lifted his eyebrows. He could hardly wait to see what Jones would say to that, but then Renny started talking again before Jones had to come up with an answer and he never found out.

"I'm sorry I got you and Inspector Tay mixed up in this, Eddie. I should never have gotten either of you involved."

"So, what happens now?"

"I'm going back to running my gallery, and I'm going to forget any of this ever happened. My grandfather's secrets died with him, whatever they were, and I'm fine with that."

"We'll have lunch and talk whenever you're ready."

"I'd like that."

Jones pointed to the second Land Rover, where a black-suited driver was holding open the rear passenger door.

"That one's for you. I thought you might want to get straight home, so I organized separate cars for you and the Inspector."

Renny turned to Tay. "Thank you for trying to help, Inspector. Please believe me, I had no idea what I was getting you into."

Then Tay got his hug, too.

He couldn't help but compare it to Jones' hug. Better? Worse? About the same? He wasn't quite certain.

"Why don't you stay in Hong Kong for a few days?" Renny

said. "I could show you some cool places I bet you've never been."

Okay, when you added that to the hug, it was better. Definitely better.

"I'd like that," Tay said. "I'll be at the Peninsula. Maybe I'll stay a couple of days."

Renny smiled. "I'll call you tomorrow."

And with a wave over her shoulder, she bounded off to the other Land Rover, got in the back, and was driven away.

"I said you'd enjoy meeting Renny, didn't I?" Jones chuckled.

Tay said nothing. He just got into the back seat of the Land Rover and closed the door.

Tay had always thought the drive into the city from the airport might be the best thing about Hong Kong.

The wide, modern expressway tracked the northern shore of Lantau Island, winding gently between the island's rolling hills on the right and the steep cliffs of the South China Sea to the left. Widely spaced streetlights on tall towers cast the road in a dim, almost otherworldly glow, but the darkness still owned the island.

The hillsides were in deep shadow, the sea rolled black into the distance, and the sky was bursting with stars. Off over there, somewhere out of sight in the island's interior, was Hong Kong Disneyland, a place Tay had never had even the smallest inclination to visit.

Neither Tay nor Jones spoke as the Land Rover's high beams bored twin shafts of yellow into the night and they drew ever closer to a teeming city crammed with seven or eight million souls, lost and otherwise. They were climbing the approach to the Tsing Ma suspension bridge when the maelstrom of Hong Kong suddenly appeared out of the darkness. Shafts of colored light from hundreds of buildings stretched toward them over the black water of the harbor.

Jones broke the silence.

"We found her."

Tay had to think for a minute before he realized what Jones was talking about.

"You mean Tilly Talbot? The writer? You found her already?"

Jones nodded.

"Then the London address she used at the hotel in Hua Hin was really hers?"

"Yes," Jones nodded again, "it was, but that's not where we found her."

"I don't understand."

"We checked that address, but the house was empty. I was told it looked like it might have been closed up for a while."

Tay took a deep breath. There Jones went with this *we* business again. Exactly who Jones was referring to when he said *we* was high up on Tay's list of things he didn't need to know, at least not for sure.

He waited in silence. He knew there was more to come, and after a few minutes, Jones told him what it was.

"We asked a friend of ours to check the departure records in Bangkok for the period around the time this woman probably left the airport there," Jones continued. "When we found out what fight she had taken and where she had gone, we canvassed hotels at her destination until we found her. Then we sent in some people to confirm that she was there, and we've been keeping her under observation since then."

The Land Rover had cleared the bridge and passed the massive container port at Kwai Chung. Just beyond Stonecutter's Island, they left the expressway and turned into the streets of Kowloon, where the Peninsula Hotel had squatted facing the harbor for nearly a century.

"Then you know where she is right now."

"We do."

Jones made it all sound so matter-of-fact. It had been

perhaps four hours since Tay sent him a copy of Tilly Talbot's passport and told him what he knew about when she had fled Hua Hin. That was all he had given Jones: a copy of her passport and an approximate time and date she had left Hua Hin in a taxi after telling the hotel she was going to the airport in Bangkok.

She was one woman running free through the entire world and she'd had nearly a week to take herself anywhere in it she wanted to go. But in just four hours, Jones had found her.

It's a small world, the cliché went, and so it was. Sometimes, Tay thought it was too damned small for him.

"You're going to make me ask, aren't you?"

Jones gave Tay a small smile. Tay could see he was enjoying this.

"Okay, Jones, I'm asking. Where is she?"

Jones' smile got bigger. He leaned forward and pointed past Tay out the car window into the neon-splashed streets of Kowloon.

"She's about two hundred yards in that direction."

Tay's mouth opened.

"You're shitting me," he said.

"I shit you not, my friend. Your girl flew directly here from Bangkok on Thai Airways and has been staying at the Langham Hotel in room 1121 ever since she arrived."

After Tay checked into the Peninsula, he and Jones settled into a pair of leather club chairs in its fabled lobby and ordered drinks.

Tay had an Irish whiskey. Jones had a Diet Coke. Maybe Jones didn't feel like having a drink, Tay thought. Or maybe he was an alcoholic and went to AA meetings. Or maybe he was just very religious. Okay, probably not that.

The lobby of the Pen, as people in Hong Kong almost always called the hotel, was one of the legendary places of Asia.

It still looked much as it did when it was built in the 1920s: an immense vaulted space the size of two basketball courts in which the antique elegance of another time has been preserved for generations to come, generations who probably don't give a stuff about the antique elegance of another time.

Gleaming marble floors, white pillars topped with gilded freezes, golden figures supporting a frescoed ceiling of gold and white, and a canopy of crystal chandeliers. They could have filmed a 1940s Fred Astaire musical there without so much as moving a chair.

"What do you want to do?" Jones asked when the drinks had been served and the white-jacketed waiter had discreetly withdrawn.

"I want to drink a whiskey, and then I may drink a second whiskey. If I'm not entitled to a second drink after today, when would I be?"

"Winston Churchill summed it up nicely," Jones said. "There is nothing so exhilarating, he said, as to be shot at without effect."

Tay couldn't help but wonder about Jones' personal experience of being shot at without effect, but asking seemed graceless, so he just looked at him and waited to see what came next.

"What I was actually inquiring about when I asked what you want to do," Jones went on after a moment, "was what you want to do concerning this woman, Tilly Talbot."

"I don't know."

"Are you going to talk to her about what she knows about Renny's grandfather?"

Tay spun the golden whiskey around in his glass and watched the way it broke the light into a swirl of sparkling crystals.

"There's something here, Jones. Something important. I can feel it."

Jones said nothing.

"I think it's something that somebody needs to find out,"

Tay continued. "At least there's a part of me that needs to find out."

"Even if Renny says she doesn't want you to?"

Tay sipped his whiskey and thought about that.

"I guess we'll cross that bridge when we get to it," he finally said.

"Goodness, Inspector, that's a terribly American expression."

"It is, isn't it?" Tay chuckled. "I suppose my genetic heritage occasionally feels the need to assert itself."

"Nevertheless, it seems to me that you are standing at the threshold of your metaphorical bridge right at this moment, and you will need to decide very soon whether to cross it. This woman is a few hundred yards from you right now, but she could disappear tomorrow, and you might never find her again."

Tay looked off across the lobby and said nothing.

"You heard what Renny said," Jones pressed. "She wants you to forget all about her grandfather."

"Yes," Tay nodded. "I heard her. And I understand why she said that."

"But what are you going to *do*, Inspector?"

Tay shifted his eyes back to Jones, but he said nothing.

"That's what I thought," Jones said.

A jazz combo started playing somewhere. Tay looked around and found it on a balcony at the opposite end of the lobby.

He sipped his whiskey and watched while they finished a very credible version of 'The Way You Look Tonight,' then slid seamlessly into 'Moonlight in Vermont.'

After a bit, he waved down a waiter and ordered another Irish whiskey. He looked at Jones, who shook his head. Apparently one Diet Coke was his limit. Who could blame him?

When Tay's second drink was served, he took a sip. Now the

combo was playing 'I Could Write a Book,' which it occurred to him was the ideal theme music for mulling over the subject of talking to Tilly Talbot, the world-famous true crime author.

"Renny is calling me tomorrow morning," he said to Jones. "I'll talk to her then and see where we are."

"What will you tell her?"

"I'll tell her you located Tilly Talbot, and that she's here in Hong Kong. I'll say I want to talk to her before we let this go."

"Because there's something important here?"

"Because there's something important here."

Tay started to take another sip of whiskey, but then he lowered his glass.

"It almost feels like an omen, doesn't it? Tilly Talbot being here in Hong Kong."

"I didn't know you believed in omens, Inspector."

Tay hesitated. It might be fun to shock Jones by telling him about his mother's occasional nocturnal manifestations, he thought, but then he quickly came to his senses. He covered his hesitation with another sip of his whiskey.

What he wanted was a Marlboro, of course. Even if he had a pack, he very much doubted they would let him smoke in here, the bastards. Tay understood how out of sync with the world he had become. He accepted it, but sometimes he resented it.

"What I believe in, Jones, is a good night's sleep."

Tay knocked back the rest of his whiskey, stood, and held out his hand.

"Good night, and thank you for everything."

"You're most welcome, Inspector," Jones said, rising and shaking Tay's hand. "But you have nothing to thank me for. You're the one doing the favor here. I won't forget it."

Tay smiled, turned away, and started for the elevator, but Jones added one more thing.

"Sleep well. No unsettling dreams tonight, huh?"

Jones' words caused Tay to stumble slightly, but he covered it as well as he could.

Had he told Jones about his mother and simply forgotten about it?

No, of course, he hadn't told him. But then how could Jones possibly know …

He couldn't know. His comment must have been a coincidence. What else could it be?

Tay didn't trust himself to look at Jones. He didn't know what his face might show, and he didn't want it to show anything, so he raised a hand without turning around, wiggled his fingers back over his shoulder, and kept on walking to the elevator.

TWENTY-FIVE

T ay tapped his keycard against the reader, opened the door to his room, and smelled the smoke.

It had to be his imagination, didn't it? He must miss smoking so much now that he had started smelling tobacco in the air even when it wasn't there. He went in, flipped on the light, and closed the door behind him.

It wasn't his imagination.

"Hello, Sam."

"Hello, John."

John August was sprawled across a loveseat at the far end of Tay's room, right in front of the big windows with a view over Hong Kong Harbor.

He was a rugged-looking man, not particularly big, but flinty and chiseled. He appeared to be somewhere in his mid-forties, although Tay had no idea how old August actually was. His face was deeply tanned, and he wore round eyeglasses with steel frames. His dark brown hair was quite long, and he had it brushed straight back against his head in a way that gave him an old-fashioned appearance that Tay had to admit suited him very well. August looked like an old-time astronaut who had retired and opened a used bookstore.

On the coffee table in front of August was an ashtray with three or four butts in it. Tay couldn't imagine where it had come from. His was a non-smoking room. There were no ashtrays in it. Still, knowing the things John August could do, coming up with an ashtray in a non-smoking hotel room was very small potatoes indeed.

"Can we just skip over the whole how-did-you-get-in-here thing?" August smiled. "I'm a little pushed for time tonight."

Tay said nothing.

August pulled himself up until he was sitting relatively straight. He crossed his legs and pointed to the armchair next to the loveseat.

"Come in, Sam. Sit down."

"It's my goddamned room, John. I don't need an invitation from you if I want to sit down."

August chuckled and produced a pack of Marlboros from his shirt pocket.

"I'd offer you one, but I heard you quit."

"I thought you'd quit, too."

"Comes and goes, Sam. Comes and goes."

Tay walked over and sat in the armchair. He remained silent while August shook out a cigarette and lit it. He took a long pull and turned his head to exhale away from Tay. Tay thought about telling him that wasn't necessary, but he didn't.

Tay had known John August for years. When he was a cop in Singapore, August had helped him out several times in ways he thought best to keep to himself. Why had John August's help been useful to Tay? Because August was ... well, Tay wasn't entirely certain *who* August was.

He was an American, that much he was sure of, and he was somehow connected to the American intelligence establishment, although not in a way anyone would have considered conventional.

After Tay was forced into early retirement and was no longer a homicide detective, August started seeking Tay's help occasionally. Only a few months back, August had enlisted Tay to help him find a young woman who had gone missing in Hong Kong. The woman's father was a prominent American political figure, but no one knew that. Not even the girl herself.

That was why the President of the United States had told August to find the girl and get her back. And to do it very quietly. The very-quietly part was why August had asked Tay for his help.

Tay knew that August was part of an organization that very few people knew existed. They called themselves the Band. Tay was happy to repay the favors he owed August. It gave him something to do and made him feel productive again. But there were things about the Band that made him uneasy.

National leaders occasionally need to do things outside the usual channels of government that they don't want anyone to find out about. But giving them that capability was a sensitive matter, particularly in a relatively open society like the United States. That was why the existence of the Band was known to so few.

Its origins stretched back to the days of Ronald Reagan. When Bill Clinton became president, however, the gray eminences behind the Band started to worry about it being exposed. They decided it would be better to move the Band entirely outside of government rather than risk falling under the scrutiny of the people who might be unsympathetic, even ready to score political points by going public with the things the Band had done.

These men set up an international business consultancy under the wonderfully bland name of Red River Consultants and moved all the functions of the Band into it. The Band continued to do the same stuff for the president and a very few other extremely senior members of government that it had always done, but now it did it without risking attracting attention from some curious Congressmen or people from the Office of Management and Budget who might wonder what some of those bland looking budget entries were really for.

The Band became a tiny group of people run by a man called, perhaps inevitably, the Conductor, with all its actual activities hidden behind Red River Consultants. And what were those actual activities?

The Band was the direct-action tool of the President of the United States. It was available to him to do some things very quietly, things that few people would ever know about such as locating and retrieving the daughter of a major American political figure from a Chinese city before China realized they had her.

John August wasn't normally in the business of conducting investigations, which is why he had asked for Tay's help in finding the woman. His role in the Band wasn't to be a detective or to collect information. He was the Band's problem solver. And Tay understood exactly what that meant.

John August solved problems the old-fashioned way.

He killed them.

"You don't look all that surprised to see me, Sam."

"Nothing you do surprises me anymore, John. How did you know I was in Hong Kong?"

"Ah, well." August took a final puff and stubbed out his cigarette in the rapidly filling ashtray. "The Hong Kong Business Aviation Center is a hot spot around here. We keep a close eye on who comes and goes through it. Imagine my surprise when I saw your name on today's list. There you were, just as big as life, and you were arriving on a plane belonging to some Hong Kong folks who are pretty well known to us."

"I've never tried to hide that connection, John. You knew perfectly well that I asked them for help when you dumped your most recent problem in my lap."

"And now you're doing them a favor to pay that back."

Tay hesitated. He didn't want to tell August any more than necessary about Renny and her grandfather, and he didn't see why telling him *anything* was necessary.

"It's a personal matter, John. It has nothing to do with you."

"Personal?"

"A guy did me a big favor. Now he's asked me to do a favor for someone he knows. We're not talking fate of nations stuff here. It's not the sort of thing you deal in."

August waved a hand as if he were clearing away smoke.

"Never mind that, Sam. It doesn't really matter why you're here. What matters is that you *are* here. I've got a problem right now that I'm not very well suited to solving. When I saw your name on that list, I thought there's the very guy who can help me."

"So you set your people to tracking down my hotel and room number. Then, instead of making a telephone call, you somehow get access to my room and ambush me here in the middle of the night."

August shrugged. "It wasn't very difficult to find you."

"I'm sure it wasn't. At least not for you."

"And what I have to tell you isn't the kind of thing you talk about on the telephone."

"It never is with you, is it, John?"

"I guess that's just the kind of business I'm in, Sam. Now, can I tell you about my problem and ask you what you think, or do you want to dance around a little more first?"

August's spy games were sometimes annoying, but they were always intriguing. Now that Tay was just another retired old fart, he had to take his opportunities where he found them.

Mattering wasn't easy anymore. The world didn't have much use for old men. Sometimes that left him feeling depressed and sometimes it just made him even more determined not to be shut out. Nobody looked at him twice these days when he walked down the street. Nobody noticed he was even there when he stood in line to pay for his groceries or waited at the side of the road looking for a cab.

He was nobody special anymore, just another old man among multitudes of old men. He was anonymous. He was *more* than anonymous. He was downright invisible.

Tay leaned back and folded his arms.

"Okay, John, let's have it."

"We were asked to pick up and protect a North Korean woman who wanted to defect through Macau. She was hot because she was a member of the Little Leader's family. The National Security Advisor wanted us to handle it because of some concern he has that the CIA's North Korea desk may not be secure."

"There's a North Korean mole in the CIA?"

August pursed his lips and wiggled one hand, palm down. "That might be putting it a little strongly. Let's just leave it at not secure, huh?"

Tay said nothing.

"Anyway," August continued, "Claire picked this woman up as scheduled and—"

"Claire's here?"

August grinned. "I knew you'd like that part."

Claire and Tay had worked together several times, and they had hit it off well. Claire wasn't her real name, of course, but it was the one she used for working with August, and Tay had never asked her what her real name was. If the circumstances had been different ... well, Tay reminded himself, the circumstances were *not* different, so why think about it?

The problem was quite simple. Tay had come to understand, if not to accept, that Claire killed people for a living. August tagged them, and she bagged them. Tay understood that, but he was still too much of a cop to get comfortable with it.

"Why was Claire involved? Was this woman on a kill list?"

"No, no, no," August waved his hands. "Nothing like that. I thought the best thing to do was let another woman bring her out. Maybe it would put her more at ease. The woman thing was the only reason I used Claire."

Tay wasn't entirely convinced, but he nodded.

"Anyway, the defector is dead now. It looks like suicide. I don't think it was, but what the hell do I know about homicide investigations? If it was a suicide, then it was. But if the NoKo's killed her right under our noses, a little payback is in order."

"What happened?"

"Claire lifted her with no problems. Then she took her back to an apartment we have in Macau to let things cool down for a couple of days. The woman was freaking out that she didn't have enough cigarettes to last, so Claire went out to get cigarettes and food. She says she was gone less than an hour, but when she got back, the woman was dead."

August shaped his right hand into a little gun, put his index finger in his mouth, and brought his thumb down.

"Where did she get the gun?"

"No idea. Maybe she had one with her," August shrugged. "She was a high-value defector, not a criminal, so Claire couldn't exactly pat her down."

"I don't understand what you want me to do, John."

"Look, Sam, I just need for you to go over everything we have and see how it strikes you. If you think it was a suicide, I'll back off, file and forget. But if you think the woman was murdered, I'll go down a different road."

Tay had no difficulty working out what that meant.

"You'll need to talk to Claire. She can tell you what happened better than I can since she was there, and she can get you the autopsy report and location photos." August's face broke into a grin. "You wouldn't mind talking to Claire, would you?"

Tay didn't take the bait. It annoyed him that August thought he had something to hold over Tay's head. Yes, Tay thought Claire was attractive and good company, and they had gotten along well, but so what?

This would have been a good time for a Marlboro. At least it would have been in a prior life, so why not now? All he had to do was point to August's pack, and he'd have one. All this stop-smoking-for-the-sake-of-your-health stuff was bullshit anyway. You had to die of something, didn't you?

But Tay didn't point to August's pack of Marlboros, and the moment passed.

"I'm a little busy right now, John. I'd be happy to help, but I just don't have time to take on anything else."

"That's no problem. Hell, the woman's dead. She's not going anywhere. This is something I need to figure out eventually, but there's no big hurry. Let me have Claire get in touch and she can give you what we have. Look at everything when you have the time. No rush."

Tay shrugged. He didn't say yes, but he didn't say no either, and he knew August would take that as a yes.

"Hey," August suddenly said, slapping both knees with his open hands and standing up, "where are my manners? You just got in so you must be tired, and here I am keeping you up."

Tay rose, and they said their goodbyes.

"I'll have Claire get in touch with you tomorrow," August said as he went through the door.

Tay nodded.

And then August was gone.

T ay closed and double-locked his door, and then stood silently, thinking.

What the hell was that all about?

Because he would bet a whole bunch of money that it *wasn't* about a North Korean defector who had either committed suicide or been murdered in Macau. Even if that part of

August's story actually had some truth in it, and Tay wouldn't have been willing to make book on that either, there had to be something else going on here, too.

Having August materialize in his hotel room and pair him up with Claire within a few hours of him turning up unexpectedly in Hong Kong was just too much of a coincidence for Tay to buy.

August was working some other angle he couldn't see yet. Had to be.

So, what did John August *really* want?

TWENTY-SIX

Tay woke late the next morning. He lay quietly in bed for a few minutes, smelling the lingering odor of John August's Marlboros.

At least he was entering the new day reasonably certain he had not dreamed August's unexpected appearance the night before. He had not dreamed about his mother either that he could remember. Something about that left him feeling mildly disappointed.

He ordered a pot of coffee and some toast from room service and was just finishing his first cup and smearing orange marmalade on a slice of toast when Renny called. She asked if he would like to come over to her gallery. Tay quickly said that he would, but then he started wondering if he had perhaps sounded too eager.

Renny gave him an address in Wanchai, which he knew was somewhere on the other side of the harbor. She said she wouldn't be there for about an hour herself, so they agreed he would come at noon.

That gave him plenty of time to finish his breakfast, read the *South China Morning Post*, and get dressed. It even gave him time to consider what to do about Tilly Talbot now that he knew where she was.

A true crime writer who didn't want to stay around and find out about the murder of someone she had almost certainly been working with to produce a book? That only made sense if she thought what Harry Black had told her was what got him killed, and that knowing it might get *her* killed, too. He must have told Tilly Tabot things that had frightened her deeply, and Tay wanted to find out what those things were.

But that raised a tricky problem.

Tilly Talbot was hiding out. She was on the run. A strange man knocking on her hotel room door wouldn't go down well, and his fake Interpol credentials wouldn't be of any use either. She was a writer who no doubt had ways to check his credentials, and she would quickly find out his creds were fake. Then she really would run, and he might never find her again.

If Renny approached her instead, he thought, *that* might work. Not only would an approach by a woman feel less threatening than one from a strange man, but how could she refuse to talk to Harry Black's granddaughter? Since she knew that Black had been murdered, that was simply the decent thing to do.

Besides, she was a journalist. She would be curious whether Black's granddaughter could add something to whatever it was she already knew.

Yes, Tay was pretty sure Renny approaching Tilly Talbot would work, but how was he going to persuade her to do that after her declaration that she wanted no more to do with any of this?

Tay had followed his instincts all his life, and every instinct Tay had was screaming at him that Harry Black had been involved in something important.

Even his mother was telling him that.

If you persist in digging into the death of Harry Black, you will release forces that will fundamentally alter the way people see the world.

That sounded almost Old Testament. You couldn't get much more important than that, could you?

He knew perfectly well that hadn't really come from his mother, of course. If it had come from his mother, he could easily have ignored it. He had ignored his mother most of his life, just as she had ignored him.

But Tay knew it was his own subconscious speaking to him through the imagined appearance of his mother's ghost. Tay might not trust ghosts, but he trusted his subconscious. It knew things. And sometimes it told him what those things were.

The problem was that he didn't know how to explain all of this to Renny so that it would make sense. He had to convince her to set aside her misgivings and help him find out what her grandfather knew that made him so dangerous to somebody that they murdered him, but he certainly wouldn't do that by telling her that his mother's ghost had appeared and insisted something important was at stake here. She would think he had completely lost his mind.

But if he didn't tell her that, he had little to offer that might change her mind.

Trust me?

He had never found that to be a persuasive way to get anyone to do anything, and he had no reason to think Renny would either.

As it turned out, he needn't have worried. Even as he was thinking about it, the problem was preparing to solve itself.

T ay ordered a hotel car, but he was a little embarrassed when he went downstairs and found a dark green Rolls-Royce waiting for him.

He asked the doorman to get him something less ostentatious, but the doorman told him all the Pen's hotel cars were dark green Rolls-Royces. He was very polite about it, but Tay noticed he explained it in a way that strongly implied he could hardly believe Tay could be unaware of that.

The car carried him along the edge of the harbor, through the grimy street of Tsim Sha Tsui, and into the Cross Harbor Tunnel. Tay had never ridden in a Rolls Royce before, and he had to admit it was a swell way to cruise Hong Kong. It was like being borne through a mass frenzy on a velvet cushion. Outside the car, there was clamor and stink, struggle and conflict, discord and strife; but inside the big car, the world was utterly tranquil.

Wanchai was a lot like Tsim Sha Tsui, but with slightly wider streets. It had once been the heart of Hong Kong nightlife, at least for foreigners. Ever since the classic 1960s movie in which William Holden had taken up residence in a cheap Wanchai hotel, met a troop of good-hearted whores, and fallen in love with Nancy Kwan, Wanchai had been the place to which generations of visiting sailors had flocked looking for a Suzie Wong all their own.

Spiraling real estate values had squeezed out most of the old boozers and their ramshackle habitats had been replaced by soaring glass and steel commercial towers with designer shops and pricey restaurants on their ground floors.

A handful of the old places had survived, but these days they were more of a historical oddity than they were a naughty destination for travelers. The few punters who still made their way to them were less likely to find them staffed with bar girls than they were with bar grandmothers.

Renny's gallery occupied a large and doubtless expensive space on the ground floor of a building called the China Overseas Centre, which faced Jaffe Road right behind the St. Regis Hotel. Tay insisted the driver drop him off and take the Rolls Royce back to the hotel. He could get a taxi when he was ready to return. Being conveyed across Hong Kong in a Rolls-Royce was one thing. Having one hovering at the curb waiting for him was quite another.

The gallery was all white walls, black marble floors, and chrome track lighting. Tay paused just inside the door and took in the paintings he could see hanging on the freestanding panels scattered around in the space. They were very big, and very colorful, but depicted no shapes or objects that Tay recognized.

Abstract contemporary art did nothing for Tay. He had always been of the view that art had the responsibility to depict *something*, even if it wasn't immediately clear what that something was. He didn't require a painting to have the realism of John Constable to be acceptable. Monet was certainly within that realm, and even Picasso was in there, too, if at the far outer margin. But this...

"I already sense that you're unlikely to be buying anything today," Renny said, as she walked toward him.

Tay might not like the art, but he liked it fine when Renny put her arms around him and gave him a hug. When she topped it off with a kiss on the cheek, he decided this might turn out to be a pretty decent day after all.

"I guess contemporary art isn't my thing," he said after he had milked the hug as long as he could. "Do you have any Van Gogh's in stock?"

Renny giggled, and Tay felt a sudden rush of unreasoning delight at being able to raise a laugh in a pretty young woman.

It suddenly occurred to Tay that maybe he should take advantage of this moment of good feeling to blurt out his story about finding Tilly Talbot in HK.

Could he pitch the idea of Renny approaching her as a favor to him, perhaps? After all, he had agreed to help Renny. He ought to be able to ask for something in return, particularly when it wasn't that big an ask.

"Look, Renny, there's something I need to tell you. When Jones and I were riding in from the airport together last night, he—"

Tay suddenly registered the look on Renny's face, and he

stopped talking. She looked uneasy, maybe even a little frightened. Surely, he wasn't responsible for that, was he?

"Come back to the office," she said. "I need to show you something."

Tay followed her through an almost invisible door, down a short corridor, and into a comfortable room. A love seat and two wingback chairs were grouped around a coffee table at one end. At the other end was a glass and chrome table desk with some kind of expensive-looking chair and two black metal horizontal filing cabinets behind it. There were no windows. Instead, big canvases that looked like the ones on display out on the main floor of the gallery covered the walls.

The desktop was mostly empty. On one side, there was a silver Apple laptop with the lid closed, and in the center was a medium-sized DHL shipping box. It had been opened, and a small parcel wrapped in brown paper and a white letter-sized envelope had been removed from it.

"DHL delivered that when we were in Hua Hin."

Tay shifted his eyes from the desk to Renny's face.

She did look frightened now. There was no doubt of it.

And then he found out why.

"The package and the letter that were in the DHL box are from my grandfather."

TWENTY-SEVEN

"I don't understand," Tay said.

"Neither do I. Not really."

Renny picked up the brown-paper-wrapped parcel and the white envelope and took them over to the seating area. She put both down on the coffee table and sat in one of the wingback chairs. Tay followed and sat in the other.

She pushed the envelope across the table to him.

"Go on," she said. "Read it."

Tay picked up the envelope. It was heavy and looked expensive.

Engraved in the upper left-hand corner was the name of the sender: *Rosenthal, Becker, and Kasem, Attorneys at Law*.

Below that was an address in Bangkok.

Tay opened the flap, slid out the single sheet of stationery inside, and unfolded it.

It bore the law firm's letterhead and, below that, four short paragraphs of text.

Dear Ms. Couvier;

*Please accept my most sincere condolences for the loss of
your grandfather. This firm has worked with him on several
matters over the years and I knew him and liked him. He was
a very fine man.*

*Your grandfather recently left the enclosed parcel with us for
safekeeping. He instructed us that, if he died or became inca-
pacitated, we should convey it to you, and he provided us
with your business address in Hong Kong for that purpose.*

*We have just learned that he passed away near his home in
Hua Hin several days ago. Therefore, with this letter, we are
executing his instructions.*

*We have no knowledge of the contents of the package. Your
grandfather left it with us exactly as you see it now. Whatever
the contents may be, we can provide you with no further
information concerning them.*

Yours sincerely,
Ira Rosenthal
Attorney at law

T ay read the letter twice to be certain he hadn't missed
anything, then he refolded it, placed it back in the envelope, and returned the envelope to the table.

He waited for Renny to say something more, but she didn't.
Her eyes appeared to be fixed on some point just over his head.
He would have thought she was examining some detail in one
of the paintings, but her eyes were soft and unfocused, and Tay
knew whatever she was seeing wasn't in the room with them.

He shifted his gaze to the small parcel on the coffee table. It
was entirely wrapped in heavy brown paper and sealed with

sturdy-looking packing tape. He could see no markings of any kind on the wrapping.

Tay waited for Renny to break the silence, but she said nothing and just continued to stare over his head. Eventually, he grew impatient and broke the silence himself.

"Would you like me to leave now so that you can open the package in private?" he asked.

He saw the focus come back into Renny's eyes and she looked at him for a moment as if it surprised her to find he was there.

"What are you talking about?"

"The package," Tay said. "I assume it's something personal. I asked if you want to be alone when you open it."

"I'm not going to open it," Renny said.

"I don't understand."

"That seems simple enough to understand to me. I'm not going to open the package. I don't want to know what's in it. I already know far more about my grandfather than I want to know."

"I see," Tay said, although he didn't.

Renny pointed at the little parcel.

"Go ahead," she said. "Take it."

"And do what with it?"

"Whatever you want. Open it. Throw it away. Present it to the British Museum for all I care."

"Whatever is in that package is something that your grand-father wanted *you* to have. It makes no sense for me to take it."

"Look, Sam, my grandfather had secrets. I get that. I just don't want to know what they were."

Tay was pretty sure that was the first time Renny had ever called him by his first name. He only wished that the first time could have come at a better moment.

She waved her hand at the little parcel lying untouched on the table.

"Take it. If you do open it and it turns out to be some kind of personal keepsake like a pocket watch, I'd be happy to have it. But if it's something that explains what he was involved in that got him killed, just keep it to yourself. I will not let him unload whatever he did on me."

Tay was nonplussed at Renny's insistence that he take the parcel, and before he could decide how to respond, she got up and walked around her desk to one of the black metal cabinets behind it.

She opened the bottom drawer, rummaged around in it, and returned with a small orange Hermes shopping bag. She scooped up the parcel, dumped it into the shopping bag, and handed the bag to Tay.

Tay took it.

It was an automatic gesture on his part rather than a decision, but he didn't see what else he could do.

"There's something we need to talk about," Tay said, putting the shopping bag down at his feet. "You remember I asked Jones if he could check that London address the hotel gave Max for Tilly Talbot? Just to see if she had gone back to London?"

Renny nodded.

"Well, she wasn't in London. I had told Jones that the hotel in Hua Hin had arranged a taxi for her to the airport in Bangkok, and on his own initiative he used his contacts to check the flights leaving Bangkok just after the time she would have gotten there."

"Eddie seems to know people everywhere."

He does indeed, Tay thought, but he left it at that. He didn't know how much Renny knew or suspected about who Jones was, but if she didn't already know he was high up in the Chinese triads, Tay would not be the one to tell her.

"Jones found out what flight she boarded in Bangkok, and he knows where she is now."

Renny said nothing.

"Strange as it might sound, she's right here in Hong Kong."

A half smile appeared on Renny's face.

"Seriously?" she said. "That's quite a coincidence."

Then she saw the expression on Tay's face.

"You don't think it's a coincidence, Sam?"

"I don't know. Maybe. Maybe not. I'd sure like to ask her."

Renny chuckled. "Well, she shouldn't be too hard for you to find. After all, there are only eight million people in Hong Kong."

"She's in room 1121 of the Langham Hotel in Kowloon."

Renny stared at Tay.

"You can't be serious."

Tay nodded.

"More of Eddie's work?"

Tay nodded again.

"Wow, the next time I lose my car keys, I know who I'm going to call."

Renny made a throat-clearing noise and looked away, but then almost immediately she looked back.

"I don't see what any of this has to do with me, Sam," she said. "I told you I'm done with my grandfather."

"I'd like to talk to this woman, Renny. We think she was working on a book that somehow involved your grandfather, and it can't be a coincidence that somebody murdered him right after she started talking to him. Whatever he was telling her got him killed, and I want to know what it was."

"Why?"

Tay knew Renny would ask him that, but he still hadn't decided what to tell her.

Just saying that he thought whatever her grandfather was telling this woman was something important wasn't nearly enough, and telling her that his dead mother had claimed it was something downright earthshaking was far too much. The former made him sound lame, but the latter made him sound crazy.

He went with lame over crazy.

"If it was something important enough for your grandfather to be killed over it, Renny, I think it's too important to let it die with him."

"Why do you care one way or another, Sam?"

Atonement was the first word that came to his mind. Past sins and old failures to pay for. But he didn't say that, of course. He didn't say anything at all. He just gave his head a little shake.

Renny hesitated. After a moment, her eyes softened and they shifted back to watching whatever it was she was seeing just over Tay's head.

"Okay," she said when she looked back at him. "Talk to her if you want to. It has nothing to do with me."

"Actually, it does," Tay said, "I need your help."

"I don't see why."

"This woman is on the run, Renny. She was so panicked by your grandfather's murder that she left Hua Hin as soon as she found out about it and went straight to the airport in Bangkok. She appears to have jumped on the first flight she could get out of Thailand and has been hiding out here in Hong Kong ever since. How do you think she's going to react if some strange man knocks on her door and tells her he's there to ask her about Harry Black?"

"And you think me knocking on her door would be different?"

"A woman approaching her would be less threatening. You know that's true."

Renny chewed on her lip, but she said nothing.

"Besides, you're Harry Black's granddaughter. When she finds that out, she'll probably be eager to talk to you."

"But why would she believe me? I could be anyone. I have no way of proving I have any connection to my grandfather."

"Yes, you do."

Renny looked at Tay and waited.

"You remember those blank notebooks we found in your grandfather's safe? You told me you were going to take one as a keepsake. You've still got it, haven't you?"

Renny nodded slowly.

"I'm willing to bet that he had made notes in those books concerning whatever it was he and Tilly Talbot were talking about. Remember, the dust inside the safe made it look like another stack of notebooks had been taken out of the safe? I think he either gave those notebooks to this woman or at least showed them to her. She'll recognize the notebook you have as being identical to the ones your grandfather had."

"There're a lot of *if's* and *maybe's* in that, Inspector."

Tay noticed that he was *Inspector* again rather than Sam. That wasn't a good sign, was it?

"It's the best idea I've got," he shrugged. "It's certainly a better idea than me knocking on this woman's door and telling her I'm investigating the murder of Harry Black. She'd probably brain me with the bedside lamp and run screaming down the hall."

Renny looked away and rubbed at her cheek with her open palm. Tay waited. He had made the best case he could. She would either help him or she wouldn't. If she wouldn't, he'd just have to take his chances and approach Tilly Talbot by himself.

"Okay," Renny said when she shifted her eyes back to him, "I guess I can see that. You helped me when I asked you to. If this is what you want to do, I have no right to say I won't help you now."

"You have every right."

Renny offered a very small smile.

"When do you want to talk to her?" she asked.

"As soon as possible. We don't know how long she'll be staying at the Langham, and there's no reason to take a chance on losing her. Later this afternoon? This evening?"

"How will you even know when she's in the hotel and when she's out? Maybe she's shopping or at a restaurant."

"She hasn't gone out since she got here."

"How do you know that?"

Tay hesitated.

"Please don't tell me Eddie has somebody watching this woman," Renny said.

Tay said nothing.

Renny just shook her head.

TWENTY-EIGHT

W hen Tay got back to his room at the Pen, he put the orange Hermes shopping bag on the desk and stood looking at it with his arms folded.

Was he going to open Renny's package?

Maybe.

Okay, probably.

But that didn't mean he wasn't troubled about it.

Whatever was inside the package had been meant for Renny by her grandfather, certainly not for him, and he felt like opening it was stepping over a line. He could well be involving himself in family matters he knew nothing about. Tay didn't even like dealing with family matters of his own. Intruding into someone else's made him very uncomfortable indeed.

Renny had agreed to meet him in the lobby at five, so they could walk over to the Langham together and take a run at Tilly Talbot. Maybe he ought to wait until she got here and open the package in front of her.

But how, exactly, would that change anything?

Sometimes, when he started overthinking things like this, Tay became deeply annoyed with himself. He could only imagine how other people felt about it. Overthinking was his single most annoying personal trait, although he realized he had many other personal traits that were vibrant competitors for that title.

No wonder women lost interest in him after the briefest acquaintanceship. He really couldn't blame them. Sometimes he even lost interest in himself. And this was one of those times.

Before the usual spasms of self-doubt completely paralyzed him, Tay grabbed the package out of the shopping bag, walked over to the sofa by the window, and sat down with it. He turned it over in his hands and examined it carefully. It was small, about the size of a compact cigar box, and slightly more rectangular than square. It weighed very little. The thick brown wrapping paper was neatly creased around all four sides of the box and sealed in place with the sort of brown strapping tape that movers used to seal shipping boxes. There were no markings of any kind on the paper.

The hotel had provided the obligatory fruit bowl on the coffee table in front of the couch and a knife and a fork were arranged with a white cloth napkin on a small plate next to the basket. Tay scooped up the knife before he could change his mind and slit the tape securing the flaps on the package. Then he laid the package on the coffee table and carefully unfolded the wrapping paper.

Being meticulous in the handling of anything that might be evidence in a case was deeply ingrained in Tay from decades of homicide investigations. He did it out of habit when he opened the package, although he knew in this instance it didn't matter. Even if there was evidence to be had here, which almost certainly there wasn't, no one cared about it.

What Jones wanted was for Tay to finger whoever shot Harry Black and who had sent the shooter. He wasn't interested in building a case. There had been no talk of evidence. All he wanted was a name. Or perhaps two names. And, as he had said, he would take it from there.

And what Renny wanted from Tay was for him ... well, now it appeared she wanted nothing from him at all.

That meant that his meticulous handing of Harry Black's package served no purpose at all, but Tay handled it that way anyhow.

T he box inside the wrapping paper was disappointingly ordinary. It was dark blue plastic with a tightly fitted lid. It looked like a box that had contained something that Harry Black had purchased, and since he thought it was a good box that he might find a use for someday, he had shoved it into a drawer until that day came. And then it did.

Tay lifted the box and leaned back on the couch. He couldn't resist shaking it gently from side to side. As far as he could tell, nothing in the box moved because he heard no sound.

He was stalling, of course, and he knew it. Once he saw what was in the box, he would have to decide whether to tell Renny about it, and that was not a decision he relished making.

Oh, for God's sake, he told himself, *just get on with it, you tedious wuss!*

Tay lifted the lid with one hand and tilted the box with the other so that he could look inside without touching whatever was there. He saw what appeared to be a piece of ordinary white copy paper crumpled into the bottom and tucked into the ends to form a bed to keep the contents from moving around.

Lying in the center of the bed of crumpled paper were two tiny tape cassettes and a plastic stick that Tay recognized as a USB thumb drive. He knew next to nothing about computers, but he knew what a thumb drive looked like even if he had only the dimmest idea of how to use one.

There was something anticlimactic about opening the box and finding the tape cassettes and a thumb drive. He certainly hadn't expected a photograph of somebody with *This is the man who murdered me* written on the back. Still, he had expected at least to open the box and learn something he had not known before, but he had learned nothing. Instead, it had turned into a matter of delayed gratification, something with which he felt like he already had a lifetime of experience.

Before he would know whether there was anything here to help him understand why Harry Black was murdered, he needed two devices. He needed a computer to see what was on the thumb drive, and he didn't have one. As for the microcassettes, to listen to them he would need one of those old-fashioned handheld tape machines, the kind he had once used to record witness statements. He could have taken the one from Harry's Black's safe, but there hadn't seemed to be any reason to do that. Now he wished he had taken it anyway, of course, but he hadn't.

Could he buy one? Tay was pretty sure miniature cassette recorders were obsolete and hadn't been made in at least a decade or two, but surely he could get one somewhere, couldn't he?

He was in Hong Kong in the middle of Kowloon where Chinese, Indian, and Arab merchants had for generations hustled a dazzling array of electronic goods to tourists out of tiny shops in a hundred grimy alleyways off Nathan Road. If he could buy a handheld microcassette player anywhere on the planet, he could buy one right here.

Tay scooped up the two cassettes and the thumb drive, shoved them into his pocket, and headed out to do some shopping.

N athan Road splits the Kowloon Peninsula like a fault line. A wide roadway choked with traffic, it runs in a straight line from the harbor all the way to Boundary Street, which once marked the borderline between the British colony and China. It's lined from end to end with hotels, office buildings, restaurants, and shops, and people throng its sidewalks day and night.

It was the first road built in Kowloon back in the mid-nineteenth century when the Qing Dynasty ceded the land to the British as part of the Crown Colony of Hong Kong, and it is still the most important road in Hong Kong. The section closest to the harbor was once a magnet for visitors and for generations it was known as the Golden Mile. As with most things, however, the world moved on. Visitors now swarm the whole of Hong Kong, not just the tip of the Kowloon Peninsula, and the Golden Mile has lost its luster.

Rather than going out the Pen's grand front entrance with the portico and the circular driveway, Tay left the hotel through the rather more modest exit at the back that led out to Middle Road. Half a block up at Nathan Road, he turned left and began looking for electronics shops. There were not as many as he remembered, but there were still a lot more than you would find in most places.

The first shop Tay ducked into was a long, narrow gallery with counters on both sides and floor-to-ceiling glass cases behind the counters. The latest electronic devices were on display: telephones, laptops, tablets, headsets, and all sorts of things that Tay couldn't even begin to identify. The presentation of electronic goods was tidy and well-ordered, and they glittered expensively under the shop's bright lighting.

That was not what he was looking for.

The next shop was only a few doors down and appeared more promising. It was less brightly lit and a bit grimy. Goods were heaped haphazardly into the display cases below the counters. A small army of what appeared to be Indian shop clerks were thrusting the various items at any potential customer who showed the slightest interest in anything.

Tay waited patiently until a space at the counter opened and then he stepped up and raised a hand to attract the attention of a clerk. It took several waves to do it, but eventually one clerk detached himself from the scrum and came over to Tay. The man was a young Indian in an open-necked white shirt who was wearing far too much aftershave. He did not smile.

"What you want, sir?"

Tay fished one microcassette out of his pocket and laid it on the counter.

The man's head didn't move, but his eyes shifted down to the cassette.

"No have," he snapped and started to move away.

"Wait," Tay said, holding up his hand palm. "I don't want cassettes. I want to buy a player that this cassette will fit."

"No have," the man said again, and this time he added a vigorous head shake for emphasis.

"Do you know where…" Tay began, but the man had already moved down the counter to a customer who seemed to offer more potential.

It was coming back to him now. Hong Kong was not a place for leisurely browsing or initiating conversation about the merits of differing products. It was a place for buying.

What you want?

I have.

You pay me now.

Welcome to Hong Kong.

B ack out on Nathan Road, Tay continued strolling north, checking out the electronics shops. When he spotted Chungking Mansions on the other side of the road, he realized he was exactly where he needed to be.

Chungking Mansions is a seventeen-story building on what is probably the busiest corner in Kowloon. For decades, it has been the Hong Kong gathering place for the Indian, Pakistani, Nepalese, Bangladeshi, African, and Middle Eastern merchants who made up Hong Kong's commercial subculture. As well as selling to the public, the stalls in the building did a thriving business catering to wholesalers shipping goods to Africa and South Asia, which meant a variety of used and not infrequently stolen goods passed through the hands of the Chungking Mansions vendors. Tay had once heard somebody claiming that a quarter of all the electronic goods and telephones in Africa had at some point been sold at Chungking Mansions.

Its cheap guest houses have made it a legendary haunt for backpackers and low-budget travelers of all nationalities, and the rabbit warren of curry restaurants, electronics shops, ethnic bistros, illegal barbers, clothing stores, and money changers that have sprouted to service the building's throngs of visitors has become renowned all over the world. Inevitably, of course, Chungking Mansions also became ground zero for foreigners at the fringes of the Hong Kong drug trade and a refuge for criminals, scammers, and illegal immigrants of every kind.

The building also has a reputation for being a fire trap with its ancient electrical wiring, blocked fire stairs, and grimy hallways mounded with rubbish. It was the bottom end of the Hong Kong retail trade, and the bottom end was exactly what Tay was looking for. If the obsolete tape player Tay needed to listen to Harry Black's microcassettes still existed anywhere on earth, he knew it would be somewhere in Chungking Mansions.

The noise and the smell hammered him the moment he walked through the entrance. A babble of voices shouting in unfathomable languages assaulted his ears while the mingled odors of curry and unwashed bodies assaulted his nose. It was not a place he wanted to hang around any longer than he had to.

Tay moved through the labyrinth of little stalls looking for a likely vendor and letting his eyes glide over the merchandise on display. He tried to move with the throngs trolling the stalls and remain as inconspicuous as possible, but no potential customer was inconspicuous to the traders working the crowd in Chungking Mansions.

"Over here, sir! Best quality! Best prices, sir!"

"Where you from, my friend?"

"Special price for you, sir!"

Tay ignored the entreaties of the vendors and kept moving through the stalls. Edging away from the worst of the noise, he found himself at the rear of the main retail area and in a space where the stands were even less imposing than they were up in the front.

His eyes fell on a Chinese man sitting on a high stool behind a flimsy plywood counter that was covered with electronic junk of all kinds. The man looked ancient. He had a deeply lined face, rummy black eyes, lank gray hair that hung to his shoulders, and a wispy white beard that looked as if it might have been glued to his chin.

Tay caught the old man's eye, but the man remained expressionless and gave no sign that he had either noticed or cared. Tay liked that. He hated aggressive hustlers like the vendors in the main area, and the air of peace that surrounded the elderly Chinese man drew Tay toward him. He walked over to the counter, took one cassette out of his pocket, and laid it on the counter in front of the old man.

The man eyed the little cassette. He pulled back his lips, sucked his teeth, and made an odd whistling noise, but he said nothing.

"I want to buy a machine I can use to play that tape," Tay said.

The old man thought about it for what seemed to Tay to be a very long time.

"No have," he eventually allowed, speaking so quietly that Tay had to strain to hear him.

"Do you know where I can get one?"

The old man said nothing. He remained completely still. Only his eyes moved, shifting from the cassette to Tay's face and back to the cassette again.

"Could you get a player for me?" Tay asked. "One that would play this cassette?"

The old man's face creased into a look that Tay couldn't read, and then his eyes shifted up to Tay's face.

"Can."

"When?"

"Soon."

"Today?"

"Tomorrow."

Tay waited. He knew there would be more. There was.

"You come back," the old man eventually said. "Eleven o'clock. Tomorrow. I have."

"Okay."

"You pay now."

Tay raised an eyebrow. "Pay now?"

The old man nodded slowly. "One thousand dollar."

Tay was flabbergasted.

A thousand goddamned dollars for an obsolete tape recorder?

Did he look like that big a sucker?

Tay opened his mouth to protest, but then abruptly he closed it again. The man was talking about Hong Kong dollars, of course, not Singapore dollars or, God forbid, American dollars.

One thousand Hong Kong was only about one hundred thirty US dollars. That was still probably ten times what the old guy was going to pay for the recorder wherever he planned to get it, and Tay knew he could doubtless wheedle and bring the price down quite a lot, but it wasn't worth the bother. He wanted to hear what was on the cassettes, not pass the afternoon bargaining with Confucius' younger brother.

Tay sorted through the Hong Kong currency he had bought at the hotel that morning before leaving for Renny's gallery and picked out one of the slightly oversized yellow $1000 notes. He stretched it out and used both hands to hold it up in front of the old man's face.

"Tomorrow morning?"

"Yes."

"Eleven o'clock?"

"Yes."

"And the machine you get me will play that cassette? You promise?"

The old man nodded and his face creased again, but this time it shaped itself into a very small smile.

"Cross my heart," the old man said.

Tay laughed. What else could he do?

He handed the man the $1000 note, retrieved his cassette from the counter, and put it back in his pocket. Then he took out the thumb drive and placed it where the cassette had been.

"Now I need a laptop I can use to see what's on that," Tay said.

The old man picked up the thumb drive and inspected the connector on the end, then he slipped off his stool and bent down. Tay heard him moving things around underneath his counter, and when he stood up, he was holding a white plastic laptop. He placed it on the counter and turned it toward Tay.

Tay knew next to nothing about computers, but even he could tell that the laptop was an Apple, and he knew it had to be fifteen or twenty years old. It was so old it wouldn't have surprised him to find a label on the bottom that said, **If found, please return to Steve Jobs.**

"Does it work?" Tay asked.

The old man went under the counter again, and this time he emerged with what appeared to be a charger. He pushed its plug into a power board and then plugged the cable into the laptop. Flipping up the laptop's lid, he pushed a button at the top of the keyboard. They both watched in silence as the laptop ran through its start-up sequence and ended on a blue screen with a few unidentifiable icons scattered across it that Tay thought looked surprisingly bright for such an old laptop.

Tay knew nothing about thumb drives except that you pushed them into some kind of socket on laptops like this, then clicked on the icon, and it opened. Or it didn't.

Depending on all sorts of things about which he had no understanding at all.

He picked up the thumb drive and looked for the place to plug it in. When he didn't immediately find it, the old man reached out with a gnarled forefinger and tapped at a spot on the left side of the laptop. Tay shifted the drive to his other hand and pushed it into the socket the old man indicated. It slid in smoothly, and after a few seconds, an icon appeared on the screen. Tay didn't know what the icon was supposed to be, but it had to be something that represented the thumb drive. Below it was a label that read Untitled.

Tay started to click on the icon, but then he stopped himself. He had no idea what was on the thumb drive, but whatever it was, opening it in the middle of the hubbub of Chungking Mansions was probably a lousy idea.

"How much?" Tay asked, pointing at the laptop.

The old man looked contemplative. Tay imagined he was trying to envision either the amount of money in Tay's pocket or the balance in his bank book.

After a suitable amount of contemplation, the old man finally delivered himself of a determination.

"Five thousand dollar," he said.

"Two thousand," Tay snapped.

He'd be damned if he was going to let this old guy play him for a sucker twice.

"Four," the man immediately snapped back.

Tay pulled out his Hong Kong currency and counted it, turning his body far enough away from the man to keep him from counting along. He had three more Hong Kong $1000 notes, and he separated them out and stuffed the rest of the currency into his pocket.

He turned back to the man and spread the three yellow notes out on his counter.

"Three thousand. That's it. No more."

The man instantly smiled and nodded. "Okay."

Tay realized he'd probably been had again, but he didn't care that much. He needed to see what was on that drive and this old laptop would let him do that. Besides, he had made his stand, hadn't he? He had gotten the guy down from five thousand to three thousand. It was the principle of resistance that mattered, not the actual amount of money he had saved.

At least that was what he told himself. And it might even be true.

The old man collected the three notes, folded them, and slid them into his shirt pocket. He closed the laptop's lid, then put it and the charger into a white plastic bag and handed the bag to Tay.

"I'll be back to get the tape player tomorrow," Tay reminded him. "Eleven o'clock."

The old man nodded gravely, then abruptly his wrinkled face split into a big grin.

"Cross my heart."

Tay laughed again, turned away, and headed toward Nathan Road to walk back to the Peninsula.

TWENTY-NINE

Tay was just passing a Starbucks and contemplating the possibility of a mid-afternoon coffee when his telephone rang.

He didn't remember taking his phone with him when he left the Peninsula on his shopping expedition, so he patted his pockets and discovered to his annoyance that he had both his phone and the burner Jones had given him.

Had he somehow become one of those people he habitually scorned, the sort whose phones had become such an extension of themselves that they automatically took them everywhere they went? God help him, he hoped not.

When he pulled both phones out of his pocket, he saw it was his own phone that was ringing, not the burner, and the screen was displaying Unknown Number.

Tay normally ignored unknown numbers when his phone rang, although truthfully it didn't ring all that often with either known or unknown numbers. He considered ignoring it this time, too, but he had a lot going on right then and he decided perhaps he ought to answer.

"Hello?"

Tay heard a chuckle from the other end of the connection.

It was a woman's voice, one that was pleasantly low-pitched and warm.

"I can feel the reluctance dripping from just that one word. You almost didn't answer, did you?"

"Claire?"

"It's been too long, Sam."

Tay wasn't sure that was true. There had been a time when he had held out some hope for a relationship sprouting with Claire, but it had turned into the sort of relationship he seemed destined to have with every woman who attracted him: ambiguous, equivocal, and undefined.

Worse, he had no doubt August thought Tay's interest in Claire was something he could exploit to leverage Tay's attention whenever he needed it. He hoped Claire didn't feel the same way, but he knew she very well might.

"How are you, Claire?"

"I'm good, Sam. Life goes on. You win a few, you lose a few. You know how it is. You?"

"I'm good."

Tay had to raise his voice to be heard over the yelping of a siren in a police van that was forcing its way through the traffic on the other side of Nathan Road.

"You must be outside somewhere."

"I'm just walking back to the hotel."

"Then I won't keep you. John asked me to fill you in about the North Korean defector I lost in Macau and get your take on whether it actually was a suicide. Maybe we could have dinner tonight and I can run the whole story by you?"

"I wish I could, Claire, but I'm really busy right now. Couldn't this all wait a few days? John said it wasn't urgent."

"I think John was mostly trying to be polite. I'm a little under the gun here. If this was a suicide, then it was, but if someone murdered our defector instead, then I need to get moving on it and see if we can pin down who's responsible."

"Who else would it be but North Korea?"

Claire hesitated. "I'd rather not talk about that on a cell phone, Sam. We can go into all that tonight."

"Look, Claire, I'm sorry, but I just can't do it tonight. I have a lot on my plate right now."

"What are you working on?"

Claire's question was casual enough, but something in her voice set off an alarm in the back of Tay's mind. She sounded almost too casual, as if she was working hard to come across as matter-of-fact when that was something she really wanted to know.

Was *that* what this was all about? Was August trying to find out what he was doing in Hong Kong? But why would he care? August wasn't the sort of man to be nosey without having a specific reason, and how could he have any reason to wonder what Tay was up to?

Surely, John August had never heard of Harry Black and couldn't care less about some old man who had lived alone in Hua Hin for nearly thirty years. August dealt in the fate of nations, not the travails of retirees living out the last years of their lives in some small town on the Gulf of Thailand. Was there something else going on here that Tay knew nothing about?

That had to be it. August always had *something* going on, and most of the time, it was something that no one else knew anything about.

"It's just a favor for a friend who asked for some help with a family issue, Claire. Certainly nothing you'd care about."

Close enough for government work, Tay thought to himself.

And, to his relief, Claire let it go.

"So," she went on, "if dinner tonight won't work for you, when *can* we meet?"

"I'm not sure, Claire. Let me call you in a couple of days and we'll —"

"How about lunch tomorrow? Look, Sam, I'm not going to take no for an answer a second time."

Tay knew Claire well enough to know that was true.

"There's a great Cantonese restaurant in the Peninsula called Spring Moon," she continued before he had the chance to say anything. "Let's say ... what? Noon tomorrow?"

Without being rude about it, Tay knew there was no escape, and he wasn't willing to be rude to Claire. It bothered him that Claire probably knew that and was taking advantage of it, but whether or not it bothered him, he still couldn't see any diplomatic way out.

"I won't have very much time," he said after his mind had riffled through the alternatives and he realized he had none.

"I'll talk fast. Thanks, Sam. I appreciate this."

They said their goodbyes, and Sam returned his telephone to his pocket.

He had no doubt something was going on here that he didn't understand, but he didn't see that it was worth worrying about. When Claire and August got around to telling him what they wanted from him, they would tell him, and whenever they told him, he could decide then what he thought about it. Whatever it was lurking in the background here, it had nothing to do with him, and it certainly had nothing to do with figuring out why Harry Black was murdered. So why waste any time worrying about it?

What Tay needed to do right now was to find out what was on that flash drive and the cassettes that Harry Black had left with his lawyers. It had to be something significant. No one went to that kind of trouble to pass on vacation photographs and a few old Celine Dion tracks.

Tay would bet the reason Harry Black was murdered was right there on the flash drive and the tapes. Unless it wasn't.

Well, he would know soon enough.

Tay quickened his pace toward the hotel.

. . .

W hen Tay got back to his room, he pulled the cassettes and the flash drive out of his pocket and dumped them on the desk. Then he took the laptop and charger out of the plastic carrier bag and sat them out on the desk with them. There was an electric outlet on the wall just above the desktop, so Tay plugged the charger in there. Then he pulled the cable around and connected it to the laptop just as he had seen the old man do it.

Now that he was looking at the laptop in the quiet of his room rather than trying to examine it in the hubbub of Chungking Mansions, he realized it didn't look nearly as good as he had thought it had. The white plastic case was scratched and gouged in several places, but he picked it up and turned it over several times in his hands and couldn't find any evidence of significant damage. What bothered him most was that the laptop had two long parallel black smears across the bottom, as if a vehicle of some sort had run it over. Maybe it had.

But he had seen the laptop start up and function before he bought it, hadn't he? Besides, he didn't intend to make it one of his lifelong possessions. It was bad enough having a telephone that connected him instantly to the entire world. Having a laptop that did the same thing, only probably more of it, appalled him. He didn't own a laptop and didn't want to own one, and he was going to discard this one as soon as he had finished using it to look at the contents of Harry Black's flash drive.

As long as it worked for the next few hours, that was all that mattered. And he had seen it work, hadn't he? Of course, he had. What was he fretting about?

He opened the lid of the laptop, mumbled a brief summons to the gods of technology, and pushed the power button. A soft chime sounded and, to his great relief, the unit began the start-up process. It was slow, but Tay was so damn glad to see it running at all that it could run at any speed it wanted as far as he was concerned. He sat patiently holding the flash drive and waiting for it to finish starting up.

When it finally did, he plugged the flash drive into the connector the old man had pointed out to him. Sure enough, after a moment, the same icon he had seen back at Chungking Mansions appeared on the screen again, and beneath it was the same label he had seen before: Untitled.

Tay took a deep breath and double-clicked the icon.

A black-bordered box blossomed, and inside it there was a single line of text.

PASSWORD: _____

S hit, shit, shit.

The drive was password protected. Why hadn't it occurred to him that it might be?

Well … what now?

He had no idea what Harry Black might have used for a password, of course, and he certainly wasn't going to sit there trying to open the damn thing by typing words at random.

Probably Jones had people who would have no trouble breaking into the flash drive, but he didn't want to go down that road unless he absolutely had to. If he did that, then other people would find out what was on the flash drive and no doubt tell Jones about it before they told Tay.

Turning what might be the key piece of information over to someone else to decide what to do with it was a lousy idea. If he had learned one thing over his career, it was that you had to keep control of an investigation.

Right now, it was Tay's decision how much of whatever he found on the drive he would tell Jones about. If he gave Jones' people the drive to crack, then Jones would decide what he wanted to tell Tay about.

Then, all at once, the obvious occurred to him.

Renny knew what the password was.

Harry Black had sent this flash drive to his granddaughter. If she wasn't able to open it, it would be pointless to send it.

Whether or not she knew she knew, *she knew*. Had to, didn't she?

Of course, Renny had told him she wanted nothing to do with whatever was in the package and that she didn't even want to know what it was, so he would have to go easy there. He didn't want just to blurt out that he had found a password-protected flash drive and ask her what she thought the password might be.

She seemed to be quite set on not wanting to know anything more about her grandfather's secrets than she already did, so Tay would have to sneak up on the subject. If he could fire her curiosity a little, then maybe she would relent and help him open the drive.

Maybe Tilly Talbot would tell them something that would get Renny back in the game. Unless she slammed the door in their faces and called hotel security, which she very well might.

Tay glanced at his watch. Renny was meeting him in the lobby in less than half an hour, and then they would walk over to the Langham Hotel and try to get Tilly Talbot to talk to them.

He wouldn't mention the package to her. If she asked, he would tell her he didn't know what was in it yet. He hated to lie to Renny, but that wasn't a lie, was it? Yes, he had opened it and, yes, he knew there were two microcassettes and a flash drive in the package, but he had no idea yet what was on any of them, so he didn't *know* what was in the package, did he?

A woman he had once gone out with briefly had told Tay that every human being had some kind of superpower. Perhaps it was playing jazz piano, mastering the game of golf, or learning languages. But whatever it was, she claimed we had a moral duty to find it and develop it as well as we could.

Tay wasn't certain the woman had been right that everyone had a superpower. He had known too many people who didn't seem to have a power of any kind, let alone a superpower.

But if he had one, he knew exactly what it was.

Sophistry.

When it came to rationalization, justification, and sophistry, he was nothing less than a grandmaster.

THIRTY

Renny was waiting at a table in the lobby when Tay went downstairs at four o'clock. From the nearly empty coffee cup in front of her, Tay gathered she may have been there for a while.

"I'm sorry if I kept—"

"Don't worry about it. You said four, and it's four now, so let's just get this done. How do you want to play it?"

Most of the time, Tay had a weakness for women who got straight to the point, but in this instance, he didn't see that as a good sign. He pulled out the chair opposite Renny and sat down without replying. A white-jacketed waiter appeared at his elbow almost immediately and he ordered coffee.

He pointed to Renny's empty cup.

"Another?" he asked.

She shook her head tightly and said nothing.

Uh-oh.

Tay waited until the waiter had poured his coffee and withdrawn out of earshot, then he arranged his face in the most amiable look he could manage.

"I'm sorry if I bullied you into doing something you don't want —"

"Look, Inspector, I'm a big girl. Nobody bullies me. You agreed to help me when Eddie asked you to. It's only fair for me to return the favor now."

"If you don't mind me saying so, you seem pretty unhappy about it."

"I already told you. I don't want to know whatever my grandfather's secrets were. You do, even if I don't understand why you would."

Tay didn't know how to answer that without going down roads he had no intention of traveling, so he took what he thought was the sensible course. He drank his coffee and said nothing at all.

"Look," Renny went on after waiting for Tay to say something and then realizing he wasn't, "let's just get on with it. I assume you have a plan."

"I thought we might walk over to the Langham and go up to room 1121. Then you can knock on the door and introduce yourself."

"*That's* your plan?"

"A straight line is the shortest distance between any two points," Tay shrugged. "Or something like that."

Renny just shook her head and stood up. Tay signaled the waiter for the bill, signed it, and they left the Peninsula together.

It was only a short walk to the Langham Hotel. On the way, they passed Fendi, Giorgio Armani, Celine, Cartier, Bulgari, Givenchy, Dior, and Yves Saint Laurent. That made it pretty much a routine stroll across Hong Kong.

The Langham was old-school luxury steeped in some Chinese decorator's idea of European sophistication. The lobby was built out of what appeared to be about half the marble ever quarried in Italy, and it was furnished with velvet upholstered chairs that looked impossible for any human being to sit in. It was all wrapped up in a refined silence that would have done credit to any of the world's great libraries.

Tay had his phony Interpol credentials handy should hotel security show any interest in them, but they crossed the acre of polished marble floor to the elevators and took one up to the eleventh floor without appearing to attract any attention at all.

As they walked along the corridor looking for room 1121, Renny glanced at Tay.

"So, you just want me to walk up and knock on the door?" she asked.

Tay nodded.

"What if she doesn't open it?"

"She won't. She'll ask who you are, and that's when you'll tell her you're Harry Black's granddaughter."

"Do you think she'll believe that just because I say I am?"

"Did you bring—"

Renny reached into her purse and pulled out the notebook with the red cover that she had taken from her grandfather's safe in Hua Hin.

"Show her that. She'll be looking through the viewer in the door, and I'll bet she recognizes it immediately."

"And if she doesn't?"

Tay shrugged. "Then I guess we're out of luck unless you can come up with something good."

When they found room 1121, Tay stepped to one side so that he wouldn't be visible from the viewer. Renny started to knock, but then she hesitated and looked over at Tay.

"Are you sure?" she asked.

As Tay stood there outside the door to that hotel room, an entirely novel feeling suddenly enveloped him. It wasn't anxiety. It certainly wasn't fear. It was more of a sense of dread.

He felt creeping over him the slightly sinister conviction that something was going to happen on the other side of that door that would change things forever. Some things for the world in general, but other things for him in particular. The feeling gave him chills.

He shook it off, pointed at the glowing white button mounted in a brass bezel just to the right of the door, and murmured to Renny, "Ding dong."

Renny sighed and pressed the doorbell.

They listened to a chime sounding discreetly somewhere on the other side of the door and waited. After a few moments, they felt rather than heard footsteps approaching from inside the room and saw the viewer darken when someone put their eye against it.

"Who is it?" a woman's voice asked from behind the door.

It was a very nice voice indeed, Tay noticed. Smooth, resonant, husky, and slightly throaty, like a smoker working on the second pack of the day. Even from just those three words, Tay caught the accent, too. It was upper-class English. Oxford, Cambridge, a house in Belgravia, weekends in the country, court side seats at Wimbledon.

Normally Tay hated upper-class English accents, but the woman's slight smoker's rasp softened the plummy vowels and gave her voice a bit of working-class character. He decided he wouldn't hold her accent against her.

"My name is Renée Couvier. Everyone calls me Renny."

After a moment of hesitation, the woman's voice came again. "I'm sorry, but do I know you?"

"Are you Tilly Talbot?"

The woman said nothing.

"Because if you are, you do know me. Or at least you know who I am. I'm Harry Black's granddaughter, and I would like to talk to you."

That brought a very long silence as Tay thought it might, but the viewer remained darkened, and he knew the woman was studying Renny. She would be trying to decide whether Renny constituted a threat or an opportunity.

"How do I know you're who you say you are?" the woman asked after a bit.

Renny took the little red notebook she had taken from Harry Black's safe out of her purse and held it up in front of the viewer.

"Do you recognize this?"

That brought another silence.

"Where did you get that?" the woman eventually asked.

"Are you sure you want to do this with me standing out here in the hallway and shouting at you through a closed door?"

A few moments passed in silence, and then Tay heard the rattle of a security chain being released and the door swung open. He stepped over closer to Renny so that Tilly Talbot could see him. He did his best to look non-threatening, something that was usually quite easy for him to do.

"This is Inspector Samuel Tay from Interpol," Renny said. "He's investigating my grandfather's death."

Tay pulled out his Interpol credentials and held them up so that the woman could see them, just not too clearly. Renny knew Tay's credentials were fake, of course, but she delivered the introduction in a firm, even voice that brooked no challenge.

After two decades as a homicide detective, Tay prided himself on his ability to tell when someone was lying, but nothing in Renny's voice or demeanor would have caused his lie detector to beep. That half-pleased and half-frightened him. He would find out soon enough which was the half that mattered most.

The woman's eyes jumped from Renny to Tay and slid across his credentials, but then they went back to Renny again. He quickly returned his creds to his pocket before she thought about asking for a closer look at them.

"I asked where you got that notebook."

"There were several of them in my grandfather's safe in Hua Hin, but they were all blank. We assumed there might have been others that weren't blank and that he might have kept notes in them about whatever it was you were meeting to talk about. If he did, perhaps you've seen his notebooks or maybe he even gave one to you during your meetings. Since you recognized the notebook I have, I know one of those two things must be true."

Tay studied the woman while she thought about that. It had rattled her to find them outside her hotel room door, but that was reasonable enough. When somebody you knew was murdered, it rattled most people. When you thought you might know whatever it was that *got* them murdered, it would rattle anybody.

Tilly Talbot was probably about the same age as Renny: mid-thirties or a little older. She was small and lithe with short brown hair, and when she moved her head and shoulders they shifted in small, slightly jerky bird-like movements. Although she was wearing a blue striped shirt tucked into faded jeans, there was a stylishness to her. Her posture and carriage reflected grace and confidence. Tay had no difficulty imagining Harry Black becoming a little infatuated with her and possibly telling her more than he intended.

She made him think of a British actress from the fifties and sixties named Audrey Hepburn, but he certainly wouldn't mention that in front of Renny. He had already made one cultural reference that left him feeling older than dirt when Renny didn't have any idea what he was talking about. He generally preferred exploring new humiliations to repeating the old ones over and over again.

"How did you find me?" the woman asked.

"One of my grandfather's neighbors said she spoke to you when you came to his house on the morning he was killed. She told you he had gone down to the beach for a walk. She said you followed him."

"Yes, but how does that—"

"From that, we could place you in Hua Hin on a specific date," Tay said, taking over the explanation. "Thai Immigration records hotel registrations in a central database so we were able to trace you to the Hyatt. We learned you had checked out of the Hyatt the morning Harry Black's body was discovered and that you ordered a car to take you to—"

"Surely, you don't think that I had anything to do with—"

"No," Tay shook his head. "We know when the body was found, and we know he was shot from some distance. Both of those things rule out your involvement in his death."

"Then why are you here?"

"You've had several meetings with Mr. Black, and we know who you are and what you do. The obvious implication is that you have been talking to him about events in which he was involved during his lifetime which you think might form the basis of one of your true crime books."

Tilly Talbot looked at Tay. Her gaze was steady and even, but it gave nothing away. She remained silent.

"I think somebody wanted to stop him from telling you about whatever it was he had been involved in and they killed him to keep him from doing it. I need to know what you talked about before he was murdered. I think that will point me toward whoever was responsible."

"How did you know I was in Hong Kong?"

"Once we found out when you left Hua Hin to be driven to the airport in Bangkok, we found out what flight you took and where you went. After that, we checked a hotel registration database here in Hong Kong similar to Thailand's database, and we focused on the period right after your arrival. And here you are."

She sighed in exasperation.

"That easy, huh?"

"That easy," Tay agreed.

"And if you could do it, so could someone else."

"I'm sure they could."

"Maybe someone else who also wants to know what Harry Black may have told me."

"Maybe someone else you'd be a lot less happy to see than us."

"What makes you think I'm happy to see *you?*"

It was a good question, and Tay didn't have a good answer for it, so he just tried to look sympathetic and said nothing else.

Tilly Talbot glanced back and forth between Tay and Renny several times, obviously weighing her options.

"Well then," she finally said when she realized she didn't have any, "I guess you'd better come in."

THIRTY-ONE

Tilly Talbot's room was actually a spacious suite. It conveyed a sense of old-world elegance, as if someone had lifted it straight out of a London luxury hotel and transported it fully intact to Hong Kong. It was the kind of place Tay liked.

The bay windows were hung with gauzy sheers that fluttered slightly from the air currents set in motion by the air-conditioning. An empire-style desk was positioned in front of the windows, and Tay saw it was comfortably cluttered with pads, pens, several books, and an open laptop.

On the left-hand wall was a doorway that appeared to lead to the bedroom as well as, of all things, a white marble fireplace equipped with gas logs. That seemed to Tay a strange thing to find in near tropical Hong Kong, but he supposed the hotel's decorator didn't think the exterior temperature should constrain the appearance of charm. Did it ever get cold enough in Hong Kong to light the gas logs without cranking the air conditioning down all the way? He wasn't sure.

Mounted on the wall above the fireplace was a flat-screen television, and in front of it was a grouping of two white upholstered loveseats with a rectangular brass and marble coffee table between them. There were more books stacked on the table, a scattering of newspapers, and an iPad in a case. A large gold vase filled with pink flowers of some variety Tay couldn't identify sat on the end closest to the fireplace.

Tilly Talbot waved them to one of the love seats while she seated herself on the other.

"I'm sorry, but I didn't register your name when we were introduced," she said to Tay. "I suppose I was too surprised to be thinking clearly."

"It's Tay. Samuel Tay. Please just call me Sam."

"And remind me of your rank."

Tay hesitated a beat. He supposed it was far too late to go back, so he plunged ahead.

"Inspector."

"Inspector Samuel Tay," she repeated slowly as if she were committing his name to memory, which he was very much afraid was exactly what she was doing.

"And you are investigating the death of Harry Black?"

Another beat. "I am."

"Why?"

"Pardon me?"

"I asked why. Why is Interpol interested in the death of Harry Black?"

Tay hesitated, and Tilly Talbot just looked at him and waited.

"It isn't," he admitted. "Renny and I have a mutual friend, and he asked me to look into her grandfather's death for her. It appears the Thai police are in over their heads, or perhaps they're simply not motivated to find out what happened to her grandfather and who was responsible."

"Not motivated? Why wouldn't they be?"

"When foreigners are killed in Thailand, their deaths are generally classified as either natural causes or suicide. The Thai police have a reputation for not wanting to find out anything that might scare off the tourists."

"Then I gather this investigation is a private pursuit on your part."

"I guess you could say that. In fact, you should say that because that's exactly what it is."

Tilly Talbot thought that over.

"I got a quick glimpse of the body when I was walking up the beach," she said. "It certainly wasn't natural causes. Somebody shot him."

"They did. They killed him with a .338 rifle round fired from some distance away."

"That's a military round, isn't it?"

"It was developed as a military round, but it's more generally available now. I'm told it's a favored hunting round in some places."

"From how far away was it fired?"

"Nearly a kilometer."

"That took a skilled marksman."

"It did."

"A military-trained sniper."

"Possibly."

Tilly Talbot tapped her front teeth with her index finger and thought about that, but she said nothing.

Suddenly, she shifted her eyes to Renny. "This must sound completely heartless to you," she said. "A cop and a journalist clinically discussing the murder of your grandfather."

"It doesn't bother me. I didn't know him that well."

Tilly Talbot raised her eyebrows. "You didn't get along with your grandfather?"

"We got along fine. I just didn't know him well. I'd only met him a few times."

Tilly Talbot's face showed a small, uncertain smile.

"I don't understand," she said.

"My mother had always told me he was dead. It wasn't until after my parents were both killed in a plane crash that he tracked me down. That was when I found out he was very much alive and had been living quietly in Thailand for many years. I don't know why my mother would have told me he was dead. She must have known he wasn't."

"I think I can explain that to you."

Renny and Tay both looked at Tilly Talbot.

"If you're ready to hear it."

Renny and Tay glanced at each other and Tay gave a little shrug, so Renny shifted her eyes back to Talbot.

"Sure," she said.

But, even as she said it, it occurred to her she wasn't at all certain that she was.

"Your grandfather was a hitman for the mafia," Tilly Talbot said. "After he walked away in the 90s, he went to ground in Thailand and had been living there under a false name ever since."

Renny's mouth slowly opened, as did Tay's, but neither of them said a word. They were both too dumbfounded to speak.

"He was responsible for the murders of some of the biggest American mob figures of the 60s and 70s," Tilly Talbot continued in a voice as calm and detached as if she were discussing the weather. "Sam Giancana. Johnny Roselli. Sam Trafficante. Even Jimmy Hoffa, although your grandfather insisted he was only present when Hoffa was murdered and didn't pull the trigger."

Tay was the first to reclaim the power of speech.

"I thought you said he was a hitman *for* the mafia, but now you're saying he murdered big-time mob bosses?"

"Yes, that bothered me, too. He promised to tell me exactly who gave him the order for each of the murders he committed, but he kept putting it off. My guess is it was an internal matter with the mafia. The usual struggle between bosses for control. Harry Black obviously worked for one of them."

"You don't know who was giving him his orders?"

"Not for sure. My theory is that it must have been Carlos Marcello, the New Orleans mob boss some people claim was connected to the assassination of Jack Kennedy, even if no one seems exactly certain how."

"Why would you think that?"

"Because Carlos Marcello was one of the few major mobsters from that period Harry didn't tell me he killed."

"Who killed Marcello?"

"Nobody. He died of old age in his bed at home in Metairie, Louisiana. Given his profession, that alone is highly suspicious."

There was a silence after that. It was up to Renny to choose where this conversation went from here, Tay decided, not him, so he said nothing and waited.

Eventually, Renny cleared her throat, and both Tilly Talbot and Tay shifted their eyes to her.

"I don't know what to say," she murmured.

"You had no idea?" Tilly Talbot asked.

Renny shook her head very slowly.

"Then I'm very sorry to have dropped it on you like that. I thought you might have had some general suspicions, and I was just confirming them."

Renny shook her head again.

"How certain are you that Harry Black was responsible for these killings he told you about?" Tay asked. "Maybe he was … well, exaggerating. Or maybe age had convinced him he did things he hadn't done?"

"Look, Inspector, I make my living from a specialized area of investigative journalism: writing true crime books. The important word in that description is *true*, so I'm professionally skeptical of what people tell me. I never take a source's word for anything without confirmation."

"Then you're saying you confirmed what Harry Black told you with other sources?"

"Better. He had documentation."

Tilly Talbot looked at Renny.

"Soon after your grandfather first approached me, he gave me an old-fashioned spiral notebook with red covers. One exactly like that notebook you have."

"I'm guessing the one he gave you wasn't blank," Renny said.

"No. It contained detailed surveillance notes and plans for killing Sam Giancana. I checked the details in those notes. They were all correct, including some that had never been publicly reported. He said he prepared detailed notes for every assignment he had. He said he had other notebooks he would give me later. I had no reason to disbelieve that."

"Did he give you these other notebooks?"

"No. I never saw another notebook like the one he gave me with the plans to kill Giancana until I saw the one you held up outside my hotel room door."

"These murders you're talking about happened a very long time ago, didn't they?" Tay asked Talbot.

"Giancana and Hoffa were killed in 1975, Johnny Roselli in 1976. Sam Trafficante in 1987. Carlos Marcello died in 1993, and it was right after that Harry went to ground in Thailand. As far as I know, he was never involved in mafia business from then on, which is another reason I think he must have been working for Marcello."

"But that was thirty years ago. If Harry Black was murdered out of revenge for things he had done for Marcello, why would someone have waited thirty years to do it?"

"Maybe they had only just found out where he was," Tilly Talbot shrugged. "I really can't tell you that. What I know for sure is that Harry Black told me some stories about prominent mafia figures he said he was paid to kill decades ago, and I was shaping those stories into a book."

"Did you tape record any of those conversations you had?"

"No." Talbot looked at Tay curiously. "Why would you ask that?"

"No particular reason," Tay said.

Talbot didn't look as if she believed him, but he didn't care. They were here to get information, not to give it. He hadn't even told Renny about the tapes and the thumb drive, so he certainly wasn't going to tell Tilly Talbot about them.

"Anyway," she went on, letting it go, "the missing piece was who paid him to kill those people. Until he gave me that, there was no book."

"Did he realize that?"

"Oh yes, he understood it perfectly well, and he promised he would tell me. But he seemed to be teasing it out like it was going to be his big surprise reveal at the end of everything else. I never quite saw why he did that. It seemed pretty obvious to me who he was acting for. If it wasn't Marcello, then who was it?"

"You can't think of any other possibility?"

"No, and I've tried. I'm sure he would have eventually admitted he was working for Carlos Marcello, but then somebody shows up and kills him before he could. Someone didn't want me to know he worked for Marcello. At least, not for sure. That's not proof of a connection, of course, but I'd say that certainly raises a reasonable suspicion, wouldn't you, Inspector?"

Instead of answering Tilly Talbot's question, Tay asked one of his own.

"So, based on what he told you, we're talking here about a man who only killed mobsters. Correct?"

"Oh, I didn't say that."

Neither Tay nor Renny said anything. They just watched Tilly Talbot and waited.

"There was a killing he told me about that he never fully explained," she went on after a moment. "It wasn't a mob figure. It was … well, someone completely outside that world. Honestly, when I did some research about the background of that murder and found out who it was, it frightened me. I started wishing he had never told me about it, and I wasn't certain I wanted to know any more than I already did."

THIRTY-TWO

"**D**o you know who Mary Meyer was?"

Both Tay and Renny shook their heads.

"No, neither did I. Not when he first told me about killing her."

"My grandfather murdered a woman?" Renny asked.

Tilly Talbot looked at Renny for a moment and Tay thought he saw something like a half smile cross her face.

"That bothers you more than hearing he killed Sam Giancana or Johnny Roselli?" she asked Renny.

"Of course it does. You told me my grandfather may have killed some old mobsters who had probably killed dozens of people themselves. I wasn't happy to hear it, but at least I could tell myself that they were men who probably deserved killing. Now, you tell me he also killed some woman who wasn't connected with the mafia and you ask me if that bothers me? What do you think?"

Tilly Talbot took a breath and held it for a moment. Then she exhaled heavily.

"Maybe we should take a break," she said. "It looks to me like this is all getting a little hard for you to hear, my dear."

"You're damn right it's hard for me to hear, but I'm going to sit right here and listen to everything you can tell me about my grandfather. I came here reluctantly today. I told Inspector Tay this afternoon that I didn't want to know any more than I already do, but I felt I owed it to him to get you to talk to us. Now I've changed my mind. I want to know what my grandfather told you. I want to know all of it."

Renny looked at Tay, but he remained silent.

"Now," she went on, shifting her eyes back to Tilly Talbot, "who was Mary Meyer, and why did hearing that my grandfather killed her frighten you so much?"

Tilly Talbot shifted her weight on the couch and uncrossed her legs. Then she crossed them back in the opposite direction and leaned toward Renny and Tay.

"Mary Meyer was murdered in Washington, DC, in 1964. She was walking along the old C&O Canal in Georgetown toward a place she often went to in the afternoons to be alone. Someone shot her twice at nearly point-blank range. A black man was arrested by the DC Police shortly after she was murdered based mostly on the similarities between what he was wearing and a description of the killer's clothing given to police by an eyewitness, but there were discrepancies in the witness testimony, and there was no other evidence of the man's involvement. The jury acquitted him when he went to trial. To this day, the murder remains unsolved."

"But my grandfather told you he was responsible."

"Yes."

"He told you he killed this woman."

"Yes."

"Did he tell you why?"

"Only that he was acting on instructions that were given to him."

"By whom?"

"He didn't tell me. He promised he would, but he never got the chance."

"Assuming that he *was* going to tell you. And that he intended to tell you the truth."

"Yes. Assuming that."

Renny thought about all that for a moment.

"You said it frightened you to hear my grandfather say he killed this woman. What did you mean by that?"

"When he first told me about it, I had no idea who she was. But when I did some research and found out, I started wondering what I had gotten myself into."

"You're stalling, Ms. Talbot. Just lay it out for us. Who was Mary Meyer?"

Tilly Talbot shifted her weight on the couch again and once again went through the routine of uncrossing her legs and re-crossing them in the opposite direction. Tay could see she seemed slightly nervous. What he couldn't see was what she was nervous about.

Then she told them.

"Mary Meyer was the closest thing to royalty you could find in Washington, DC. When she was murdered, she had been divorced for only a few years from a man named Cord Meyer. Cord Meyer was a senior official at the CIA. When they were divorced, he was head of the CIA's Covert Action Staff. Her sister was married to Ben Bradlee, the editor of the Washington Post who later became a media celebrity from the Post's coverage of the Watergate scandal. Her best friend, her room-mate at Vassar, was married to another senior CIA official, James Angleton, the Agency's infamous Director of Counterintelligence."

Tay had become a spectator to the conversation between Tilly Talbot and Renny, which was fine with him. As a spectator, he could sense shifts of tone and nuances in the narrative that he might have missed had he been a participant. He liked being a spectator. He was comfortable in that role. It was what he was good at.

That was why Tay knew before Renny that something more was coming, and that it was likely to be something big.

It was.

"In 1976, the Washington Post published a major story confirming rumors that had been floating around Washington ever since Mary Meyer was murdered. Mary Meyer had been President John Kennedy's mistress from the time he entered the White House until he was assassinated in 1963. Although Kennedy was an infamous womanizer, by all accounts he was genuinely in love with Mary Meyer and shared with her intimate details of events in his presidency that were known to very few people."

"But why would that—" Renny began.

"There's more," Talbot interrupted. "Most of Mary Meyer's friends knew she kept a diary, and those who knew about her affair with President Kennedy suspected she recorded many of the things he told her. Some of those things were secrets so big they could never be allowed to become public. Her sister, the one who was married to the editor of the Washington Post, knew that Mary sometimes took her diary to the place where she appeared to be going on the afternoon she was murdered and wrote in it there. But she didn't have the diary with her when her body was found."

Renny and Tay looked at each other, but Talbot went on before either of them could gather themselves enough to ask any questions.

"When her sister learned the diary was missing, she went to Mary's house to locate it and make certain it didn't fall into the wrong hands. She found James Angleton, the counterintelligence chief of the CIA, was already there. He had already found out about her murder somehow, gotten into her house, and was searching for the diary. He didn't find it. When Mary's sister got rid of him and subsequently searched the house for the diary herself, she didn't find it either. To this day, no one knows what happened to that diary."

"Are you saying my grandfather murdered Mary Meyer because someone wanted her diary, and he took it?"

"It's a reasonable suspicion. I just don't know for sure."

"Did you ask him?"

"Yes. I did."

"And what did he say?"

"I didn't ask him if he'd taken the diary. I asked him who he had given it to. He just smiled at me. Then he said, 'Maybe later.'"

If there had ever been a moment in Tay's life that cried out more loudly for a Marlboro, he couldn't remember what it was, but of course, he didn't have any. How could he have been so stupid? The gesture he had made in giving up smoking was looking more idiotic to him by the second.

"This is a lot to take in," Renny said.

"I know it is. I'm sorry to dump it all on you like this."

"I can see now why hearing about my grandfather killing this woman frightened you."

"Yes, I thought I was dealing with internal power struggles in the mafia and some mobster murders, but all at once I realized this was something much bigger and much scarier."

"I'm going to have to think about all this for a while," Renny said. "I still don't see how it all fits together."

Neither did Tay, but he was certain there was some awful unifying narrative here.

Part of him wanted to know what it was, of course, but part of him just wanted to walk out of that hotel, get on the first plane to Singapore, and go back to smoking Marlboros in his garden. He felt safe and at peace there. He did not feel at peace here, and when he thought about the tape cassettes and the memory stick waiting for him back in his hotel room, he felt anything *but* safe.

"Do you want to hear my theory?" Tilly Talbot asked.

Renny nodded, but Tay remained still and silent.

"I think Carlos Marcello sent your grandfather to murder Mary Meyer and steal her diary. Robert Kennedy and the Department of Justice were trying to deport him. He had even been accused of somehow masterminding President Kennedy's assassination. I think Marcello thought he could use the diary to protect himself. You know about Robert Kennedy's involvement in a scheme to get the mafia to work with the CIA to assassinate Fidel Castro, don't you?"

"I remember hearing about something like that," Tay said, "but I always thought that was just another crazy conspiracy theory."

"No, it was true. That happened. Robert Kennedy was involved in setting it up, and the mafia bosses the CIA worked with to coordinate the plot were Sam Giancana, Johnny Roselli, and Sam Trafficante."

"Those are the three men you said my grandfather confessed to killing."

Tilly Talbot nodded.

"Oh my," Renny said.

"I think Carlos Marcello was the man who was actually behind the whole CIA-mafia connection," Talbot continued, "and Marcello interpreted the whispers connecting him to President Kennedy's assassination as a warning to keep quiet about what he knew. That was why he wanted Mary Meyer's diary. He was certain Kennedy had talked to her about the plot and Robert Kennedy's involvement. I think Marcello got that diary and used it to blackmail the White House, the Department of Justice, and the CIA into leaving him alone."

"You're saying my grandfather made it possible for this mobster to blackmail the government of the United States?"

"Exactly. Then he had the other men who knew the truth

killed. Which was why he died peacefully in his bed rather than in prison or from some hired killer's bullet."

"This man blackmailed the *CIA*?"

"Marcello threatened to reveal the evidence that proved a conspiracy between the CIA and the mafia to assassinate Fidel Castro. That evidence was Mary Meyer's diary. The diary that your grandfather took from her after he killed her. Of course…"

Tilly Talbot shrugged and made little popping sounds with her lips.

"…that's just my theory. We'll never know for sure. Your grandfather was the only one who did know, and someone killed him to make certain he didn't tell anyone else."

"There's somebody else who knows," Tay said.

"Why would you say that?"

"Because somebody killed Harry Black to shut him up. And whoever that was must have known what he was going to tell you."

Renny looked at Tay.

"My god," she said. "This isn't over, is it?"

Tay just shook his head.

THIRTY-THREE

W hen Tay and Renny left the Langham, they walked back toward the Peninsula Hotel.

They didn't have a reason to go to the Pen, not really, but it was where they had been before they had gone to the Langham to talk to Tilly Talbot and, with no sense of what they should do now, a sort of natural gravity had simply reversed their direction of travel. They followed Peking Road to Ashley Road, then turned right toward Middle Road, which would take them to the back entrance of the Pen.

They didn't talk much. Each of them was struggling separately to put what they knew now together with what they had known before, and then roll it all up into something that made sense. Tay had always believed that to be one of the most fundamental of all human drives: to understand the things we know. Otherwise, what point is there in knowing those things?

The smell of automobile exhaust, sewage, unwashed bodies, and stale cigarette smoke was the smell of Hong Kong's sidewalks. Tay usually found the mixture nauseating, but now the occasional whisper of tobacco, stale or otherwise, was a welcome respite.

Tay had never wanted a cigarette so badly in his whole life.

Why had he ever given up smoking? He knew the answer to that, of course, but at that moment, the choice felt cowardly to the point of foolishness. He had few genuine pleasures in life. To discard one of them, hoping it might somehow prolong his life, was absurd. Why would he want to prolong it if he had to give up his limited pleasures to do so?

Tay caught a glimpse of Renny out of the corner of his eye. She was dressed in a no-nonsense style, a white shirt and loose coffee-colored slacks, plain clothes that somehow seemed elegant on her. He wondered if it might be something in her carriage that he found so appealing. Her back was straight as a marine drill sergeant, yet she moved with an offhand grace. Was it possible to be attracted to a woman because of her posture? Surely not.

Renny was a lovely woman, simple as that, and Tay was unmistakably drawn to her, but that just made the pain and unhappiness on her face even more difficult for him to bear. He felt like he should say something to her. After all, he was the one who had pulled Renny into the conversation with Tilly Talbot in the first place. If it hadn't been for him, she would never have heard any of those things about her grandfather.

But now she *had* heard them, and Tay felt responsible for that. It made the unhappiness she was suffering now his responsibility.

"You know," Tay began with no clear idea where he was going to end up, "it's possible none of those things your grandfather told her were true."

Renny turned her head only far enough to glance at him, but she said nothing.

"He was trying to convince this woman to write a book with him," Tay hurried on. "Maybe he'd been around some of the people he was telling her about for some reason and then he embellished his stories to make himself sound more important than he was. Or maybe he just made the stories up completely."

Renny kept looking at him, and Tay started feeling uncomfortable.

"Everyone wants his past to matter," he finished quickly. "Maybe your grandfather had nothing to do with the mafia and invented those stories to make himself sound important."

"Are you just playing devil's advocate here, Inspector, or do you really believe that might be true?"

Good question, Tay thought. He wasn't entirely sure which it was himself.

At the next corner, Renny suddenly stopped walking and turned to face him.

"I think I'll take the MTR back from here."

She pointed to an entrance into Hong Kong's subway system that was just across Middle Road next to the Kowloon Hotel.

"At this time of day, it will get me home a lot faster than a taxi."

Tay had been about to ask Renny if she wanted to have dinner with him at one of the restaurants in the Peninsula, but now he gathered she didn't. For a moment, he considered asking her anyway. Then he decided it would just end up embarrassing either her or him, probably both of them, so he only nodded and said nothing.

"I don't want to talk about any of this right now, Sam. Let me think about it overnight, and I'll see how I feel when I wake up. Call me tomorrow and we can talk about it then."

"You haven't asked me if I opened that box that you gave me."

"No, I haven't."

For a moment, she looked as if she was about to say something else, but then she gave her head a quick shake.

"Tomorrow," she said.

Then, to Tay's complete astonishment, Renny suddenly threw her arms around him and hugged him hard. He thought she smelled wonderful, a mixture of lilacs and soap, and her body tucked so perfectly into his that it felt as if it had been there a hundred times before. If he understood women better, perhaps he would be able to tell whether it was just a friendly hug, or if it might be a romantic hug, but a call like that went well beyond both his experience and his ability.

"Thank you for everything, Sam. It's meant the world to me that you went right down the line for me on all this."

That sounded to Tay like a sort of goodbye, but before he could gather himself to ask whether that was what it was, Renny turned away, dodged through the traffic on Middle Road, and disappeared down the steps into the MTR station.

Tay raised his arm to wave, but Renny never looked back.

He lowered his arm again and walked up Middle Road toward the Peninsula Hotel, feeling a little pathetic.

T ay couldn't think of anything else he could accomplish until tomorrow and he wasn't particularly hungry, so he went back to his room feeling very much at loose ends.

He needed a tape player before he could listen to the cassettes, and he wouldn't have one until tomorrow. He needed a password before he could find out what was on the thumb drive, but he didn't want to ask Renny about one until he had heard the tapes and had some idea why her grandfather had wanted to get the tapes and the drive to her. There was something on those tapes, and it was something important.

Every investigation Tay had ever done had holes like this, times at which nothing was happening, and the only thing he could do was to wait around for something to happen in the future. At least, this time it was clear what he was waiting for, which was a far greater level of clarity than he normally enjoyed. But even that clarity didn't make him feel better.

Investigations ran on momentum, so he hated coming to points like this. Once you get things moving, it was important to keep them moving. When things stopped, more often than not, everything you had done up until then turned to a pile of crap.

Tay sat on the couch, found the television remote, and flipped through the channels with little interest. Eventually, he settled on BBC News and lowered the volume until it was just a murmur in the background. He was no fan of BBC News, but the hotel television system only gave him a choice of BBC or CNN, and nothing was worse than the smug, know-it-all Americans on CNN.

He thought again about his decision not to have dinner. He still wasn't particularly hungry, but eating was something to do, wasn't it? And he hated having nothing to do.

He located the room service menu, had a momentary seizure at the prices, and scanned through it looking for something appealing that wouldn't require him to mortgage his house.

When his telephone rang, he was glad for the interruption. It would have to be Renny, he thought. Who else could it be? And knowing she had called him almost the moment she got home made him smile.

"Hello?"

Silence.

"Hello? Can you hear me?"

More silence.

Tay took the phone away from his ear and looked at the screen. It was dark, but he could still hear the phone ringing.

What the hell?

All at once he realized it wasn't his phone ringing at all, but rather the burner phone Jones had given him. Unless it was the wrong number, he now had a little doubt about who was calling him, and it wasn't Renny.

"Hello?"

"I hope I'm not calling at a bad time, Inspector."

Tay was not a man overly fond of telephone calls, so any call he received was pretty much coming at a bad time. But, of course, he didn't tell Jones that.

"No," he said, "it's fine. I was just about to order room service and have an early night."

"Ah, does that mean you have already wrapped this thing up and just haven't gotten around to telling me about it?"

Jones chuckled slightly, apparently to show he was only joking and intended no criticism of Tay's investigation.

"It means I have found more pieces to the puzzle, but I still have absolutely no idea how to put them together or what I'll see when I do. I'll have more pieces tomorrow. Maybe everything will become clearer then."

"Have you spoken to that writer we located for you yet? The one you thought Renny's grandfather was talking to about writing a book?"

"Renny and I spent some time with her this afternoon. We were right to think he was working with her on a book, but they were just getting started. She had met him only a few times."

"What was there about this man that made her think he was worth a book?"

"She said he claimed to have been a hitman for the mafia."

Jones chuckled. "Seriously?"

"He seemed to have this woman convinced," Tay said, "and I think she's a pretty tough sale, but there is no objective evidence that it's true. It's simply what he told her."

"But he was quite an old man, wasn't he? And he'd been living in Thailand for a long time."

"That's true. The killings he told her about date back forty or fifty years."

"Did she know anyone specific he claimed to have killed?"

"Oh yes. She had names, all right. Sam Giancana, Johnny Roselli, and Sam Trafficante. He also said he was involved in the murder of Jimmy Hoffa, although he insisted he wasn't the trig-german on that one."

Tay wanted to tell Jones enough to satisfy him that progress was being made, but not so much that he would push for *more* progress to be made, and for it to be made faster. So he decided not to mention Mary Meyer.

Even if it were true that Harry Black had killed Mary Meyer, Tay didn't yet understand how that fit in with killing mafia bosses, anyway.

He certainly wasn't all in on Tilly Talbot's theory that Carlos Marcello was blackmailing the CIA to keep himself from being deported. That sounded more like a plot for a really lousy novel than it did a real-world possibility worth taking seriously.

"That seems doubtful to me," Jones said. "Those were the most powerful mafia bosses of the 70s and 80s. Who could order men like that killed?"

"She thinks it was Carlos Marcello, but her only evidence for that seems to be that Marcello was the one top mob boss from that era who ended up dying in his bed."

There was a silence while Jones thought that over.

"Even if some or all of this is true," he eventually said, "and this man was killing other mob bosses at the behest of Carlos Marcello, I don't see how that explains why somebody would want to murder him now. Who in the world would care now about getting revenge for the death of some mafia bosses nearly fifty years ago? None of those people matter anymore. The mafia doesn't even matter anymore. I should know."

Tay wasn't about to ask Jones why he should know, although he had no difficulty guessing.

Instead, Tay said, "I don't have an answer for that. Not yet. But I think I will soon."

He could have told Jones about the tape cassette and the thumb drive, but he wasn't ready to do that either. He wanted to know what was on them first. Then he would decide what, and how much, to tell Jones about them.

"Give me a couple more days," Tay said. "I feel like this will all come together soon."

"Do you really think so, or are you just saying that to make me feel better?"

Tay stayed silent.

"That's what I thought," Jones said.

There was little more of substance to talk about after that, so the two men soon said their goodbyes and Tay went back to listening to the BBC murmuring in the background.

He picked up the room service menu again and started reading it one more time from the beginning.

THIRTY-FOUR

Tay put the room service tray outside in the hallway, shut off the television, and went into the bathroom to get ready for bed. When he came out, he stood by the desk and looked down at the two cassette tapes and the thumb drive lying there.

There was something about the whole mafia hitman story that didn't feel right to him. Tilly Talbot believed it, but he thought she probably wanted to believe it.

She wrote true crime books for a living, so she was at least a little predisposed to believe crime stories when someone told them to her. She couldn't get a book out of trying to prove the stories she had been told weren't true. There was only a book there if they *were* true.

A retired mafia hitman living quietly in a beach resort in Thailand shot down by a sniper over forty years after his last hit? It sounded like a terrible movie made by some streaming service you never heard of and starring some largely forgotten television actor you thought was dead.

If the mafia hitman story were true, why had Harry Black gone to all the trouble of arranging for a lawyer to send these two cassettes and this thumb drive to his granddaughter if something happened to him? Did he *expect* something to happen to him? Did the cassettes and the drive prove one mobster had hired him to kill other mobsters?

And if they did, why would he be so eager to show a woman who was his only living relative that he was a hired killer who had worked for organized crime?

That didn't sit right with Tay. It didn't fit what little he had learned so far about Harry Black. There was something else here, something entirely different from that. He just didn't have a clue what it was.

Tay eyed the cassettes and the thumb drive again. He missed the time when people kept journals and diaries, often in beautiful leather-bound books. When he found something like that had been left behind by a murder victim, he knew it would help him solve their homicide.

Now he had a murder victim who had left behind tape recordings and a digital drive, and he had to have electronic equipment to see what the man was saying. It reminded Tay yet again that this was a twenty-first-century world, and he was a twentieth-century man. Maybe nineteenth.

He was getting morose now and he knew it. That sometimes happened at night after another day wound down. He had far fewer days in front of him than he had behind him, he knew perfectly well, and that understanding brought with it an ever-increasing sense of urgency. He felt like he had to make each day he had left count for something. This one had counted for very little.

He was nowhere yet with understanding Harry Black's murder. He still didn't know why someone would want Black killed, let alone who it was who killed him. He had gotten involved in trying to find out only because Jones had asked him to get involved, not because it was his responsibility. He supposed it didn't really matter all that much if he ever figured it out or not. He wasn't a cop anymore. He was no longer accountable for delivering justice.

And yet...

He felt responsible now anyway. He felt responsible to Jones because he owed him, perhaps more than he could ever repay, and now he felt responsible to Renny too because ... well, just because. Most of all, he felt responsible to himself. He had agreed to take this on, and he owed himself an outcome, one that made sense of something that right now seemed senseless. He had never left the things he took on half-done, and he wouldn't start now.

Maybe whatever was on those tapes and that drive would point the way to an explanation. Or maybe they would just dig him deeper into the swamp he was wading through. He would know tomorrow which it was. There was nothing he could do tonight to make that happen any faster.

He gave up worrying about it, cut off the lights, and went to bed.

"Wake up, Samuel! We have to talk."

Tay considered refusing to open his eyes, but that never worked. When his mother was alive, it had been hard enough to deflect her from any course of action on which she was settled, but now that she was dead, it was like trying to stop a charging bull by waving a red flag. Good luck with that.

"Do we have to do this tonight, Mother?"

"Yes, Samuel, we do. Now wake the fuck up!"

"Language, Mother! Language!"

Tay opened his eyes and pulled himself up until he could rest his back against the bed's headboard. A dim glow filled his room, and his mother sat watching him on the foot of his bed.

Uh-oh.

"No light show tonight, Mother? I do so look forward to the disco ball thing you do sometimes, and the cloud of fireflies is wonderful, too."

"I swear, Samuel, I don't know why I bother. All the effort I put into coming here to see you, and all I get from you in return is sarcasm and jokes. I'm your mother, you putz. Show a little respect!"

All the effort she put in? What did that mean? His mother made it sound like the dead were subject to the same temporal aggravations and indignities the living had to suffer when they traveled. Surely not. There had to be *some* advantage to being dead.

He decided to keep things simple. He took the high road.

"I'm sorry, Mother. You're right. Let me begin again."

Tay cleared his throat and arranged his face into a look so pious it would have done credit to a casket salesman extolling his wares to the family of the late deceased.

"How are you, Mother? I'm delighted to see you."

"No, you're not. Don't overdo it."

Tay realized his mother was looking quite prim. She was sitting very straight with her legs crossed, and she was wearing a gray suit with silver buttons that looked like a Chanel knock-off. Did they have knock-offs on the other side? He decided he'd better not ask.

"You look very nice tonight, Mother."

"Thank you."

"Very…"

Tay searched briefly for the right word.

"… professional. You look as if you're scheduled for a court appearance today. *Are* you scheduled for a court appearance today?"

"Don't be an ass, Samuel. I'm here to help you, so I thought a professional appearance was appropriate."

"You're here to help me?"

"Yes."

"Help me do what?"

"To solve this case you're working on, of course."

"Why would you want to do that?"

"Because I'm your mother. What are mothers for?"

"I've often wondered that myself," Tay murmured.

"What did you say, Samuel? Speak up, boy!"

"I said I would appreciate any help you can give me."

"No, you didn't."

Tay rolled his eyes and tilted his head back.

"Okay, here's what we're going to do," his mother continued. "First, I want you—"

"Hold on, Mother. You're about to give *me* instructions about how to conduct an investigation?"

"You're not getting anywhere, are you? Maybe somebody needs to."

"I'm always happy to listen to people who know what they're talking about, but with the greatest of respect, I have to say that's not you."

"I have some ideas."

"I have one, too. Harry Black must be somewhere over there where you are. Why don't you just find him and ask him what happened?"

"I've already done that."

"*What?*"

"I talked to him this morning. He's a delightful man. Quite handsome for his age, really. If he were only a few years younger … well, he's not, so why think about it?"

Wait a minute, Tay thought. Ghosts are romantically attracted to other ghosts? How could that be? If ghosts became emotionally involved with other ghosts, did they start ghost families and have little ghosts? The idea raised metaphysical questions so convoluted that even Tay hesitated to consider them.

"Anyway," his mother continued, "Mr. Black wasn't any help. He doesn't know what happened. One second he was there walking on the beach, and the next second he was here."

Tay knew he was being baited into asking where *here* was, but past discussions with his mother about that had never gone well and he was far too weary to have another one right now.

"I also asked Harry if he had any idea why someone would want to kill him, and he said he didn't, but I think he's lying about that."

"*Harry*? It's Harry now, is it? A moment ago it was Mr. Black."

Tay's mother said nothing. She just looked at him until he started feeling uncomfortable.

"How would you know whether he was lying?" Tay went on, deciding that a change of subject might be the better course. "You don't have any experience determining when people are lying."

"Of course, I do. I raised you. You were a terrible child."

"I never lied."

Tay's mother gave out a snort so loud he actually flinched.

"I can't tell you how much I'm enjoying this witty banter, Mother, but it *is* the middle of the night and I've had a very tiring day. Would you please get to the point so I can go back to sleep?"

"You are so disrespectful, Samuel, that I swear sometimes you make me want to shoot myself, but I'm already dead, so what good would that do?"

Tay laughed despite himself. "Good one, Mother."

His mother looked at him and smiled.

"Yes," she said. "It was rather good, wasn't it?"

She uncrossed her legs, re-crossed them in the opposite direction, and folded her arms.

"I haven't given up on Harry yet," she said.

"In what sense do you mean that, Mother?"

She ignored him, as he knew she would.

"Harry knows something," she continued, "and I'm going to get it out of him."

"I hear waterboarding is quite effective."

"No," she said, "I thought about that, but being afraid of drowning won't work on someone who's already dead."

Tay saw his mother wasn't smiling, so he just nodded and said, "Good point."

"There is one other thing I have to tell you before I go, Samuel, but you're not going to like it."

"You think I liked all the things that came before this?"

His mother ignored that, too.

"You're trying to find out two separate things here. The first is why Harry was killed, and the second is who killed him. Is that right?"

"And the first thing," Tay nodded, "will almost certainly lead to the second thing."

"That doesn't matter."

"It matters very much to me."

"Now please listen to me, Samuel. Are you listening to me?"

"Yes, Mother, I am listening to you."

Tay's mother fixed him with a stare so intense that it felt slightly unnerving.

"It is right and important that you pursue the question of why Harry was killed, and I'm sure you will find enough in those tapes and on that thumb drive to make that clear."

"How did you know about—"

His mother waved him into silence.

"It is right and important because you will expose the truth of something that has been hidden for a long time and people are entitled to know the truth about it."

"You mean that Carlos Marcello was blackmailing the White House and the CIA to keep himself from being deported?"

His mother cocked her head at him and gave him a look of utter astonishment.

"Is that what you think happened?" she asked.

"That's what the facts I know tell me happened."

"Then you know the wrong facts, Samuel. This is bigger than that. Much bigger than that."

"What are you talking about, Mother?"

"That's all I can give you. You'll have to find out the rest for yourself."

"I thought you warned me that no one would thank me for doing that."

"They won't. But since when is the test of whether you *should* do something, whether you are thanked for doing it?"

It surprised Tay to hear his mother say that. It didn't sound like her. Was she mellowing in her old age? Then again, could you say that people who were already dead were old? That didn't sound right at all.

"But here is the point I want you to take to heart. Are you listening to me, Samuel?

"Yes, mother, I'm listening to you.

"Once you find out why poor Harry was killed, you must stop pursuing the matter. Do *not* try to determine who killed him. You would pay a personal price for finding that out, and it is a higher price than you can afford."

Tay had no idea what that meant, and he was sure his puzzlement showed on his face.

"You don't understand, do you, Samuel?"

Tay just shook his head.

"You are obsessed with finding out the truth and, in your profession, that is an admirable quality, but you never spare a thought about what consequences the truth may bring with it. Sometimes the truth can do more harm than good. And I'm telling you that, in this case, that harm will fall personally on you. I don't want to see that happen."

"We're edging into the fortune cookie thing again, Mother. Can you just tell me plainly what you mean?"

"I've already said more than I'm allowed to."

What did *that* mean? Was his mother required to submit the things she told him in advance and get approval for them? And, if so, approval from *whom*?

"I'm going to have another talk tomorrow with Harry, but my guess is you will find the answer in those tapes and on that drive before I wheedle it out of him so it won't be necessary for me to come back and spoon-feed it to you. You're good at what you do, Samuel. The very best. Even I have to admit that you're about the smartest man I ever met."

Tay was so dumbfounded at hearing that from his mother that he didn't know how to respond.

"Cat got your tongue, Samuel?" his mother chuckled.

"I'm speechless, Mother. I had no idea that was what you thought."

"Well, I hope you enjoyed hearing it because you're not likely ever to hear it again. It might not be possible even if I wanted to say it again sometime, which I probably wouldn't."

"What does that mean?"

"Surely you understand that these little meetings of ours can't keep happening forever. When I move on, we won't be able to meet like this anymore."

"Move on? Move on to where?"

"Ah well, now you're getting into spiritual questions that, if I may say so, are well above your capacity to understand. You don't do spiritual very well. Never have. That's why I stick to the fortune cookie stuff with you. It's more your speed."

"Mother, that's—"

"Toodeloo, Samuel," his mother interrupted, raising one hand and wiggling her fingers at him. "And remember, do *not* try to find out who killed poor Harry. It would achieve nothing, and it would cause you great personal harm."

The glow in his room flickered and then slowly faded to darkness like stage lights do just before the curtain came down.

Tay was alone again. His mother was gone, as gone as if she had never been there at all.

Which, of course, she hadn't been.

THIRTY-FIVE

ay arrived at Chungking Mansions at precisely eleven o'clock the next morning, elbowed his way through the mobs of Pakistani and African traders, and stood in front of the elderly Chinese man who was supposed to be getting him the tape player.

The man was on his stool behind the plywood counter looking exactly the way he had when Tay had been here yesterday. He was even wearing what looked like the same clothes. For all Tay knew, he might have been sitting there all night without ever moving at all.

Tay had brought one cassette with him to make sure the tape player worked the way it was supposed to. He took the cassette out of his pocket, held it up, and wiggled it.

The old man looked at him without expression.

"Fifteen minutes," he said.

Tay made a show of looking at his wristwatch.

"You said eleven o'clock. It's now just after eleven o'clock."

"Fifteen minutes," the old man repeated. "Maybe thirty."

Tay gave the man a hard look, but that didn't seem to bother him in the slightest.

"So, you give me discount for being late, huh?"

The old man snorted, and even Tay had to smile slightly. He could see there was nothing to be gained from badgering him.

"Okay," Tay shrugged, "another fifteen minutes."

"Maybe thirty. You go away. You come back."

"Then I'll come back in thirty minutes. Thirty minutes, right?"

Now the old man cracked a smile.

"Cross my heart."

Tay chuckled and made his way back out to Nathan Road to look for somewhere to kill a half hour.

The only possibility he saw that seemed at all promising was a Starbucks just across the road. He didn't want to go to a Starbucks. There had never been a time in his entire life that he wanted to go to a Starbucks. Starbucks was far too American for his taste. But he had to kill a half hour somehow, and he certainly didn't want to pass it in Chungking Mansions being hustled by the Pakistani and the African merchants, so he sighed in resignation and crossed Nathan Road.

He ordered a small black coffee, which appeared to annoy the woman behind the counter. He imagined she had been expecting him to order one of those milkshake-like creations piled with whipped cream and streaked with colored syrups that everyone in Starbucks seemed to drink instead of actual coffee, but he pretended not to notice her scowling at him.

He took his coffee over to a counter that ran along the front window and perched himself on a stool. He sipped the coffee, which he had to admit was better than he expected, and watched the passing parade on Nathan Road. Every few minutes he glanced at his watch, willing it to move faster.

Tay was back in front of the old man's plywood table at exactly eleven-thirty, and he saw that the man was no longer alone. With him now was a skinny little boy who couldn't have been over twelve or thirteen years old. He was wearing grimy khaki shorts and a wrinkled T-shirt with a badly faded version of Andy Warhol's famous portrait of Mao on the front, the version in which Mao's fluorescent green face made him look as if he was about to be seriously ill. Both the boy and the old man were peering down at what the boy held in his hands.

When the old man noticed Tay, he grabbed what the boy was holding and slapped it down on the counter. It was a microcassette recorder that looked very much like the one Tay had used years ago to record interviews with witnesses. It was a little scratched and battered, maybe, but then so was Tay.

"You try," the old man said.

Tay fished the cassette out of his pocket and picked up the recorder. The eject button was in the same place the one on his old recorder had been, and when he pressed it, the cassette compartment popped open. He snapped in the microcassette he had brought with him, closed the compartment with his thumb, and pressed the button marked *PLAY*.

He was both pleased and a little relieved to hear sound coming from the tiny speaker. It was a man's voice, somewhat faint and tinny, but Tay quickly hit the *STOP* button. He had no intention of playing any more of the tape in public than he needed to confirm that the machine was working. And it seemed to be working just fine despite having had some hard wear.

Tay felt around the base of the machine until he found the battery compartment. He slid a thumbnail into the slot and pulled it open. The batteries looked clean, so maybe they were relatively new. He briefly considered getting a new set anyway and then rejected the idea. The machine was working the way it was. Why take a chance on jinxing it?

He ejected the tape and returned it to his pocket.

"Thank you," he said to the old man.

The man produced another of his white plastic bags from somewhere and slapped it down on the counter in front of Tay.

"Free!" he barked, and then he grinned.

Tay laughed, rolled the little recorder up in the plastic bag, and pushed it into his trouser pocket. Then he gave the old man a nod and started back to the Peninsula.

T ay was anxious to get back to his room so he could start listening to the tapes, but the delay in picking up the recorder had left him without enough time to do that before meeting Claire for lunch. He could always cancel the lunch, he supposed, but he had to admit he was curious about what Claire and August really wanted from him.

The story about the North Korean defector who may or may not have committed suicide had an unmistakable odor to it. He supposed it was at least possible that was actually what Claire wanted to talk about, but he doubted it. There was something else. He was sure of it. At least he had already told Claire he was busy and would have to keep their lunch short, so maybe he could find out what she really wanted and get back to the tapes fairly quickly.

When Tay reached the Peninsula, he took the staircase in the lobby up to the first floor and walked into Spring Moon at five minutes after twelve.

The main dining room was decorated in a style he thought of as Hollywood-Chinese. A polished wood floor, big-character Chinese calligraphy on the walls, hundreds of blue and white ceramics displayed in glass showcases, and large round tables with turntables in their centers for serving the big Chinese families that frequently gathered in places like this. There was also a slightly more intimate mezzanine running around three sides of the room with smaller tables lined up alongside a wood and glass railing.

He spotted Claire waiting for him at a table in the far back corner of the mezzanine. It was the same table he would have chosen if he had gotten there first, the sort of table you picked when you didn't want anyone to overhear your conversation and you certainly didn't want anyone to come up behind you by surprise. Claire had her face tilted down toward the screen of her telephone and she hadn't noticed him yet, so he stood quietly and watched her for a moment.

Tay's involvement with women over the years could be divided into three categories. *Actual Relationships*, the smallest category by far. *Almost Relationships*, a slightly larger category, but still quite small. And *No Relationship at All*, which included pretty much every female he had ever encountered throughout his entire adult life.

Claire fell into the *Almost Relationships* category. For a while there, it looked as if she might be on her way to moving up into the *Actual Relationships* category, but that never happened. And Tay understood exactly why it hadn't.

What Claire did for John August and the Band made him uncomfortable. Claire killed people. Of course, she only killed people the most senior political leadership of the United States had decided needed killing, so she wasn't a criminal. Tay supposed she was something more akin to a soldier. But he was a policeman — okay, an ex-policeman — and he had all sorts of difficulty wrapping his mind around the idea of engaging in an intimate relationship with a stone-cold killer.

Nevertheless, he had to admit that Claire looked fantastic today, and that gave him pause. Maybe he had made a mistake. Maybe he could learn to overlook her professional side.

Claire was tall for a woman, and she was lean and fit-looking. Today she had her long blonde hair pulled back into a ponytail. She was wearing black jeans, black ankle boots, and a white dress shirt with the sleeves rolled up. It was hardly a feminine look, but it suited Claire perfectly.

Tay wasn't certain he was allowed to notice an American woman's appearance these days. Americans had been getting goofier and goofier about that sort of thing for the last few years, and he had the impression now that just thinking an American woman looked attractive would get you five to ten in San Quentin. Well, he thought, to hell with it. I'm in Hong Kong now, not New York, and I'll think whatever I damn well want to think.

Suddenly, Claire looked up and glanced toward the front of the restaurant. When she saw Tay there, she lifted a hand in greeting and unleashed a dazzling smile. He tried to keep his response neutral and professional, but it was hopeless. He smiled back in a way that he knew left no doubt he was glad to see her and started for the stairs.

The whole while Tay was climbing the stairs to the mezzanine, he was fretting.

Should he kiss Claire or just shake her hand? It would only be a kiss on the cheek, of course, but that was still well beyond the bounds of the air of neutral professionalism he felt he ought to maintain here. A handshake was much more appropriate between colleagues, wasn't it? Well, they weren't exactly colleagues, of course, but maybe the handshake was still the better choice.

"Hello, Sam," she said when he arrived at the table, and then she hit him with another of those luminescent smiles. "I've missed you."

Tay bent down, kissed her on the cheek, and seated himself at the table. Fuck neutral professionalism.

"Hello, Claire."

"I hope you don't mind," she said, "but I've already ordered for us. You said you were busy, and I thought it might save some time."

Tay didn't mind. He had heard the place had a Michelin star and he could write what he knew about high-style Cantonese food on the back of their Michelin star and have enough room left over for his laundry list.

He and Claire slid into the usual inconsequential chit-chat while they were waiting for their food to be served, but Tay quickly tired of the bullshit.

"So," he said, "killed anybody interesting recently?"

Claire burst out laughing. It was a nice laugh, Tay had to give her that, but he tried to keep his face empty rather than show too much appreciation for it.

"Now that's the Sam Tay I miss. Never afraid to say what's on his mind."

"It was a serious question, Claire."

Just then, an entire corps of waiters arrived bearing the food Claire had ordered, and that took her off the hook. The food was served with considerably greater ceremony than Tay figured lunch at a Chinese restaurant merited, Michelin star or not. At the prices this place was probably charging, however, he figured the delivery of every dish probably ought to be accompanied by an entire uniformed brass marching band.

Claire's selection was a bit on the excessive side, Tay thought. Sliced abalone with jellyfish, lobster dumplings, honey-glazed barbecued pork, Australian rack of lamb with Sichuan pepper, braised lobster with crabmeat, and — just in case they were still hungry — roasted Peking duck.

The food was wonderful and worthy enough of attention to push away any thought of a serious conversation while they ate. Tay didn't have the heart to spoil the meal with too much reality, so he said nothing of any substance until he had popped the last morsel of Peking duck rolled up in a soft pancake into his mouth and wiped the excess plum sauce from his lips.

"Now that you've softened me up with an expensive meal," he said then, "are you ready to tell me what this is really all about?"

"It's about exactly what John told you it's about. I've got a dead North Korean defector on my hands I think committed suicide. The problem is, I'm not certain it was suicide, and we don't have anybody who knows enough about investigating suspicious deaths to tell us for sure. John thought you might do that for us."

"I'd be happy to help if I can, Claire, but I already told John that I'm a little busy right now. I just don't know when I'll be able to get to it."

"What are you working on that's keeping you so busy, Sam?"

Claire put the question was such an elaborate casualness that she might as well have fired off a volley of skyrockets to underscore its importance. Just as Tay had suspected, John August wanted to know what he was doing in Hong Kong, and he thought Claire would be more effective at wheedling it out of Tay than he would.

"Is there actually a North Korean defector, Claire?"

"What do you mean?"

Claire's eyes slid away from Tay's and examined the remaining lobster dumplings with sudden fascination.

"Of course, there's a defector," she said. "Why would I tell you there's a defector if they weren't a defector?"

Tay chuckled. "You are a terrible liar, Claire."

She took a brief stab at looking indignant, but when she realized what a bad job she was making of it, she shook her head, leaned back in her chair, and laughed.

"Okay, Sam, you got me. John wants to know what you're doing in Hong Kong. He's afraid you may be working on something that might put us at cross-purposes, and he asked me to find out for sure."

Tay didn't see that it would do any harm to tell Claire and August what he was doing, but just on general principles, he didn't much like people asking him. If they had to ask, they probably didn't need to know.

"It's a personal matter, Claire. A favor for a friend of someone who once did something important for me."

"Can't you tell me something about what it concerns so I can put John's mind at rest?"

"I'm taking a fresh look at a homicide. This woman's grandfather was murdered in Thailand, and Thai cops aren't usually very diligent about investigating the killing of a foreigner. She wants to know why her grandfather was killed and who was responsible. I'm trying to find out for her."

"Are you making any progress?"

Tay had reached the limits of what he was prepared to share with Claire and August about Renny's grandfather, so he finessed.

"I promise you it's nothing that rises anywhere close to the level of matters you and John deal with. I'm just a simple investigator from Singapore, Claire. I do cop stuff. I don't get involved in all that fate-of-mankind stuff you and John do."

Claire started to ask another question, but Tay rushed on before she could.

"Look, I hate to eat and run, but I have a lot of commitments today. Just tell John he wouldn't have the slightest interest in what I'm doing here, but I appreciate him buying me this elaborate meal all the same. The next time he's in Singapore, dinner is on me."

Tay got quickly to his feet before Claire could find a way to wrest back control of the conversation. He gave her a peck on the cheek and turned to walk away.

"Sam," she called after him.

He could have pretended he didn't hear her and kept walking, but that was far too rude a thing for Tay even to consider doing. He stopped and glanced back.

"Will I see you again before you go back to Singapore?" Claire asked.

"If you like."

"I would like."

"Then we'll figure out a way to make that happen."

As it turned out, Tay didn't have to figure out a way to make that happen. It happened anyway. Just not quite in the way Tay might have wanted it to happen.

THIRTY-SIX

W hen Tay got back to his hotel room, he laid everything he needed out on the desk before he began. The two cassette tapes, the thumb drive, the tape player, and the laptop.

He examined each of the cassettes carefully, but there was nothing written on either of them and no indication at all of the order in which Harry Black intended for them to be played.

He had used one of them to test the player back at Chungking Mansions, but he couldn't tell now which one that had been, so he picked one of the two cassettes at random, slipped it into the recorder, and pressed PLAY.

The spools began to turn, but all Tay heard coming from the speaker was a soft hiss. He fast-forwarded a little, then hit PLAY again, but the hiss continued.

Was it possible this tape was blank? That didn't make any sense. Harry Black had put in place a careful plan to get these cassettes to his granddaughter if anything happened to him. He certainly wouldn't have done that for a blank cassette. There was something here, somewhere.

Tay recalled a murder case he'd had years ago in Singapore in which a telephone call recorded on a cassette tape had been a key piece of evidence. The problem was that the tape had deteriorated from age to the point that the conversation was mostly unintelligible. The experts had testified then that cassette tapes only had about a thirty-year life. Tay couldn't recall the details, but it had something to do with the magnetic coating that contained the data becoming detached from the binder holding it to the tape as the cassette aged.

Were these cassettes so old they had begun deteriorating? He supposed they could be. Tape cassettes like these had been around since the 1970s. These particular cassettes could be fifty years old.

Tay stopped the recorder, removed the cassette, and examined it again. He saw nothing that might indicate its age. It looked almost pristine, as if it had just recently been taken out of its wrapper.

That was when it occurred to him that the tape cassette and whatever was on the cassette didn't have to be the same age. Harry Black could have rerecorded an older cassette several times, moving the material on it to progressively newer and newer cassettes.

The mob killings for which Black claimed responsibility had occurred in the 1970s and 1980s. Was it possible that these tapes somehow proved his involvement in those murders? Could they be tapes of conversations in which somebody was giving him instructions to commit those murders?

Of course, it was possible.

And could he have rerecorded those conversations on new cassettes to preserve them from deterioration?

Certainly, that was possible, too. The quality might have degraded a little with each rerecording, of course, but probably not enough to render whatever was on the original tape completely unintelligible.

But if that were true, Tay asked himself, why was he hearing nothing on this tape but background hiss?

Perhaps the rerecorded material was shorter than the

cassette allowed for. If the recording only occupied part of the space and he was listening to the portion of the cassette Harry Black had left blank, that would explain the hiss. If Tay recalled correctly, these little tapes ran for thirty minutes and had two sides. After the first thirty minutes, you ejected the cassette and reversed it, and you had another thirty minutes to work with on the other side.

There had to be something here, Tay told him, and the only way he could be certain to find it was to play the tape all the way through on both sides until he did.

He snapped the cassette back into the recorder, placed it on the desk in front of him, and pressed PLAY again. He folded his arms and settled in to listen.

A half-hour later, there was a *CLICK*, and the spindles in the cassette stopped turning.

Tay had heard absolutely nothing on the tape but that damned hissing sound. It had been positively soporific. He made a mental note that he may have just discovered the world's most effective technique for inducing mental paralysis. The next time he had difficulty getting to sleep, he was going to play a blank tape cassette and he was certain it would cause him to nod right off.

Tay ejected the cassette, turned it over, and snapped it back into the recorder. He hit PLAY again, and almost immediately he found what he was looking for.

Harry Black had recorded on the second side of the tape and left the first side blank. Had that been some kind of security measure or just confusion on his part? Tay didn't know, but he supposed it didn't matter. This was what Harry Black wanted to get into his granddaughter's hands if something happened to him.

It was a conversation between two men. Was one voice

Harry Black's? Tay assumed it must be, but the only way he could be certain was to ask Renny to identify it.

The problem with that was that she had been quite adamant she didn't want to know what was in the box her grandfather had sent her and had made Tay promise he wouldn't tell her. First, Tay would have to break that promise, and then he would have to convince Renny to listen to the tape to identify her grandfather's voice. Tay wasn't at all sure she would be willing to do that.

Maybe it didn't matter because the voices Tay was listening to were mostly unintelligible. He was no expert in such matters, but it sounded to him like the original recording was old and degraded when Black rerecorded it on this cassette and that had left the conversation broken up in such a way that it made very little sense.

Tay rewound the second side of the cassette to the beginning and listened again to what was there.

Hissssssssssss.
Voice 1: … is stupid.
Voice 2: We have to know for sure.
Voice 1: Know for sure? What the fuck does that mean? Know for sure?
Voice 2: What are you talking about? It means exactly what it sounds like it means.
Voice 1: So you don't trust me? After everything I've done, now you don't trust me?
Voice 2: Of course, I trust you.
Voice 1: Then why the hell—
Voice 2: Look at it this way. This is history. We must record it as history. Are a couple of photographs too much to ask for history?
Voice 1: I don't want to be history. You be history, man. You're the man of position here. I'm only the shooter. I'm just manual labor. When you told me …

Hisssssssssss.
Voice 2: ... nothing to do with ...
Hisssssssssss.
Voice 1: No, no, no. There's no way...
Hisssssssssss.

I t went on like that for several minutes. It felt to Tay like it could be a conversation between Harry Black and somebody else about the murders he claimed he committed, maybe even a conversation with whoever was giving Black his instructions, but there wasn't enough there to say for sure.

Perhaps Black had recorded the conversation as some kind of insurance so that he could threaten to expose where his instructions had come from if he ever needed to protect himself. If that's what it was, and one voice was Harry Black's, then it was the other voice that mattered, and Tay had no way of identifying the other voice.

Then Tay heard something that caused him to sit up straighter.

Hisssssssssss.
Voice 2: We don't want the body found. We just want him to disappear.
Voice 1: I'll take care of it.
Voice 2: If the body is ever found ... well, just don't let it be.
Voice 1: Are you telling me how to do my job now?
Voice 2: I'm not telling you how to do your job, I'm just telling you—
Voice 1: Look, Cork, I've done much tougher—
Voice 2: I know you have, but—
Voice 1: An eight-hundred-yard shot—
Voice 2: Don't ever speak about that. Not even to me.

*Voice 1: Talking about that one makes you nervous, doesn't it,
Cork?*
Voice 2: Don't speak about it even when you're joking.
Voice 1: Who says I was joking?
*Voice 2: I do. You had to be joking since you weren't there. I
wasn't there. Are we clear on that?*
*Voice 1: (makes a snorting sound) Sure, man. I wasn't there.
You weren't there. Nobody was fucking there. It just
happened all by itself.*
Voice 2: What makes you think—
Hisssssssssss.

O ne guy called the other guy *Cork?* What the hell kind of
name was *Cork?*

A nickname? Like a cork in a bottle? Maybe that meant the
other guy was a drinker. Or maybe it meant he never drank at
all. Could be either, Tay supposed. Or neither.

He listened carefully to the rest of the tape, but that was the
highlight. The rest was just more of the same disconnected stuff
about killing and bodies and a lot more hissing. Then, after six
or seven minutes, the snatches of conversation ended and there
was nothing more but the hissing of blank tape all the way to
the end.

He listened to the other tape, both sides, beginning to end,
and heard more of the same. There were several more refer-
ences to *Cork*, but nothing that was any more specific than just
that name. If it was a name. It occurred to Tay that what Black
must have thought mattered was the voice. It was the voice that
could identify the other man, the one being called Cork, and he
had a lot of samples of it. Anyone who knew the man could
probably ID him from his voice.

Assuming, of course, one guy actually *was* somebody named

Cork, and Harry Black was the other guy. Maybe that wasn't true. Maybe Tay was letting his assumptions run away from him.

Tay picked up the thumb drive and looked at it. Was another piece of the puzzle on it? Something that pointed to who this person called Cork was? Had to be, didn't there? Otherwise, what was the point of making elaborate arrangements to get it to Renny?

But Tay knew looking at it wasn't going to help him find out what was on it. He needed the password, and he was sure Renny knew what that password was. Maybe she didn't know she knew what it was, but she knew.

Why in the world would her grandfather leave an encrypted thumb drive to be sent to her after he was dead if she didn't know how to open it?

THIRTY-SEVEN

Renny answered her phone on the second ring.

"We need to talk," Tay said.

"Uh-oh. I can't think of any conversation I've ever wanted to have that began with the words *we need to talk*."

"I have all the pieces of the puzzle here in front of me right now, but I need your help to put them together."

"We already know what you'll see if you do. Tilly Talbot told us. My sweet old grandfather murdered people for the mafia."

"I think there's more to it than that."

"If there is, I don't want to know about it. I already know far more than I want to."

"I'm asking for your help here, Renny. I think that's fair."

"Look, Sam, I appreciate your dedication to figuring this out, but—"

"The box your grandfather sent you contained two audio tapes and a thumb drive."

That brought a silence on the other end of the phone, which was what Tay expected. When Renny spoke again, her voice was tight.

"I thought I made it clear that I didn't want to know what was in that box."

"I'm just telling you, there were two tapes and a drive in the box. I'm not telling you what's on them."

"Good."

"The reason I'm not telling you that is because I don't *know* what's on them."

Tay let the silence stretch out after that. He was counting on Renny's natural curiosity to draw her out, and it worked.

"What do you mean you don't know what's on them?" she asked.

"The two cassettes have been degraded by some deterioration, but they appear to contain conversations between two men. The deterioration breaks the conversations up so that they don't make much sense, but the same two men's voices are on both cassettes. I'm pretty sure from the context that one man is your grandfather, but I don't know who the other one is. Does the name Cork mean anything to you?"

"Cork?"

"Yes. Maybe it's a nickname."

"I've never heard of anybody called Cork. Not from my grandfather, not from anybody else."

"Then there's this thumb drive. It requires a password to open it. You know what the password is."

"*What?* Until you just told me, I didn't even know there was a thumb drive in that box. Why in the world would you think I know the password for it?"

"Because your grandfather went to quite a lot of trouble to make certain you would receive it if anything happened to him. Why would he do that if you didn't know how to open it?"

That brought another silence. Tay waited her out.

"Okay, I'll give the password to you on one condition."

Tay said nothing.

"You must promise me you'll never tell me what's on that drive."

"If that's what you want."

"That's what I want."

"Okay, I promise."

Renny cleared her throat. "The password is probably MH1717072014."

"Wait a minute," Tay said, opening and closing the desk drawers until he found a pad of notepaper and a ballpoint pen. "Now, one more time, please."

"MH1717072014."

"Capital M, capital H?"

"Yes."

"Why would you think—"

"My grandfather gave me a thumb drive once with pictures of my parents on it. He had locked it with a password, and that was it."

"It just seems odd that you remember such a complicated —"

"It's the flight my parents were on when they were killed plus the date the plane was shot down over Ukraine. Malaysia Airlines flight 17, MH17, on 17 July 2014. 17072014."

Tay cradled the telephone between his shoulder and his cheek and pulled the laptop toward him. He opened the lid, inserted the thumb drive, and waited for the password box to appear. When it did, he typed in MH1717072014 and waited.

He didn't have to wait long.

The password box disappeared and a directory appeared on the screen listing several files labeled only with combinations of letters and numbers that were meaningless, at least to Tay.

"That worked," he said to Renny. "I have the drive open."

"Remember your promise?"

"Yes, I remember. Thank you for helping me."

"I don't know if I've helped you or not, Sam. I'm certain I'm better off not knowing any more than I already do about my grandfather. That might well go for you, too."

"So I've been told."

"Really? By whom?"

Tay doubted Renny believed in ghosts, so quoting his mother to her didn't seem to be a very good idea.

"I just meant in general," Tay said. "People are always telling me I'm too nosey."

Renny said nothing. Tay doubted she believed that was what he had meant at all, but she wanted the conversation to end, so she let it go.

"I've got to run, Sam," she said. "A customer just came into the gallery."

Tay didn't believe that either, but he pretended to, so he let that go, too.

And that was where the conversation ended. With a matched pair of gentle lies. Not venal lies, not lies meant to foster deception, but only lies intended to function as a social lubricant. Lies intended to deflect conflict about things that really didn't matter.

Unless they did.

A fter Tay ended the call, he opened the first of the five files in the thumb drive's directory.

He wasn't sure what he expected, but he didn't expect this.

The file contained nothing but about two dozen completely unremarkable black and white photographs. They were photographs of buildings and streets in some city Tay didn't recognize. From the automobiles and the way people on the streets were dressed, it looked to him as if the photographs dated back quite a few years. Maybe to the 1960s or even the 50s. He also thought the city was probably an American city since the cars looked American.

One picture showed a curving road next to a small park, and something about it made Tay pause and look at it more carefully. Had he seen that photograph somewhere before? He didn't know how he could have, but he felt a sense of remembrance looking at it. He had spent very little time in America, so he doubted he had been there, wherever *there* was. Then what was it he recognized? Why would that street and that park seem vaguely familiar to him?

Another photograph had the look of the downtown shopping area in some medium-sized city. Not New York or Chicago certainly, but a smaller city. Boston, maybe, or San Francisco. He peered at the signs he could see, but the photograph was slightly out of focus and he couldn't make out any of them.

Tay went through all the photographs again from the beginning searching for recognizable landmarks, but he didn't find any. Just nondescript, medium-sized buildings and a four-lane road with sidewalks on both sides. The photographs were all framed in such a way that whoever had taken them seemed to have been more interested in the street than the city, but Tay couldn't see why. It was just a street. There was nothing interesting about it at all.

The second file yielded another harvest of snapshots. These were also in black and white, and they all showed the interior of some office building. It was a rather ordinary-looking building, and it appeared as if the photos must have been taken on a day when the building was closed since there were no people in any of the photographs. Just empty offices, rooms with plain wooden furniture, and windows hung with Venetian blinds. Beyond the windows, city streets were visible six or eight floors below.

One photo looked as if it was taken from higher up, perhaps from the roof of the building, but it showed the same small park and curving road he had seen in the street-level photograph in the first file. In the distance, beyond the park, was an overpass that looked as if it carried railroad tracks. The curving road disappeared through an underpass beneath it.

The third file contained about a dozen photographs of a man and a woman who looked to Tay like they were probably Americans. These photographs also seemed to be from the 1950s and 60s. Most of them were also in black and white, but a few were in color. Sometimes the man and woman were shown together and sometimes they were shown separately.

The man was tall and slim, studious looking. He wore big glasses that sat heavily on his thin face, and his hair was short and combed into a traditional style with a part on the left. The woman was blonde and quite glamorous. In most of the photos, she held a lighted cigarette.

There was something about the photos that spoke of wealth and privilege in a time now gone. The man and woman both had a look that Tay associated with the East Coast upper class in America, the closest thing that America had to an indigenous aristocracy. He couldn't say what it was that made him think that, but he knew it when he saw it.

There were photographs of lawn parties and dinners with attractive, well-dressed people smoking cigarettes and sipping cocktails. Everyone was slim and relaxed and projected the air of casual sophistication he associated with the rich and well-born. American glamor. Hollywood without the movie stars.

Tay was about to close the file and move on to the next one when he saw an icon at the end of the list of documents that differed from the other icons. He clicked it, and something that mimicked the appearance of a notepad opened on the screen in front of him.

There were just four words written on the pad.

CORD AND MARY MEYER

Mary Meyer was the name of a woman Tilly Talbot said Renny's grandfather confessed to killing.

She also said hearing about that murder had frightened her because Mary Meyer had been President Kennedy's mistress, and she may have kept a diary that detailed things Kennedy had told her over the years, things that some people didn't want to see the light of day.

And Cord Meyer?

Cord?

Cork?

Could it possibly be?

Tay felt a sudden chill.

He clicked slowly back through the photographs again until he came to one that caused him to stop and scrutinize it more closely. It was a photograph of a party on the lawn of a manor house that looked like something straight out of *The Great Gatsby*.

In the foreground, Cord and Mary Meyer stood with their arms around each other lifting their drinks in a toast, and in the background, a crowd of other people were doing the same thing.

Tay realized now that those toasts were being directed toward a painfully thin young man with a shy smile and an unruly mop of hair who was waving them off with an upraised hand. His hand was partially blocking his face, so Tay hadn't recognized the man the first time he glanced at the photo.

But now he knew who it was.

He was looking at the young prince in his youth, the man who one day would become one of America's most famous presidents. He was looking at a photo of Cord and Mary Meyer raising their glasses in a toast to John Fitzgerald Kennedy.

T ay knew next to nothing about the internet and less than nothing about using it to do research, but after a brief struggle, he managed to connect to the hotel's wi-fi system. And he did know what Google was.

He googled the name Cord Meyer and waited a few seconds while the screen redrew.

The first entry on Mr. Google's list was for a Wikipedia article, which was close enough for Tay. When he read it, his mouth opened.

Wikipedia identified Cord Meyer as a high-level operative for the CIA. Cord and Mary Meyer had been divorced just before the period in which her affair with Jack Kennedy was supposed to have begun.From the late 50s through the mid-70s, the time during which Harry Black was supposedly killing people for the mafia, Cord was engaged in running black operations for the Agency.

Tay had just heard two tapes in which somebody, almost certainly Harry Black, was receiving instructions to carry out those killings. Those instructions came from a man he had thought Harry Black was calling *Cork*, but now he would bet Black was actually calling him *Cord*.

That's why Harry Black wanted his granddaughter to have these tapes and this thumb drive if something happened to him.

Harry Black wasn't killing people for the mafia.

Harry Black was operating under the instructions of Cord Meyer.

Harry Black was killing people for the CIA.

THIRTY-EIGHT

Tay read through the articles about Cord Meyer that appeared on the first page of his Google search results. He glanced through the second and third pages of the search results, but he couldn't be bothered to read anymore. The list of search results just went on and on and looked to be more of the same.

Instead, he searched Google for Mary Meyer and read the first page of articles listed under her name, too. They were mostly about her murder. Two shots, one to the back and one to the head, both leaving the sort of muzzle stippling that showed the shots had been fired at point-blank range.

Her murder had all the hallmarks of a professional hit, but the best suspect the DC cops could come up with was a hapless black man named Raymond Crump who was arrested about a quarter mile from the crime scene. There was no forensic evidence linking Crump to the crime, and Crump didn't even remotely match any of the descriptions given by witnesses, so the jury acquitted him when he went to trial. The whole thing smelled to Tay like a fit-up, one hastily thrown together to cover up something else. He had seen a few fit-ups in his time, but not many this clumsy and inept.

Could it be true that back in the 60s the CIA had killed Jack Kennedy's mistress to get their hands on her diary and whatever revelations it presumably contained about things Kennedy had told her?

Every available account of Mary Meyer's murder seemed to point to the same thing: a well-planned and carefully implemented execution, one consistent with the methodical preparations that Harry Black had made for the other murders he had told Tilly Talbot he committed.

Tay had to admit that some articles turned up by his Google search were pretty nutty stuff. Cord Meyer seemed to be a lightning rod for an entire menu of conspiracy theories. From reading some of that stuff, you would think Meyer was personally responsible for everything from the crucifixion of Jesus Christ to the assassination of President Kennedy. Compared to some of the things people had tried to blame Meyer for, the murder of his ex-wife was relatively small potatoes.

Still, all of it wasn't nutty. Some of what he read was eerily consistent with what Tilly Talbot claimed Harry Black had told her. If that really was Cord Meyer on the tape cassettes giving Black his instructions, Tay had something extremely dangerous here. The sort of thing some people might kill to keep secret.

Of course, that was exactly what somebody *had* done, wasn't it? They had killed Harry Black when he started talking to Tilly Talbot about writing a book.

Now Tay knew what it was Harry Black was going to tell Tilly Talbot.

That could well be a problem for him.

A *big* problem.

Tay became so absorbed in his reading that he lost track of time. When he eventually looked up from the laptop screen, he was surprised to see it was dark outside. Beyond his windows, the skyscrapers of the financial district shot shards of colored light across the black waters of Hong Kong Harbor and the twinkling lights of the Star Ferry moved ceaselessly back and forth between Kowloon and Central.

He stood and stretched. Then he walked to the window and stood looking out at the harbor but seeing nothing. His mind was on the pieces of the puzzle that was Harry Black.

What did he actually have? he asked himself.

Did he have proof that Harry Black was undertaking contract killings at the direction of a high-ranking CIA operative who was charged with conducting black operations for the Agency? Did he have proof that a high-ranking CIA operative even sent Harry Black to kill his ex-wife to retrieve a diary that might contain revelations damaging to the CIA?

No, he didn't have proof.

What he had was evidence.

It was powerful evidence, that was true, powerful enough to be believed, but it fell short of proof. To become proof, an eyewitness had to come forward. Someone who was directly involved. Someone who could say, *Yes, this is true, and I know it is true because I was there.*

That was exactly what Harry Black was about to do.

And then somebody murdered him.

Tay shook his head. He was going around in circles, wasn't he?

He walked back to the desk and sat down again with no clear idea what to do next, but when he looked at the laptop screen, he remembered there were still two files on the thumb drive he hadn't opened yet.

He clicked on the first.

Another list of files with .jpg extensions. More photographs.

Tay half expected another set of pictures of buildings and streets. He hadn't yet figured out what the first ones he had seen were supposed to be, so he didn't see how more of the same was going to do him any good.

He started opening the files one after another, anyway. They were not photographs of buildings and streets.

They were photographs of handwritten pages in a notebook.

The images were too small for him to read the handwriting. He struggled for a moment, looking for a way to increase the size of the images, but didn't know how to do that. Surely there was a way, he thought. Computers can do anything, can't they? But whatever the way to do it was, it was well beyond his limited expertise.

There were a lot of images, fifty or more, and Tay kept on methodically clicking through them, trying to find one with handwriting large enough for him to read without increasing the size.

He found one.

It was a page with nothing on it but something printed in the middle of it in very large letters.

June – August 1963

It looked like a title page for one section of a long, chronological narrative.

Like a diary.

Could these photographs be pictures of pages from Mary Meyer's long-lost diary? Did they prove that Harry Black had once held it in his hands? And how would that be possible if Harry Black's story that he had murdered Mary Meyer wasn't true?

Maybe these weren't pictures of Mary Meyer's diary at all, Tay reminded himself. Maybe they were pictures of something else entirely.

Bullshit.

He was looking at Mary Meyer's diary. He could feel it in his bones.

Again, not proof exactly, even if these *were* pages from her diary. But it was more evidence.

And the evidence was accumulating.

Tay opened the fifth and last file.

More pictures. The same mysterious curving road and small park he had vaguely recognized in the first batch of photos.

But the angle of these photos was different. Instead of being from ground level, these photos had been taken looking down on the road and the park from what appeared to be a few floors up in a building. Five or six, certainly. Maybe even a bit higher.

They had been taken through a window and he could see the edges of the window frame in most of them. The window was an old-fashioned double-hung sash window that had been pushed open from the bottom. There was a wide sill, the white paint flaking and peeling from years of exposure to the sunlight coming through the window.

Tay clicked slowly through the photos. They all appeared to be substantially the same. The same road, the same park, the same railway overpass in the background.

The only real difference was from one frame to the next more people had gathered along both sides of the road. They looked as if they were waiting for a parade to pass.

The next photograph pulled Tay up short.

It was a photograph of a man holding a rifle with a telescopic sight. The man's right arm was extended out of the frame in a way that made it apparent he was holding the camera himself. A selfie taken long before the word selfie came into vogue.

Tay thought the way the man held the rifle was called port arms: the stock in his left hand and the barrel resting in the crook of his left elbow. His face was only partially in the frame, but Tay could tell he was young and somewhat bland and forgettable in appearance. He was wearing a khaki shirt and pants like the ones that service station attendants used to wear.

Was the man Harry Black? Tay would bet that he was, but Renny would know for sure.

In the final photograph, the rifle barrel was resting against the wooden windowsill with the road, the park, and the gathering crowds visible just beyond it. The angle of that photograph differed slightly from those that came before, and now Tay could see in the background a building that faced the little park from across the road.

Seven stories tall. Red brick. Arched windows outlined with white brick on the top floors. An enormous billboard with a digital clock on the roof. The billboard was yellow with red letters.

HERTZ RENT A CAR

In that single moment it all crashed together.

Suddenly Tay saw everything.

He felt faint.

Dear God, he thought.

Oh, holy shit!

Now he realized why the pictures of the road and the little park looked so familiar.

The Texas School Book Depository.

Dealey Plaza.

Elm Street.

The railroad overpass.

The grassy knoll.

Those were places that defined a location everyone in the world over fifty years old had seen in photographs and on film a thousand times.

On November 22, 1963, at 12:30 p.m., Lee Harvey Oswald

presumably assassinated President John F. Kennedy at that spot by firing three shots at his motorcade from a sniper's nest on the sixth floor of the Texas School Book Depository.

That's what the crowds in the photos were gathering for. They were waiting for Kennedy's motorcade to pass.

Tay looked again at the photograph that showed the digital clock on the big Hertz billboard.

It read 12:25 p.m.

H arry Black's photographs of Dealey Plaza and the crowds waiting to cheer President Kennedy were taken through an open window in a building that overlooked the road on which his car was about to pass. They were taken five minutes before John Kennedy was shot in the head.

But the building where the barrel of a sniper rifle with a telescope sight rested on the windowsill overlooking the route of Kennedy's motorcade could *not* be the Texas School Book Depository from which Lee Harvey Oswald had fired. The Texas School Book Depository was plainly visible right outside the window.

I'm just the patsy, Oswald told the Dallas police before Jack Ruby shot and killed him less than twenty-four hours after President Kennedy died.

Over the decades that had passed since then, Oswald's claim had given rise to an uncountable number of conspiracy theories about who was responsible for killing President Kennedy.

Some of those theories were crazy. Some of those theories were not so crazy.

Now Samuel Tay was a member of a very small club: the people who knew for certain that Oswald had told the truth. He really had been just the patsy.

Harry Black shot John Fitzgerald Kennedy. He even photographed himself preparing to do it.

And if Harry Black shot John Fitzgerald Kennedy, and if

Harry Black was working for Cord Meyer at the CIA, then that meant …

Tay could barely even form the thought.

He had been certain from the beginning that using a sniper to kill Harry Black had been a message.

Now he knew what that message was.

And he knew who it was from.

THIRTY-NINE

Tay sat staring at the laptop's screen for a long while without moving. He was too dazed to do anything else. He felt like he had passed through a portal to a parallel dimension. One in which all the truths of his universe were false, and all the fables were true.

Later, he would be unable to remember how long he had been sitting there when the ringing of the doorbell shocked him back into the present.

He must have forgotten to put out the Do Not Disturb sign. That was all he needed right now. Some maid wanting to put a chocolate on his pillow.

He walked to the door and opened it, his mouth half open to tell her to go away.

But it wasn't a maid outside his door.

It was John August and Claire.

"Can we come in, Sam?" August asked.

"This isn't a good time."

"Oh, I think it's an excellent time," August said as he brushed past Tay into the room.

"Well, fuck you, John."

"Yeah, fuck me."

Claire followed August inside. She sat at the end of the couch while August sprawled in the chair in front of the window. Tay thought she looked a little uncomfortable. He wondered why, but then he shifted his attention to August.

"What is this all about, John?"

August pointed to the other end of the couch. "Come on over and sit down first, Sam. Let's all just relax."

"I told you the last time you were here, John. It's my fucking room. I don't need an invitation from you to sit down."

"Oh dear, Sam, now don't go all testy on me. We're about to have an important conversation."

"And what is this important conversation going to be about? More bullshit about Korean defectors?"

"No …"

August's eyes floating around Tay's hotel room, found the cassettes and tape player lying on the desk, and then came to rest on the open laptop next to them, the thumb drive still sticking out of its USB port.

"Why don't we talk about a man I think you know as Harry Black?"

Tay walked over to the couch and sat down.

"Why are you interested in Harry Black, John?"

"Because of the book he was writing with that English lass."

"Why in the world would you care about that?"

"Because if he had published the book he was writing with her, it would have created a problem."

"What kind of problem?"

"His book could have caused people to believe that the government of the United States has been lying to them for over fifty years and is continuing to lie to them today. That kind of problem."

"Why is that a problem? Because it's true?"

"Yeah," August nodded, "particularly because it's true."

"I still don't see what that has to do with you."

"I was told to make certain his book didn't get written."

"Told by whom?"

"By the man we work for."

"And who is this man you work for?"

"Come on, Sam, you know who we work for."

"Is the Band still working for the White House?"

"I couldn't possibly comment on that."

"So, the man you're referring to would be the President of the United States?"

August said nothing.

"You're telling me the President of the United States wanted Harry Black prevented from writing his book?"

"I'm sure you can understand that he couldn't just stand by and allow stories like Harry Black was going to tell this woman to get out there in public."

"Particularly since the stories Harry Black was telling this woman were all true."

"Yeah," August nodded, "particularly because of that."

August had a small leather bag slung over one shoulder. It looked well-used, even a little scratched and battered, but it was still stylish. August wouldn't have had it, Tay thought, if it hadn't been stylish.

August pulled the strap off his shoulder and set the bag in his lap. With his right hand, he lifted the flap, dipped inside, and emerged holding a stack of four small notebooks with red covers. He dealt them out onto Tay's coffee table, side by side, with the confidence of a blackjack dealer sitting on a pair of aces.

Tay knew what the notebooks were. They were Harry Black's notes about the other murders he had committed. He was certain no one had gotten into Harry Black's safe before they had, and he figured Black had moved the notebooks somewhere else, but it looked like he had been wrong about that.

Tay lifted his eyes from the notebooks and looked at August for a long time.

"You killed him, didn't you, John?"

"Oh no, not me."

"But you know who did."

August nodded.

"You going to tell me?"

August slowly inclined his head toward Claire.

"I'm management," he said. "She's labor."

Tay tried to keep his face empty when he looked at Claire, but he was certain his dismay showed all over it.

Claire looked back at him without expression. She said nothing.

"Then that was you on the motorbike, too, was it, Claire?" Tay asked. "That was you shooting at me in front of that restaurant in Hua Hin?"

"You've heard the old joke, haven't you, Sam?" Claire offered a smile that looked both weary and, Tay thought, a little embarrassed. "How do you know when a professional shooter likes you? He misses."

"Or, in this case, *she* misses."

Claire nodded slowly.

"My mother warned me about this," Tay said. "She told me I shouldn't try to find out who pulled the trigger."

"I thought your mother was dead."

"Yes, she is, isn't she?"

Claire looked puzzled, but she said nothing else.

. . .

A ugust took a deep breath and let it out again.

"How did you find all this out, Sam?"

"I'm a detective. I detect."

"I should have guessed. If anyone could, it would be you. I just didn't think anyone *could*."

Tay said nothing.

August pointed to the cassettes and the tape player lying on the desk.

"I was wondering if there was something like that out there somewhere. I guess I should have known there had to be. And that you'd find it."

Tay still said nothing.

"Have you listened to the tapes, Sam?"

Tay nodded.

"All of them?"

Tay nodded again.

"What's on them?"

Tay thought that over. He couldn't see the point of lying about it.

"They're tapes of Cord Meyer giving Harry Black instructions to kill people."

"Wow," August said, "that's even worse than I thought it might be."

August scooped up the four red notebooks, stacked them together, and pushed them back into his shoulder bag.

"Who's heard the tapes other than you?"

"Nobody."

August looked skeptical. "You're telling me that writer gave you those tapes without ever listening to them herself?"

"She didn't give them to me."

"Then where did you get them?"

"I got them from Harry Black."

Now August looked bemused. "That doesn't make any sense."

"Actually, it does. He left them with his lawyer to be sent to Renny in the event anything happened to him."

"So this lawyer heard them."

"No, Black left the lawyer a sealed package. The lawyer simply followed his instructions and sent the package to Renny when you killed her grandfather. He had no idea what was in it."

"Has Renny listened to the tapes?"

"She gave me the package without opening it. She said I could open the package or throw it away, but she didn't want me to tell her what was in it."

"That seems … strange."

"Not really. She says she already knows more about her grandfather than she wants to."

"And how much is that?"

"She knows what Tilly Talbot told us."

"Which is?"

"Which is that Harry Black killed several prominent people, mostly mob bosses, in the 60s, 70s, and 80s. Talbot and Black had only just gotten started on the book he wanted her to write about him, so she didn't have many details."

"Did she give you any names?"

"Sam Giancana, John Roselli, Sam Trafficante, Jimmy Hoffa. Although Black insisted he hadn't been the triggerman for Hoffa."

"Any others?"

"A woman named Mary Meyer who was murdered in 1964. Talbot says Mary Meyer was John Kennedy's mistress, and she kept a diary in which she recorded some indiscrete conversations with Kennedy. Her theory is that the mafia killed Mary Meyer to get her diary. They intended to use it to blackmail the government into getting Robert Kennedy and the Department of Justice off their backs."

"How could this woman be sure that Black wasn't just feeding her a lot of bullshit?"

"She says she was skeptical at first, but he gave her one of those red notebooks with his planning notes for the murder of Sam Giancana. Black was a very organized and methodical guy. He seemed to think history required him to leave a convincing record of what he had done."

"Not an outstanding character trait for a hired killer, huh?"

"He promised Tilly Talbot he would give her proof of the other killings. I think he intended to turn over the notebooks you have right there to her, but he never got the chance."

"Did he tell this woman who hired him to kill these people?"

"He kept holding that back, too. He said it was part of his big finish. Her theory is that it was Carlos Marcello."

"I like that," August smiled.

"She thinks Harry Black was a hitman working for somebody high enough up in the mafia to have other high-up people killed. Since Marcello was the only one in that generation who died in his bed, she figures it must have been him."

"So that's what she thinks, is it? Harry Black was a mafia hitman working for Carlos Marcello? And that's all she knows?"

"She said he told her he had a really big finish for her, one that would make her forget all about the mobsters he had killed. He called it the crime of the century."

"But he never told her what it was?"

Tay shook his head.

"So, she has no idea what he was talking about. And she never told Renny. Or you."

Another shake of the head.

"But you've figured it out anyway, haven't you, Sam?"

Tay said nothing.

August pointed to the laptop on the desk next to the tape cassettes. "That memory stick was in the package with the tapes?"

"Yes."

"What's on it?"

"Photographs. Harry Black documented everything."

"Everything?"

"Everything. His preparation photos from Dallas are on it. Photos looking down on the route of Kennedy's motorcade just before it arrived are on it. Photos of the building he was shooting from are there, too."

"That's it?"

"Oh, no. My personal favorite is the photo of him holding a rifle, followed by a photo of the same rifle pointed out an open window toward the street where the motorcade is about to pass. In the background, you can see the time on the Hertz billboard on top of the Texas School Book Depository. He took that one five minutes before he shot John Kennedy."

August sighed.

"Well … shit," he said.

"So, what happens now, John?"

"Now? Nothing happens. It's over."

Tay frowned. That didn't sound right.

"This woman doesn't have enough for a book," August went on. "The granddaughter doesn't know any more about what Black may have done than the writer does. Harry Black is dead and there's nobody left to tell the story. It's over."

"You're forgetting something."

"Oh? What's that?"

"You're forgetting about me. I know everything."

August smiled.

"Ah, Sam, but you're not going to tell anyone. You're almost a member of the Band yourself. You've run operations with us before. The White House vetted and approved you. You're one of us."

"I'm nothing like you, John."

August chuckled. "You're a lot more like me than you want to admit, my friend."

"What are you going to do if I decide to spill the beans?"

Tay pointed to the tapes and the thumb drive. "After all, I've got some pretty dramatic proof."

August chuckled again. "Yeah, but I'm going to take all that with me when I leave here, and you're going to let me."

"I am?"

"You are."

"Why would I do that?"

"Because you don't want to tell this story to the New York Times or anybody else. If you did, it would make you the most famous man in the world, and it would destroy the granddaughter. And I know exactly how much you don't want either of those things to happen."

"Maybe I place a higher value on the truth than you do. High enough to make it worth all that."

"You shall know the truth and the truth will set you free? Something like that?"

"Yeah, something like that."

"You don't really believe that shit any more than I do, Sam."

Tay thought about everything for a moment, and then he said, "What if you're wrong, John?"

"About what?"

"About me. What if I decide this is a story important enough to tell despite what it would cost to do that?"

August pursed his lips and looked at Tay without saying anything.

"What would you do then, John? Kill me, too?"

August glanced at Claire who was expressionless, then he looked back at Tay.

"Probably not."

Suddenly his face split into a big grin.

"At least, not unless we really had to."

FORTY

J ohn August and Claire left Tay's room soon after that.

August picked up the two cassettes, unplugged the drive from the laptop, and dropped all three into his pocket.

He pointed to the cassette player and laptop.

"Just to be on the safe side," he said to Claire, and she collected those, too.

Tay didn't try to stop them.

Nobody shook hands or said goodbye.

After they had gone, Tay sat for a long while on the sofa without moving. He stayed in the same spot where he had been while August and Claire were there. He had no reason to, but he could think of no reason to move, either.

After a while, it occurred to him he wanted to see people and hear noise. He wanted to remember that he still lived in a world where people went about their lives, neither knowing nor much caring about the kind of secrets for which he had become an involuntary custodian.

He went downstairs thinking he might have a whiskey or two, maybe get something to eat, but when he got to the lobby, he realized he neither wanted whiskey nor food. Instead of sitting down, he kept walking straight out through the lobby doors and over to Nathan Road. He turned left and headed north toward … well, he didn't know where he was going.

On the other hand, he didn't much care either.

H e walked at a steady pace, methodically covering ground. At the far northern end of Kowloon Park, he came to the Tsim Sha Tsui police headquarters, and he stopped on the sidewalk and stood looking at the building.

There was nothing remarkable about it. It was just a building. It could have been any building, but the fact that it was a police station reminded him how much he missed being a policeman.

Now that he was no longer a policeman, he felt unmoored. Everybody had to be something, didn't they? And a policeman was the only thing he had ever been. So what was he now? He really had no idea.

He had gotten involved in all this in the first place only because Jones had asked him to help Renny and his hunger to be a policeman again had pushed him into agreeing. After Tilly Talbot told Renny the story of her grandfather being a mafia hitter, Renny had decided she didn't want to know anything else. That appeared to be that as far as Renny was concerned, so he probably didn't have to worry about whether he was willing to tell her the truth or not.

Jones was another matter entirely.

Would Jones accept the mafia story and leave it at that? He had no idea.

And, worse, he had no idea what he would do if Jones wouldn't.

.   .   .

Tay waited for the light and joined the swarm of pedestrians crossing Austin Road. Just on the other side, he spotted the red and green sign of one of the 7-Eleven stores that dotted every neighborhood in Hong Kong. It suddenly occurred to him he was thirsty, so he went inside and hunted through the refrigerated cabinets in the back until he found a can of Coke Zero.

Tay took the Coke up to the cash register to pay for it. While he waited behind another customer who was counting his change, always a wise thing to do in Hong Kong, his eyes came to rest on a rack mounted on the wall right behind the cashier. It was where they kept the cigarettes.

The other customer left, and Tay stepped up to the counter and put down the can of Coke. The clerk was a painfully thin and slightly stooped Chinese woman of indeterminate age. She looked as if her spindly frame was simply not strong enough to keep her completely vertical.

"I haven't smoked in over six months," Tay told her.

She looked at the can of Coke, but she didn't look at Tay.

"I had a bit of a health scare," he went on anyway. "Really shook me up. I quit cold. Haven't missed it a bit."

The woman punched the price of the Coke into the keyboard of the cash register without responding.

"But what the hell?" Tay said. "Who wants to live forever, right? Certainly not in a world like this."

He pointed past the woman to the rack behind her.

"Give me a pack of Marlboro Reds."

The woman reached back with a practiced motion, pulled out a pack, and dropped it on the counter next to the can of Coke.

"Do you have any matches?"

Now the woman shifted her eyes to Tay, but she said nothing.

"A box of matches? You know…"

Tay pantomimed the striking of a match and the lighting of a cigarette.

"Gotta have wooden matches to light a cigarette," he said. "No other way to do it right."

The woman continued to look at him, saying nothing.

Tay tried again.

"Box of *match-is*?"

He broke the word into two distinct syllables, spoke it a bit more loudly than was strictly necessary to make it heard, and embellished his pantomime to the point that it came close to attaining the status of method acting.

Nothing.

"Okay," Tay shrugged, "It's important for a man to be flexible."

He pointed to a clear plastic tub underneath the cigarette display that was filled to the brim with plastic disposable lighters.

"Give me one of those," he said. "A green one would be nice. Going green is the thing to do these days, don't you think?"

The woman looked at Tay for another moment without expression, then she turned, dipped down into the plastic tub, and pulled out a lighter. It was red.

She hesitated, thought about it, and dropped it back. She pawed through the tub until she found a green one and added it to Tay's other purchases on the counter.

Then she made a sort of snorting noise and gave Tay a big grin, her wrinkled lips peeling back unevenly from a mouth that appeared to be missing as many teeth as it contained.

Tay paid, waved away the plastic bag the woman offered, and scooped up his purchases in his hands.

Out on the sidewalk, he split open the pack of Marlboros with his thumbnail, peeled back the top, and inhaled the intoxicating aroma that every new pack he had ever opened gave off. He shook out a cigarette and lit it with his new green lighter.

The first pull was glorious. He hadn't realized he had missed smoking so much. He was certain he could feel the particles of nicotine passing from his lungs into his capillaries, flowing out into his arteries, and infusing him with energy and purpose. He took another long draw. It only got better. He felt ten feet tall.

Tay tossed the unopened can of Coke in the first trash barrel he saw and continued walking north on Nathan Road. He smoked with a determination that suggested any interference would result in violence.

There was only one thing that might make it better, he thought. If he could somehow spin the world back and reset it to the way it had been before he had ever heard of Harry Black. But the truth is an ugly bastard. Once the damn thing gets out of its box and starts strutting around in public, it won't go away. No matter how much you might wish for it to, it won't go away. It's up to you to figure out a way to live with it.

Maybe, Tay thought, if he smoked another Marlboro after this one, he would figure it out

Maybe, if he smoked another Marlboro after this one, he would find a way to accept whatever this lying, dying old world had in store for him next.

Someone else could try to save it.

Wasn't going to be him.

Over and out.

A year passed, more or less.

Tay thought of it as a pleasingly dull year, one made up mostly of books he read, Marlboros he smoked, cups of coffee he drank, and walks he took through the peaceful streets of his gracious old nineteenth century neighborhood.

One unexpected thing did happen. The Singapore Police went through one of its periodic reorganizations. A woman Tay knew was promoted to Senior Assistant Commissioner and appointed Director of the Criminal Investigation Department.

More important, she knew Tay, and she had less interest in his inability to get along with his superior officers than she did in his ability as a criminal investigator. She hadn't exactly offered him his old job back, but he thought that might be coming. She had invited him to consult with CID investigators on several cases, and there had even been some talk of appointing Tay as one of Singapore's representatives to Interpol.

Wouldn't *that* be ironic?

During the year, Tay heard from Renny twice when she came to Singapore for art auctions at Sotheby's. The first time she had been in town, she invited him to lunch. The second time, she suggested they meet for coffee. There was no third time, and Tay got the message. She never mentioned her grandfather on either of the occasions he saw her. He got the message about that, too, so neither did he.

Jones telephoned a few times, but the nonsense of sending Tay a burner phone to receive his calls was never repeated. Mostly Jones inquired politely about Tay's health, and Tay assured him that he was fine. Jones didn't ask Tay any further favors so the limits of their acquaintanceship didn't have to be tested. He never mentioned Renny or her grandfather to Tay again, so Tay didn't mention them to Jones either.

Tay never heard from John August or Claire during the year. Not once. Not about anything.

He largely put Harry Black out of his mind. Oh, he thought about him occasionally, mostly when he saw some mention in the news of something that caused everything to come back to him again, but he never felt even the slightest temptation to discuss what he knew with anyone.

Sometimes he even wondered if he really knew what he thought he knew. Maybe, he told himself, he had misunderstood some of the things he had discovered and jumped to a conclusion that was at least partially wrong.

Then something completely unexpected happened, and it propelled Harry Black right back to the very front Samuel Tay's consciousness.

O ne late afternoon when Singapore's heat and humidity were particularly smothering, Tay decided he would walk up to his favorite bookstore and pass a pleasant hour or two wandering its aisles.

Kinokuniya was the largest bookstore in Singapore by far. It was on the third floor of the massive Takashimaya shopping mall on Orchard Road, just a short stroll from Tay's house, and he had spent many a happy hour poking through its stacks and browsing a few of the half million or so books on Kino's shelves.

As in many bookstores, the first thing you saw when you went through the door was a scattering of tables displaying the store's newest and hottest titles, as well as a good many titles that were neither new nor hot but that publishers paid the store to display prominently.

Tay generally didn't bother looking at the titles on the front tables. They simply didn't hold any appeal for him. When it came to reading, he wasn't a bestseller kind of guy. He was far more likely to leave Kino with a biography of Metternich or a history of Japan in the eighteenth century than he was with a novel by David Baldacci. Actually, he didn't remember *ever* reading a novel by David Baldacci, and he had absolutely no intention of starting now.

This time, however, something drew him to stop at Kino's front tables and scan the titles the store was pushing. His eyes skipped over most of the covers on display without any interest until one caught his eye.

At first, he thought he must be imagining what he thought he was seeing, so he looked away, and then he looked back.

He was not imagining it.

The cover was mostly black and white, but the author's

name screamed out from the top of it in giant capital letters in a shade of purple so vibrant that it made the name look as if it were battery powered.

TILLY
TALBOT

Tay bent forward and peered more closely at the cover.

The title of the book was at the very bottom since apparently the publisher thought the author's name was the bigger draw. It was printed in white rather than the electric purple used for Tilly Talbot's name, and the typeface was much smaller, but he had no difficulty seeing every word of it.

WHO THE HELL
IS HARRY BLACK?

Tay didn't pick up the book, but he stood there quietly and stared at it for a long time.

Oh crap, he muttered.

A NOTE FROM THE AUTHOR

A number of people played important roles in making this a better book.

In particular, I would like to thank Michael Parnell, Jacqueline Beard, Rob Carnell, Tony Hall, Tony Grey, and Col. Rich Buickerood, all of whom read and provided notes on my early drafts.

I profited enormously from being able to tap into their collective knowledge of all sorts of things, especially firearms and long-distance shooting, and I drew on many of their suggestions in the final shaping of this book. I am also grateful for their ability to dig out those annoying typos and formatting errors that creep into every book no matter how much I try to avoid them. I am in their debt.

One other thing.

This is fiction, folks. I make this stuff up. I hope it feels real, but it isn't.

There are people and places here who *are* real, but Harry Black isn't one of them. He is as much a product of my imagination as are Samuel Tay and his mother.

The reason I got into the fiction business in the first place is that novelists have no responsibility for digging out and reporting truth. I'm not writing history here. I'm not trying to convince you of anything. I have no idea who actually assassinated John F. Kennedy.

I just know for sure it wasn't Harry Black.

Unless, of course, it was.

Jake Needham

JUST ONE MORE THING

I hope you enjoyed reading WHO THE HELL IS HARRY BLACK? I have to admit it was an awful lot of fun to write.

If you would be willing to recommend it to other readers, I'd be grateful. When you like a book and post a short review on Amazon to tell others that you liked it, you give me a really big hand up in reaching new readers.

Your review doesn't have to be long. Just a couple of sentences will do the job. What really counts is the rating you give the book and the fact that you took the time to recommend it in the first place.

All you have to do is go to the Amazon page for WHO THE HELL IS HARRY BLACK? and scroll down a bit to get to the review section. Then click the **Write a Customer Review** button that's over there on the left side of the page.

It really would be a great help to me. Thank you.

A PREVIEW

THE INSPECTOR TAY NOVELS - BOOK 1

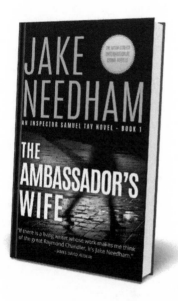

There are seven books in the
Inspector Samuel Tay series.

Here's the first chapter
of the book that introduced him.

THE AMBASSADOR'S WIFE

CHAPTER ONE

THE FIRST AND most important truth about Singapore is this. It is hot. It is nasty, stinking, sweaty hot.

Inspector Samuel Tay had been born in Singapore and he would probably die in Singapore, but he had never come to an accommodation with the savage heat and the sadistic humidity. If he owned both Singapore and hell, he would rent out Singapore and live in hell.

How had people survived in Singapore before they invented air conditioning, and why would they have even tried? He had absolutely no idea.

Tay took out a handkerchief and wiped the sweat from his face while he waited for the light to cross Orchard Road. As he did, his gaze lifted, and he eyed his destination with distaste.

The Singapore Marriott was a thirty-three-story octagonal-shaped tower crowned by a gigantic Chinese-style roof that loomed over the corner of Scotts and Orchard Road. He assumed the roof was supposed to make the building's appearance more local by making it look vaguely reminiscent of a traditional Chinese pagoda.

What it really made the building look like, Tay thought, was a giant dildo. Worse, the stupid roof was green with a huge red ball right at its peak. The Marriott not only looked like a giant dildo, it looked like a giant dildo wearing a green rubber with a red pom-pom tied to its tip.

Merry fucking Christmas everybody.

It broke his heart sometimes, this city of his. Back before the

Marriott was there, a traditional Chinese department store had stood on that very corner.

It was a glorious building with graceful, iron-arched galleries supported by tiled colonnades wrapped around each of its five floors. Tay remembered the mysterious air those galleries had cast over the whole building, the way they obscured its interior in dim shadows and infused it with a soft, dreamlike light.

On every floor the windows had been covered by dark green wooden shutters. As Singapore's warm winds blew through the building, those shutters had clacked and clattered together with a sound that came back to him with absolute clarity even after almost forty years.

Buildings like that were all gone now, as gone as if they had never existed, and his city had become a place he did not know, somewhere he had never been. For nearly fifty years, the people who decided such things — the bastards — had been tearing down glorious structures just because they were old. Sometimes they even replaced them with new structures touted as modern versions of whatever it was they had replaced. They never were, of course. They were nothing really, other than just new.

Through the merciless grinders of progress, the soul of a city had passed, reluctantly accompanied by Tay's own soul, and each of them had emerged as... well, what? He really had no idea.

Sometimes Tay thought he could close his eyes and see everything again just as it had been before, back when he was eight years old and Singapore was still thrilling to him, but he wasn't sure he really could. Was he seeing something he actually remembered, or was he only seeing something he hoped he remembered?

The older Tay got, the harder it was for him to be sure.

SERGEANT ROBBIE KANG was waiting for Tay just inside the lobby of the Singapore Marriott. Kang had black hair and a fair complexion and he was wearing his customary short-sleeved white shirt with a button-down collar and a pair of dark chinos.

"Have you looked at the scene yet, Sergeant?"

"No, sir." Kang shoved his glasses up the bridge of his nose with his forefinger. "Not yet. All I know is we've got a deceased woman upstairs. A homicide."

Tay did not ask why Kang was already certain it was a homicide.

"Well, let's take a look then," was all he said.

Kang hesitated.

"What?"

"They say it's messy, sir."

Tay watched Kang's Adam's apple bob up and down as he swallowed.

"Very messy."

That answered his question about why Kang was certain it was a homicide, but it also introduced a slightly sensitive element into the conversation.

Tay did not like messy. He and Sergeant Kang didn't talk about it, but Tay knew Robbie Kang realized it all too well. He really did not like messy.

Tay had never before had to deal with a woman found dead in one of the city's five-star hotels, not even a neatly expired woman let alone one who had become deceased in a manner that someone felt compelled to describe to Kang as messy. And he really wasn't enthusiastic about doing it now.

Even after nearly twenty years as a policeman, each time he approached the scene of a violent crime he struggled against a squeamishness he feared might one day master him altogether. For years, he had watched his colleagues out of the corner of his eye searching for someone else who shared his secret weakness, but he had found no one. As far as he could tell, his colleagues thought nothing of spending an afternoon poking around the charred corpses of two children killed in a suspicious apartment fire and then going straight out for a rare steak.

Tay couldn't do it. Whatever gene might be required to achieve that sort of detachment, he lacked it.

For a fleeting moment, Tay toyed with telling Kang that he could no longer bear any of it. He would not on this day stand gazing down at broken bones, unsupported flesh, and extruded innards. He would not squat down next to a glistening heap of blood and tissue, poke at blood-drenched clothing, and try to still his pounding heart while he fought against nausea. He would not do that again. Not ever again.

But Tay said none of that.

He just did what he had done a few hundred times before and would no doubt do another few hundred times more. He shrugged and followed Kang toward the crime scene.

Inside the elevator, Kang pushed the button for the twenty-sixth floor. Tay heard a slight humming sound and the elevator doors slid closed.

As he and Sergeant Kang levitated in an air-conditioned hush, Tay tilted his head back against the polished wood paneling and shut his eyes.

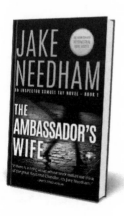

Available in both paperback and ebook editions
from all Amazon stores worldwide

THE INSPECTOR SAMUEL TAY NOVELS

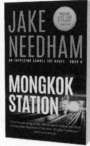

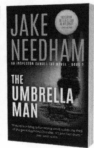
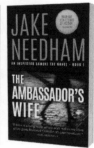

They steer a tight ship in squeaky-clean Singapore. No dissent, no opposition, no criticism. Disneyland with the death penalty somebody once called it.

Samuel Tay is a little overweight, a little lonely, a little cranky, and he smokes way too much. He's worked almost his entire life as a senior homicide detective in Singapore CID, and he's the best investigator anyone there has ever seen.

Problem is, the senior officers of CID don't much like Tay. His father was an American and there's something about him that's just a little too American for most Singaporeans. Tay knows they'll get him someday, and eventually they do.

That's when a whole new world of unexpected possibilities opens for Samuel Tay.

THE AMBASSADOR'S WIFE - Book 1

THE UMBRELLA MAN - Book 2

THE DEAD AMERICAN - Book 3

THE GIRL IN THE WINDOW - Book 4

AND BROTHER IT'S STARTING TO RAIN - Book 5

MONGKOK STATION - Book 6

WHO THE HELL IS HARRY BLACK? - Book 7

THE JACK SHEPHERD NOVELS

Jack Shepherd was a well-connected lawyer in Washington DC until he tossed it all in for the quiet life of a business school professor at Chulalongkorn University in Bangkok.

It was a pretty good gig until the university discovered the kind of notorious people Shepherd had gotten involved with in his law practice. That was when they suggested he'd probably be happier somewhere else.

These days, Shepherd lives and works in Hong Kong where he's the kind of lawyer people call a troubleshooter. At least that's what they call him when they're being polite.

Shepherd is the guy people go to when they have a problem too ugly to tell anyone else about. He locates the trouble, and then he shoots it.

Neat, huh? If his life were only that simple.

LAUNDRY MAN - Book 1

KILLING PLATO - Book 2

A WORLD OF TROUBLE - Book 3

THE KING OF MACAU - Book 4

DON'T GET CAUGHT - Book 5

THE NINETEEN - Book 6

"THE BIG MANGO is a classic!"
-- Crime Reads

$400 million is in the wind, ten tons of cash, the result of a bungled CIA operation to grab the foreign currency from the Bank of Vietnam when the Americans fled Saigon in 1975.

A few decades later, the word on the street is that all that money somehow ended up in Bangkok and a downwardly mobile lawyer from California named Eddie Dare is the only guy left alive who might still have a shot at finding it.

Eddie knows nothing about the missing money. At least, he doesn't think he does. But so many people claim he's got an inside track that he and an old marine buddy named Winnebago Jones decide to head for Bangkok anyway and do a little treasure hunting. What do they have to lose, huh? Their lives, as it turns out.

From the Big Apple, to the Big Orange, to the Big Mango. You have to admit it has a kind of nutty logic to it. Bangkok is about as far from California as Eddie can go without sailing completely over the edge of the world.

Although, at times, he wonders if that isn't exactly what he *has* done.

THE BIG MANGO

available in both ebook and paperback editions

MEET JAKE NEEDHAM

Jake Needham is an American lawyer who became a screen and television writer through a series of coincidences too ridiculous for anyone to believe. When he discovered how little he actually liked movies and television, he started writing crime novels.

Jake has lived in Asia for over thirty years and has published fourteen novels that have collectively sold nearly a million copies. He has twice been a finalist for the Barry Award for the Paperback Mystery of the Year and once a finalist for the International Thriller Writers' Award for Ebook Thriller of the Year. He and his wife, an Oxford graduate and prematurely retired concert pianist, live in Bangkok.

Every month or two, Jake sends out one of his famous *Letters from Asia* to those readers who have asked to receive them. He often talks about the real people, places, and things that appear in his novels in fictional form and sometimes lets his readers know about new books he has coming soon or suggests books by other writers that he thinks they might like. If you want to be one of those readers who receive Jake's letters, go to this web address and give him the email address you'd like for him to use:

www.JakeNeedhamNovels.com/letter-to-readers

Ebook edition ISBN 978-616-603-878-1

Trade paper edition ISBN 978-616-603-877-4

Made in the USA
Middletown, DE
27 December 2023

46881465R00217